CJ Parsons was born in Britain and grew up in Canada. She graduated from Montreal's McGill University with a degree in psychology and went on to earn a graduate degree in journalism. She worked as a newspaper reporter at Canada's *Globe and Mail* before moving to Hong Kong, where she became a columnist at the *South China Morning Post*.

After returning to Britain, she moved into television news, working as a broadcast journalist for both the BBC and CNN International. She also spent two years covering crime, seeing first-hand the disturbing forces that drive people to kill, something that inspired her first novel, *When She Came Back*, published by Headline in November 2020.

CJ is now senior producer at CGTN. She lives in north London.

THE WINNER

C.J. PARSONS

ONE PLACE. MANY STORIES

HQ
An imprint of HarperCollins*Publishers* Ltd
1 London Bridge Street
London SE1 9GF

www.harpercollins.co.uk

HarperCollins*Publishers*
Macken House, 39/40 Mayor Street Upper,
Dublin 1, D01 C9W8, Ireland

This edition 2024

1
First published in Great Britain by
HQ, an imprint of HarperCollins*Publishers* Ltd 2024

ISBN: 9780008613952

This book contains FSC™ certified paper and other controlled sources to ensure responsible forest management.

For more information visit: www.harpercollins.co.uk/green

This book is set in 11/15.5 pt. Minion by Type-it AS, Norway

Printed and Bound in the UK using 100% Renewable Electricity at CPI Group (UK) Ltd, Croydon, CR0 4YY

To Mum, aka 'Purple Grandma'

PROLOGUE

This is it, Elliot thought, as his brain registered that the car was no longer clinging to the sharp curves of the coast, that he had overshot the last turn and there was now nothing beneath the wheels but air. *This is the end of my life.*

The fabric of time seemed to stretch, the car floating above the North Sea in slo-mo, its windscreen blurry with rain.

Then a gut punch of panic knocked the breath from him.

Rosie.

His head turned to the passenger seat; she was staring at the windscreen through splayed fingers, a clichéd image of a girl watching a horror film, mouth gaping in a silent scream as the car flew forward, riding a fading wave of momentum.

The sky vanished from the windscreen, replaced by a view of waves crashing against rocks. Elliot's stomach swooped into his throat as they fell.

There was a deafening crash, a high-pitched squeal of protesting metal, and he was flung forward, the seatbelt cutting into his chest, face slamming the airbag.

Then nothing. Silence. Darkness.

Was he dead already? Was this death?

It could have been seconds or hours before the pain came,

telling him that he was still in this world. He could hear rain falling on metal. Waves smashing the shore.

Alive. I'm alive.

He inhaled and pain knifed him in the chest, fading as he exhaled. He breathed in and the stab came again. Was that a broken rib?

Elliot was hanging forward in his seat, his back to the sky, only the seatbelt preventing him from falling, face first into the airbag.

Rosie.

He turned his head slowly, painfully, towards her.

Her upper body was sagging against the seatbelt like a puppet on slack strings, her face suspended just above the pale mushroom of the airbag, eyes closed. He could see a starburst of fractured glass on the window beside her, and only blackness behind it. Elliot reached across to touch her dangling wrist. Felt the flicker of a pulse beneath the skin. Waves of dizziness were breaking over him, sending white dots swarming across his vision, so at first he thought her face was half masked in shadow. Then his mind cleared for a moment and he saw that the layer of darkness was blood. She must have cracked her head against the side window on the way down.

She'll die if I can't get out of here.

He took a breath, winced in pain. Stared hard at the windscreen, trying to see what lay beyond it. But his vision doubled and all he could make out was darkness on the other side. Panic launched a fresh assault as he pictured the car trapped beneath the waves. Imagined water spilling in through the seams of the windows. Drowning slowly in the dark.

Inhale . . . pain. Exhale . . . relief.

With a Herculean effort, he raised his head until it made contact with the seat back, the movement unleashing a sick dizziness and an unnerving sensation of loose parts shifting and skidding inside his skull. Something trickled across his lip and he licked it away without thinking. It was slick and salty in his mouth. Blood.

Inhale . . . pain. Exhale . . . relief.

He turned his face slowly towards the driver's door, the broken shards sliding and clicking in his head, dread filling him as he imagined what he might see through the side window.

Please don't let it be water.

And sobbed with relief. The window was webbed with cracks but still intact, a diagonal of deeper darkness cutting across the bottom, warped by the rain wriggling along the glass.

Rock. He could see the surface of the sea boiling just beyond it, perhaps half a metre below. Elliot could feel his mind starting to function properly again, his cerebral cortex coming back online, wresting control from the crazed jangle of his limbic system. And now, at last, he was able to do what psychologists did best: analyse.

So, the front of the car was wedged between a couple of the giant rocks jutting out of the sea just beyond the cliff's base. The doors were held shut so he'd have to escape through the back, climb up to the road.

Was that really possible, though? How steep was the cliff? It might be better to call for help and wait here until it arrived. He looked at Rosie again, for signs that she might be coming round. And noticed something that sucked his breath away. Now that his vision had cleared, he could see that the wall of the car beside her had caved in. The metal bulged obscenely, reaching halfway across her lap. Jesus. He tried to pull her out from under it, but she was stuck tight, her lower body pinned down by warped metal. It would take equipment, experts, to prize her free.

Assuming it's not too late for her. Because of you.

The thought whispered around his skull. He pushed it aside.

His mobile. Where was it? It had been in his jacket pocket as usual, but when he groped for it now, it was no longer there. He closed his eyes – a mistake; the world tilted and lurched like a funfair ride – then quickly opened them again. The phone must have fallen out in the crash and skidded to the lowest part of the car: the front. He would have to navigate around the airbag to reach it.

Don't panic, his cortex admonished. *There's no need to rush.*

Except that wasn't really true, was it? Because a realisation was creeping up on him. There hadn't been any rocks sticking out of the water when they'd driven along this road a week ago, at the start of their Highlands holiday: Rosie had taken photos from the window and they'd admired them later, in the hotel.

There hadn't been any rocks because the tide had covered them. He forced himself to remain calm as the implication of this sank in. Was the tide coming in now?

There was a dripping sound from somewhere in front of him. He leaned left then right, trying to see around the airbag.

Inhale . . . pain. Exhale . . . relief.

The windscreen was cracked at the base and water was travelling across the dashboard in rivulets, dripping down into the footwell. He became aware of the sound it made: the plink of liquid on liquid. He stretched his legs towards the space beside the pedals and felt the cold clutch of water around his ankles. If he'd dropped his phone, it was submerged now.

Think-think-think.

What about Rosie's? She usually kept it in her canvas bag.

The bag she had tossed onto the floor at her feet. Under water now, like his phone.

The waves were becoming more aggressive, pushing shards of

glass out of the jigsaw in the windscreen, gushing in through the gap at the bottom. Slowly but surely, seawater was filling the car. It was only a matter of time before the entire front section, including the seats they were strapped to, became completely submerged.

'Rosie, *wake up!*'

Nothing. Not a flicker of response.

He grabbed at her arm and her one exposed leg, yanking with all his strength. But it was no use.

He needed to get out of here. Climb to the road and flag down a car. Would he make it, though? Even getting to the cliff's base would be a major achievement, battered by waves on the sharp rocks.

Still, he had to try. He couldn't just stay here, waiting for the tide to bury him.

He looked at Rosie. What would happen to her? This was an isolated stretch of coast, they had passed only a few other cars in the last hour. How long would it take for rescuers to arrive? How far was the nearest hospital, the nearest fire station? The cold hard fact of the matter was that help probably wouldn't arrive in time.

Then a cold voice slid across his thoughts, whispering, *She brought this on herself, though, didn't she? If she hadn't said those things, we'd be safe right now.*

Elliot considered her profile. Now that the wave of panic had passed, he felt oddly dispassionate. Empty. He watched fresh blood trace a sideways line across her face. Listened to the dripping of water filling the footwell.

Plink-plink-plink.

Getting louder. Faster.

CHAPTER 1

'What are you hiding in your sleeve?' Heather demanded.

The boy turned and gave her a sly smile. Eric Shulman: a budding psycho if ever there was one. Different from the school bullies whose bravado was a thin covering for the gaping wound of their hellish insecurities. No, Eric was a different breed entirely. He didn't seem to be masking anything except a dark, unnerving blankness.

'Sorry, what did you say, Miss?'

The recreation zone was noisy with lunchtime shouts, shrieks and laughter. So she supposed it was possible that he genuinely hadn't heard her question.

Possible.

But unlikely.

'That packet I just saw poking out of your jacket sleeve. I'd like you to take it out. Right now.'

Any other Holland Park Upper student would have backed away, or at most, stood his ground. But not Eric. He moved a step closer, the reduced distance emphasising the difference in their heights. Fifteen years old and already towering over her.

'That's a big accusation, Miss, to make without proof. Because everyone has rights. Even the police aren't allowed to search people without a good reason.' He took out a piece of gum, popped it into his mouth and began to chew, releasing a smell of mint. It mingled with the skunky scent of cannabis clinging to his jacket. 'Last time I checked, teachers didn't outrank police. And you're not even a proper teacher. Just a trainee.'

Arrogant little bastard.

She was dimly aware that her leg was throbbing again: a sick, thudding ache, as though the bone itself were swelling and contracting with each beat of her heart. The pill must have worn off already. Swallowing, she pointed to Eric's cuff, where the packet of drugs – it had to be drugs, didn't it? – was concealed. The tip of her finger touched his sleeve.

'I can see that—'

Eric's hand whipped up and grabbed hold of her wrist. He leaned down, filling her nostrils with mint. Hissed in her ear.

'Don't. Touch. Me.'

And suddenly Heather was afraid. Afraid of this oversized teenager with his dark, glittery eyes and his insolent slouch, the posh accent stretched out into a drawl. His grip tightened. Heather's eyes darted around the recreation area. There were supposed to be two of them on duty, damn it. Where the hell was Steve? Probably drinking coffee in the staffroom, the lazy shirker.

She pulled herself to her full height, which, at five foot three, didn't really achieve much. Then she looked Eric straight in the eye, speaking with all the authority she could muster.

'Let go of my wrist immediately or I will report you to the head.'

'Oh dear,' he said, without a trace of concern. 'Do you think I'll get chucked out?'

And he laughed. Because of course they couldn't get rid of him. Not without turning off the money tap that had sent donations flowing into the school's coffers from the first day Eric Shulman (heir to the Shulman media dynasty) had sauntered through the gates. Shulman money had paid for the shiny new equipment in the lab and the flashy computers in the 'coding corner'. It had turned the neighbouring plot of land into the tennis courts that were the jewel in Holland Park Upper's PE crown.

Which meant that Eric would never be permanently excluded no matter what he did. If Heather's eight months' training at the school had taught her anything, it was that the wealthy occupied a sort of parallel universe where the rules didn't apply, floating through lives of beauty and ease while people like her trudged below, clocking up hours, toeing the line.

'Let go this second, or . . .' She cast around desperately for a suitable threat, but her mind had gone blank. Then, from somewhere to her left, came the sound of footsteps.

'Stop it, you dickhead.'

Heather turned to see Dean Mitchell, the big-mouthed, big-hearted boy who lived two floors down from her, in number thirty-four.

He squared up to Eric, not quite as tall, but broad.

Eric released Heather's wrist, long fingers migrating to his school tie, adjusting the gold clip.

'Well, well, if it isn't Bursary Boy.' Eric's gaze flicked from Dean to Heather and back again. 'You two are neighbours, aren't you? From the same estate.' The way he said the word, dragging out the 's', made it sound dirty.

'Yeah.' Dean leaned in closer, reducing the space between them to just a few inches. Eric didn't move. 'Have you got a problem with that?'

'Not at all. I love the literary references. Shakespeare Estate, housing blocks named after his great works. So highbrow.' He looked Dean up and down. 'I guess that must make you Othello, since you couldn't really play anyone else, could you? So is Miss Davies your Desdemona? I bet—' The school bell's clang covered the next words.

The sound broke the spell he'd somehow managed to cast, reminding Heather that this was her place of work. That, heir or no heir, she was in charge. And she wasn't about to let him get away with grabbing hold of her like that.

'Eric, you're coming with me to the head's office. Now.'

He gave her his slow, contemptuous smile. 'Whatever you say, Miss.'

'Thank you for your help, Dean.' She gave him a nod of approval. He was one of the good ones: a boy who held open doors and tidied away his lab equipment without having to be asked. 'I'll handle things from here.'

He gave her a nod back.

As Heather marched Eric across the playground, she was looking towards the moment when he would be forced to reveal the contents of his jacket sleeve with satisfaction. They might not be able to get rid of him for good, but drugs on school premises would mean mandatory exclusion for at least a week. Which was something, at least. As far as she was concerned, they would all be better off without Eric around. Some of the teachers liked to preach that there was good in all the children, that it was just a difficult age and no one knew what was really going on at home. But Heather didn't buy it. No, Eric Shulman was just a spoilt, nasty little shit, simple as that.

It was only much later, as she was walking home, that it suddenly occurred to her to wonder how he knew where she lived.

CHAPTER 2

CelebRater Blames 'Spiked Juice' For Drink-Driving Arrest

By London Post Entertainment Correspondent Angus Fitz

CelebRate star and self-proclaimed 'recovering alcoholic' Ozzie Jacobs has spoken out about his dramatic fall off the wagon, claiming to be the victim of a spiked drink. His two years of sobriety ended on Saturday night in a drunken bar fight, a high-speed car chase and a fatal collision between his Ferrari and a beloved ginger cat named Katie.

'When I got to the New Heights I ordered pineapple juice like I always do,' Jacobs said in a Celeb TV interview. 'But I swear someone must have put something in my drink because I started to feel really weird. The next thing I knew, I was slamming vodka shots and taking swings at people who were trying to stop me from driving. When some mates followed me in their cars, to make sure I got home OK, I sped up to try and escape them. I feel terrible about running over the cat. I love animals and I'm so sorry I made someone lose a pet. But I have lost absolutely everything.'

Jacobs has certainly lost followers – putting his financial future at risk. The Triple F's twice-a-month social media lottery awards winners a cash prize of £5,000 a week for life, along with six months of fame as one of a dozen 'Winfluencers' on CelebRate, the UK's most popular app and website. But there is a caveat: winners whose follower numbers fall below half a million during their six months on the platform forfeit those lifetime payouts, and are often catapulted, jobless, back into their old lives. The rule was originally created to ensure that winners made every effort to engage with fans and attract followers – and sponsorship money for the company – while they were featured on the site. But it later became a way for fans to express their disapproval for perceived bad behaviour, as Jacobs is now discovering. He began the week with more than six and a half million followers, making him the site's top-rated Winfluencer. But his numbers plummeted after two pieces of mobile phone footage surfaced online, the first showing his drunken confrontation with police. The second, more damaging video, shows a crying child cradling the body of her dead cat. Jacobs now has fewer than 600,000 followers.

'We're only allowed to back three CelebRaters,' former Jacob fan Marie Howe said, referring to the contest's practice of limiting the number of Triple F stars its users are permitted to follow at any one time, 'and I'm not wasting one of my follows on someone who drink-drives.'

Since winning the social media lottery four months ago, Jacobs has spoken openly about his difficult journey to sobriety, raising awareness of youth alcoholism and winning millions of followers in the process. He had even been tipped *to appear alongside Triple F celebrity Noah Fauster as the co-host of a star-studded documentary on the history of the contest.*

'This is a very sad day for Ozzie, for the Triple F and for me personally,' Fauster said. 'Ozzie is my friend. He fought a long and difficult battle against alcohol addiction. It is heart-breaking to see that alcohol won in the end. I just wish—'

*

'Catching up on the important news of the day, I see.'

Heather nearly dropped her phone as Steve spoke right next to her ear. She had been alone in the staffroom making coffee when the news alert about Ozzie Jacobs popped up on her screen, drawing her in.

'Jesus, Steve, can you not sneak up like that? I never hear you coming.'

'No one does. I'm like a ninja.'

The coffee hadn't finished brewing but Steve yanked the pot from its slot and filled Heather's mug, then his own. 'So Ozzie's in the Drop Zone. I guess that means there's going to be an extra draw this month to replace him.'

Her eyebrows shot up in surprise. 'You're a CelebRate fan?'

Steve foraged in the staff biscuit tin, face lighting up as he discovered a Hobnob near the bottom. 'Of course not. The whole concept of winning fame is ridiculous. My interest in the Triple F is purely academic. As an IT professional—'

'Do trainee computer science teachers count as IT professionals?'

Steve leaned a shoulder against the wall as he dipped the biscuit in his coffee. 'The point is, I inhabit the world of IT. Which allows me to appreciate the platform's innovative flourishes.' He gave her a sideways look. 'Contenders' Corner, for example.'

Heather's breath caught. Oh God. She kept her features neutral, telling herself it was highly unlikely he'd spotted anything; there were two million of them on there, after all.

'I like the search function,' Steve continued, 'the way you can narrow down the wannabes by geographical area, job or even hobbies and interests. I put in "bricklayer" and "origami" and got three hits. Then he gave her a Cheshire cat grin and her stomach sank. 'So . . .' Steve waggled his eyebrows. '"Class Act . . ."'

Heather flinched. Looking at it on her laptop screen after a few glasses of wine, the tagline had seemed witty, a playful reference to her career – her almost-career. Her delayed career. But hearing the words out loud, in Steve's Mancunian drawl, the catchphrase sounded silly and vain.

'It's easy to poke fun, but I'd like to hear you come up with a clever way to describe yourself in five words or less.'

'Hey, don't get me wrong, the taglines are the best bit.' He dragged fingers through hair that looked like it had come straight from a pillow. 'There was a fat taxi driver who went with "Driving Women Crazy". And my personal favourite, "Boob Job Girl." You can imagine what she looked like. Still, what the tagline lacked in wit and wisdom it more than made up for in accuracy and . . . scale.'

Heather started to laugh before quickly stopping herself. She mustn't encourage him. Steve was her best mate at Holland Park Upper – maybe even her best mate full stop, though she'd never admit that to him – and she sometimes feared it was only a matter of time before he ended up on the wrong side of an HR tribunal.

It wasn't that he was a bad bloke; far from it. He just needed to start acting his age. He was thirty-one, after all, eight years older than her. Heather had given up asking why he'd come to teacher training so late in life, what he'd done before. She could never get a straight answer. And anyway, she was just glad to have someone older along for the ride on her first induction year; it made her feel less self-conscious about the other student teachers being younger than her. Heather's original classmates had finished their two-year placements, taken off their trainee wheels and ridden off into proper teaching jobs across the country. Leaving her behind.

She sipped her coffee. 'Poor Ozzie. Imagine what that must be like, having everything you've ever wanted, money, fame, excitement. Only to end up right back where you started.'

Steve swallowed a bite of Hobnob. 'He isn't where he started. His old employers won't want him back now that he's a famous drunk. And he will have given up his old flat. So when he gets booted out of his posh pad, he'll end up like the other dumped CelebRaters – living with his parents, drinking too much, desperately trying to cobble together an independent social media career, but unable to because he's been labelled a loser. And he wouldn't be able to compete with CelebRate's flashy features and celebrity livestreams anyway.'

Heather frowned, considering this bleak assessment. She didn't condone drink-driving, obviously, but it did seem a bit unfair to lose everything over one mistake. 'He's really unlucky,' she said. 'I can count on one hand the number of winners who've been cut off like that. The rest get to do whatever they want for the rest of their lives and never worry about money again.'

Steve was watching her closely, blue eyes narrowed. He wasn't bad-looking, in a rumpled, skinny sort of way, the narrowness of

14

his hips accentuated by his habit of wearing oversized trousers belted at the waist.

'What would you do if you actually won?'

'Do?' Heather smiled as she imagined having £5,000 a week to spend as she pleased, swanning around parties and premieres, her every move followed by fans keen to share in the experience of swapping a small, ordinary life for a wealthy, glamorous one. Never feeling forgotten or invisible. 'Spend money. Quit work. Dance naked in a fountain of champagne.'

'Then what?'

'What do you mean?'

'You quit your job, you dance naked – cheers for the mental image, by the way.' His eyes did a quick up-down flick of her body and she felt herself flush. He wouldn't be looking at her like that if he knew what was hidden beneath the calf-length dress. 'You run around every posh shop you can find. Then what do you do?'

Heather shrugged. 'Travel, I guess? And go to . . .' Where did rich, famous people go, aside from clubs and parties? The front rows of pop concerts? Celebrity fundraisers? '. . . events. Eat in expensive restaurants.' She drank her coffee, watching him curiously. 'Why? What would you do?'

He dunked the last piece of Hobnob. 'Drink too much, try cocaine and develop a taste for it. Shag women who secretly hate me but are after my money. In short, go off the rails.' Some of the biscuit must have fallen into his coffee because Steve swore suddenly and plunged his fingers into the liquid to try and rescue it, the heat making him withdraw his hand immediately.

'Well, at least you have a plan.'

'What can I say? I know myself. I'm weak and superficial and horny. If I won, they'd have to rename it the Quadruple F . . . fame, fortune, followers . . . fucked.'

'Shh.' Heather shot a worried glance across the staffroom. Bad language was practically a criminal offence at Holland Park Upper. But the real teachers must still be in their weekly meeting with the head. 'Well, I think being rich and famous would be amazing.' She drained the dregs of her coffee, which had a sharp, burnt taste. 'Doing exactly what you want, when you want, not a moment wasted. Loads of people wanting to know you and be part of your life, hanging on your every word.' She could feel her leg throbbing like a rotten tooth. She would pop to the loo and take a pill before her next class. 'I would love every minute of it.'

'I don't know, Heather. You might not be so desperate for fame if you actually knew what it was like.' For once, Steve spoke quietly, and there was a look on his face she'd never seen before, as though a shadow had slipped across it.

'How would—' The bell drilled into her sentence. Damn. Was it that time already?

Steve put his cup in the sink. Sodden bits of biscuit debris mottled the bottom.

Heather peered at it. 'Do you really need to submerge them like that?'

'Yes. A wise man once said, "Tea's too wet without biscuits". Same goes for coffee.'

'A wise man?'

'My grandfather; an aficionado of the Hobnob.'

She washed her own cup and placed it upside down on the tea towel lining the counter, raising an eyebrow at Steve when he made no move to do the same.

'Didn't your mother teach you to clean up after yourself?'

'Nope,' he said cheerily, breezing towards the door. 'She's not that kind of mother.'

Heather tried unsuccessfully to picture Steve in a family setting. 'So what kind of mother is she?'

He shot her a smile that didn't touch his eyes. 'The kind you only talk about to your therapist.'

CHAPTER 3

'He's running a bit late,' Suzie said, speaking over her shoulder as she led Elliot through the base of the six-storey glass pyramid that was the Triple F headquarters. She had glossy blonde hair worn in a tight knot. Had they met before? He had trouble telling the Triple F executive assistants apart: they all wore the same company-issued grey trouser suits and pulled-back hair. 'I'll take you to the Blue Lounge. He'll meet you there.'

'Thanks.' Elliot had been told that the pyramid shape of the Triple F building – or 'HQ' as it was called by the people who worked there – had been chosen to represent the narrowing journey upward from the wide base of the general public to the two million-odd trying their luck on Contenders' Corner, to the Final Fifteen, ending with the single high point of the winner. The top floor was taken up by the CEO's office and, for reasons no one had been able to explain, the five floors below it were colour-coded: blue, red, yellow, green and orange.

Elliot followed Suzie through the Hub: a large, open-plan office in the middle of the ground floor bisected by a wide corridor, allowing a stream of people to pass through the middle. Rows of workers were seated at computers on either side, speaking into headsets, making the room feel like a call centre. Elliot slowed, tuning in to one of the phone conversations.

'As you know, Becky is now third in the ratings, so if you want her to wear your jacket you're looking at the premium Top Trio price. If that's outside your budget, Alison is 20 per cent off today, but she has fallen to eighth, so obviously her influence isn't on the same level as . . .'

Elliot paused to look up at the giant flat-screen monitor on the wall, which was displaying a slide show of images from the CelebRate homepage: women with upswept hair emerging from exclusive boutiques with shopping bags on their arms. Men with gelled-down hair emerging from limousines with women on their arms. A square-jawed gambler at a roulette wheel whose female companion wore bunny ears and not much else.

Suzie came to stand beside him, following his gaze. 'Our latest crop,' she said. Elliot watched as one image after another filled the screen: different people engaged in variations of the same activity – the shameless parading of wealth. He wondered what part of human nature fuelled this desperate desire for affirmation, for envy, even from total strangers. 'I started my Triple F career in this department,' Suzie was saying, 'back when Winfluencer Sales was much smaller. We had to call up fashion designers and restauranteurs and give them a whole pitch about why they should want to have our winners seen with their brand. But now *they* contact *us*. It's true, what the press has been saying. The Triple F is reinventing the way influencers are made and marketed.' Her smile sprang up, as though activated by a switch. 'Have you heard we're looking at a stock market floatation next year? Exciting times for the company.'

'Yes, selling fame is clearly a very lucrative business.'

The smile vanished as abruptly as it had appeared. 'We're not *selling* fame. You have to win it. Everyone who enters has the same chance, right up to the screening stage.'

Elliot's fingers tightened around the handle of his briefcase, which contained the latest batch of screening documents, dividing the finalists into greens, ambers and reds: those equipped to cope with the intense scrutiny and upheaval that came with winning the social media lottery, those who might be okay but would need careful monitoring and those likely to fall apart under the pressure.

'Yes,' he said, 'but you have to pay for that chance.'

'Ten pounds is a small price for a shot at being rich and famous. And you raise your social media profile just by getting posted on Contenders' Corner, so even the non-winners get value for money.'

Elliot raised an eyebrow. '"Non-winners?"'

'Didn't you get the email? That's what we're calling them now. Brand Management thinks "losers" sounds too negative.'

'Right.' Elliot had had a very clear goal in mind when he'd taken this job, a motive that no one else knew about. But at times like this, he found himself wondering whether it was really worth it.

*

'Ah, Dr Leyton!'

'Hello, Noah.'

The Blue Lounge was a glorified cafeteria full of fake Edwardian furniture. Chandeliers hung from the ceiling and a suit of armour stood in the corner, appearing to keep watch over the beverage station, with its pyramid of champagne glasses. A sloping window overlooked a rock garden bordered by a 'living wall' of ferns, designed to conceal the uninspiring view of the car park beyond.

'I got you an orange juice. Do you have the files?'

Elliot opened his briefcase and took out a plastic folder containing the finalists' assessments. He tossed it onto the table in front of Noah, seated on a blue sofa. The wall above him was covered in arty photographs of Triple F winners. Noah himself appeared in three of them – looking glamorous and handsome at a film premiere, astride a horse, sharing a joke with Scarlett Johansson at a fundraiser. He was the only winner featured more than once. But that was to be expected. Noah was the contest's first and most popular winner, the only one with a permanent CelebRate profile, consistently attracting more than seven million followers. After his six months had ended, he'd stayed on to become the contest's poster boy and celebrity spokesman – as well as its executive consultant and mentor to the winners. Noah Fauster was the North Star in the contest's ever-changing universe, remaining in the spotlight while the six-month-long conveyor belt of fame rolled past.

Elliot joined him on the sofa. 'So I assume the Triple F will be having an extra draw to backfill Ozzie?'

'A "bonus round", yes.'

'It's disappointing, what happened. Ozzie seemed to have adapted well. Though it was always going to be a risk, selecting a finalist with such a long history of alcoholism.'

'To be fair, he hadn't touched a drop in years.' Noah gestured towards the plastic folder. 'So what have you got for me today?'

Elliot took out the five files inside: his share of the fifteen people randomly selected from the millions of Contenders' Corner wannabes. 'Not a great batch, I'm afraid. A young widower whose wife died only a few months ago, clearly still grieving.

A nineteen-year-old with deep-seated insecurity and symptoms of anorexia. Definitely a self-harm risk. A girl with anger management issues. An electrician – unmarried, no girlfriend – who scored well, but whose parents died in a fire at his sister's house five years ago. The sister survived and he blames her for their deaths, so they aren't speaking. No family support, in other words.'

Noah's face fell. 'Don't tell me you've red-lighted all five?'

'No. The last one is a young woman who graduated from university last year but has been unemployed ever since, which is good: no difficulty transitioning to a life without work. Stable family background. Excellent scores on adaptability metrics.' He picked up the file labelled 'Candidate 2340', handing it across. 'She's a green.'

Elliot picked up the orange juice Noah had given him. Like all the cold beverages, it came in a champagne flute, to represent the luxury life they were marketing. Elliot found it annoying. The glasses were too damn small.

Noah glanced at the front of the file. 'The numbers mean nothing to me. What's her tagline?'

Elliot sighed. The catchphrases were included with the files so that, in theory, they might provide an insight into the contestant's self-image. But in reality, they were all just vapid nonsense.

'"Reaching for the Stars".'

'Oh.' Noah's tone was sour.

'I know. It's meaningless, but most of the slogans are.'

'No, it's not that. I know which one she is now and . . .' He sighed. 'Did you look up her profile on the Final Fifteen?'

'No. I never look at that. And I've recently stopped looking at CelebRate as well. Nothing of any psychological value is ever revealed there. It's all just empty posturing. People prancing around at parties, showing off their handbags.'

If Noah was offended by this assessment of the world he represented, he didn't show it.

'Well, allow me to enlighten you.' He reached inside his jacket and took out the miniature tablet he always seemed to keep there, tapping the screen and then handing it across. 'There.' Elliot took one look at the photo and knew that Candidate 2340 would never win. She was perhaps twenty, with a plump face and plain features framed by wisps of mouse-brown hair.

'I guess she might work as a makeover candidate,' Noah said doubtfully. 'Remember that fixer-upper from last year's Christmas batch? We did the full transformation – nose job, boobs, the lot. She wound up looking fantastic and the fans ate it up.'

'Maybe,' Elliot said, not buying it for a moment. He remembered the girl Noah was talking about. Big nose, flat chest and a terrible hairstyle. But also large doe eyes and a heart-shaped face. The potential for a Cinderella-style transformation – just in time for Christmas – had been obvious from the get-go. But Candidate 2340 had small eyes and big features softened by excess fat. She would never be beautiful or even pretty.

Noah reached for the other four files, using the taglines to match them to the photos on the finalists' page. He paused when he came to the electrician with the dead parents. Elliot had rated him amber, mainly because he knew it annoyed his bosses when too many of the finalists were red. Noah scanned the documents. 'He took ballroom dancing lessons, likes mountaineering and white-water rafting – all of which look great in photos – and he's included "beautiful women" on his list of hobbies.' His eyes drifted back to the face on the screen. 'Good-looking, working-class hero with an adventurous streak and a twinkle in his eye.' He looked at Elliot, eyebrows raised. 'Maybe he has some strong friendships, so doesn't need to rely on his family for support?'

Elliot drank a mouthful of juice. 'We've seen how winning can disrupt peer groups. A strong family unit tends to be the one constant as Winfluencers make the transition from their old lives to their new ones. But it's obviously not my call. If you want to gamble on an amber, it's up to you.'

Noah gathered the files and tucked them into the leather satchel at his feet.

'Well, it's not really my decision, of course,' he said, which both of them knew wasn't true. Noah had a knack for picking winners who drew in followers – and therefore advertisers. So if he told the selection department that one of the finalists looked like 'a good fit', the matter was pretty much decided. 'Let's just hope the other two shrinks' – Noah must have seen Elliot wince at the word because he said quickly – 'sorry, "psychological screeners", had better luck with their five and give us some good greens to choose from.'

'Yes.' Elliot swirled his tiny portion of orange juice around its ridiculous champagne glass, thinking, *the world would be a better place if this building, and everything it represents, was wiped from the face of the earth.* He smiled at Noah. 'Let's hope.'

*

Heather could feel Eric's eyes drilling into her like dark knives, twisting with hate and resentment. She lifted her chin, meeting his gaze with a level stare. She was posted just outside the classroom, watching the kids surging through the hall in noisy waves and trickles, keeping an eye out for scuffles, bullying or illicit mobile phone use. The head's office was just a few doors down and Eric was standing right outside it, flanked by his parents. His week-long suspension was up and the three of them had been summoned for a discussion about the terms of his return and a reminder of the school's strict anti-drugs policy. As if any of it would make a blind bit of difference. Heather's gaze moved to Eric's mother, who was smoothing her platinum fringe. Heather had seen the woman at parents' evenings, school concerts and science fairs: slim and perfect, with salon-fresh hair and designer outfits. Every inch the wife of the generous benefactor. What was it like, Heather wondered, to glide through life like that, shopping for clothes without checking the price tags, weekends spent drinking champagne and eating canapés, never having to feel lonely or forgotten? She experienced a sour twist of envy before reminding herself that Mrs Shulman's life couldn't be all sunshine and roses – not with Eric as her son.

Heather switched her attention to the husband who had, until now, been an unknown quantity: an invisible source of largesse, whose name was synonymous with wealth. In the flesh, he was shorter than she'd expected. Square-jawed and square-shouldered, hair buzzed to a shadow on his skull, minimising the impact of a receding hairline. He had the same dark eyes as his son. He turned them on Heather now, thick brows gathering. She gave a small nod of acknowledgement; he was a parent after all, she had to be professional. But his face didn't change. His dark eyes duelled with hers, refusing to break away, sending out a chill. Then came a shriek, followed by a girl's voice shouting 'Get that away from me, you arsehole!' Heather turned, relieved, to mediate a dispute involving a rubber spider. The next time she looked towards the head's office, the Shulmans were gone.

Heather sat in front of her laptop at the kitchen table, considering her Contenders' Corner profile. With Ozzie the cat-killer gone, the number of Winfluencers had fallen below twelve, triggering a bonus round that could take place at any time – generating a new list of finalists. So she wanted her profile to look its best . . . just in case. She considered the photo on her screen. It was flattering, no doubt about that: her head tilted, long chestnut hair straying across one cheek as she turned the page of a text book. But she needed to change the tagline. Class Act. How had she not noticed how braggy that sounded? She ran through various career-themed alternatives – Staying in School? Educated Guesser? – but they weren't any better. Of course, the slogan didn't *have* to be job-based. But what else could she pin herself to? She'd been a keen swimmer once, had even won a few medals. And used to love dancing. But that was all in the past. She spoke a little French, played a mean game of Monopoly and had dabbled in ceramics just long enough to create a scroll-shaped vase and a set of mugs, all of which dribbled when used. And that was it. God, was she really that dull? She swiped through the photos linked to her post. Three. The minimum. And even that had been a struggle, given that she'd only had the last seven or eight months to draw from – months where her days were usually divided between teaching at the school and sitting on the sofa, watching reality dating programmes over a ready meal. Beyond that lay the dead zone of the previous two years, and she certainly didn't want anyone seeing what she'd looked like then. Maybe—

She jumped as a sound came through her laptop's speaker,

like a flourish of trumpets. She could hear it being echoed on her mobile phone on the kitchen table. The screen filled with an image of exploding fireworks, a message rolling across it in flashing letters. 'CONGRATULATIONS! YOU'RE A FINALIST!'

*

When it faded away she found herself flooking at her own picture among fourteen others, on a page headed 'The Final Fifteen'.

There was a stunned moment of disbelief. Then a crashing wave of adrenaline. She was a Triple F finalist! *Oh my God. Oh-my-God-oh-my-God-oh-my-God.*

Heather jumped up from the sofa, her body suddenly unable to contain all the excitement surging through it. She had been chosen: one of only fifteen people randomly selected out of nearly two million! She let out a shriek of pure joy before clapping her hands over her mouth.

She couldn't just stand here, alone with this momentous news. She needed to share it. Grabbing her keys, she shot out the door, not even bothering to put shoes on. She was only going three doors down, after all. Heather lived in one of the identikit housing estates built in the days when the government had decided everyone needed a front door that led outside in order to feel happy and fulfilled and satisfied with their place in society. So they had put up giant brown blocks of flats fronted by row upon row of doors with a narrow walkway running in front of them. Heather's was hemmed by a low wall scrawled with graffiti, for residents to lean against as they looked out across the park that formed a borderland between their scruffy edge of Shepherds Bush and the rarefied atmosphere of Holland Park. Heather often paused on her doorstep to admire the white-pillared doorways on the other side of the park, Porsches and Jaguars parked out front, wondering what her life would be like if she lived over there. What *she* would be like.

The light was on in the frosted kitchen window beside Debbie's front door. Heather knocked and a moment later, her friend was standing in the doorway wearing her favourite wig: the orange-tipped one that went all the way down her back. Debbie had decided years ago that she didn't have the time or energy to manage her thick Afro hair so had buzzed it short and bought an extensive wig collection instead – eleven at last count – which she swapped from day to day, to the delight of the toddlers she took care of at the Ladbroke Grove nursery where she worked.

'Hello, lovely.' She beckoned Heather inside. 'I don't know what's just happened, but that is clearly a face bursting with news.'

Bursting. That was exactly the right word. And not just her face: her heart was bursting with excitement and her mind was bursting with thoughts and her body was bursting with trapped energy.

'Wine?'

'I'm assuming that was a statement and not a question.'

Debbie waved her towards the sofa before disappearing into the tiny kitchen off the living room. Heather put fingers to her lips and noticed they were trembling. She breathed in through her nose, telling herself to calm down as she released the air through her mouth. It was silly really, letting herself get so worked up. One in fifteen. It was never going to happen. But still . . .

'There you go.' Debbie reappeared with a bottle and two glasses, which she placed on the coffee table. She bent to fill Heather's glass before pouring her own and settling down beside her on the squashy brown sofa. 'You have the wine. Now spill the tea.'

Heather flirted briefly with the idea of building suspense, but found she couldn't wait another moment.

'I'm a Triple F finalist!'

Debbie's jaw dropped. 'No *way!* You're in the Final Fifteen, the FF?' She took a swig of wine, eyes wide. 'Well FFS!' And she laughed, one of the deep Debbie laughs that seemed to come right from her core. 'Babe, that is *amazing*! I've got to see this for myself.' She leaned across the coffee table for her tablet – an iPad knock-off with a cracked screen she was always meaning to get fixed – and switched it on, drumming her fingers against it until the Final Fifteen appeared. She nudged Heather playfully in the ribs with an elbow as she clicked on her photo. 'Get you, girl! What a hottie! A face made for CelebRate. And "Class Act" . . . cute!'

'I'm not going to be on CelebRate because I'm not going to win,' Heather said, more to herself than Debbie. Now that the initial surge of excitement had passed, reality was setting in. She needed to manage her own expectations, not get carried away. The higher she let her hopes rise, the further they would have to fall when the winner was announced next week.

But Debbie had no such doubts.

'Well, I heard they choose the person who gets the most clicks on the Final Fifteen page. And that should definitely be you. You're much better looking than these others.'

'That's just a tabloid theory. The Final Fifteen are chosen randomly but no one really knows exactly how the winners are selected.' Heather leaned over the tablet and examined the fourteen other faces: her rivals. She tapped on a blonde posing beside a surfboard in a bikini, long hair bouncing around her shoulders.

Her body was sun-gold and blemish-free. A video began to play, showing the surfer riding a wave that slowly curled itself around her. 'And anyway, I'm nowhere near as pretty as this girl.'

She drank a mouthful of wine, feeling some of her excitement drain away.

'Please,' Debbie scoffed, waving a dismissive hand above the surfer's image. 'She's just a generic blonde. Your look has depth. It's more interesting. And check out Blondie's tagline: "Surf's Up". She's clearly too thick to understand the basic instruction to describe *yourself*. She's just describing the condition of water.' Debbie flicked back to the homepage, where the scrolling Top Trio banner showcased images of the three most popular winners. Heather scanned the row of moving thumbnails just below it: livestream links to parties and premieres where Winfluencers were in the thick of the action, chatting with their followers and passing along their questions to celebrities in real time. Heather's eyes paused on the middle thumbnail, showing Jim Munson, the number two-rated CelebRater, speaking to Kate Winslet in what appeared to be a castle, tapestries and swords displayed on the stone wall behind them. Hollywood A-listers milled in the background drinking champagne. Heather watched Jim clink glasses with the film star, feeling as though she was peeking through a tiny window into another, more dazzling world. Debbie put the tablet on the arm of the sofa. 'I bet you'll win.' She parked her heels on the coffee table. 'Have you thought about what you'd do? Would you stay on at the school?'

'I shouldn't think so,' Heather said, and was surprised by a twinge of regret. Good Lord. Did she actually *like* her under-paid, underappreciated, unglamorous job? Spending her days force-feeding science to teenage brains too jam-packed with crushes and gaming strategies to make space for anything else; patrolling the recreation zone like a prison warden; trading anecdotes about terrible students over terrible coffee in the staffroom? True, she had always wanted to teach, had thought it would be fun – rewarding even. But that was more than two and a half years ago, when her career was still on track.

'A full-time celebrity. Imagine!' Then Debbie frowned, making her whole face change. 'You'll leave your flat, won't you? All the winners move to posh houses.' She put a hand to her mouth, eyes sheening with tears. 'I'll miss you!'

Heather leaned over to give her friend a hug. 'Don't go getting all emotional about something that isn't going to happen. And even if I did win – which I won't – we'd still see each other. You'd just come over to my luxury pad for a visit and our wine would be poured by one of my many hot male servants. Dressed only in boxers and bow ties, as per the boss's orders.' She laughed, but Debbie didn't join in.

'No. Once you're rich, you'll have a new life with new people. You'll forget all about me.'

'Don't be silly,' Heather said. 'I'm not the sort of person who would drop her friends just because of coming into money. What do you take me for?' She raised her glass, feeling her excitement returning. One in fifteen. She'd told Debbie it would never happen. But those actually weren't terrible odds. 'To good luck and good mates!'

'Cheers to that.' Debbie was smiling again as their glasses clinked.

CHAPTER 4

It's a matter of finding the tipping point. Of knowing which buttons to push. They all have weak points, wounds that can be reopened. I've seen to that.

It's quiet in my study. No sound but the tap of my fingers moving across the keyboard. I slowly become aware that it's dark outside. When did the sun go down? I've been so absorbed in my work, hunting through the chat boards for the perfect spot, that I didn't register the fading light. Now the only source of illumination is my computer screen, casting a frosty glow across the stack of papers beside it. The one on top is a printout of an article about my current target, showing him emerging from a club with a blonde on his arm. The one underneath it contains the secret he's been hiding.

I decide to start with Celeb Chat: a thread entitled 'Loveable Rogue'. It's full of the usual stuff about how he may be a ladies' man, but at least he's honest and up front about it, how he's cutting a swathe through the female population with a cheeky grin and a wink. I select one of the comments then tap 'Post Reply'. I write, *Ran into an old mate of Jim's named Desmond, who says he's 'a real man's man'.*

I've chosen my words carefully. To the site's censors and fans, the comment will sound innocuous – banal even. But not to Jim. A few more of these sprinkled around CelebRate and the fan boards he's sure to be monitoring, and he'll begin to panic, wondering who I am and what I know.

CHAPTER 5

When Heather got back from Debbie's the first thing she did was go through her messages. Dozens of DMs and emails had arrived over the last hour, including one from the Triple F itself, loaded with attachments: forms, background questionnaires and psychometric tests to be printed off, filled out by hand and sent back via the contest's private courier service; the Triple F was famously paranoid about online security. There was also a warning not to speak to journalists at this stage in the process. The *London Courier* must surely be aware of this edict but was having a punt anyway; they'd DMed her, requesting an interview. And a Channel 4 producer wanted to record Heather's 'journey' and be with her, cameras rolling, when the winner was announced. Just as well she wasn't allowed to say yes to that one. She didn't want to risk having her look of crushed disappointment captured on film. Her inbox was filled with well wishes from people she hadn't heard from in ages; college friends who'd left her messages on read were now congratulating her on making it into the FF, suggesting drinks to celebrate. She read through them all, smiling. Then she reached the last unread email, sent an hour before the finalists had been announced. The sender's name was listed simply as

'E', the web address a jumble of letters and numbers tagged to a Gmail account. Weird.

Then she opened it and her smile fell away. The message was short, but those eight words were like a splash of icy water, sluicing away the warmth that had come with the deluge of greetings and well wishes.

'Watch yourself, bitch. Or I'll make you sorry.'

*

'Do you think I should call the police?' Heather glanced around the staffroom to make sure no one was eavesdropping. But the proper teachers were bunched together on the chairs by the window, heads bent in a tight circle of gossip.

Steve broke off a finger of KitKat bought from the shop beside the school and bit into it, forehead creasing as he chewed. Heather wondered if he was surprised she'd come to him with this. He probably assumed she had other, closer friends outside of work. And not so long ago, he would have been right. She used to have a whole posse of college classmates to drink with, laugh with, confide in. But not any more. These days there were only two people she felt she could turn to in a crisis: Debbie and Steve. She had chosen Steve because, for all his flaws, there was a core of strength there, a practicality.

'Don't waste your time on the police,' he said. 'They won't do anything. The internet is overrun with trolls. People get messages like this every day. But I do think you should find out who sent it. If you want I can track them down using the IP address.'

'You can?' She lifted an eyebrow.

'Have you forgotten that I am a computer educator?'

'Isn't your job mainly telling teenagers not to run off with chatroom strangers and making sure no one's getting around the porn filters?'

'Mock if you must, but I happen to have created my own online gaming platform, called "Blood and Guts", which has attracted a respectable following.' He took another bite of KitKat. 'I don't like to brag, but I'm kind of a genius.'

'It's a shame you don't like to brag. You have such a talent for it.' She gave his arm a teasing elbow nudge and received a side-smile in response. Then the first bell rang, marking the end of lunch.

'Back to the salt mines,' Steve said, putting his dirty mug in the sink, ignoring her pointed look as she washed her own. 'Don't worry. I'll find your troll. Leave it with me.'

CHAPTER 6

'Look,' Debbie said, as Heather carried two glasses of wine towards the sofa. 'It's almost time.'

Heather's eyes flew to the station clock on her living room wall. The week since the finalists were announced had gone by in a blur, her emotions swerving between crashing waves of excitement and queasy swells of anxiety. But now, finally, the moment of truth was here. In less than two minutes, the latest Triple F winner would be announced. A fresh burst of adrenaline rode through her, bringing a sick, jittery feeling. She sat down next to Debbie, handing her a glass. Placed her phone face down on the coffee table. Gulped her wine.

'I won't win,' she said firmly. 'One in fifteen. Not great odds for someone who's not naturally lucky.'

'But you *are* lucky,' Debbie said. 'You've already made it through the luck part. Once you're in the finals it's not about that any more. It's about being selected.'

Selected. She wondered how much of that process was down to the forms she'd printed off and filled out, the hundreds of multiple-choice questions. There had been personality tests, intelligence tests, tests to gauge adaptability, reasoning, emotional stability.

And the background report. Pages and pages of probing questions about Heather's life, her family, her past relationships. She had sat for a long time staring at the document headed 'Traumatic Life Events,' with its instruction to write down 'incidents, relationships or accidents that may have disrupted the course of your life or had a strong negative impact on your psychological well-being.' She'd sat with her pen suspended over the paper for a long time before jotting 'N/A' and quickly turning the page.

Heather watched the minute hand's glacial creep through the final sixty seconds. Until it was pointing straight up. It was time.

Then came the now familiar flourish of trumpets from her mobile, still lying face down.

She stared at it, suddenly afraid to look. Did that sound mean she was the winner? Or did they use the same sound to thank the losers for playing and let them know a different finalist had been chosen?

And just for a moment, a strange thought whispered round her skull.

Be careful what you wish for.

'Aren't you going to go pick that up?' Debbie was staring at the handset with wide eyes.

'Yes.'

But Heather remained perfectly still as her phones began to ring, first her mobile, then the landline, not moving a muscle as they went to the answering service.

Then immediately started ringing again. And again.

That was how she knew she'd won.

CHAPTER 7

Heather stood nervously in front of the main entrance of the Triple F's headquarters, unsure what to do next. She'd never been here before, though she'd seen the building's image countless times on TV and online: a billion-pound glass pyramid located on the border between Chiswick and South Acton, designed by a famous architect lured out of retirement by the contest's CEO. She reckoned they must have full-time window cleaners because the glass walls gleamed in the late-April sunshine, the reflected light powerful enough to make her squint. Heather glanced at the time on her phone – 10.41, nearly twenty minutes early. She looked around for somewhere to pass the time, but this was one of those weird pockets of London where shops and terrace houses suddenly gave way to warehouses, scrapyards and car parks. She had walked here from the Tube station along a path beside the tracks, passing nothing but a Big Yellow storage depot and a furniture warehouse. There was a fountain out front – three intertwined metal Fs surrounded by water and blasted by spray, but no bench on which to sit and admire it. She had just decided to see if she could wait in the lobby when the building's glass doors parted to reveal a blonde woman of about her age wearing a fitted grey trouser suit, hair pulled back in a tight knot. Her smile gleamed with fresh lip gloss.

'Heather Davies?'

'Yes.'

'Hello, I'm Melanie. Can you come this way, please?'

The butterflies that had been performing acrobatics in her stomach for the last fifteen hours picked up speed, batting their wings against her insides.

When Debbie had finally convinced Heather to 'pick up that bloody phone!', she was greeted by the same image of exploding fireworks that had appeared when she'd become a finalist. But this time the words superimposed over it said, 'Congratulations! You are THE WINNER!' A volley of emails from the Triple F had followed in its wake, telling her what steps came next, and about her various appointments at the contest's headquarters. But she hadn't bothered reading any of those at first because she was too busy dancing around the living room with Debbie, flinging her arms in the air, shouting out no mores – 'No more shopping in the reduced section of Tesco!' 'No more travelling by bus!' 'No more showering at work to save on hot water!'

Her phone wouldn't stop ringing; she'd had to switch it off, leaving it to collect more messages from reporters she wasn't allowed to speak to and old acquaintances she hadn't heard from in years. And her brother, of course. No sign of her mother, but she probably hadn't heard, living where she did.

Excitement had kept Heather awake all night, staring at the ceiling, with its comma-shaped mystery stain. Her life, after being mothballed for two years, was now surging ahead on rocket fuel, propelling her into a future where millions of people would watch her every move and hang on her every word. Where each day would bring exciting new adventures. She would earn more in two months than her former classmates made in a year. So in a way, it was like winning time itself, reclaiming the years that had been stolen from her.

Melanie led Heather along a wide corridor that cut through the middle of the ground floor, steeped in natural light. Workers rushed past, their movements filled with purpose. Heather felt some of her excitement give way to insecurity. Everyone looked expensively dressed and immaculately groomed, making her suddenly conscious of her unfashionably long skirt and Primark blouse, the hair tied back in a scrunchie: more schoolgirl than socialite. She should have gone with her first instinct and worn it down.

Melanie had told her their first stop would be the make-up artist's studio, followed by the 'hair centre'. After that, Heather would receive her 'F-phone' – packed with camera filters and editing software – and be given a 'selfie tutorial' on making the most of it. Then there'd be her first of three media training sessions, a meeting with her image consultant and a professional studio photo shoot. Last, but definitely not least, a 'get to know you' chat with Noah, the famous face of the contest, who would act as her mentor, guiding Heather through her Triple F journey. The thought sent the butterflies into a frenzy; she was about to meet Noah Fauster in the flesh!

'I don't usually wear much make-up,' Heather said as she was led into a room dominated by a mirror framed with globe-shaped lights. There was a long make-up counter beneath it covered in blushers and brushes, tongs and straighteners, creams and sprays. 'I'm a bit concerned about the emphasis on wearing it.'

Melanie patted her arm. 'There's no need to worry. Sandra will help you master a look for every occasion.'

The make-up artist was friendly, explaining each brush and sponge stroke as she went: how she was counterbalancing a sallow tinge that Heather hadn't been aware existed and using shade to narrow the look of her nose and soften her chin, since they were apparently in need of narrowing and softening. Heather was taught the correct technique for applying mascara – she'd been holding the mirror at completely the wrong angle – and which brush to use when blending eyeliner. The lesson was videotaped so that Heather could follow along every morning. Every morning! The session had taken well over an hour. Then she was sent to the hair centre, where the scrunchie was whipped away and her hair was 'reimagined' by a French hairdresser named Jean-Paul, who transformed it into a series of upswept waves. He bustled off straight afterwards, saying he was late for a colour consultation.

Presumably she was supposed to wait in the hair centre until either Melanie or the selfie trainer came to collect her. She sat in the salon chair, staring at her reflection, barely recognising the face there. She had been transformed into someone else: a wealthy, glamorous woman, the kind who bought her clothes in Harrods when they weren't even in the sale. It felt strange, looking into a mirror and seeing a different version of herself staring back.

'What do you think?'

The door to the room was outside the mirror's range and must have opened soundlessly because the male voice caught her off guard, making her pulse jump.

A man – the selfie trainer, presumably – crossed the room to stand behind her, staring at her reflection, his gaze unnervingly direct. He was older than Heather – mid-thirties, perhaps – with skin so pale it was almost translucent. His dark hair stuck up at the front and, unlike everyone else she'd seen so far, he was wearing casual clothes; a grey cardigan open to reveal a T-shirt showing a blocky green figure that she recognized, thanks to her students, as a Minecraft character. He wasn't at all what she'd been expecting. Though, to be fair, she hadn't even known selfie trainers existed until today.

'How does it feel?' he asked, nodding towards her reflection.

She touched her hair, meeting his eyes in the mirror.

'You mean the makeover?'

'Yes.'

'I think Sandra and Jean-Paul did a great job.'

'That's not what I'm asking.' He considered her reflection with a look of intense concentration. 'How does it feel seeing yourself like this?' His irises were a shade of grey she'd never seen before: so pale it made them appear luminous, like some underground creature whose eyes glowed in the dark. 'It's a strange notion, burying the skin under layers of coloured liquid and powder. Putting on a mask.'

It seemed an odd thing to say for a man whose job revolved around creating flattering surface images. It took her by surprise, making her drop her guard.

'Men should be the ones who wear make-up,' she said. 'That's how it works in the animal kingdom.'

'I wasn't aware that animals wore make-up.' He said it deadpan, not a trace of a smile. Then he placed his palms on the back of the salon chair, leaning against it. He didn't touch her, but she was aware of his proximity, like a force field, entering her personal space, disrupting the signals.

'Nature's own built-in make-up,' she said. 'Colours that appear when they're old enough to mate. Have you seen those baboons with red and blue faces? Like 1970s eye shadow – completely over the top. And peacocks, with their fancy feather jewellery. Males desperate for female attention, trying to be flashy.'

'To be fair, not all of nature's flash is males on the pull. Some of it is aposematism.'

'Oppose . . . What?'

'The displaying of bright colours by poisonous animals. It's a warning to predators, a way of labelling themselves as toxic.'

'I wish humans had warning colours like that. I could have avoided my last relationship.'

He tipped his head to one side, mouth flickering in an abbreviated smile.

'You're funny,' he said. 'That's good.'

'You're brainy. That's better.'

They looked at each other in the mirror, not speaking until the silence began to feel loaded. Heather was about to ask him if he had her new handset so they could start the session when the door flew open and Melanie glided in, eyes aimed down at the tablet in her hand.

'Apologies for the delay. The selfie trainer is ready, so—' Then she looked up, saw the man behind the chair and stopped abruptly. 'Oh.' There was a pause. The man's eyes flicked sideways to briefly register Melanie's presence, before returning to Heather's reflection. She stared back at him, puzzled. If he wasn't the trainer, then who was he? Melanie ran a palm over her hair, appearing flustered.

'Sorry, I didn't realize . . . Was there something you needed . . .'

'I came down because there are some issues with the server I need to attend to.' He aimed a nod at the mirror. 'I will leave you to continue your orientation.'

And he walked swiftly from the room.

Issues with the server. So he was from the IT department. That explained the white skin and Minecraft T-shirt: a tech nerd, pale from too many hours bathed in screen light. Should she ask Melanie for his name? The thought surprised her. It wasn't as if he was attractive, certainly not in any conventional sense. But there was something about him, something . . . what was the word? She pictured him standing behind the chair, eyes locked on her mirror-self. *Compelling.*

As soon as they were alone, Melanie was back on form, cool and businesslike.

'So,' she said as Heather got up from the chair, 'I just spoke to Noah and he's really looking forward to meeting you.'

Heather's excitement returned, flip-flopping inside her. Was this really her life? Being transformed by the country's top hair and make-up artists, then meeting a man whose face was plastered across websites, TV screens and magazine pages?

'What woman *wouldn't* look forward to meeting Noah Fauster?' she said. 'I feel like I'm in a dream. I just hope I'm not going to wake up!'

Melanie laughed, revealing a row of surprisingly pointy teeth. 'Don't worry,' she said. 'We'll make sure you never wake up.'

*

'It's all about allowing others to share in your journey.' Noah rested his elbows on his knees, hands loosely clasped as he leaned forward on the sofa. 'You have been given a very rare opportunity to exchange a life of toil and daily struggle for a glamorous new one: a life that most people can only dream of.' He looked at her intently across the low table. 'Every time you post on CelebRate, you offer the less fortunate a small piece of that dream.'

Noah Fauster was handsome. So handsome, in fact, that Heather was having trouble concentrating on what he was saying. She kept staring at his eyes, wondering if they really were that impossible blue-green colour – surely those must be tinted contacts? – and at his hair, which was dark, but with lighter, bronzy glimmers that caught the light. Cheekbones that could have been chiselled by Michelangelo. Jesus, who actually *looked* like that? She'd seen his picture before – obviously, who hadn't? – but experiencing him in the flesh was like watching a statue step off its pedestal and stroll over to shake your hand.

'Don't you agree?' he asked, catching her off guard.

'Yes,' she bluffed. He'd been saying something about the rules concerning sponsored products; refusal to feature them in posts could result in banishment from CelebRate and the severing of weekly payments. But then he'd started talking about copyright law and her attention had drifted. She shifted uncomfortably in the armchair, crossing her legs then quickly uncrossing them in response to a bolt of pain. They were seated in a lounge filled with blue furniture and beautiful people chatting, laughing and clinking champagne glasses over plates of what appeared to be mostly salad.

'Good,' Noah said. 'Although the Triple F is a generous benefactor to a range of charities, it is, at the end of the day, a business. And by participating, you are consenting to become part of that business model.' He flashed a grin. 'But since your so-called "obligations" consist of wearing top designer gear and eating for free in some of the world's best restaurants, it's not exactly hard graft.'

'No.' Her leg was getting worse and she fidgeted in the arm-chair, trying unsuccessfully to find a more comfortable position. The photo shoot had put too much strain on her knee – all that spinning and kicking. She needed a top-up now, before the pain dug deeper.

Heather slipped the pill container from her pocket then laid her jacket across her lap, screening her hands under it as she twisted open the vial and fished out a pill. Then she pretended to cough, placing a hand to her mouth and popping the pill inside, washing it down with her flute of sparkling water.

Mission accomplished. She relaxed against the armchair, now able to focus on what Noah was saying.

'Once you've moved house . . .'

'Yes, I plan to start looking for a place soon.'

'Tomorrow, ideally. You need a home that fits with your new image and lifestyle. But don't worry, you won't have to lift a finger. Your image consultant will liaise with the property division and show you a selection of suitable addresses, arranging for the mortgage to be paid directly out of your winnings. We're talk-ing about multimillion-pound homes.' He picked up his flute of orange juice. 'Isn't that exciting?'

'Incredibly exciting.' Heather nodded as she added some additional 'no mores' to her list. No more water that changed temperature mid-shower. No more sitting on a park bench in good weather, wishing she had a garden. No more loud music coming through the walls at all hours. Her home would be spacious, serene and beautiful. She felt a soaring sense of wonder. She had been given a second chance at life. And she intended to grab it with both hands.

Noah drank some juice. 'Have a think about what your dream

home looks like. Is it modern or historic? What's most important: big garden, great view, central location? The rest, I'll leave to our experts, who will be messaging you shortly.' He glanced at her new handset on the table between them. 'How was the tutorial? F-phone all set up?'

She picked it up, glancing at the screen.

'All good, though I'm having trouble adding my Instagram, X and TikTok accounts. I can't find them on the app list.'

'That's because they're not there. CelebRate is a safe space; we've installed AI software that scans DMs for abusive content, deleting them automatically and blocking the sender. But we can't safeguard the content on other platforms, so we don't allow them onto the handset. Obviously we can't control what apps and sites you choose to use on your private tablet or computer, but the F-phone is designed to keep you safe and keep you focused exclusively on your CelebRate notifications and DMs. Believe me, that will give you more than enough to stay on top of.'

'Fair enough.' She thought of all those posts and messages. People talking about the things she did, said and wore. It was simultaneously exciting and nerve-racking.

Noah put down his orange juice. 'Tomorrow the highlights from today's shoot will be posted in the Big Reveal, then you don't have to do anything for the rest of the week except enjoy your new life.'

Heather was familiar with the 'Big Reveal' – a scrolling, music-bedded gallery of glamorous, professional photos and videos introducing the newest winner, accompanied by snippets of biographical info, like the trailer for an upcoming film.

Heather Davies, coming soon to a cinema near you!

After that came a six-day gap, as anticipation and curiosity built, then the new star would appear in selfie form, showing off the wonders of their new, Triple F lifestyle, primped up and Prada-clad, grinning with delight. Most of the girls seemed to wear skimpy outfits such as crop tops and short skirts. Obviously she wouldn't be doing that. And if the contest tried to pressure her into putting on something more revealing, she'd say she was a feminist and didn't want to be objectified. They couldn't argue with that, sponsors or no sponsors. Everything was going to be fine. Better than fine; *amazing*.

'I'm here today to give you an overview of your new life as a Winfluencer – what to expect from us and what we expect from you.' Noah folded his hands, tone turning serious, less like an excited game show host telling the winner about their prize. 'But I'm also here as your mentor. It's a role I've taken on because I believe it's critically important. You are entering a period of enormous change. And even good change – let's be honest, *fantastic* change – can be stressful and there are likely to be occasional bumps along the way. So if you need anything, a shoulder to lean on, an ear to bend . . . I'm never more than a phone call away. I've DMed you my number, please add it to your contacts. No problem is too big or small.'

Heather felt a rush of gratitude, mixed with shame at having reduced this man to a two-dimensional figure: all surface, no substance. Noah Fauster was clearly a kind, empathetic person who deserved to be appreciated for more than just his looks.

'Thank you, Noah.'

'Any time.' He tilted his head. 'I think that covers everything. Unless there's something you'd like to ask me?'

She considered the backlog of questions that had been building up all day: would she always have to wear this much make-up?

49

What if she just wanted to stay home one day, sit on the sofa and do nothing . . . would she still have to submit three pictures or videos? And most important of all, what if no one liked her posts? What if no one liked *her*? The future she was being offered was so bright, so beautiful . . . what if she messed it up? Bands of anxiety were tightening around her ribs, making it suddenly feel as if there wasn't enough air inside this blue room, with its sealed, sloping glass.

She could sense Noah watching her as she hunched forward, doing her breathing exercises – in through the nose, out through the mouth – until she felt calmer.

'Sorry.' She sat back against the blue armchair, face hot with embarrassment. 'I'm not feeling a hundred per cent.'

He leaned over to pat her hand. 'I know it's a lot to take in. Trust me, it's perfectly natural to feel overwhelmed. But don't worry. You won't be posting for another week. This will all feel more normal by then.'

'I'm sure it will. I don't know what's wrong with me.'

'There's nothing wrong with you. You just need some time to get used to all the big changes that are happening in your life. So I suggest you go home and relax. Can I walk you out?' Noah got up from the sofa, crooking his elbow so she could take his arm: a surprisingly old-fashioned gesture for a man still in his twenties. She rose to stand beside him, slipping her arm through his, feeling shy and self-conscious bathed in the glow of his fame and beauty. Admiring glances followed Noah as they walked through the tables.

'Thanks again, Noah – for all your help.'

'It's what I'm here for. You can contact me any time, day or night, any time you're worried or afraid.'

'"Afraid"?' She turned to look at him, taken aback. 'What do I have to be afraid of?'

'Sorry, I misspoke. I meant to say "nervous".' He led her out into the corridor, with its thick blue stripe running along one wall. 'There's nothing to be afraid of here. Nothing at all.'

CHAPTER 8

They all have secrets. They paint a pretty picture to fool the world, but the secrets are there, hiding beneath the shiny surface like toxic sludge, just waiting to be drawn to the surface.

I fold my arms behind my head and consider the man in the photo pinned to my study wall. He's managed to hold it together so far, keeping up appearances, smiling for the cameras. For the ladies. But he knows his past is rising up through the muck, unburying itself. He's scared. And scared people do stupid things.

I use the phone tracker, watching him head east, a black 'F' moving along a map. It stops and I expand the view so I can see exactly where he is. The Fox and Hound, a pub in the middle of nowhere. Not even a gastro pub. A traditional boozer, the kind with dart boards and microwaved curries and carpets that smell of spilt beer.

'You're trying to get away, aren't you, Jim?' I say softly to the photo on the wall.

He wants a break from his new life, with its glitzy parties and unfamiliar clothes. The cameras, following his every move. He's retreating into the familiar, the comfortable. The anonymous. He's doing that because he's fraying under the pressure. *My* pressure.

I log in to the account I use for situations like this. Send out a few emails.

Then I return my attention to the tracker, with its now motionless F.

He wants to escape. But I won't let him.

CHAPTER 9

When Heather walked through the school gates on Monday, a cheer went up from the Year 9 girls loitering beside the bicycle rack.

'Congratulations, Miss! You looked dead glamorous on the Big Reveal!'

Heather gave them a sheepish grin and a small wave. They were all right, those girls, if a bit noisy during chemistry lab.

They weren't the only ones staring. Heads turned as she pushed upstream through the river of students in the main hallway, towards the relative tranquillity of the staffroom. A boy from her Year 8 set performed a dramatic double take as she passed.

'Do my eyes deceive me, or is there a CelebRater in our humble hallway?' He whipped his phone from his blazer pocket and held it up, clearly filming her. 'Quick, someone unroll the red carpet!'

'Very funny, Winston. Now put away the mobile before I confiscate it.'

She didn't hang around to make sure he'd done as he was told. She'd been too excited to sleep properly all weekend, so desperately needed a coffee. But as soon as she entered the staffroom, all conversation immediately ceased, like in one of those scenes in old Westerns where the baddie steps through the batwing doors and everyone inside stops and stares. Then someone began to clap and a couple of others joined in and the next thing she knew, everyone was applauding her.

Everyone except Steve. He was leaning against the wall beside the coffee machine, forehead contracted, lips sucked in. He looked . . . worried. Why? What was going on? She tried to make eye contact but his gaze flicked down to the cup in his hand.

Heather was starting to feel annoyed as she headed towards him. What was his problem? Couldn't he at least pretend to be happy for her?

But her way was blocked by the crowd of teachers. Normally, they barely registered her existence outside the classroom; she was, after all, just a lowly trainee on her first induction year – here today, gone tomorrow. Now, though, they couldn't seem to get enough of her, grabbing her arm as she passed, aiming a fusillade of questions her way.

'How do you feel?'

'Does Noah Fauster look as good in real life?'

'Are you going to post a video of the school?'

'Is this your last day?'

Heather smiled vaguely without replying, but her reaction to that last one caught her by surprise. In her fantasies of winning, this job was always part of the past, with no place in her glamorous new life. But now she found herself wondering: did she really want to abandon teaching forever? True, it was a slog. A low-paying, high-stress career whose main benefit was widely considered to be the large number of days that you didn't have to actually do it.

So why this unsettled feeling in the pit of her stomach at the thought of walking out of this building, never to return?

The coffee pot was nearly empty by the time she finally made it through the gauntlet of teachers. Steve hadn't moved from his position against the wall. She stood facing him, eyebrows raised, waiting for him to say something.

'So?' she said eventually.

'So.' He raised his mug in salute. 'Congratulations. You got what you wanted.'

'Thank you.' She beamed, hoping to draw him into her excitement. 'Can you believe it? I actually pinched myself this morning, to make sure I wasn't dreaming. Until now, I thought that "pinch yourself" thing was just an expression.'

'Well, don't go turning to self-harm just yet.' He drank some coffee. 'That doesn't usually start until a few months down the line. No point getting ahead of yourself.'

His words set off a kick of anger. Normally she found Steve's cynical humour amusing and was happy to join in. But today she just wanted him to drop the negativity and behave like a proper friend: congratulate her, give her a hug and tell her he was excited for her.

'Jesus, Steve, for once can you—'

'Okay, I have to ask, because we're all wondering . . .' Alison Matthews, who taught art, had appeared at Heather's elbow. 'What on *earth* are you doing here?'

Steve put down his mug, gave Heather a small pat on the shoulder – which wasn't like him at all – and ambled away.

She turned to face the art teacher, an ageing hippy with a long, grey plait and a bright paisley blouse. She had been teaching at the school for decades and had, until now, barely said two words to Heather.

'What do you mean what am I doing here? Where else would I be? Class starts in . . .' – she glanced at her watch – 'ten minutes.'

'Yes, but you don't need to work any more. You're rich and famous. In case you haven't noticed, celebrities don't tend to spend their days training for low-paying jobs.'

Heather felt a stab of annoyance. Interfering cow. What business was it of hers?

'I wouldn't just disappear without speaking to the head first and working through my notice. I have a duty to the students.' She turned away to open the cupboard door above the sink, scanning the shelf for a fresh box of sugar cubes.

'Isn't your duty to your "followers" now?' The art teacher's laugh was half snort. '"Followers"! It sounds like you've started a cult!'

'I have, now that you mention it.' She spotted the sugar on the top shelf and reached for it, looking over her shoulder as she deadpanned: 'Rap music sermons, multiple husbands and chocolate fountain baptisms. Can I offer you a membership pack?'

Another snort-laugh. 'That's so fun—'

The door to the room opened and the head herself strode through. Kate Robbins was a no-nonsense woman with sensible shoes, low-maintenance hair and a series of generic, interchangeable suits. She never entered the staffroom unless she had an announcement to make, preferring to stay in her office, bent over paperwork.

Yet here she was.

The buzz of chatter died away. Miss Robbins scanned the room, head swivelling like a searchlight, stopping when it landed on Heather.

'Miss Davies,' she said. 'We need to speak.'

*

It was dark and threatening rain as Elliot headed across the Triple F car park. The Zoom meeting about American franchise plans had dragged on. The main source of the hold-up was a Texan executive who had taken a dislike to the proposed name – TF USA – complaining that it sounded 'like a bad Scrabble hand'. He refused to let it go and the debate had consumed the better part of an hour. Or rather, the worse part. By the time Elliot had finally begun his talk about the role of psychological screening, most of the audience were tapping on their phones, no doubt warning partners and spouses they were running late.

Elliot was halfway to his car when he saw a flicker of movement at the edge of his vision. He turned to the source and saw a figure duck down, hiding behind the hulking shape of an SUV. Elliot's heart went into a wild dash.

Someone was following him.

He was suddenly conscious of how poorly lit and isolated the car park was; a barren field of concrete interrupted by half a dozen cars, a self-storage depot and furniture warehouse on the other side, both shut for the night.

Should he go back to HQ? Call 999? Or try to make it to his car, hope that he was able to get inside and lock the doors in time? From his left came the sound of a heavy tread. His pursuer had broken cover. Fear kicked in and instinct took over. Elliot ran towards his car as it began to rain: fat drops that fell sporadically. The footsteps were behind him now, growing swifter. There was no doubt about it; he was being chased. Elliot's feet slammed the tarmac. But he wasn't fast enough. The footsteps were getting louder. Nearer. Elliot's mental calculations were automatic. His pursuer – mugger? Carjacker? Killer? – was closing in too fast. He would be caught the moment he stopped to open the car door.

But if he kept running, tried to loop back to the Triple F building, he would be overtaken before he reached it. There was only one thing left to do.

He wheeled around suddenly to face his pursuer, shoulders back, chin raised – a purposefully dominant pose. He caught a fast-moving glimpse of a man in a hoodie bearing down on him.

'What do you want?' Elliot managed to keep the fear out of his voice, speaking loudly to project authority and reverse the power dynamic, hoping to throw his would-be attacker off balance, literally as well as mentally.

It worked. The sudden change of direction caught the man by surprise, his momentum carrying him forward so that he only just managed to keep himself from crashing into Elliot, pulling up awkwardly, arms pinwheeling. And now, Elliot was able to see his pursuer's face.

'You!' Elliot pulled a palm across his forehead as relief flowed through him. Because this was a known quantity, rather than a shadowy stranger. The frantic kick of his heart began to slow. 'Jim, what are you doing here?'

Jim Munson had been exiled from CelebRate the day before, after an image of him punching a police officer was splashed across the front page of the *London Mail* under the headline 'Fame, Fortune . . . Fights.' He was now facing criminal charges, a red line for the contest. Elliot had been summoned to a meeting about Jim's case where Noah had kept peppering him with questions. Or rather, the same question in various different forms ('Dr Leyton, do you have any idea why this would happen, why he suddenly went off the rails?'). Because Jim had been going from strength to strength, his follower numbers rising, every post liked by a million fans, always striking the right balance:

sharing his successes without sounding braggy. Easy banter and a smile that never looked fake. And then, to top it all off, the chance to front an advertising campaign for hair gel that would have spread his face across YouTube channels and TV screens. There was even talk of featuring him alongside Noah on the next Triple F promotion – a first for the contest, since Noah had always appeared solo – sparking rumours that Jim was going to be offered a long-term role.

So Noah had kept asking *why*. Why would Jim squander it all on one night of alcohol and violence?

Elliot had spoken earnestly about the pressures of the contest and delayed reactions to social upheaval. The psychometric tests weren't perfect, he'd said. Sometimes you couldn't predict who would snap. They had seemed to buy it.

Now, standing in the watery glow of the car park lights, Jim Munson looked terrible. Greasy hair framed an unshaven face and the skin beneath his eyes was bruised with fatigue.

'I need to talk to you, doc. In private. Not' – he jerked his head in the direction of HQ – 'in there. I've spent enough time in that building today.'

The rain meant business now, launching itself from the clouds to hiss against the tarmac and drum on the roofs of cars. Elliot hated the rain. It brought up bad memories, negative associations.

He considered the wretched man in front of him.

'How did you know I was here?'

'I came out after my HR meeting and spotted your car. I've seen you in it, leaving after group.'

Elliot glanced over his shoulder at the distinctive shape of his silver Porsche. He hesitated, torn. Jim had crossed a line by ambushing him in the car park. The proper course of action would be to tell him – coolly and politely – that if he wished to talk he could make an appointment for a session at Elliot's private practice in Notting Hill. Anything else would appear odd, perhaps even suspicious. But he wanted to find out what Jim was so desperate to tell him. The information could prove useful down the road.

He ran a mental risk assessment. Reached a decision.

'All right. We can talk in my car.'

*

'Everything was going so well.' Jim raked fingers through his rain-soaked hair. The Porsche was still in the car park. Elliot had turned on the inside light so he could watch the other man's face.

'Yes,' Elliot said. 'At the last group session, you appeared to have adapted successfully to your new life.'

A vigorous head-bob of agreement. 'It's true. I was flying high, loving every minute of it. Until . . .' He trailed off. Frowned.

'Until . . .?'

His hands became fists against his thighs. 'It started with these public posts. Hinting at something in my past. Nasty stuff.'

'Well, as you know, trolls are an unfortunate side effect of fame. Everyone at the Triple F has experienced—'

'No, not like that. I had trolls from the get-go. Jealous tossers slagging me off to make themselves feel better. No. This was different.'

'In what way?'

'Whoever posted those messages knew things about me. Secret things.'

'Such as?' He frowned as Jim shook his head, scattering drops of rain on the soft leather upholstery. 'I can't help you if I don't know what's going on.'

Jim stared straight ahead, not speaking, for what felt like a long time. Then he nodded. 'Okay . . .' His gaze dropped. 'Such as . . . the fact I slept with a man. Only once, when I was really drunk a couple of years ago. Just . . . to see.'

'As an experiment.'

Jim's head whipped back up, eyes narrowing. 'That's exactly how I think of it! How did you know?'

Elliot cursed himself inwardly. The last thing he needed was for Jim to start asking awkward questions.

'You'd be surprised how many people try out different experiences when they're younger: it's far more common than most people think. But you are concerned that this episode from your past could become public?'

'Yeah.' The head-bob again. 'The troll obviously knows about it. He keeps dropping hints on CelebRate and some of the fan sites. He doesn't use a first name, just a generic initial and the surname "Know". Which is obviously his sick little joke, to tell me he "knows" my secrets. The first post was right after I got offered the hair gel advert. Me, on the telly! I was so happy. Then I saw what he'd written and . . .' Jim's forehead buckled. 'After that, everything started falling apart.'

Elliot considered how best to react. He had always known there might be situations like this, when his official role conflicted with the demands of his secret project. He decided the best course of action was to respond as though he truly was just another Triple F psychologist, with no other motive for being at the contest. It wasn't as if anything he did at this point would make a difference anyway; the damage was already done.

'So you feel it would hurt your image if this information were to come to light?' he said. 'Because there have been several highly successful LGBT winners – men as well as women – who have attracted huge followings and . . .'

'I'm not gay!' Jim's voice rose with each word until he was shouting, the volume amplified by the small space. Then he closed his eyes and took a deep breath. 'I did that . . . tried that . . . one time in my whole life. And I've shagged hundreds of women.'

I'll bet you have, Elliot thought. *Classic overcompensation.*

Jim hunched forward, cradling his head in his hands, fingers burrowing in his wet hair. 'But anyway, that's not all of it. This troll knows other stuff too.'

'Such as?'

'I hit my girlfriend. Just the once, back when I was drinking too much. I'd lost my job, so I was feeling low, worthless. She called me a limp-dicked loser. It struck a nerve, you know? And I just . . . lashed out. Gave her a black eye. I felt terrible the second I'd done it, begged her to forgive me. But she left. And I don't blame her. I was lucky she didn't press charges.'

Elliot already knew this story too, though he wasn't foolish enough to let it show this time. The two incidents were clearly linked; Jim had issues with repressed homosexuality, which had led him to lash out at the woman in his life for failing to turn him straight. Instead of accepting his sexuality by coming out, he drank too much, battling his demons and anyone else who got caught in the crossfire. Elliot looked at the man's wretched face, profiled against the yellow-orange mist of condensation. Contempt rose in his throat. Millions of people had struggled and sacrificed for the legal rights and social acceptance that were now Jim's for the taking. But instead, he was whimpering in fear at the thought of his secret becoming public. Elliot found it pathetic.

But Elliot's face betrayed none of these thoughts as he said: 'So tell me more about these posts. What exactly did they say?'

Jim blew out a puff of air. 'That he'd spoken to a bloke with the same name as the man I had the . . . the thing with and that he'd said I was "a real man's man".' Another one said, "Jim's a heavy hitter with the ladies". And he left a comment on a fan forum, where some girls were speculating about my taste in women, what colour eyes I liked. And guess what Mr Know had to say about that?'

Elliot said nothing, his face impassive.

'He said "I hear he likes girls with black eyes".' Jim burst into tears then, a wrenching, wheezy sound. 'Everything was perfect, until . . . Those comments changed everything. Made me jumpy and paranoid. I couldn't sleep. I kept trawling through chat boards and gossip sites late into the night to see if there was anything else out there, wondering when he was going to stop being sly and start spilling my secrets all over social media.'

Elliot ran a hand along the side of the steering wheel; he liked the feel of the leather against his palm. 'Why don't you tell me about the incident with the police officer.'

There was a gulping sound and a couple of sharp breaths as Jim appeared to gather himself.

'I arranged to meet an old workmate at a pub we used to go to because I was sick of all the fancy clubs; I just wanted somewhere quiet and normal. Like before. But a bloke there recognized me and said, "Shouldn't you be off somewhere posh with all the other wannabe celebs?" Then he said that the only reason he could think of for me to come to some dodgy, out-of-the-way boozer was because I was up to no good, maybe meeting someone I didn't want the fans to know about – someone who didn't fit with my image.'

'And you believed him to be this Know person?'

'Yeah. I started screaming at him to get away from me, threatening to kill him. He was just a drunk tosser talking shite to impress his mates, but I was drunk too and I suddenly thought, it's *him*. He's followed me here so he can taunt me in person. By the time the cops showed up, I was totally out of control.'

Jim's eyes were aimed at the windscreen, now veiled with condensation. Rain hammered the roof. Elliot considered the information, weighing possible responses.

'Have you reported all this to HR? Or Noah? Explained the situation?'

A snort. 'Explained that I went mental and hit a cop because I'm a woman-beating queer? No chance. I only told you because I know you can't say anything on account of patient confident . . . confident . . .'

'Confidentiality.'

'Yeah. But there's no one else I can talk to. And I'm scared. What does this bastard want? And more to the point, how does he know all my secrets?'

'Did you confide in the ex-girlfriend you mentioned about your . . . sexual experiment?'

'No! God no. It can't be her; she doesn't know.'

'What about the gentleman from your . . . encounter? Did you tell him about having hit your girlfriend?'

'No.' He shook his head firmly. 'No matter how drunk I was, I would never tell anyone about that. Especially not someone I . . . you know, fancied. It must have been a hacker.'

'Hacking into . . . what exactly?'

'My home computer.' Jim rubbed his forehead with his fingertips. 'I keep a journal there. In a Word document. Been doing it since I was a kid. Just thoughts about the day, things that have happened. The computer is password-protected but . . . I don't know, maybe someone got in?'

Elliot traced a line across the condensation on the windscreen. 'Isn't the more likely explanation that the messages came from someone you know, who wants to hurt you? Who have you confided in about both of these . . . incidents?'

'No one.' Jim turned to face Elliot, shoulder propped against the seatback, eyes wide and haunted. 'That's what's so scary. I haven't told a single living soul. Aside from you. But it couldn't be you, because you only found out tonight.'

'Yes, that's right.' Elliot nodded, keeping his features flat and his tone neutral. Even as a child, he'd always been a gifted liar.

*

Heather twirled in front of the mirror, admiring the way the bottle-green fabric swished around her calves as she moved. She felt giddy, like a teenager shopping for her prom dress, humbled by the glamour of it all. Was this really her life, browsing Bond Street's most expensive boutiques, trying on clothes and buying whatever she fancied, transforming her appearance with a wave of her Triple F credit card?

'What do you think?' she asked the shop assistant, a French woman named Claudette who had recognized her from the Big Reveal. 'It's for my first post, so I want to get it right, since this is now my job.'

It felt strange saying that, after so many years focused on becoming a teacher. She had hoped to stay on at the school a bit longer, to give herself a chance to get used to the idea of leaving

– or at the very least, to say a proper goodbye to her students. But the head had been very firm. 'Your presence here is too distracting,' she'd told Heather, 'now that the children see you as some sort of celebrity, so I think it would be best for everyone if you went immediately.' So Heather had gathered her things and left, walking out of the building alone, while everyone else was in class.

'Green is an excellent colour on you,' Claudette said, as Heather turned around to show her how the dress looked at the back. 'I think that suits you the most out of all the ones you've tried on.'

'Okay then.' She performed one last twirl, pivoting on her good leg. 'I'll take it!'

'Excellent. How about the jacket and shoes? And the scarf? I think the scarf pulls the outfit together.'

'Yes, I'll take those too.' She looked through the open door of the changing room, at the shed clothes piled on a velvet stool, scanning them for anything she'd overlooked. 'What about the navy trousers?'

Claudette shook her head. 'They were not so good. The waistline is too low for your body. You have a high waist.'

'In that case, I'll take everything except the trousers.'

She beamed at the French woman. After nearly two hours in the shop, Heather felt as though they had bonded. Claudette had been so helpful, agreeing to take pictures with the F-phone. She had snapped several of Heather browsing, and now took another of her smiling at the till. Then standing in the doorway, wearing the green dress, arms held out sideways to display all the shopping bags. Claudette handed back the phone.

The moment of truth had arrived. It was time for her first post.

'Which one should I use?' Heather asked, flicking through the images. Claudette had said she was a big CelebRate fan, so she must have ideas about what worked best. Plus she was from Paris, which made Heather assume she had style and taste.

'I like the one holding all the bags. You look like Julia Roberts in the shopping scene from that old film, *Pretty Woman*.'

'Hmm. Didn't she play a prostitute in that?'

Claudette shrugged. 'Yes, but nobody cared that she was a prostitute because she looked so beautiful.'

'Ah, I do love a film with a strong moral message.' Heather considered the suggested photo, adrenaline spiking her blood; she was about to take the plunge, submit her first post . . . and become a real Winfluencer. 'It *is* a good picture.' She thought for a minute before writing the caption: 'I can't believe these lovely things are all mine! I feel like Julia Roberts in *Pretty Woman!*'

She showed it to Claudette, who nodded approvingly. Then Heather took a deep breath and tapped 'Post Image'.

She stood staring at the 'Post Submitted' message on her phone, heart hammering. There was a delay – the Triple F's image-vetting process – followed by a ping from her CelebRate app as the picture appeared. She had done it; she was officially a Winfluencer! She experienced a moment of relief . . . but only a moment. Because self-doubt was hot on its heels. What if no one liked her? A sick, nervy feeling began churning in her stomach, overlaid with flashes of panic.

A few long seconds passed. Then a message appeared on the screen: 'londongal427 liked your post'. A moment later, there was another one. And another. 'Three likes!' she shouted out. 'Already! No . . . wait. Seven! Thirteen!' She stared at her phone in wonder. People she'd never met before were looking at her picture right now and cheering her on, welcoming her into their social media lives. It was an oddly emotional moment.

'Congratulations,' Claudette said. 'Everyone is going to love you.'

'Do you really think so?'

'Of course. Because you look so beautiful.'

Heather beamed at her, though she knew it wasn't really true, that she was hiding the ugly parts of herself. But Claudette had no way of knowing that.

*

'Fine,' Heather said, 'send me your bank details and I'll transfer the money across.'

'Thanks, sis,' Ronan's voice said. '"*Sis*"'? Seriously? When had he ever called her that? 'I'm telling you, I've got a good feeling about this one. It's my lucky break. I just know it.'

How many times had her brother said those words, Heather wondered. Why couldn't he just get a bar job, like all the other wannabe actors, so he could keep himself afloat while freeing up his days for auditions? But she had long ago stopped asking that question. Ronan would only make excuses about needing the time and 'creative space' to write his own one-man show. The fact of the matter was her brother thought he was too good for ordinary work. He wanted to be a star and refused to settle for anything less. 'Give the audience what it wants.' That was his 'mission statement'. The problem was audiences didn't seem to particularly want *him*.

'We should go out for dinner,' he said. Was it her imagination, or was his accent becoming posher as the call progressed? 'Somewhere fancy, since you're living the high life now. Just two siblings out on the town. We have a lot of catching up to do.'

'That's certainly true, since I haven't seen you in nearly two years.'

'Has it really been that long?'

'It really has.'

'Well, I was out of the country a lot. Remember I went on that tour to Goa with Drama in Motion? My monologue was a huge hit.'

'That tour lasted four weeks. You were gone ten months.'

'I met a girl there. I was in love. How was I supposed to know she'd turn out to be a psycho?'

Heather closed her eyes, breathing in through her nose and out through her mouth until her anger had faded, leaving behind only a vague sadness. She had hoped, at first, that Mum leaving might draw the two of them closer. But it had only blown them further apart. She no longer recognized the brother who'd built her tree forts and danced beside her in the bedroom as they sang pop songs into hairdryers.

'I need to get going, Ronan.'

'Okay, but what about meeting up this weekend? We can take some selfies for your feed. Your followers would love me.' Heather closed her eyes. Her brother had been calling relentlessly from the moment he'd discovered Heather was the newest addition to CelebRate. But back when time had hung on her like a weight, thick and immobile, he was nowhere to be seen.

'We can talk about it later.'

'But I—'

'Goodbye, Ronan.'

CHAPTER 10

It's been a long day and I'm tired, but I need to get this done before bed. Things are moving fast for her, so I can't afford to wait. I consider the woman's photo, pinned next to Rob's on my study wall. Is she beautiful? I certainly don't think so. But maybe that's because of what I know about her. When I look at those thick-lashed eyes and full lips, I don't see glamour or smouldering sexuality. I just see damage. But damage is good. I rely on it.

There are so many things I could do, places I could go. Probably best to start simple, see how she reacts, take it from there. A public comment should do the trick. I read through the latest CelebRate posts on the big Celeb gossip sites, hunting for a good jumping-off point. I can't be the one to instigate the conversation. I'm flying under the radar – for now at least. I come across a photo of her hugging a little girl – her goddaughter, apparently – both of them wearing matching sunglasses with tiger-striped frames, laughing at the camera. 'Wow, look at her!' says one of the comments underneath. 'She would be SUCH a cool mum.'

Perfect.

I click on the speech icon. Write, 'I know a girl named Ellie who might have something to say about that.'

Hit 'Reply'. Then I sit back in my chair with my arms folded behind my head.

Job done.

CHAPTER 11

It was strange seeing the Shakespeare Estate from the other side of the park. It looked different somehow, shabbier, drained of life. Heather had been excited to discover that one of the homes along the familiar Holland Park border was in the Triple F's property portfolio. How many times had she gazed across at those white-pillared houses, wondering what it would be like to live there? So actually being inside one felt surreal.

She turned away from the window and refocused her attention on the room in which she now stood. It was big. Her whole flat would have fitted inside it. She turned in a circle, taking in the oak floors and built-in bookshelves, the working fireplace with its frame of carved marble. The Victorian mouldings and crystal chandelier. Amazing to think that this place could be hers. None of the teachers she'd studied with would ever be able to afford a house like this, no matter how many years they worked. She had felt so left behind when they'd all headed off to their first teaching jobs, spending the last eight months earning proper salaries while she struggled through her first induction year. Now, though, it was *her* turn to leave *them* behind.

She headed upstairs to explore the rest of the house, starting with the 'family bathroom', with its walk-in shower at one end and

Bolivian marble bath at the other, marvelling at the warmth of the tiles underfoot, courtesy of underfloor heating.

She checked each of the five bedrooms in turn, ending with the largest, whose giant skylight was displaying sun-rimmed clouds that disappeared, with the touch of a button, behind a motorized ceiling blind. The master en suite was stylishly modern, all dark granite and shining chrome, but for Heather, the bedroom's main highlight was concealed behind a top-mounted door in the middle of one wall. She actually gasped out loud when it slid aside to reveal a huge walk-in wardrobe, complete with shoe display shelves, gliding drawers and more rail space than she could ever hope to fill.

Heather felt as though she was floating as she headed back down the curving staircase to the living room, where Lara, her image consultant, stood waiting by the rear window.

'So?' Lara asked. 'What do you think?'

Heather beamed. 'It's absolutely stunning.'

Lara nodded. 'I think so too. It's a perfect house for hosting.'

Heather looked at her, puzzled. 'Hosting?'

Lara's perfectly arched eyebrow rose. 'Dinner parties? Or cocktail barbecues in the back garden. This room will make a great entertaining space.'

'Ah. I was thinking more about my day-to-day life, sitting by the fireplace with a cat on my lap. I love cats, but didn't think it would be fair to trap one in my poky flat.' She wandered over to the fireplace, fingers travelling along the mantel above, tracing the cool, smooth marble.

'I can source you a gorgeous Persian to go with this room,' Lara said. 'Fully certified, of course. Only the best.'

'Really?' She looked at the floor, a broad expanse of gleaming oak. 'Sure, why not? I like Persian rugs. I've never had one before.'

Lara's laugh sounded perfectly managed, flawless in pitch, volume and duration. 'I meant a Persian *cat*. You mentioned wanting one?'

'Ah.' Heather felt foolish; Lara must think she was an idiot. 'Thanks, but a rescue cat will do me fine. It can have a fabulous new life, just like me.'

Lara pulled a face, making her nose wrinkle. 'That's sweet, but you're going to be taking a lot of photos here, so you need to consider how *everything* in your home looks, whether it fits with your brand. And trust me, when you see a chinchilla Persian kitten, you will literally fall in love.'

Heather wasn't really a fan of puffy cats, but she was in far too good a mood to argue. 'Sure, why not? No harm in looking.'

She circled the room, picturing her future here. Getting ready for nights out at concerts and premieres. Chatting to fans as she wandered through the rooms doing livestreams. *Hosting*. She wondered: who were these people she would host? Heather couldn't really picture Debbie and Steve in this enormous, white-pillared house with its chandeliered 'entertaining space'. But soon she would have new friends, Winfluencers like herself, carefree and full of fun.

She returned to the window overlooking the garden and tried to open it, frowning when it wouldn't budge.

'Why is this sealed shut?' She could hear her voice rising, becoming shrill. 'I won't live in a house with sealed windows. I have to be able to let the air in.'

Lara gave her a puzzled look – no doubt thrown off by the sudden change of tone – then joined her at the window.

'I think it's just paint. The house was recently redecorated. Hang on.' She grabbed onto the bronze handles at the base of the frame and yanked hard, gritting her teeth. The window rose with a sharp squeal of protest. Heather felt something inside her unclench as a breeze drifted in from the back garden, carrying the scent of blossoms.

'There you go,' Lara said brightly.

'Thanks. Sorry I overreacted. I used to . . . stay somewhere with windows that wouldn't open. I don't ever want that again.'

'Of course.' Lara nodded. 'I totally understand.'

I very much doubt that, Heather thought. But she wasn't letting those thoughts follow her into this day. She circled the room again, fingers trailing along the built-in bookshelves, excitement swelling inside her until she could barely contain it.

'I love it,' she said. 'And I kind of like that it's not too far from where I live now.'

Lara's nose wrinkled again – perhaps in response to the mention of the Shakespeare Estate.

'Yes, the property division bought a couple of places on this street to sell on to CelebRaters. It's considered a good Winfluencer location because the facades are beautiful and the road is wide but doesn't get much traffic, so it's easy to film from the front. Plus it's good value, by Holland Park standards, because of its proximity to' – her eyes flicked towards the back window, with its view over the park – 'the edge.'

Heather pressed her lips together, unsure whether to be amused or insulted. 'Well, edge or no, I love it.'

Lara nodded. 'Good. All you have to do is say the word and it's yours. Literally right away. The company will set up your mortgage and give you an advance on future income to cover the deposit. And because it's part of the Triple F's property portfolio, you can live here as a renter until the sale is finalized.'

'That's okay. I don't mind staying where I am until the deal goes through.'

Lara's forehead scrunched and she made a little 'mm' sound. 'Well, the thing is . . . we'd kind of like to get you into your new home as quickly as possible.'

'"We"?' she echoed, as Lara led her out of the living room and down the stairs. Heather trailed after her. 'Who is this "we"?'

'The Triple F family!'

They were back where the house tour had started – on the basement or 'garden floor', with its granite kitchen island and pearl-grey stone tiles, the handle-free cupboards that opened at a touch ('Italian design,' Lara had whispered, as though it were a secret. 'Literally the best.'). There was a giant glass wall at the back, framed in timber, overlooking the garden.

'The whole point is to showcase your new lifestyle,' Lara said. 'You can't do that if you're stuck in a tiny flat. And think how this place would look on CelebRate! You can use the image-string function to make a sequence as you literally move up in the world, maybe throw in a video of you walking from room to room, talking to an interior designer about what furniture you want. Run some music under it. It will be amazing!'

The image consultant pushed a button hidden in the timber frame and a glass panel slid aside, creating an opening to the garden. At the far end, a willow dipped leaves in a tiny pond, overlooked by a wrought-iron bench. Lara's mobile phone rang and she retreated into the kitchen to answer it, allowing Heather to explore in peace. She sat on the bench, looking up at the house. It was the kind of place a celebrity might live in. She closed her eyes and tilted her face to the sky. She felt as though she was living in a fairy tale, a magical kingdom where dreams became real. She walked back across the grass to the kitchen. Lara was leaning against the fridge, tapping out a message on her phone. She looked up as Heather approached.

'The word,' Heather said.

'Sorry?'

'You asked me to say the word if I want this place. And I do.'

'Oh.' Lara's laugh tinkled. 'I get it. Funny.'

Heather looked around at the beauty and luxury surrounding her on all sides. A wave of euphoria crested through her, making her dance around the room, arms raised, just to release some of it. She'd just taken a pill, so it didn't hurt at all.

'You've made a really good choice,' Lara said when Heather returned to her side, giddy and a little breathless from her victory jig. 'You are literally going to love living here.'

'Yes,' Heather said. 'I literally am.'

CHAPTER 12

It's like being in a film, Heather thought. *The Great Gatsby*, perhaps.

Dozens of tiny lights were scattered like stars across the ceiling above the bar area of the New Heights, casting the VIP crowd in a golden glow. A row of handsome bartenders, identically dressed in black, shook cocktails and poured drinks while the latest *Britain's Got Talent* winner sang a throaty number on a discreet stage tucked in the corner. Debbie Limon, the UKTV news presenter, was leaning against the bar, chatting with an actor Heather recognized from an ITV crime drama. The Triple F's private club occupied the entire top floor of a sleek Chiswick high-rise not far from the contest's headquarters, its pool and roof garden offering panoramic views across London. Heather had seen this place in a thousand posts, back when CelebRate had been a daily source of comfort and longing: a fantasy realm where life was being lived to the full, somewhere beyond the sealed windows. And now, here she was, a part of the scene.

Anticipation was whirling inside her as she looked around at all the beautiful people tossing their hair and laughing, sipping drinks, eating the 'nibbles' being circulated on silver trays. Heather had spent a lot less time on CelebRate since starting work at the school, but she still recognized most of the Winfluencers. There was Sasha, she of the enormous earrings, standing beside Leonora, who read tarot cards and seemed to eat nothing but tapas. And Amir, the handsome rollerblader with a passion for Japanese anime. She fiddled nervously with her hair. Was she really one of these people now? It didn't seem possible.

Then a familiar voice said, 'Champagne?'

Heather turned and looked up at Noah, who had appeared beside her like a genie, two fresh glasses in his hands.

'Always.'

He handed her one before raising the other in a toast. 'To your first Triple F mixer event. The first of many.'

'Cheers to that.' They clinked glasses and drank in a mirror-image motion. Then she held up her flute, admiring the bubbles. 'Does the novelty of drinking champagne ever wear off?'

He appeared to consider the question. 'It's not what I drink at home. But I always have it in public because champagne captures the spirit of the Triple F lifestyle.' He tilted his head. 'And speaking of luxury lifestyles . . . how are you enjoying your new place?' He must have seen the startled look on her face because he chuckled and said, 'As a mentor, I always keep an eye on the newbies, make sure they're settling in okay.' He nodded approvingly. 'It's a beautiful home. You have excellent taste.'

'Thank you. I still can't believe it's mine. I feel like the police are going to show up any moment and arrest me for squatting.'

He laughed softly. 'I remember that feeling. Give it time. You'll be surprised how quickly you get used to it.' A photographer appeared beside them. There were a lot of them circulating. Flashes kept going off in the corner of her eye, like a storm on the horizon. Noah put his arm around Heather's shoulders and they smiled at the camera. The photographer took out a notebook and got as far as 'So who—' before Noah interrupted with, 'Dolce and Gabbana dress, Miu Miu handbag. My suit is Hugo Boss.'

'Ta.' The photographer jotted it down before melting back into the crowd.

Heather looked down at her red dress. 'How did—'

'You bought it with your Triple F Visa. We monitor fashion purchases so we can let the designers know that a Winfluencer has chosen something from their label, then offer them the opportunity to have the images featured more prominently on CelebRate. For a price, of course. Fabulous dress, by the way. Sure to bring in new followers. You're doing so well, Heather. That video tour of your new place has already attracted more than 100,000 likes.'

Heather felt a glow of pride. She'd thought about asking Debbie or Steve to come round and help her record the video. But the thought of parading her new wealth in front of them made her feel uncomfortable, so instead she had made it herself, using one of those selfie sticks she'd always found irritating. And she'd been pleased with the result.

'I'm glad you like it. Who would have dreamed that people would want to watch me wander around my house pointing at curtains? It's . . . Oh wow, is that Simon Cowell?'

Noah glanced round. 'Oh yes, I'd forgotten he was coming. We've been discussing a possible collaboration.' He tapped the side of his nose. 'But please keep that under your hat. I should probably go have a quick word with him, if you don't mind?'

'Of course! I'll see you later.'

The moment Noah stepped away from her, Heather began to feel self-conscious. She clutched her champagne glass as she wove past the groups and pairs of made-up, dressed-up people, searching for an entry point into a conversation. But no one paid her any attention. A photographer aimed his lens her way and she looked towards the door, a smile arranged on her face as though greeting a new arrival. The flash went off.

Okay, she decided as the photographer moved past. Time to be brave; she was going to have to break into one of the glitzy circles and introduce herself.

'Hiya. You're Heather, aren't you?' She turned to see a petite brunette with a short pixie cut, dark purple lipstick and a long black T-shirt dress with netting at the hem that made Heather think of cobwebs. A small diamond stud winked at the side of her nose. Heather remembered seeing a post of her riding a motorbike, but couldn't remember her name. 'I'm Tessa. Come on.' She took Heather's hand and led her away from the bar. 'I'll introduce you to a couple of people. The first mixer always sucks. Like being the newest monkey in a zoo where all the other animals know each other and you have no idea where the predators are kept.' Tessa stopped in front of a pair of women Heather recognized from the Top Six, a heavily made-up blonde with inflated lips and a sour-faced brunette in a sequinned dress.

'Ladies, allow me to introduce the Triple F's fresh meat. Also known as Heather. Heather, these are Analise and Grace.'

Analise – she of the filler-pumped smile – gave her a cheery wave but Grace narrowed her eyes, scanning Heather from top to toe.

'You did that house tour video,' she said. 'Bit weird, showing people your loo. I never do that.'

'Well, it's not like I was using it at the time.'

'Still. The *idea* of using it was there.'

Tessa grabbed a canapé – salmon on some sort of tiny pancake

– from a passing tray. 'Yeah,' she said, waving it in the air. 'As soon as I see someone's loo the first thing I do is close my eyes and imagine them having a huge dump.' She popped the canapé in her mouth.

Analise burst out laughing but the sequinned brunette glowered.

'Oh, lighten up, Grace.' Analise elbowed her playfully. 'I'm sure Heather isn't trying to steal your USP.'

'No, I'm . . . sorry, what *is* your USP?' Heather received a frown in response. Grace clearly thought she should have known that already.

'I'm an interior designer. Every couple of weeks I redecorate my living room in a totally different way and post images and videos, with design tips about getting the most out of your space. People love it. I'm fifth in the ratings.' She tossed her hair. 'One point eight million followers.'

'Every couple of *weeks?* Wow. You must spend a fortune on furniture.'

Grace gave her a look that conveyed just how big a moron she thought Heather was.

'Well, obviously I don't buy it myself. It's donated by sponsors.' Grace fluttered her eyelashes. 'You *do* know the Triple F has sponsors . . . don't you?'

'Course she knows,' Analise snapped. 'Stop giving the poor girl such a hard time. She's only just arrived.' She turned to Heather, giving her a conspiratorial wink. 'Grace is just upset because some weird, experimental designer is sponsoring her, so she has to put his rubbish in her house.'

'His specialty is clear plastic inflatable furniture, filled with coloured balls,' Tessa said, making no attempt to hide her amusement. 'Bubble-gum pink.'

Grace closed her eyes, as though battling pain. 'My other sponsor is a replica antique furniture company. How am I supposed to marry a classic Georgian look with . . . *that*?' She shuddered. 'You know what? I promised myself I wouldn't think about this tonight. And frankly I don't think either of you are being the least bit supportive. I'm going out for some air.' And she stalked off towards the double doors to the roof terrace.

'Wow,' Heather said, watching her leave. 'Emotions are running high.'

'Well, inflatables will do that to a person.' Tessa waved over a waiter and Heather swapped her empty flute for a fresh one.

'To be fair to her, it does suck when the sponsors are bad,' Analise said, selecting a glass from the tray. 'I'm not really a fan of this eye shadow. I would much rather have worn my own.'

Heather tried to check out the offending shadow but it was difficult to see, screened as it was behind a dense forest of lashes.

'So is make-up your USP?'

'Yeah, I'm a beauty vlogger. Make-up and hair.' Analise touched her long, blonde mane. 'I'm not remotely good-looking, if I'm being honest. It's all smoke and mirrors. Well. Smoke, mirrors, filler, hair extensions, eyelash extensions.' She patted the top of her impressively proportioned chest. 'Silicone. You should have seen me before my boob job: talk about raisins on a breadboard!' Heather laughed. She had initially been put off by Analise's fishy pout and trowelled-on make-up, the boobs swelling above a dangerously low neckline. It was a look that made her think of the blow-up dolls in sex shops. But now she found herself warming to her. It seemed like she was simply an appearance-conscious woman who didn't like the way she looked so had set out to change it. Analise drank her champagne. 'My slogan is "beauty is a choice". The point being that you can still have it, even if you don't come by it naturally. You just have to work a lot harder.'

'"Beauty is a choice",' Heather repeated. 'I like it. Surprisingly philosophical-sounding, for a make-up vlog slogan.'

'Thanks! Obviously the trolls have torn it to shreds, but then they tear everything to shreds.' She rolled her eyes.

'Yeah, I'm not looking forward to that side of things,' Heather said.

Analise shrugged. 'They come with the job so you just have to ignore them. Like living on a nice street with dog turds on the pavement. You learn to step over them, not let them stick to your shoe.'

'I do love your way with words, Analise,' Tessa said. 'Your poetic use of symbolism and simile.'

'Well, I was once referred to as "the Bard of Beauty". Also "Botox Barbie" and "Fish-Faced Freak", but we'll just throw a veil over those.'

'Jesus,' Heather said, horrified. 'People actually called you that?'

Analise waved a dismissive hand. 'Trolls can be divided into two groups: bitter, middle-aged women whose lives haven't panned out quite how they'd hoped, and sexually frustrated men overeating pizza in their parents' basements, venting their rage at womankind for not fancying them. You can't let them get to you, or you'll end up like . . .' Her voice trailed off.

Heather leaned closer, curious. 'End up like who?'

Analise shot a look around her, as though to check that no one was listening. 'Remember Kay Burns?'

Heather nodded. 'She was the top-rated CelebRater, what, a year, year and a half ago? But then something happened, some scandal, and she fell into the Drop Zone.' She frowned. 'What was it again?' She snapped her fingers as the memory surfaced. 'An SS uniform! She wore one to a costume party.'

Analise nodded. 'Yes, that's what everyone *says*. But I met her ex-boyfriend and he said the photo – posted anonymously, obvs – must have been faked because Kay's biggest secret was that her Austrian great-grandparents were Nazis. Kay could have laughed the whole thing off as a case of bad-taste-joke-meets-AI-technology, but then her family's Nazi past was outed on social media at the same time and she totally lost the plot. Stopped going out, started drinking too much. Drugs too.' Analise's face was grim. 'Last I heard she was in rehab.'

'Deepfakes are scary,' Tessa said . 'Remember Omar? He swore he never even met the prostitute in that sex video. And then there was Sara Kalin.'

'I used to follow her,' Heather said. 'She came across as a saint, doing all that charity work with children. Loved by everyone. But then she was caught on camera screaming abuse at a toddler. I unfollowed her myself when I saw it.' She rotated her champagne glass by the stem, frowning. 'You're saying that video was AI-generated?'

'We'll never know for sure.' Tessa threw back her own glass of champagne as though it were a tequila shot. 'Sara swore it must have been, but she didn't stick around to try and prove it. She fell into the Drop Zone, then ran away to Australia and hasn't been seen since.'

Heather grimaced. The conversation was taking some of the shine off her mood. Imagine living a life of Triple F luxury one minute, adored by everyone, blissfully assuming you'd never have to worry about money again. And the next minute you were out in the cold, jobless, homeless and reviled. Jesus.

Analise gave Tessa a playful punch on the arm. 'We better stop! You know we're not supposed to talk about depressing stuff at mixers. Plus we're scaring Heather.'

'No, I want to know the risks,' Heather said. 'Forewarned is forearmed and all that.'

Tessa shrugged. 'Well, don't worry. Most trolls aren't that smart. Mine seem content to spend their days thinking up colourful new ways to call me a dyke. I *wish*! Men are the *worst*. Lesbians are so lucky.' She glanced at her chunky watch, a man's Rolex. 'I better shoot. I've been roped into a late-night radio interview. Some feminist bollocks about women rejecting male ideals of hotness.' She rolled her eyes. 'As if I'm taking some big moral stand every time I get dressed, when really I just like boots and have a bit of a goth streak. But I'm planning to do a podcast series after my six months are up, so it's good to get my voice out there.'

'Yeah, I should probably go too,' Analise said. 'I have to get my lip gloss special posted before I go to bed.' Heather watched her tap the Going Places app on her screen to summon a Triple F car, noticing that she selected the more discreet Mercedes option, rather than a sports car or limo. 'How about you? Staying or going?'

'I don't have any other commitments and this is my first mixer so . . .' She looked around at the glittering crowd and heard the *Britain's Got Talent* winner introduce a new song. 'I'm going to stay a bit longer. Soak it up.'

A waiter passed by carrying a magnum of champagne, pausing to top up Heather's glass.

'Don't you just love champagne?' Analise said. 'It's like drinking stars.' She leaned over and gave Heather a goodbye hug, releasing an unsubtle, floral scent. 'I liked talking to you. Maybe we could meet for a coffee?'

'Yes, let's do that. Thank you for taking pity on a lost newbie.'

Then Tessa summoned the New Heights' famous glass lift and the pair of them stepped inside, Analise blowing her a kiss as the door slid shut.

Heather looked around, pleased with how the night was going. Her chat with Analise and Tessa had left her feeling more confident, like she really did belong here. Then she saw Grace returning through the terrace doors. She had no desire to restart *that* conversation. May as well head outside herself, take a look at the roof garden.

A breeze lifted Heather's hair as she stepped out through the double doors. The terrace was spread across two levels, evenly split between the roof garden and the pool, a slab of glowing turquoise flanked by deck chairs. There was no one in the water. Heather walked along a path through potted trees twinkling with strings of lights, and leaned against the low wall running along the roof's edge. London spread itself around her, its glow staining the dark. Beyond Chiswick Park, the skyscrapers of Canary Wharf speared the night. She wondered how many people were inside them right now, working late, sweating over deadlines while she was here, surrounded by beauty and music, drinking champagne.

'Miss Davies? Is that you?

Heather turned in surprise. It felt strange, hearing someone call her that outside the school. A woman of perhaps forty was standing in front of her, holding a drink in one hand and lifting a cigarette to her lips with the other. Heather recognized her from somewhere, but here, out of context, she was struggling to place her. The woman was wearing a simple midnight-blue dress that skimmed her body, stopping just short of her silver high heels. Her thick platinum-blonde hair was cut at an angle, short enough at the back to reveal the base of her neck, long enough at the front to touch her shoulders. But what stood out about her was the way she held herself. The lack of self-consciousness, of effort. It separated her immediately from the crowd of Winfluencers. This woman wasn't trying to appear elegant or glamorous. She simply was.

Then she smiled, a cold lip-twist that Heather recognized immediately. She had, after all, seen it many times before. On the face of Eric Shulman.

'Mrs Shulman. Hello.'

The blonde dragged on her cigarette, tipping back her head and blowing smoke at the sky.

'Please. Call me Veronica.'

'Okay.' A pause. 'Call me Heather.'

Mrs Shulman – Veronica – cocked her head, sending a lock of hair across her cheek. Heather wondered briefly whether she was going to have a go at her for getting Eric into trouble. But she quickly dismissed the idea. The woman was all careless insouciance; it was hard to picture an abrupt gear switch into protective-mother mode.

'Congratulations. Eric told me you'd won.' Veronica Shulman placed her glass on the edge of the wall – not champagne: a tumbler of clear, iced liquid with a lemon wedge – then leaned an elbow beside it, the cigarette still smouldering between her knuckles. 'Are you enjoying it, the money, the attention?'

'Well, yes. Who wouldn't?'

Veronica didn't reply. Another drag. Another plume of smoke.

'Eric says you've quit.'

Something about her choice of wording, the abruptness of the delivery, made Heather feel defensive. 'I left my job at the school, yes. I didn't really have a choice. And anyway, being a Winfluencer is actually quite time-consuming. There are events to attend and posts to . . . to . . .'

'Post?' Veronica finished, lips curling into that Eric smile. She picked up her drink and took a long slug, making the ice cubes tinkle. 'And you're certain that was the right decision?'

Heather blinked in surprise. She wasn't sure exactly what she'd been expecting at the start of this conversation: perhaps a sly reference to Eric's troubles at school or a rattle through the standard pleasantries – congratulations-on-your-win, the-school-won't-be-the-same-without-you, nice-seeing-you – before the socialite glided back inside. But definitely not this.

'The right choice?' she echoed. 'Are you implying that I should have stayed on as a trainee teacher even though I don't need the money any more?'

Veronica lifted a milky shoulder. 'Money isn't everything.' A hard suck on the cigarette. 'Believe me.'

Heather looked at her for a silent, processing moment before deciding to tackle the elephant in the room. 'I would have thought you'd be glad to get rid of me, given the trouble I've caused your son.'

Veronica's lips twitched sideways. 'Eric causes trouble for Eric. And unlike the other teachers, who don't want to risk upsetting the applecart where my husband's donations are concerned, you weren't afraid to call him out.' She raised her drink again, took another slug. 'I wish more teachers were like you. Eric might be turning out differently if he didn't go through life feeling untouchable.' She gazed down into the half-empty glass. 'At school, anyway.'

'Have you said this to the head? If the teachers knew you felt that way, they might not be so . . . hesitant . . . about disciplining him.'

She laughed softly, turning towards the glowing city, propping her forearms on the wall, cigarette dangling over the edge. An orange ember broke free, drifting down through the darkness towards the car park below.

'I can't. Edmond takes a different view.'

'Edmond?'

'My husband.'

'Ah. Is he here?' Heather glanced towards the bar, scanning the crowd, on the lookout for a broad figure with close-shaved hair.

Veronica Shulman shook her head. 'No. He's invited to all the Triple F events – he's a major shareholder, plus his company works closely with the contest's charity wing – but he hates parties. So he sends me instead.' She drew on her cigarette. 'Fame. Fortune. Followers.' She drawled the words. 'Did it start as a joke, do you think, making a theme out of F words?'

'Fucked if I know,' Heather deadpanned.

Veronica smirked, tapping ash over the wall before turning to look her in the eye. 'Do you have a boyfriend?'

Normally the question would have annoyed Heather. Her relationship status was, after all, none of this woman's business. But something about the way she asked, the cold matter-of-factness of it, made her reply anyway.

'No. I don't.'

The older woman nodded, as though this were the right answer.

'I'd keep it that way if I were you. I'm not convinced men are worth the bother. You can have children without them now, if you're maternally inclined, so it's entirely possible to skip them altogether.'

Heather considered this statement, wondering whether it was meant to shock her, before deciding that it probably wasn't meant to do anything. She was starting to get a read on Eric's mother. And she was fairly sure that, right now at least, Veronica Shulman didn't care how she came across.

'True. But they are useful for sex.'

Veronica laughed, a throaty laugh that was probably the product of too many cigarettes but still sounded seductive.

'You raise a fair point.' She took another drag, blew more smoke at the sky. 'So, science.'

Heather waited for her to say more, but she didn't.

'Yes? What about science?'

'You teach it. Taught it.'

'Not fully. I've done a few lessons with the whole class as part of my training. But mostly I ran small group lessons with the bottom set.'

'With my son.' Her voice was flat, giving nothing away.

'Yes. With Eric.' He hadn't caused too much trouble during those sessions. Mostly, he'd just stared at her vacantly. At first, she'd found it unnerving. But after a while, she'd learned to ignore him.

'I studied physics at uni,' Veronica said. 'Science is a way of thinking much more than it is a body of knowledge.'

'Carl Sagan,' Heather said. 'I love that quote. I recited it to my students.'

'I know. Eric told me.'

Heather's mouth fell open. Of all the unexpected things Veronica Shulman had come out with during the course of their conversation, this was the most surprising. Eric Shulman had gone home after school and quoted her to his mother. Did that mean he'd actually been listening during those bottom-set lessons, when she'd thought he was just trying to psych her out with his stare? Dear God, had he actually been *learning*?

'You're a good teacher,' Veronica said. 'You have a talent for it. It seems a shame to throw it away so you can spend your days taking photos and spending money. The novelty of that will wear off sooner than you think.'

'I'm not a teacher. I am . . . I *was* . . . a trainee on my first induction year. And you have no way of knowing whether I was good or not.'

'I have Eric.'

'Eric actually told you I'm a good teacher?' She could hear the disbelief in her own voice.

The throaty laugh came again, carrying a hint of scorn. 'Of course not. He's a teenage boy, and a selfish, entitled one at that. He would never think to put it in those terms. But he talks about your lessons, the ideas you've presented. You inspire him to think. That's not happened with any of the others. And now that you've left, it might never again.'

It took Heather a few moments to reply. Veronica Shulman's words were spinning inside her, crashing up against the assumptions she'd made about her least favourite pupil.

'I'm sure that's not true,' she said eventually. 'There are plenty of teachers far more experienced than me who . . .'

'Don't worry, dear.' Veronica patted her arm. 'I'm not trying to make you feel guilty about your life choices. I'm just being maudlin about my own career path-not-taken because I've had too many G&Ts.' She looked down into her now empty glass.

'Speaking of which, I'm going to head inside and get a refill. Care to join me?'

Heather considered the offer, before deciding she'd had enough. The long day was finally catching up with her. She wanted to go home, kick off her shoes and collapse onto her beautiful new sofa. Watch a bit of rubbish TV then go to bed.

'Actually, I think I'm going to head off.'

Veronica nodded. 'I should probably do the same, but then my husband might still be up so I'd have to talk with him and that would be terrible.'

Heather smiled, assuming this was a joke.

But Veronica Shulman didn't smile back.

*

The Going Places app was up and running on Heather's F-phone; she'd used it on the way over, summoning a limo to bring her here from the Triple F building after her 'pre-mixer consultation' with Lara. So all she had to do was tap the app, select a car and wait to be whisked home by a discreet driver in a traditional chauffeur's cap.

But Heather found she didn't fancy it. She wanted some fresh air first, to clear her head and reflect on the night. She could summon a car later.

Heather was walking along a path bordering Acton Green Common, enjoying the smell of fresh earth and pine, when her leg began to throb. Hardly surprising, given that she'd been on her feet since the last pill. Best take another one now, before the throb sharpened into something nastier. She reached into her jacket pocket for the discreet vial, an unlabelled white cylinder she had bought in Muji. But it wasn't there. Had she put it in her handbag instead? She rummaged through the Miu Miu clutch, first pushing, then clawing through the pile of new beauty products, but she reached the bottom without finding it.

A wave of panic broke over her. Where the hell were her pills? She'd definitely had them in the Triple F building. She'd taken one in the loos near Lara's office, marvelling at all the products on offer in the make-up area. What had she done with them after that?

Think, Heather, think.

She'd had the make-up area to herself and was fairly sure she remembered putting the container down while she checked out the various sprays. She'd been using one of them to fix her hair when the driver called to tell her he was outside, waiting to take her to the party. She remembered hastily reapplying lipstick before rushing off. She must have left the container on the make-up table. Tomorrow was Saturday; the building would be closed. As would her doctor's surgery, which ruled out an emergency refill.

Fresh panic raced through her. Because she knew where she was headed. By morning, the throbbing would have given way to the other pain, as though some savage animal were trapped inside her leg, trying to claw its way out.

Shit-shit-shit.

She closed her eyes and took a deep breath, reaching for calm. She was only a short walk from the Triple F building. Maybe there was someone working overnight who could let her inside, a cleaner or security guard. It was worth a try.

*

A few upper-floor windows were still lit when she arrived at the glass pyramid – a good sign. She was limping heavily as she passed the now silent fountain, with its trio of Fs, and stood in front of the main entrance. Had it really only been two weeks since she'd first walked through those doors? It felt like months; so much had changed. She gave the double doors a push, but they didn't budge. There was a card sensor mounted on the wall beside them and above that, a metal panel with a speaker and a large button labelled 'Reception'. Heather pressed it firmly. She heard a trio of rising notes, just audible through the glass doors. She waited, breath held, for someone to appear. But no one did. The place was locked for the night; no one was getting in or out without a staff pass. She walked slowly around the outside of the building, with its walls of sloping glass, bordered on two sides by rock gardens. The spiky plants and stunted trees looked weird in the darkness. There was a car park at the back and a breeze raced across it as she stepped out of the shelter created by the side of the building, making her hunch her shoulders inside her jacket. Without the sun, the May air couldn't hold the heat.

She was limping along the edge of the tarmac, past the back of a free-standing 'living wall' separating the car park from the pyramid, when she heard a loud metallic clang and a man's voice shouting. She moved towards the sound and saw that the rear wall was interrupted by the entrance to a cargo bay: a sloping ramp leading down to a concrete cavern in which a white van was currently parked. A pair of workmen in fluorescent vests were removing paint buckets and rolls of plastic sheeting from the back, not bothering to close it. She hesitated, unsure what to do next. She had come here propelled by fear, not thinking beyond her urgent need to get her pills. Now though, the scale of the challenge was beginning to sink in. The Triple F was famous for its tight security, so these men would be under strict orders not to let anyone inside. She could, of course, ask them to go and retrieve the pills for her, but even if they were prepared to remove items from a high-security building, they were bound to ask for her ID and make a record of it. Then there would be awkward questions about why a winner who'd left the 'regular medications' section blank on her finalist's health questionnaire had shown up in the middle of the night on a desperate hunt for pills.

She watched the men carry the paint and plastic rolls through a door that had been propped open with a bucket. They must be coming back soon, or they would have shut the van. Heather glanced at her Gucci watch. Twelve-thirty a.m. Weird time to be doing decoration works. Her eyes returned to the open door. She could slip through it, retrieve the pills and be on her way in a matter of minutes . . . assuming the men weren't painting just inside. But if that were the case, wouldn't she be able to hear them? She listened for the sound of chatter and footsteps. Nothing.

There was no other way; she had to try. Heather moved towards the door with as much speed as she could manage, her heavy footsteps setting off flares of pain. If the workers came back and saw her, there would be no dashing off across the car park towards the station. Unable to run, she would be caught easily. Then explanations would be demanded. Maybe even police summoned.

Adrenaline was spurring Heather's heart into overdrive as she stepped across the building's threshold into the basement. The workers had taped a sheet of plastic to the floor, which crackled with each step. It was a small space containing only a pair of lifts facing each other and a door to the stairwell. Pieces of plasterboard were stacked against the far wall, along with paint buckets and a roll of the plastic sheeting. Should she risk the lift? If the doors opened for another passenger, she would be trapped. No. Best take the stairs.

The stairwell reeked of fresh paint, making her feel slightly dizzy as she slowly made her way upwards, wincing with every step. She paused when she reached the ground floor, gathering herself for the next flight. She pictured the white container, relief in a bottle, camouflaged among the beauty products on the make-up counter. Then came a terrible thought: what if the Triple F cleaners packed everything away at night, locking all the products in a cupboard? Her breath quickened in alarm.

One more flight and she would find out, one way or the other. Heather looked up the stairwell, building her determination. Right. Onwards and upwards. The smell of paint grew stronger as she neared the first floor – the walls were still damp; the workmen must have finished here not long before. She was sweating by the time she reached the door. It was propped open with a large tin of paint, presumably to let the fumes disperse. On the other side would be the yellow-lined corridor leading to Lara's office, with its framed posters of successful Winfluencers whose images she'd moulded, her bookshelves stacked with guides to the perfect hairstyle, the perfect home, the perfect answers to questions from the press. A few doors down from that was the photographer's studio. The loos were directly opposite.

But when she hobbled out through the stairwell door she saw something that made everything inside her sink: a wide, blood-red stripe ran along the corridor's wall. She cursed herself. Why had she been so sure Lara was on the first floor? It wasn't as though she'd looked it up and pressed the lift buttons herself; the receptionist had escorted her. Yellow must be the next floor. Which meant another flight of stairs.

Heather felt like crying. She had already pushed herself too far, the pain progressing from dull ache to sharp twinge to the lightning flashes that made her want to scream. Those pills were her only escape. She leaned her back against the wall and closed her eyes. She would have to risk the lift. She was limping more slowly now, gritting her teeth as she hobbled over to the button, which glowed green at her touch. Then she waited, heart hammering. There was no sign of life from the offices around her. Whatever Triple F work was carried out on the first floor apparently didn't overflow into the night. There was a ping and the lift doors slid open. Heather lurched inside, dragging her leg like a dead weight. Then saw something she hadn't noticed before. Beside the numbered buttons was a sensor pad, like the one outside the main doors. The kind that could only be activated by a staff pass. She tried simply pressing the button for the second floor but there was no response. She stabbed at the others. Nada. Despair wrung her insides. She couldn't work the lift, but she couldn't use the stairs either, not with her leg in this state. She was trapped. Heather slammed her palm against the lift wall. *Damn-damn-damn.*

Suddenly the doors slid shut and the lift began to rise. She blinked in confusion. What was going on? Why had it suddenly decided to start moving? The answer came to her in a cold slap of dread. Someone on a higher floor must have summoned it. Which meant she would be caught, facing whoever it was, when the doors opened. Her thoughts tumbled with panic. What should she do? Try to bluff her way out? Say she'd left a sponsor's product behind after agreeing to pose with it tonight? But that wouldn't explain how she'd got in without a pass. The lift stopped on the second floor.

Her heart drumrolled as the doors slid apart. Then her eyes widened in surprise as she found herself staring at a familiar face.

*

The IT man from the make-up studio stood looking at her quizzically through the lift's open doors. If he was taken aback to find her there in the middle of the night, he gave no indication. He simply raised a pale eyebrow and said, 'We meet again.'

'Yes. I . . .' She grappled for the right response. But his unexpected appearance had thrown her completely off balance, sending her thoughts scattering.

Pull yourself together, a voice in her head admonished. *Act natural!*

She pushed back her shoulders and pulled up a smile, heart slamming against the walls of her chest.

'Hello.' What was his name? Had he told her? If he had, she couldn't remember it. So she just said, 'You're working late.'

'Yes.' The doors began to slide shut and he put out a hand to stop them. 'Are you getting out on this floor?'

'Oh, ah. Yes.' She stepped out into the lobby, with its thick yellow stripe running along the wall. He must have summoned the lift, but made no move to get inside. 'I was leaving but needed to use the loo first.'

An idiotic thing to say. Why would she travel to a different level, when there must be toilets on every floor? Her mind raced ahead. He was sure to ask what she was doing here at this hour. What was she going to say?

But he didn't ask. Instead he put his hands in the pockets of his navy cardy and said, 'Would you like me to show you around?'

'That's a kind offer, but I don't want to keep you late. Well. Later.'

'You aren't. I'm a night person. I wasn't planning to go to bed for a while yet.'

'Also I . . . I've pulled a muscle. I can't walk far.'

'I'll keep it short then. The most interesting room in the building is on this floor anyway. Mere steps away.'

'Ah. Okay, well in that case . . . sure. But first . . . I really need the loo.'

'Of course. I'll wait here.'

*

The pills were still there – *thank God, thank God* – the plain cylinder mingling with the surrounding bottles of powders and creams. She took two – this was an emergency, after all – chasing them down with water from the sink. They wouldn't kick in for twenty minutes or so, but just knowing they were in her system, working their magic, made Heather feel better immediately. She put on a fresh coat of lipstick, smiling at her reflection, relief sinking through her. Everything was going to be okay.

Her limp wasn't as bad when she rejoined IT Guy. He moved slowly, allowing Heather to keep up as he led the way to an anonymous-looking door around the corner from the lifts. There was a keypad mounted beside it. She watched from the corner of her eye as he tapped in the code: 10-09-08. Like a rocket countdown. Then came a click as the lock was released. Heather felt a small thrill as she stepped across the threshold into the forbidden space.

The room was windowless, with a long table in the middle surrounded by chairs, a computer at one end. Her guide didn't switch on the lights, but there was really no need to; the wall to their left was covered by a giant screen displaying a shifting collage of images and videos that bathed the room in a soft, multicoloured glow. Heather transferred all her weight onto her good leg as she looked around for the source, eyes settling on the computer. IT Guy stood facing the lit wall, his back to her.

'I like coming here at night,' he said without turning, silhouetted against the kaleidoscope of photos. 'That's when you get to see what's really going on. The raw, uncensored truth.'

She realized she'd been staring at him and shifted her attention to the screen instead, homing in on individual images. CelebRaters. A video of a woman she recognized as Kiera – an ex-baker who posted photos of elaborately decorated cakes – popped to the surface and began to play. Heather watched as Kiera launched herself at a handsome Triple F chauffeur holding open the door of a limousine. She made a clumsy attempt to snog him but he took her by the shoulders, gently detaching her. She snatched off his cap and hurled it angrily into the road, nearly losing her balance, clearly drunk.

The video was replaced by a still picture of a good-looking, tattoo-covered man shouting at a dog, his face twisted with rage. Then came the former flight attendant whose tagline had been 'High Flier', sticking out her tongue and lifting up her top, flashing her boobs for the camera.

'Wow,' Heather said, as a photo of Robert, an ex-builder from the Top Trio, popped up from the collage to fill the screen. He was passed out on the table of a posh restaurant, a pool of vomit beside him. 'Just . . . wow.'

'It's not easy adapting to this world. At night, you see what happens when society's guardrails are suddenly removed, all at once.'

Heather's eyes jumped from one image to the next with growing amazement. So this was what other Winfluencers got up to after they were done posing at Triple F mixers. Sneaking into a locked building seemed tame by comparison.

She moved forward to stand beside IT Guy. The pills must have kicked in because the steps were easier now, the pain receding into the background.

'Where do these come from?'

'Members of the public take them and send them in, hoping to have them posted on the site. But you won't find them there. See how they're all framed in red? That means they haven't been vetted yet. The frame turns black once they're published. Only you and I can see these. In the morning, a team will go through everything submitted overnight and post the ones that are usable. But most of them aren't. Because it's late and everyone's drunk or coked up or both. Most of them are like this.'

A man in an alleyway mashed groins with a girl in fishnet stockings, pressing her up against the wall. Her arms were stretched above her head and her skirt was rucked up around her waist.

'I feel like I should look away.'

He turned his head towards her. 'And yet you can't. Because here before you is what happens when the rules suddenly cease to apply. No eight-hour workday. No family to feed or bills to pay. Just acres of free time and enough money to make every whim a reality. Pure id. There's something compelling about it.'

'You come here at night a lot.' She had meant to phrase it as a question, but it came out as a statement.

'Yes. This is messy, unvarnished reality. What actually makes it onto CelebRate is just a pretty veneer for the advertisers. An idealized vision of what happens when ordinary people are subjected to sudden wealth and fame.'

'Subjected?' She turned to look at his profile, eyebrows raised. He was still facing the screen. It threw moving patterns of light across his pale skin. 'That's an odd choice of word. You make it sound like a punishment instead of a reward.'

'It's not a reward, it's a "prize". Rewards are something you earn. Like fame used to be; the product of hard work and struggle, of striving, competing and improving. This . . .' he circled an open palm in front of the screen, 'is something entirely different. Fame, hijacked by people who have done nothing to achieve it yet somehow feel they deserve it, who feel that everyone should want to watch them, not as they perform a live concert, unveil a new work of art or act in a film, but simply engage in the mundane activities of their daily lives: shopping, partying, eating a piece of cake. It makes no sense whatsoever. But it's fascinating.'

Heather was about to object – she was one of these people, after all – when her own image appeared on the screen, delivering a jolt of surprise. It showed Heather leaning against the wall of the roof terrace, a champagne glass between her fingers. She was looking at Veronica Shulman, whose head was tipped back as she pulled on her cigarette, exposing a milky length of throat.

'Someone's been sneaking unauthorized photos, I see,' IT Guy said. 'You're encouraged to take selfies at the mixers, but third-party pictures like this are only supposed to be shot by official Triple F photographers.' He considered the image for a moment. 'I like it. The expression on your face is very . . . pensive. You can see the intelligence at work behind your eyes, trying to make sense of the woman you're with. She surprised you somehow.'

Heather stared at her own face on the screen, the widened eyes and S-shaped crease of her brow. The slightly parted lips.

'No way. You can't possibly be getting all that from this photo.'

He looked straight at her then, leaning ever so slightly closer, making her heart quicken. She was suddenly conscious of how tall he was: well over six feet. And perhaps 'skinny' wasn't the right word to describe him. More . . . lean.

And Heather suddenly found herself wondering how it would feel to be with *him* in an alleyway, up against a wall with her skirt around her waist. She gave her head a shake. God, she must be desperate, harbouring fantasies about a prison-pale IT guy who clearly had a voyeuristic streak.

His eyes were fastened on hers. 'Are you saying I'm wrong?'

'I'm saying you're guessing. A lucky guess, but still a guess. Or maybe you saw a video of the party and caught some of our conversation.'

He shook his head firmly. 'No. Nothing more than this image was needed. It's all right there, spelled out in the crease of your brow, the tug of your lips. And above all, the flash of realisation in your eyes.'

Heather clasped her hands behind her neck as she digested this. Jesus, did her face really give so much away? She was going to have to work on that, try not to be so transparent when there were cameras around.

'Don't worry,' he said, as though reading her thoughts. 'No one else would have seen all that. Reading faces is sort of a hobby of mine. And anyway, most people aren't sufficiently interested in the inner workings of someone else's mind to pay close attention. They're far too busy obsessing about how they're being perceived by others.'

Her gaze returned to the photo by the roof wall, London's lights scattered across the background. And her own face, reflecting the discovery that Veronica Shulman wasn't the woman Heather had assumed her to be, the trophy wife skimming effortlessly along the top tier of society. That she was actually someone clever and complicated. Disappointed.

'I like that photo,' she said.

'So do I. Want to post it?'

'I thought that was up to the . . . what do they call censors around here?'

'VMCs. Visual media curators.'

'Yes. Them.'

'It is supposed to be. But the computer they use is right there and I am able to access the system.'

'Oh you are, are you?'

'Yes.' He leaned sideways to speak into her ear, their bodies not quite touching. 'Want to know my password?'

'Yes.'

She stood staring straight ahead at the screen, acutely conscious of his proximity, of the fact that if she leaned ever so slightly to the right, her shoulder would make contact with his.

'Why? Because you like being able to control things . . . or because you like knowing secrets?'

'Both.'

He must have tilted his face towards her because for a moment, she could feel his breath against the hair just above her right ear, like the faintest breeze, before he suddenly moved away. She experienced a small jolt of loss.

'All right then.' His voice was coming from behind her now. 'Join me.'

She turned to find him standing over the computer. Heather briefly considering turning on the overhead lights to better see what he was doing, but decided against it. She liked the semi-darkness, with its shifting colours. She crossed the room to stand beside him, watching the screen as he clicked an icon labelled 'CelebRate Filter'. A login page appeared. She watched him type 'FFFCEx' next to 'User Name'.

'What does the "CEx" stand for?' she asked, hoping to find out his name without asking. It felt too late for that now.

But he ignored the question, instead asking one of his own. 'Would you like to take over?'

'Yes.'

He stepped aside and she took his place, putting her hands on the keyboard. 'Password please.'

'What's it for?'

She frowned, confused. 'What's *what* for?' She stared at the blinking cursor in frustration. 'I thought you were going to tell me your password?'

'I just did. WhatsIt4? No spaces, W and I capitalized, no apostrophe, number four, question mark at the end.'

'Interesting choice,' she said, keying it in.

'It's an interesting question.'

There was a three-note chime, then the wall collage was briefly mirrored on the computer screen before fading out to reveal rows of thumbnail pictures and videos framed in red. She scanned them until she found the one showing her with Mrs Shulman. *Veronica.* Clicked on it. A pop-up box appeared: 'Select this image?'

She clicked 'yes' and another box appeared. 'Publish to CelebRate?' Underneath were two buttons: 'Publish' and 'Cancel'. Heather could feel his pale eyes watching her.

'Ready to share yourself with the world?'

She rolled her eyes. 'Please. I'm posting a picture on social media, not joining an international prostitution ring.'

He laughed then, for the first time since she'd met him, a surprisingly deep sound at odds with his narrow frame.

She let the arrow hover over 'Publish', savouring the moment: standing in semi-darkness with a man whose name she didn't know, in a room she shouldn't be in. About to break a rule and steal a little power.

'This is forbidden,' she said, turning her head to look him in the eye.

His eyebrows rose. 'Excuse me?'

'My favourite word in the English language. I make a point of saying it whenever I do something that's against the rules. One should never waste the opportunity to use a favourite word.'

She was still holding his gaze as she clicked the mouse. A few seconds passed. Then the photo filled the screen on the wall. A message box appeared over it saying 'Image Published'. A moment later, the picture shrank back down to join the crowd of photos and videos around it, now framed in black. A number counter appeared in the top right corner, scrolling upwards: 2 . . . 5 . . . 11 . . . 19.

'That's how many views it's had,' he said. They watched together in silence as the number raced higher, passing 100 in a matter of seconds. His eyes were still on the screen as he said, 'Unbutton.'

'Excuse me?'

His eyes moved to hers. 'My favourite word. "Unbutton".'

'Ah, but that's cheating. You have to say it in context.'

He gave her his slow crawl of a smile. 'All in good time.'

CHAPTER 13

'I cannot *believe* you didn't invite me along,' Ronan said. 'Angus Brimes was there! Do you have *any* idea what that man could do for my career?'

You don't have a career, Heather thought, holding the phone slightly away from her ear so that she didn't have to hear her brother's voice at full volume. *You're an unsuccessful, untalented actor who should have given up and found a real job years ago.* But there was no point telling Ronan that. It would only turn into an argument, one she'd had in many forms, over many years, more times than she could count.

'It was just a CelebRate mixer. The winners have to go so we can be photographed together dressed up and holding drinks. We're not supposed to invite *anyone* along.'

Ronan began speaking in that whiny tone she hated, his 'poor-me' voice.

'I just think it would be nice if you thought about someone else for a change. About your own flesh and blood.'

She stared dully out the back window of her bedroom, eyes moving past the garden wall to the playground beyond. It was after seven, so the families had gone home for dinner. The only occupants were a couple of teenage girls, sitting on the swings, chatting. Talking about boys, no doubt. Younger versions of herself and Debbie. Her eyes moved past the playground to the estate. She scanned the rows of windows, wondering what was going on behind them. At this time of day, the smells of cooking would be drifting out onto the walkways, Indian curries mingling with Bolognese sauce and the Caribbean aromas of jerk chicken and escovitch fish.

'That's totally unfair, Ronan, and you bloody well know it. I gave you money and tried to send some to Mum, but she refuses to accept it. Says she has no use for it, living the way she does.'

'Well, that is true. Mum doesn't need money. So if you want to send her share my way . . .'

'I gave you my entire £5,000 from last week.'

'Yes, but you have plenty more where that came from. And five grand doesn't go far these days . . .'

'Doesn't it?' Her tone was acid.

'I can tell you're about to get nasty so I'm going to go now.' She hated the wounded self-pity in his voice, hammed up, like his stage acting. What little of it there had been.

'Fine by me.' And she ended the call, robbing him of his exit line.

Heather could feel a bad mood brewing as she shoved the phone in her pocket. Bloody Ronan. Why did he have to ruin everything? She looked around her bedroom, at the cardboard boxes piled up against one wall. Lara had offered to send over a 'creative unpacker' – who knew such a job existed? – to help go through them, offering advice on where to place things. But the boxes felt like presents and Heather had wanted to open them herself, savouring each surprise.

She went downstairs and sat on the sofa, a new purchase from a designer furniture shop in Chelsea. She had taken one look at the curved lines of wine-red velvet and fallen in love immediately. Her tablet was lying on the seat and she picked it up, logging on to CelebRate. She knew from the ratings alerts on her F-phone that she was currently seventh – a nice safe, solid position – but she wanted to see how the other Winfluencers were doing, who had risen to overtake her and who was slipping down the ratings. She was pleased to see that the photo with Veronica had already attracted more than 30,000 likes. Heather scanned the comments below. Most of them were positive, focusing mainly on her clothes and hair. Someone thought her heels weren't high enough for the dress and someone else thought she looked better in green than red, but there was nothing about the expression on her face, the captured moment of realisation. IT Guy was right. People didn't notice such things.

She thought of coloured light shifting against pale skin.

Unbutton.

There was no point denying it: odd-looking or not, she fancied the man. Which meant she couldn't keep calling him 'IT Guy'. Heather went onto the Triple F corporate home page and clicked the tab labelled 'Our People'. It took her to a list of departments: 'Our Board', 'Our Sales Team', 'Our Creative Team'. Ah. There it was: 'Our Tech Team'.

She scrolled down the photos, well over a dozen people. Not surprising really, given that the Triple F was, at its essence, a website and app. Her eyes hopscotched from one face to the next, hunting for the familiar grey gaze. But she reached the end without finding him. Weird. Perhaps he was new and hadn't been added to the site yet? She thought of his casual confidence moving through the building.

I like coming here at night.

No, he wasn't new. Maybe she'd misunderstood his role and he wasn't in IT after all. She returned to the list of teams. Tried 'Creative'. But he wasn't there either. None of the other departments seemed likely, but she worked her way through them one by one, just in case. No luck. She tossed the tablet aside. Oh well.

She fancied a glass of wine. Grabbing a bottle from the cupboard – no, she corrected herself, hearing Lara in her head, not the cupboard, the 'Fendi Casa wine bar' – she crossed to the back window, placing the bottle on the sill as she lifted the sash. The temperature had dropped and cool air flowed in. The teenagers were gone, leaving the swings empty and motionless. The low-hanging sun spilled shadows across the playground and cast the estate beyond in honeyed light.

Suddenly, Heather didn't want to drink alone. She wanted to drop round to Debbie's, tell her about IT Guy . . . or whatever he actually was. Moan about her brother. Debbie would roll her eyes and tell Heather she was far too soft where Ronan was concerned. That family or no family, she should have told him to shut the hell up.

She stared at Shakespeare Estate. Well, why not? If she cut across the park before it closed she could be at Debbie's door in less than ten minutes. Which was nothing. They were still neighbours really. Putting the wine inside her bag – correction: her Mulberry Millie tote – she grabbed her keys and headed out the door.

Heather was humming to herself as she walked through the park's east gates, along the path between the immaculately groomed flower beds – was it her imagination, or was everything better tended on this side? – towards the shuttered refreshment stand. Its roof stuck out like the beak of a giant cap, supported by a wooden beam at one end, four picnic tables sheltering beneath it. The playground was just beyond, then the west gates that would take her to the estate.

As she approached the picnic tables, Heather became aware of brisk footsteps behind her. So she wasn't the only one using the park as a shortcut. She entered the shadowy space under the snack stand's roof. The semi-darkness made the picnic tables look skeletal, like the bleached bones of animals. When the footsteps suddenly drew closer, she felt her heart quicken. The man – it had to be a man with a heavy tread like that – sounded like he was heading straight towards her. A flare of panic went off and she sped up instinctively, sending a bolt of pain through the back of her leg, causing her to stagger. She hadn't even made it past the tables when a hand grabbed her wrist. Heather shrieked as the momentum made her swing round to face her pursuer.

He was of average height, with a square skull and a blocky forehead that jutted above his eyes. A bulbous nose spread too wide, not so much broken as smashed to a pulp at some point, never to regain its original shape.

'Heather,' he gasped. 'Heather Davies!'

She struggled to push past her fear, to calm down and think rationally. Maybe he was harmless. Someone she'd met and forgotten, who was simply keen to say hello. She looked at the hand, like a vice around her wrist. It didn't look harmless. She could hear the quiver running through her voice as she said, 'I'm sorry, do I know you?'

'No, not yet. But *I* know *you*. I'm your biggest fan.'

'Fan?' Heather echoed.

'Yes. I love your photos and videos. Every one of them. You're so beautiful. Not like the others. You're *real*. Natural. I . . . I've been thinking about you a lot.'

She took a deep breath, composing herself. Just a fan. An overly enthusiastic follower who had recognized her and become carried away with excitement. Noah had warned her there would be people like this. An 'occupational hazard,' he'd called them. She heard his voice in her memory now, giving instructions on how to handle these situations.

Be polite but firm. Establish your boundaries in a way that doesn't cause offence or anger.

'Hello,' she said. 'I'm glad you've enjoyed my posts. What's your name?'

'Bill.' His gaze crawled up and down her body, making her feel queasy and exposed.

'Hello, Bill. It's nice to meet you. Could you let go of my wrist, please? You're . . . I guess you don't know your own strength because you're actually hurting me.'

'Sorry.' He loosened his grip but didn't release it. 'I just don't want you to go running off right away. I've been waiting for hours, you see.'

The queasy feeling twisted deeper, burying itself in the base of her stomach.

'Really? Waiting where?'

'On the pavement opposite your house. Walking up and down. Hoping you'd come out.'

'How did you know my address? Because I never revealed—'

'I saw the park through the window on your moving day video and this is the only street in the area with houses looking directly onto it. So I narrowed it down to six possible addresses and watched all of them. I'm a patient man so I just hung around, keeping an eye out. Until finally, there you were!'

'Oh, I . . .' She swallowed. 'That was . . . clever.'

'It's because I wanted to talk to you. *Needed* to.'

'Okay. Well, I'm here now, so . . . why don't we walk across the playground together? Have a nice chat.'

He shook his head. 'No. I think we should stay here.' His hand felt like a manacle around her wrist. Her thoughts sped. It was nearly time for the park to close. The man who locked the gates should be arriving any minute. He would come over, tell them to leave. And that would be Heather's chance. She would shout to him for help. Unless he came late, *too* late . . . or not at all. He was unreliable; it was well-known around the estate. He'd sometimes drink too much in the evening and pass out, leaving the gates unlocked all night.

Fear was clawing at her chest but she fought it off.

'Okay, we can chat here then. But I'm afraid I only have a few minutes. I'm on my way to visit a friend and she'll worry if I don't show up soon. She might even call the police.'

'I doubt your friend cares about you as much as I do. Would she wait around for four hours just to get a glimpse of you?' He shook his head. 'No. It's because I'm devoted. And I think that sort of devotion deserves a reward.' He was dragging her nearer as he said this, so close she could smell his breath: stale coffee overlaid with mint. Revulsion made her recoil reflexively. She could attack him, scratch and punch until he let go of her arm. But then what? She couldn't run; he would recapture her easily. And this time, he'd be angry.

Think, Heather, think!

'Would you like to join me and my friend for drinks? The three of us could have a glass of wine together. Then maybe you and I could go somewhere afterwards for a private chat.' Heather knew she was blowing Noah's 'boundary-setting' rule for dealing with ardent fans, but this one had clearly crossed the line between fan and stalker. At this point, she would have said anything to get away.

But he wasn't so easily deterred. 'No, I don't think so. We can have a nice, private chat right now. On the bench under the willow.'

And he began dragging her past the climbing frame and towards the tree, with its thick curtain of leaves. He could do anything to her under there; no one would see.

'No!' she shouted. 'Let go of me right now or—'

She was interrupted by a metal squeal – the west gate opening; it had needed oil for years – followed by a male voice, young and familiar-sounding, calling out, 'It's still open! C'mon!' Then footsteps, indistinguishable words and laughter.

Heather couldn't see whoever had just come in; her back was to the gate. But right now, they represented her best chance of escape.

Bill was still pulling her along by the arm, lips compressing into a line of displeasure as she resisted, digging in her heels and leaning back with all her weight.

She turned her head towards the gate, where she could hear more laughter, and shouted at the top of her voice. 'Help me! I'm being attacked!'

The laughter stopped abruptly.

'It's fine,' her captor shouted. 'She's my girlfriend. This is just a . . . a little misunderstanding.'

'He's lying!' Heather screamed. 'Help me! Please!'

There was a beat of silence. She had time to think that have-a-go heroes were thin on the ground in London, that the next sound she heard would probably be the gate's squeak as whoever was out there decided this was hassle they didn't need.

Please help me.

The grip on her wrist tightened.

Then footsteps again, not hurrying away – *thank God, thank God* – but running towards her.

'Let go of her!'

The fingers released their grip suddenly, as though her skin had turned white-hot. But she could still feel him beside her, like a shadow. She felt paralysed as he whispered in her ear, the sensation of his breath sending a chill right through her.

'I'll be watching for your posts.' And before she had time to react, he was gone, leaving only empty air beside her. She could hear him running, sending loose pebbles scattering as he dashed back towards the east gate.

'Miss Davies? Are you okay?'

She couldn't recall ever having been so grateful to see someone. Dean Mitchell, her teenage saviour. Again. His older brother appeared beside him a moment later. Jake, was it? Similar features to Dean, the same wide, dark eyes and curved cheekbones, the same short dreadlocks sticking straight up. She looked at the pair of them standing there, wearing matching expressions of concern and felt gratitude rising inside her. She resisted the impulse to pull them both into a hug.

'I'm fine.' But her legs clearly disagreed, because they suddenly seemed to be made of water. She sat down quickly on the grass, afraid she might collapse if she didn't. The two brothers looked at each other.

'What happened?' Dean asked. 'Did he really attack you?'

She swallowed. Nodded. 'Yes. Well. He was trying to . . . drag me away.'

Dean frowned, clearly struggling to work out exactly what

this was all about, who the man was and why he'd gone after her. 'Maybe you should call the police?'

But now that she was starting to calm down a little, Noah's instructions were coming back to her.

If you ever get into any trouble with fans, call me. There are . . . consequences to calling the police now that your life is open to the public. So it's best to weigh all the options first.

'Thanks, Dean. I'm sure I will. But there's someone else I need to speak to first. And right now, I just want to get home.' Her eyes moved to his brother. 'Would you two mind walking me?'

The siblings exchanged a puzzled frown. There were, of course, plenty of people on the estate who would avoid calling the police at all costs. But the boys had clearly assumed she wasn't one of them. Because she was part of the system, a humming cog in society's machine, trying to stop young people from falling through the gaps. Or at least, that's what she'd been at the school.

'Okay, Miss. If you're sure that's what you want.'

CHAPTER 14

Heather's heart began to race the moment she stepped out through her front door. She had spent the night slipping between dreams in which she was being chased but couldn't run, and the morning hunched over her laptop with the blinds drawn, reading fan comments and catching up on other CelebRaters' posts. By two-thirty she was starting to feel trapped. She needed to go for a walk, stretch her legs, get some air.

Stop hiding.

Her eyes dashed up and down the street, searching for the lurking figure of a man. No one. Just a father pushing a pram and an elderly couple strolling hand in hand. Her fear turned to anger as she walked away from the house. Some of it was aimed at the man in the park. But most of it was directed at herself. When she'd spoken to Noah, he'd told her that Bill the fan was just a sad, desperate loser who had become fixated on a stranger's photos. And it was true. So why was she giving him so much power over her?

It began to rain as she headed towards Holland Park Avenue, slowing as she passed a lilac-painted house near the end of her street. There was a lilac convertible parked directly in front. A coincidence, surely? She couldn't imagine any of her posh neighbours intentionally matching their cars to their houses.

Then, from the direction of the house, came the clatter of high heels, an erratic gait. Heather turned to see a woman struggling down the front steps dragging a wheeled suitcase, head bent, face hidden behind a curtain of blonde hair.

'Can I help you?' Heather asked, dashing up the stairs and grabbing the bottom of the case. The woman lifted her head, revealing her face.

Analise.

After their chat at the New Heights, Heather had watched a few of the make-up artist's vlogs. The Analise in those videos had been articulate and relatable, with a dash of self-deprecating humour.

The Analise in front of her was a mess.

Her mascara was smudged, leaving dark blotches under her eyes that made it look as though she'd been punched. Her inflated lips had been outlined and painted red at some point, but she must have been drinking since, because most of the colour had been washed away, leaving only the crimson frame. One of her hair extensions had pulled free and become caught in her collar, where it hung dejectedly.

'Hello, Analise!' Heather took hold of the suitcase, carrying it down the last few steps to the pavement. 'I had no idea you lived so close to me. Are you off on holiday?'

Analise stumbled down the stairs, staggering sideways when she reached the pavement, clearly drunk. She squinted at Heather, eyes widening and narrowing as though trying to bring her into focus.

'Hey, you're Heather from the party! You looked so pretty in that red dress. I forgot to tell you I liked your tagline in the Final Fifteen. "Classy Girl". So cute!'

'Class . . . never mind. Look, are you . . . okay?'

Analise gave her head a firm shake, sending the rogue hair extension sliding to the pavement.

'No. It's fair to say that I am *not* okay. I can't get away, you see.' She grabbed Heather's shoulders, filling her nostrils with the smell of alcohol as she leaned in close. 'Did he get to you too?'

A dark thought blasted through Heather like an icy wind. The man in the park. What had he done to Analise?

I'm your biggest fan.

She should never have let Noah talk her out of going to the police.

'Who?' she demanded urgently. 'Has someone hurt you? What did he look like?'

But Analise was shaking her head, swinging it all the way from one side to the other.

'I can't see him. But he's everywhere.' Then she leaned forward and whispered into Heather's ear, holding on to her arm, long nails digging in. 'Watch out. He knows everything.'

'*Who* does? Tell me what's going on!' But a car had appeared beside them, a Triple F Mercedes. Heather was surprised to see Noah step out of the back. He did a double-take when he saw her standing on the pavement next to Analise.

'Heather . . . I didn't know you two were friends.' He looked down the street in the direction of her house. 'Although I guess you are practically neighbours.'

The rain was coming down harder now but Analise didn't seem to notice. She stood swaying beside her suitcase, which had somehow fallen onto its front. Noah picked it up and carried it to the boot, placing it inside. Then he took Analise by the arm and gently guided her towards the car, holding the back door open. But she didn't get in.

'Are you coming there with me, Noah?'

'Oh. Actually, Analise, I wasn't planning . . .'

She started to cry immediately, noisy tears that she didn't bother to wipe away. 'I'm scared! I need you!'

He put an arm around her shoulders. 'In that case, I will come with you and stay until you're settled in. There's no need to feel scared.' She nodded, tears still flowing as she hugged him around the waist before ducking inside the car. 'Just give me one second, Analise. I need a quick word with Heather, then we'll be on our way.'

His face was grim as he led Heather a few steps down the pavement.

'What's going on, Noah?' she whispered. 'Is it—' She swallowed. 'Did someone do something to her?' She pictured Bill the fan pacing this very street, perhaps waiting for Heather, but seeing Analise instead. Recognising her from CelebRate. Falling in step behind her. If Bill had done something, it was all Heather's fault for not reporting him.

Noah took a compact umbrella from an inner pocket. It sprang open at his touch and he held it above Heather's head, protecting her from the rain. 'I'm afraid Analise has had a . . . setback.' He blew out a puff of air. 'Okay, let's call a spade a spade. A breakdown. She's struggling to cope with the trolling aspect of Triple F life.'

'Trolling?' Heather frowned, remembering Analise's dismissive shrug. *You learn to step over them, not let them stick to your shoe.* 'She didn't seem bothered about trolls when we spoke at the party. She sounded . . . fine. Happy.'

'Well as you can see, she's not fine and happy now. So she's going to spend a few days in a very discreet mental health facility to help settle her nerves and get her back on track. I'm only telling you this because of what you've just witnessed. It's very important that this doesn't become public, so you cannot tell anyone or, God forbid, say something on social media. Doing so would cross a red line for the contest, resulting in immediate removal from CelebRate and the severing of payments. Analise needs time and space to recover. With a little luck, she'll bounce back stronger than ever and no one need ever know.'

The threat of exile made Heather draw a shocked breath.

'I won't say anything. But I don't really understand the need for secrecy. Can't Analise just admit to her followers that she's struggling?'

Noah sighed. 'I don't think she'd get much sympathy, do you? Here's a girl who has been handed money and fame on a plate, freaking out because there's one downside, a downside that she would have been well aware of going in. There's a real risk that her popularity would evaporate – and with it the amazing opportunities that have come her way. Three million followers. A spot in the Top Trio, which as I'm sure you're aware means a lot more media attention, not to mention higher-paying, more prestigious sponsors. Netflix has been in talks with us about a series based on her vlogs. Why risk it?'

Heather nodded. He had a point. 'But won't the fans notice she's gone quiet on CelebRate?'

'There are some unused vlogs and photos we can post to keep things ticking over until she gets back.'

Heather looked towards the car. The windows were reflective glass, so she couldn't see Analise's face.

'I don't understand how this happened so fast. She seemed so upbeat at the mixer.'

'I guess she was keeping her true feelings buried.' Noah glanced towards the car. 'I'd better go. We've got a long drive ahead of us.'

'Okay. Thanks for telling me. It's kind of you to go with her.'

'It's nothing. I just wish I could do more.' Heather trailed behind as he returned to the car, watching as he opened the door. She caught a brief glimpse of Analise, wild-eyed and tear-stained, as he ducked inside. Then the door closed and all she could see was her own rain-warped reflection in the window as the car pulled away.

*

'Have you lost your mind?' Steve said, waving a chip in the air. 'Why the hell didn't you go to the police?'

Heather poured sugar into her coffee. 'Noah Fauster advised against it.'

They were sitting at the window table in Joe's Café, a greasy spoon across from the school. She hadn't thought about where she was going after the encounter with Analise. She had simply walked, sticking to familiar, busy streets, refusing to give in to the impulse to keep looking over her shoulder.

And somehow – whether through subconscious desire or simple habit – she had ended up outside the gates of Holland Park Upper. It was almost time for the final bell and she'd retreated into the café, ordering chips and a sandwich, watching the students pour out in a tumble of youthful energy. There was a pause after the teenage tide had ebbed. Then the teachers trickled out. Steve had spotted her in the window, joining her inside and helping himself to her chips.

'Noah Fauster?' he echoed, pouring ketchup onto the edge of the plate. 'Who's he?'

'How can you not have heard . . .? Never mind. He's the contest's representative and the winners' mentor. He said this stuff's pretty common and that we have to expect some hassle from overly enthusiastic fans, especially at the beginning of our time on CelebRate. He says there are a couple of women and one bloke who pop up at every event he's scheduled to attend, begging to speak to him. So just one is . . . not so bad.'

'Yeah?' Steve dipped a chip in ketchup before putting the whole thing in his mouth, frowning as he chewed. 'Do his three grab him and try to drag him off?'

'Maybe "drag" was too strong a word.' She sipped her coffee. 'It's not like he actually hurt me or anything. And there's no reason to believe he wasn't telling the truth about just wanting to talk. I probably overreacted because I'm not used to it.'

Steve gave her a level stare. 'Okay then, allow me to recap: a stranger waits outside your house for hours, chases you across an empty park in the dark, then grabs hold of you and starts dragging you against your will to a secluded area . . . and you're saying "no harm done"?' He massaged his temples with his fingertips as though trying to stave off a brewing headache. 'That's completely bonkers.'

Steve had ordered a coffee and the conversation paused as the waitress brought it over. Heather waited until she was gone before continuing.

'It's an occupational hazard.'

'"Lottery winner" isn't an occupation.'

'Yes, it is,' she said defensively. 'I'm a Winfluencer.'

He tore open a sugar packet and emptied it into his cup. 'Riiiiight.'

'Don't be like that. It's actually a lot of work. Not in the same way as teaching, obviously, but there's more to it than you'd think.'

'Going to parties and then posing for pictures at those parties is not work.' He stirred the sugar, spoon clinking against the cup. 'Fame is not—'

'Can we change the subject, please?' She could see Steve was heading off on one of his rants and she didn't want the conversation to descend into an argument. What could a trainee computer teacher possibly know about the challenges and pitfalls of fame? 'Why don't you catch me up on the gossip at school? Go on, spill.'

There was a pause as she watched him reverse course, pulling himself back from the path of confrontation. He stirred his coffee.

'Okay, let me think . . . Oh, Angus has *finally* come out of the closet, to the surprise of no one.'

'God, was he supposed to be a closet case? It never crossed my mind that he might be straight.'

'Well, it clearly crossed his, because he made a big announcement in the staffroom and looked quite crestfallen over the lack of interest.'

'Aw. Shame. I might send him an email congratulating him and feigning surprise. Any other news?'

'Rumours persist of a torrid affair between the new geography teacher and the librarian. They were spotted arriving at work together last Monday.' He put down the coffee mug and leaned back in his chair. 'Oh, and I've started seeing your replacement.'

Heather ate a chip as she tried to work out why this last piece of information had caused a sour feeling in the pit of her stomach. She decided it was the word 'replacement'. She'd been gone less than three weeks. Had she really been so easily replaced, her cast-off life eagerly snatched up by some stranger?

'Congratulations,' she said stiffly. 'How is she? Any good?' He raised an eyebrow and she felt herself flush. 'With the kids, I mean. Is she connecting with them?'

'Ah. That. No, not really. She says she picked the wrong age group. Should have gone with primary.' He swallowed another mouthful of coffee. 'She's right, of course. Teenagers are selfish wankers. It's the nature of the beast.'

'Yeah. You're right about that.' She was surprised to hear the affection in her voice, the nostalgia.

'Oh, speaking of teenage wankers . . .' He put down the cup. 'I got you that information.'

'Sorry?' She blinked, baffled. 'What information?'

'The IP address? The menacing message?'

'Oh. Right.' She'd completely forgotten about that. It felt like a lifetime since that email had been her top priority. After everything else that had happened, it seemed inconsequential, part of a different life. 'Of course. Thank you. Who was it?'

He cracked his knuckles. 'At this point I would like to reveal an amazing plot twist, implicating a suspect nobody could possibly have foreseen . . . but alas I cannot. It's exactly who you'd expect.'

She sighed. 'Eric.'

'That's our boy.'

Heather closed her eyes, inexplicably disappointed. Veronica Shulman's voice replayed in her memory.

He talks about your lessons . . . You inspire him to think.

Now she found herself wondering: had Eric's mother been lying? Because you wouldn't send an email like that to someone who inspired you. But why say it if it wasn't true? Heather took a bite of her sandwich, looking out of the window as she chewed. None of it made sense.

'Thanks, Steve. I feel safer knowing.'

127

'Of course.' He drained the last of his coffee, wiping his lips with the back of a hand. 'As any aficionado of the horror genre knows, there is nothing scarier than an invisible enemy.'

I can't see him. But he's everywhere. Analise, hunted eyes and clutching hands, breath sharp with alcohol. Her voice whispering. *Watch out. He knows everything.*

'Yes,' she said. 'I think you're right about that.'

CHAPTER 15

I keep tabs on reporters now. What they write, how they approach stories. Who will handle things the right way. I'm about to give one of them a gift. The question is, which one? I run through my list of names, pausing at Carlos Hayek. His latest piece was about a former children's TV presenter caught during a police raid on a drug den. Instead of sensationalising her downfall, he charted the woman's journey from TV darling to meth head with sympathy and humanity, described how she tried to become a 'proper actress', only to be told, time and again, that she lacked the talent. A sensitive piece by a gifted writer. I cross him off the list. Maybe Davina Jiel? A blunt, pull-no-punches reporter specialising in celebrity scandals. But there's a risk there. She has a strong feminist streak. This story might bring that out. Best not chance it.

I stop when I get to Wayne Cartwright. His latest article is about a bishop caught shagging a married woman in the back of his church. I read it, smirking at some of the word play; the reporter seemed to particularly enjoy the fact that the pair were caught behind a large organ. Wayne Cartwright's email address is at the bottom of the piece.

I log into the email account I use for such purposes and write to him under the subject heading 'Story Tip'. A few lines of information should be enough. I include a map, though I'm sure he could easily find the place himself, but I want to make sure he actually goes there. Words won't be enough. There have to be photos.

I tap 'Send'.

Job done. I open a bottle of whisky and pour myself a glass. Now there's nothing left to do but wait.

CHAPTER 16

'Shit,' Elliot said when Noah showed him the newspaper article.

'Shit indeed.' Noah swirled sparkling water around his champagne flute. The two of them were seated side by side on one of the Blue Lounge sofas – closer than Elliot found strictly comfortable – with a copy of the *Daily Chronicle* open on the table between them.

Cover Girl Cover-Up, the headline read, with a subheading underneath declaring: *Triple F becomes make-up vlogger's concealer, glossing over trip to mental health facility.*

Elliot skimmed through the main body of the article, which contained more make-up puns – *the contest tried to spare the cosmetic queen's blushes by keeping her stay a secret* – but not much actual information. There was a vague reference to a 'battle with depression and anxiety', but the rest was just a rehash of Analise's successful career as a Winfluencer. It was accompanied by a photo, which appeared to have been taken through a window. It showed Analise parked on an armchair in front of a television, wearing a glazed expression. Her face was bare, not a scrap of make-up. And without the rouge-sculpted cheeks, dramatically outlined eyes and fans of fake lashes, she was plain, bordering on ugly. The fish lips were parted and had an odd, purplish tinge, making Elliot think of liver.

'Even by *Chronicle* standards, this seems remarkably insensitive,' he said.

'The photo . . .' Noah said. 'That's the main issue. She looks . . .' His voice trailed off, as though unable to find words that captured the full horror of Analise without make-up.

'But surely it demonstrates the transformative powers of cosmetics and her skills at applying them?'

Noah shook his head. 'Unfortunately that's not how it works. Analise is allowed to be vulnerable and insecure, so long as she remains beautiful and exciting. CelebRate stardom is all about aspiration.' He flicked a finger at the photo. 'And no one aspires to look like that.'

Elliot glanced around the room at all the perfectly coiffed men and women posed on sofas and chairs, drinking coffees and nibbling breakfast pastries; Elliot had noticed that most of the food was left half-eaten, no doubt due to calorie concerns. He picked up his own croissant and took a bite, washing it down with tea. 'So what exactly do you expect me to do about this?'

Noah frowned into his glass. 'I want you to gently guide Analise towards the right decision. And let's be clear: the *only* decision.'

'In other words, you want me to make her think that quitting Netflix and dropping out of CelebRate a month early is *her* idea?'

Noah sighed. 'I'm afraid so. If she stays, she'll only be trolled and derided. Netflix has already asked for a meeting and clearly aims to pull out. Surely feeling that she has control over her situation, that she's the one making the decisions, would be . . . better for her mental health?'

Elliot gritted his teeth. He couldn't stand the way Noah seemed to think that having a 'mentor' title magically transformed him from ex-carpenter into psychology expert. But in this case, it worked in Elliot's favour. Because it would be useful to speak with Analise face to face, witness her reaction to news of her fall from grace. She was, after all, part of his project.

So he composed his features into a neutral expression and nodded. 'Okay, I'll speak with her.'

'Thanks, you're a star. She's being released tomorrow afternoon. And she doesn't know about the article yet. Sunny Hills has seen to that. I thought you might be the person best equipped to, um . . . enlighten her.'

Noah folded the newspaper and handed it to Elliot. The story was on page five. Was that better or worse than it being on the front, he wondered. Would she be insulted that her breakdown hadn't merited a cover story?

'Fine.' He tucked the paper inside his jacket.

'You're a star,' Noah said again.

Elliot gave him a small, stiff nod. He had noticed the way Noah used the word 'star' as a compliment, assuming that everyone shared his view that fame was the ultimate goal, the most desirable state. Most of the people in this building would probably have agreed with that assessment.

But Elliot knew better.

*

Heather waited nervously in the lobby of the Triple F building. The CEO had summoned her for a meeting. Why? What could he possibly want from her?

Duncan Caldwell was the invisible force behind the Triple F, camera-shy and elusive: an irony not lost on the press. At one point, he'd remained out of sight for so long that rumours began to circulate that he'd been dead for a month. Even this failed to draw him out. He carried on as usual, concealed within the walls of the Triple F pyramid, pulling the levers of social media power while the outside world gossiped and speculated. It occurred to Heather that she had no idea what he looked like or how old he was. Noah was the face and voice of the company, and if Duncan Caldwell had something to say, he arranged for it to be said in Noah's smooth baritone.

Maybe this meeting was to do with the incident in the park? Noah must have told him about it. Or . . . oh God, was this about her refusal to wear a swimming costume at Triple F pool parties? Lara had been very disapproving about that, telling her that all the winners were expected to pose in swimwear, that poolside posts were 'very popular with followers'. And, therefore, with sponsors presumably. Was she going to be exiled for refusing to bare her legs?

She pushed the thought away. No. She was being silly, allowing her insecurities to inflate minor incidents into issues worthy of a CEO's attention.

'Sorry to keep you waiting.' The receptionist had emerged from the centre of the ring-shaped desk to stand in front of her, a clipboard tucked under her arm. 'Mr Caldwell will see you in his office now.' Heather was led past the main lift banks in the lobby to a single lift door tucked around the corner, discreet and unmarked. The receptionist pressed a grey button, which turned green in response, before handing Heather a plastic rectangle the size of a credit card. 'Hold this against the sensor and it will take you directly to Mr Caldwell's office. Please hand it to him upon arrival.'

'Okay.' She scanned the woman's features for some hint of what might be to come, but the receptionist's face remained impassive.

It was only as Heather stepped inside the small wood-panelled space and saw the now familiar card sensor that it occurred to her, in a flash of panic, that this meeting might be about her late-night adventures after the mixer. Had he found out about her . . . her . . . what crime had she committed? Breaking and entering? No, she hadn't broken anything. But trespassing perhaps, sneaking into high-security areas. Not to mention bypassing the censors, publishing posts without permission.

She could feel her heart racing as the lift swept upwards. Then the door slid aside and Heather stepped out.

Duncan Caldwell's office looked like a 1920s film set crossed with a greenhouse. To her left was a huge wall of sloping glass that went all the way to the top of the building. On her right was a cream-coloured sofa with a bookcase beside it and an S-shaped coffee table in front of it, a small drawer tucked into each curve. There was an enormous desk in the middle of the room, its surface a blonde semi-circle of wood with a smaller black semi-circle embedded within it. The floor was carpeted in a luxuriant, pearl-grey pile. Whoever had last walked on it had left imprints in the fabric. And right now, a man with his back to her was retracing those steps, as though following tracks in the snow, stepping carefully from one footprint to the next, arms out for balance.

Heather stared at his back. What on earth was he doing?

Then he must have heard the lift door slide shut because he turned to look at her over his shoulder.

Recognition hit her like a splash.

IT Guy. Oh God. So this *was* about their late-night foray. The CEO must have summoned them here to explain themselves. Were they about to be sacked? Was she going to be cast from the Triple F kingdom, homeless, jobless and publicly shamed?

But IT Guy didn't appear remotely concerned. He continued to look at her over his shoulder, without moving the rest of his body.

'Hello, Heather. Thank you for coming at such short notice.'

Thank you for coming?

But . . . if he was the one who'd invited her, that meant . . . *No.* Surely not. She stared in disbelief. But what other explanation was there?

'You're Duncan Caldwell.'

'Yes, I am aware of that.' A pale eyebrow rose. 'Ah. So you weren't?'

'No. I thought . . .' Her eyes returned to the carpet. He was standing in an odd stork-like pose, frozen mid-stride. 'What are you doing?'

He took one last, carefully placed step before abandoning his efforts and joining her in front of the lift, running fingers through his hair.

'This carpet is new and I noticed that my steps leave imprints, which got me thinking about the nature of time, and how Heraclitus said you can never step in the same river twice. So I decided to try and occupy exactly the same space at two different times. But it's surprisingly difficult. For one thing, the imprints aren't as clear up close.'

'You could just get some of those stencilled footprints, like they have in dance schools, then stick them to your carpet so you can step on them every day, thus saving the wear of your carpet while simultaneously raising two fingers to the space-time continuum and Heraclitus.' She handed him the lift security card.

'Amazing.' He slipped the card into his cardigan pocket, eyes drifting back to the carpet. 'Who would have guessed that dance schools held such philosophical weapons in their arsenals?'

'The power of cartoon footprints has always been underestimated.'

He gave her a sharply analysing look, softened by the hint of a smile. 'Would you like a drink?'

'Yes, Sauvignon Blanc, please.' She was joking – it was still morning; she'd assumed he meant tea or coffee – but he crossed the room to a polished rosewood drinks cabinet whose double doors opened to reveal rows of bottles and a selection of glasses: tumblers, wine glasses and brandy snifters. No champagne flutes, she noted. There was a bowl of ice embedded in the bottom shelf – how did it stay frozen, she wondered – and below that, a built-in fridge section with more bottles inside. He selected one, opening it with a corkscrew and pouring two glasses, handing her one as they sat down on the cream sofa.

Heather took a sip, seeing him through new eyes. Not IT Guy. Duncan Caldwell, the CEO. She had felt reckless and mischievous that night, when the two of them had wandered the building, entering forbidden rooms, breaking rules. Like kids at school getting one over on the head teacher. Except it turned out that he *was* the head teacher.

'So are you going to tell me why I'm here?'

He raised the glass to his lips. 'I wanted to find out how you're getting on. Noah said you had an unfortunate encounter with a fan.'

The thought of the man in the park made her stomach clench. So *that* was what this was about. He must have summoned her here to reaffirm the 'hands-off' policy Noah had warned her about, to make sure she wasn't planning to involve the police. The realisation brought a feeling of disappointment paired with annoyance.

'Not a fan.' She kept her tone firm but polite. 'A stalker.'

'Aren't they more or less the same thing, aside from the level of enthusiasm and determination?'

'He watched my street for hours until I came out, followed me, grabbed my arm and tried to drag me away.' She was trying to keep her tone light but the memory of the stranger's fingers coiled around her wrist was making Heather's chest feel tight. That encounter had transformed the world she once strode through carelessly into a place of hidden predators. 'Fans just want selfies and autographs, a quick chat. He wanted *me*.'

Duncan frowned. 'I'm really sorry, Noah didn't provide details. I had no idea the incident was so serious. Have you reported it to the police?'

'I would have, but Noah said the Triple F advised against it.' She looked down into her wine glass, conscious of how dependent on the contest she had become; she couldn't afford to risk losing her weekly payments. 'Anyway, there's been no sign of him since, which hopefully means he's moved on. So no harm done, I guess.'

'But harm *has* been done.' She looked up to find Duncan staring at her intently. 'You have been shaken, made to feel unsafe. To put you at ease again, this man must be caught, fingerprinted and processed. Named, shamed and warned by the police. Surely that would make you feel better?'

Gratitude rose inside her, catching in her throat, setting off a prickle behind her eyes, the threat of tears.

'Yes. It would. But I thought that went against company policy? Noah said . . .'

'Noah needs to get out of the Triple F bubble more often. What he told you is true; the contest strongly discourages involving police in incidents with fans. The concern is that it creates an us-them dynamic, a sense that CelebRaters aren't willing to fully share their lives with followers, even though that's what they're paid to do. But this so-called fan crossed a line. He needs to be punished.'

'So is that why you called me here? To ask about the man in the park?'

'Partly. There was also a separate issue I wanted to discuss with you. Winfluencer Sales tells me you've been having issues with some of our sponsors. Refusing to wear certain types of clothing. Short skirts. Swimming costumes. I was curious as to why.'

The sudden topic switch caught Heather by surprise, throwing her on the defensive.

'There are plenty of CelebRaters running around half-naked. I thought I'd try something different, for the sake of variety.'

He stared at her with those pale grey eyes. 'That's not the real reason, though, is it?'

Heather could feel her guard snap up, nerves humming along it like an electrical fence. She put her glass on the coffee table with a firm clack.

'Look, I reached a compromise over the skirt; the designer agreed to let me wear a different one the same length as this—' she flicked the material of her calf-length dress. 'And there's no specific rule about wearing swimming costumes to pool parties so—'

'Let me be clear,' he interrupted. 'I don't give a damn what you wear to pool parties or how long your skirts are. I just wanted to hear your side.'

Heather breathed in through her nostrils and out through her mouth, telling herself to calm down. Ran palms down her skirt.

Registered the faintest pulse of pain behind her knee. Hardly anything really; a good day.

She hadn't thought about her clothing limitations when she'd entered the contest, but now that she was here, the issue wasn't going to go away. Sooner or later, she would have to explain herself. She considered the man beside her. Did she really want to share the darkest chapter of her life with someone whose name she had only just learned? They sat in silence for longer than most people would have found comfortable. But Duncan Caldwell, it seemed, wasn't most people. She took a deep breath.

'Something happened to me.' She pressed the base of her palms against her eyes. Memories were stirring, rustling in their buried cells. 'I was . . .'

A sound interrupted, a bonging, like a gong. With her nerves stretched tight, it was enough to send her pulse spiking, making her jump.

'I am so sorry,' Duncan said. 'That line is rarely used; it's reserved for absolute emergencies. Which unfortunately means I'm going to have to answer it.'

'It's okay. I can wait.'

She was shaking off the past, pulling away from it, back to the here and now: the man standing behind the semi-circular desk, speaking on the phone. She saw his features freeze.

'How, exactly? I see. That's . . . very unfortunate. No. I'll let Noah handle it.' A pause. 'I don't really care what's expected.' He pinched the bridge of his nose between a thumb and forefinger. Then he slowly put down the phone.

Heather tensed. 'Something bad's happened, hasn't it?'

'Yes.' He flexed and unflexed his hands. 'There's been a . . . a fatality. One of the Winfluencers.'

'Oh no! How? Was it . . .' She could hear the rising note of hysteria in her own voice. 'Was someone attacked?'

'No, nothing like that. This was . . . self-inflicted. An overdose of sleeping pills.'

'Oh God,' Heather whispered. 'Who was it?'

But she already knew the answer.

CHAPTER 17

The dream began as it always did, with a dripping sound.

Mum had dropped her off on the way to pick up Ronan from drama club, so it was just Heather and Dad in the house. She could feel the day's heat, making the cheap school blouse stick to her back. The sound was coming from the bathroom at the end of the corridor.

Drip-drip-drip.

Water striking water. And for reasons she couldn't define, it made her uneasy.

'Dad?' she called to the house. 'I'm home!'

Nothing. No sound but the dripping.

'Dad!' She shouted louder, the unease hardening into something sharper. 'Where are you?'

The corridor was stretching, its walls warping. The bathroom door seemed to be receding before her, but she kept moving towards it, even though her feet suddenly felt impossibly heavy, as though they'd been dipped in concrete. Slowly, inexorably, the door was drawing closer. She didn't want to see what was on the other side. But it was as if her legs didn't belong to her any more; she couldn't make them stop.

Drip-drip-drip.

Then the bathroom door was right in front of her, slowly swinging open. She squeezed her eyes shut, but her eyelids must have turned transparent because she could see right through them, could see the overflowing bath, the leaky showerhead fastened to the wall. And her dad, lying there, one arm hanging over the edge of the tub.

'Dad?' She walked towards him, the soles of her school shoes slapping wet tile.

The dome of his belly stuck out of the water like a fleshy island; he had given up trying to lose weight. There was a plastic disc washed up on its shores, the lid to his jar of sleeping pills. The rest of the container was lying on the floor, two blue ovals in its neck.

Then her gaze moved to her father's face: the hanging mouth, flecks of dried spittle at the corners. And his eyes. Wide. Blank.

'Daddy!' She tried to scream it but the word came out as a whisper. She ran to his side, dropping to her knees and shaking him, sending water sloshing over the edge of the tub. 'Wake up, *wake up*!'

*

'Wake up,' her phone alarm said in a husky male voice, pulling her out of her Saturday afternoon nap. 'Time for you to wake up, gorgeous.'

Heather turned off the alarm before it could speak again. When Lara had added a sponsor's 'love alarm' app to her phone – designed to make lonely singles feel like they were starting the day with someone – Heather had thought it was a fun idea. Now it just seemed sad.

Throwing back the duvet, Heather crossed to the back window and opened the curtains, breath coming fast, waiting for the late-afternoon sunlight to dissolve the last fragments of her dream. She raised the window and a breeze flowed into the room. When her heart had slowed from its gallop, Heather sat down in front of the mirror at her new 'vanity station'. Her reflection stared back at her, pale and sheened with sweat.

The nightmare had returned. It had been years since she'd last had it. But the news of Analise's overdose must be stirring up the old memories, sending them drifting up through the murky layers of her subconscious. Back into her dreams.

She needed to talk to Tessa. Find out what she knew.

The two of them had started exchanging DMs on CelebRate after news of the suicide broke, a rapid-fire exchange of shock and horror.

She had everything to live for. I can't believe she's gone.

I keep wondering whether there's something I could have done to help her.

*

Then Tessa had said something that made Heather stop short.

It shows you can't escape the past. It always catches up with you.

Heather had stared at that message for a long time. What did Tessa mean by that? She'd asked for an explanation, but her new friend had suddenly gone quiet. Tessa had only sent one more DM after that, saying she was off to Edinburgh overnight for a sponsor's conference but would be back for Saturday's beach party; they could speak then.

Watch out, he knows everything.

She'd spent the last three days replaying the scene outside the lilac house again and again, as though it were on a loop. Had

Analise been talking about someone from her past? Hopefully tonight Heather would get some answers.

*

The New Heights had gone all out on the beach party theme. Women in bikinis and spiky heels flirted with men in Speedos beside the pool, where a game of water polo was underway. There was a grass hut on the edge of the roof garden, in which tropical drinks were being shaken and poured. Birdcages hung from the potted palms, a parrot in each one. Flaming tiki torches lit the scene. The roof garden was covered in sand, and Heather could feel it getting inside her Jimmy Choo sandals. There was no sign of Tessa yet so Heather drifted from one group to the next, dipping in and out of conversations.

'Well, of course Jemima is devastated that she's dropped out of the Top Six. She better come up with a good PR stunt or . . .'

'. . . started using Ozempic and I'm already down to a size eight! Can you believe . . .'

'. . . sponsor bailed after that video slagging off working mothers went viral. She denies saying it but . . .'

Leonora, the tarot reader, was chatting with cake decorator Kiera and Amir, who was without his trademark rollerblades, presumably because of the sand. They waved Heather over to share a rumour that a safari park was looking to become a sponsor.

'I heard they want a CelebRater to pose with their animals!' Leonora shuddered. 'That is *so* unhygienic.'

Heather nodded to be polite, while secretly hoping the rumour was true and that the safari people picked her and let her hold a monkey.

'I like your dress,' Amir said to Heather, eyeing the raspberry cotton sheath. She beamed at him, simultaneously flattered and relieved. She'd felt self-conscious about the beach dress when she'd arrived and seen how little everyone else was wearing.

'Thanks! I like your . . .' She scanned his nearly naked body for something to compliment in return '. . . tattoo.'

Kiera and Leonora both leaned over to inspect the rollerblade on Amir's calf. 'That's so cute!' Kiera said. 'I have a tat, but it's only small. See?' She pulled up the side of her bikini to reveal a question mark on her hip. 'It's because I question everything.'

Heather checked her watch. Past eleven and still no sign of Tessa. Maybe her flight had been delayed. A waiter went by with a tray of champagne. The other three grabbed glasses but Heather found she wasn't in the mood; she'd been drinking so much of it lately. She just fancied a glass of wine.

'I'm going to the bar,' she said as Leonora showed off the Ten of Cups card inked on her shoulder blade. 'Catch you later.'

There was a crowd at the bar and it took ten minutes to reach the front. Heather tried to flag down a bartender, but they all seemed to be focused on the customers at the other end. Frustration gnawed at her. Then a familiar voice spoke directly behind her ear, lifting the hairs there.

'Sauvignon Blanc?'

She turned around, back pressing against the bar. 'Hello, Duncan.'

He had ignored the beach theme, instead wearing a blood-red polo shirt and black sports jacket. A tuft of his hair was sticking up again. He could easily have flattened it with gel and she wondered briefly whether he'd actually styled it that way on purpose, to separate himself from all the moussed and blow-dried men around him.

'I'd love one but good luck getting it. There seems to be a staff shortage tonight.'

The crowd surged forward, momentarily pushing him against her, making her pulse quicken.

His gaze held hers for a moment, before moving towards the bar. 'In that case, I'd better pitch in.' And he walked around the end of the bar to stand behind it, scanning the bottles displayed in the illuminated fridge. Seeing their boss alongside them, the bartenders snapped to attention, shooting nervous glances his way as they put on a display of speed and efficiency. Duncan ignored them as he selected a bottle, turning to face Heather across the bar as he opened it. He placed two large wine glasses on the polished bronze surface, filling them.

They drank facing each other, a long, mirror-image slug. She felt her muscles loosen as the alcohol glowed inside her.

'I thought you never attended these events.' She was dimly aware of the queue behind her, the heads craning, wondering what the hold-up was.

'I don't.'

'And yet, here you are.'

'Yes. Here I am.'

His pale eyes fixed on hers. Then a voice behind her shouted, 'Who does a person have to kill to get a drink around here?' His gaze flicked to the waiting throng. He picked up the wine bottle, topping up both their glasses before returning it to the fridge.

'I think I'll end my bartending career there. Shall we head out onto the terrace?'

'You read my mind.'

*

It was surprisingly humid for mid-May, the air like warm breath. Duncan led her to the far corner, screened behind a pair of potted palms. They stood by the wall at the roof's edge, looking out at the rows of houses and blocks of flats filled with other people's lives, all their joys and fears and struggles boxed away for the night.

Duncan turned to face her. 'So what have you and the other Winfluencers been discussing this evening?'

She thought back over the idle chit-chat about sponsors, tattoos and beachwear. And was hit by a sudden realisation.

'I can tell you what we *haven't* been talking about: Analise. You would have thought her suicide would be the main topic of conversation. But no one's even mentioned it.' Guilt and shame twisted inside her. 'One of us is dead, and everyone's flirting and drinking like nothing's happened.'

Duncan looked out across the roof with its glowing torches and caged parrots. A beach ball sailed past.

'Well, this setting isn't really conducive to the contemplation of mortality. And anyway, they're only following the rules . . . or didn't your image consultant warn you against introducing mood-deflating topics at mixers? It twists the face, apparently. Ruins photos.'

'Oh. I forgot about that rule. I guess I didn't take it seriously.' She swallowed some wine, remembering Lara's bright, chirpy tone as she went through the long list of dos and don'ts at Heather's 'pre-mixer consultation'.

Whatever happens, don't talk about anything sad or depressing when you're inside the New Heights. You don't want to get caught on camera looking like a Debbie Downer!

'Don't let the facades fool you.' Duncan's gaze moved across Heather's features, making her feel scanned and analysed.

'Analise's death shocked everyone. A woman who has been given everything she had ever dreamed of suddenly discards it all. Human nature is so contradictory. Warped by self-deception and self-sabotage.' His expression became unfocused, almost dreamy. 'It's tragic. But also intriguing.'

Intriguing. Heather shook her head, thrown by the word choice; they were talking about a young woman's death, after all. And she found it unsettling, the way he spoke about humanity as though he wasn't really part of it. But she put on a smile and said, 'Thank you for your analysis of this alien species, Mr Spock.'

He chuckled softly. 'Sorry. I've been told more than once that I need to work on my empathy. Our PR department is endlessly frustrated.'

They stood for a while in silence, gazing out at the city. Then Duncan turned to face her, eyes sweeping the raspberry dress that skimmed her body, stopping just short of her Roman-style sandals.

'You look good.'

'You're right. I do.'

He laughed then. It made his face look odd, as though his features weren't designed for it.

'You must have worried about the beach theme, knowing the other Winfluencers would be exposing themselves. That you would stand out as the only woman covering up. You were starting to tell me why that is when we were interrupted.' He looked appraisingly at her lower body. 'You limp sometimes, favouring your right leg. Is the left one damaged?'

She would have withdrawn then – told him she didn't wish to discuss it, or made an excuse and retreated to the loo – had she detected even the faintest hint of sympathy in his tone. Or worse yet, pity. But Duncan Caldwell's voice contained only curiosity. Interest. As though this were merely another facet of her character that he wished to understand.

'Yes. I'm . . . scarred.'

'May I see?'

'I don't want my leg caught on camera. And trust me, you wouldn't want to see it anyway. It's ugly.'

'You needn't worry about photographers. They are all under strict instructions to steer clear of me. And as for your injury being "ugly" . . . I disagree. People used to take pride in their battle scars. I don't understand why that's changed. Scars show you've been through something, that you have known pain and come out the other side. That you are more and stronger than you were before. Why would anyone wish to conceal that?'

And he sounded so sincere, so genuinely puzzled, that before she'd had a chance to think about her actions, she was putting down her glass and lifting up her hem, showing him what was underneath.

Duncan tilted his head as he considered the mess of flesh between her knee and the base of her hip. The turbulent surface was interrupted by a smoother patch where they'd grafted on some skin – from a 'donor', they'd told her. And she was grateful, of course she was, but the more accurate word was 'corpse', wasn't it? A dead person's skin was bound to her leg because her own had been shredded beyond repair. The surgeons had done what they could: bone grafts and skin grafts and a steel plate to hold it all together. But there were limits to their powers. The most important thing was that her leg still worked; it had been touch and go for a while there and she had been told to prepare for the possibility of amputation. So she was lucky really. But her mini-skirt days were behind her.

'May I touch it?' Duncan asked.

She hadn't expected that. Only one man had seen her leg since the accident – the result of a brief foray into online dating. She had told him she was scarred and he had said he didn't care, that she was sexy and he didn't give a toss about her imperfections. But he'd changed his tune when he'd lifted up her skirt and seen the ruin beneath. She still remembered his little gasp and the look of revulsion. She'd stopped dating after that.

But there was no revulsion on Duncan Caldwell's face. Merely interest.

'Yes,' she said. 'You can.'

Placing his glass on the wall, he bent down, long, pale fingers travelled upwards from her knee, sweeping back and forth, exploring the trenched and puckered landscape, light but not hesitant. She tensed at first, then felt herself relax. It was a strange sensation being touched there. Some of the skin had retained its sensitivity, but other parts had been numbed by the damage, so the pressure seemed to come and go, even as she watched his hand stay on her, moving along the part of herself she had been so afraid to reveal. And she found herself wondering how it would be if his hand kept right on moving, travelling upwards. A shiver passed through her and he immediately snatched his hand away, as though scalded. Her hem fell, covering the leg again.

'Sorry, did I hurt you?'

'No, I was just . . .' She shook her head. 'Not at all.'

He straightened, returning to his full height, staring at her with an intensity she found unnerving, as though trying to see right inside her head. She felt suddenly reckless, standing here with this strange man looking into her eyes as the breeze lifted her hair and the music thumped behind them. She took hold of his jacket by the lapels, rising on tiptoe, pulling him towards her. Their lips touched.

'Duncan!' a woman's voice boomed, breaking the spell, making Heather jump back. 'I can hardly believe my eyes. You're *actually* here!'

A plump blonde crammed into a tiny silver swimsuit was standing beside one of the potted palms, holding a frothy cocktail with a paper umbrella. Duncan's back must have been blocking her view of Heather because the woman's eyes popped open wide and she clutched at her chest as though Heather had suddenly leapt out from behind a tree. 'Oh! Hello, I didn't see you there.' A purple-taloned hand shot out. 'Ruth Winters. Brand management.'

Heather looked blankly at the hand for a moment. She'd almost forgotten about the party; it felt far away, disconnected from the bubble of intimacy she and Duncan had created around themselves, making the blonde's arrival feel like an invasion. She held out a hand, heart still racing from the almost-kiss.

'Hello. I'm Heather.'

Ruth pumped her hand with a firm grip, the sort of handshake used to assert dominance in board meetings. Then she sucked on her cocktail straw, considering Heather through narrowed eyes.

'What number are you?' she asked.

'Excuse me?'

'Sixty-four,' Duncan said.

Heather looked back and forth between them, baffled. 'I'm sorry, but I have no idea what you're talking about.'

'Oops, sorry. Of course you don't.' Ruth reached to give Duncan's arm a squeeze. 'We must remember not to keep slipping into shop talk, mustn't we?'

Duncan looked at her for a moment without speaking, then turned to Heather.

'We use numbers to identify the winners. The contest has been running for two and a half years now, with two winners a month, plus the occasional bonus round to replace those disqualified over low follower numbers. You're our sixty-fourth winner since the contest began.'

'Can you believe it's been that long?' Ruth sighed, edging closer to Duncan, looking up at him. 'Wherever does the time go?'

He retrieved his glass from the wall and took a sip. 'Was there something you wanted, Ruth?'

'Why would you even *ask* that? This is the first time I've *ever* seen you out socialising. Can't I just be excited that you're here and come over for a chat?' He gave her a level stare and she ran a hand over the top of her short-cropped hair. 'Okay, fine. Now that you bring it up, I was going to suggest you consider doing the *GQ* interview.'

'You mean *re*consider. Since I've already said no.'

'But it's *GQ*! The *cover* piece! You can't put a price on that kind of publicity.' She gave Heather a smile filled with unnaturally white teeth. 'He's shy, you see.'

'I'm not shy. I simply recognize that I'm not good at interviews. Are you forgetting the last time?'

'Well, I'm sure you won't make that mistake again—'

'It wasn't a mistake. It was an honest response.'

'But no one expects an honest response! This is about image and branding.'

'What did you say?' Heather asked Duncan.

'Something about my motive for setting up the company. I don't remember the exact wording.'

'Well, allow me to refresh your memory.' Ruth pulled herself upright and raised an eyebrow in what was apparently meant to be an impression of Duncan.

'"I have always been fascinated by the human appetite for fame. I wanted to control the means by which it is dispensed, completely uncoupling it from talent."'

Heather laughed. It was just so . . . bald, so utterly devoid of diplomacy or spin.

Duncan shot her a sideways glance and smiled. Heather smiled back, then turned to find the brand manager watching the two of them with a small frown.

'So are you here all by yourself?' Ruth asked. 'I can introduce you around if you're having trouble making friends. Seems silly to be wasting your time talking with management when you should be catching up with the other CelebRaters. Like going to a school dance and hanging around with the teachers all night!'

'Actually, I'm waiting for Tessa Abbot.' Heather took her phone from her bag and checked the screen. Still no DM. 'She's flying in from Edinburgh, but I guess she's been held up.'

Ruth shrugged. 'Why guess? Just check her location.'

'Excuse me?'

'Didn't anyone show you how to use Friend Finder? All the Winfluencers are on there.' She snapped her fingers towards Heather's mobile. 'Hand it over and I'll show you.'

Heather didn't like giving up her F-phone, but she wanted to see what Ruth meant so she passed it across, watching the screen as Ruth went into Settings. A moment later, she was looking at a map of London. There was a cluster of overlapping black Fs on the location of the party, along with a red, pulsing dot that presumably represented Heather.

'Looks like everyone's here . . .' Ruth said. Then, 'Aha!' She tapped on an F closing in on Chiswick from the direction of Heathrow. When she expanded the screen around it, the F was replaced by a name: Tessa Abbot. 'There she is. Just around the corner. Maybe even closer than that, since the Finder can be a bit laggy. So you'll have a friend to talk to any second now!'

'I didn't realize I was being tracked.' Heather found the discovery unsettling, but Ruth clearly didn't pick up on that because she nodded enthusiastically.

'Handy, isn't it?' She handed back the phone. 'It takes away that whole worry of "who's at the party and will I be the first to arrive?"'

Duncan must have heard the disquiet in Heather's voice because he said, 'Don't worry. The finder is no different from the apps families and peer groups use to locate each other. Most Winfluencers find it useful.'

She looked down at the screen again. Tessa's F had moved to join the others, a stacked tangle of letters.

'It looks as though she's arrived,' Heather said. 'I'd better go look for her."

*

'How was the conference?' Heather asked, after she'd found Tessa by the coat-check counter, wearing frayed denim shorts and a white vest, a leather jacket over the top.

'Gruelling. Practically slavery.'

'Really?'

'No. Not really. I just had to wander around wearing one of these girl-biker jackets, letting people take selfies with me, then stand on the side of the stage looking fascinated when the CEO spoke. Boring as hell but otherwise okay.'

155

They sat down at one of the tables lining the wall beside the dance floor. A thick, white candle flickered between them. There was no one at the other tables. It was too early for dancing and most of the other Winfluencers were by the pool. Scattered shards of yellow and white light rotated across the empty dance floor. Heather put on a fresh coat of lipstick using the illuminated hand mirror the make-up artist had given her. She looked good. But then, it was hard *not* to look good at the New Heights; its famously flattering lighting was rumoured to have cost a fortune.

'The fans seemed to like your Edinburgh posts,' Heather said, tucking the mirror and lipstick away. 'Up two places in the ratings. Seventh. Nice!'

Tessa shrugged off her leather jacket, hanging it round the back of her chair. 'Not as nice as you, though, Miss Sixth.'

Heather flushed, half with embarrassment, half with pleasure. 'Can you believe I'm in the Top Six?! I don't know what happened to lift me up a spot. I haven't done anything special.'

'You were tagged in a couple of photos with Noah. That always helps. People are probably wondering if there's something going on between the two of you.'

'Well, there isn't.' Heather watched a woman in a blue sarong walking across the empty dance floor. She looked familiar. 'Noah's great to look at, but he's not my type.'

The woman drew nearer and the penny dropped: Rebecca, the former flight attendant who'd lifted up her top in one of the late-night videos she'd watched with Duncan. Heather waved and Rebecca waggled her fingers in return before disappearing in the direction of the loos.

'Really?' Tessa looked towards the terrace doors at the other end of the club, where Noah was chatting with Nima, a 'hair artist' whose vlogs offered styling and product tips for Afro Caribbean hair. 'I thought he was everyone's type.'

Nima must have said something funny because Noah laughed. The hair artist leaned closer, placing a hand on his arm. She was wearing her hair in layers of tiny braids with a copper band at the end of each one. Creating them must have taken her most of the day and by tomorrow night the braids would be gone, replaced by something new. Still, it clearly worked: fourth in the ratings.

'Well, he's not mine,' Heather said. 'I tend to go for older men.' She passed her index finger through the base of the candle flame – a trick Ronan had taught her when they were kids – watching it flicker. 'I've been told I have daddy issues.'

A champagne waiter appeared and Heather took a glass – she couldn't face the bar queue again – watching the bubbles race for the surface, pale gold in the candlelight.

'Like drinking stars,' Heather said.

'Sorry?'

'How Analise described champagne.'

'Oh. Yeah, I remember.'

Heather looked Tessa in the eye. 'What really happened to her? Noah said Analise was trolled but . . .' – *You learn to step over them* – 'I don't believe it.' Then, remembering the edict about discussing depressing topics, 'Sorry, if you're worried about talking here, we can go somewhere else or—'

'I'm fine staying,' Tessa said firmly. 'I'm okay with most Triple F rules, but draw the line at letting them tell me what I can and can't say in private conversations when there's no one else around. As for Analise being trolled . . .' She sucked in a breath. 'Believe it. Because it's the truth. Some bastard tormented her.'

'Who?'

'I have no idea. Unsurprisingly he – or she, since trolling is an equal opportunity role – didn't leave their actual name. Just some creepy made-up one: "All Knowing".' She frowned. 'Something like that.'

'I thought Analise didn't care what trolls said?'

'This wasn't a normal troll. Whoever it was had got hold of private information about her. A secret.'

'So he – or she – outed Analise on social media?' Heather frowned, searching her memory. 'It couldn't have been *that* bad a secret, since I don't remember seeing anything about it.'

'Nothing was said directly; it was all sly and subtle. Hints that no one but Analise would have understood.'

'Do you know what the secret was?'

'I do.' Tessa took a breath that hitched in the middle. 'She called me one night drunk. Hysterical. She told me.'

'And?'

Tessa touched the corner of each eye with a fingertip. 'Like I say. It was private.'

'Fair enough.' Heather drank some champagne and they sat in silence for a while, lost in their own thoughts as music and laughter swirled all around. Then Heather began to speak.

Later, she would wonder what had possessed her to spill her guts to a woman she'd known such a short time. Whether wine and champagne had eroded her judgement. Or whether Tessa simply happened to be there when the pressure inside finally reached critical. Because Heather had never talked about the day her father died. Not to her friends. Not even to her family. The grief had always felt too dense to cut up into words, an immovable weight lodged in her core. But as she looked at Tessa's face, dragged down by sorrow for her lost friend, not caring how it made her look or whether it broke a rule, something inside her shifted.

'When I was fifteen, I came home from school and found my father in the bathtub. He'd overdosed on sleeping pills.' Tessa drew in a sharp breath, then placed a hand on hers. 'I called an ambulance. Did CPR. But it was too late. He'd swallowed most of the vial so . . .' She shook her head. 'He'd always had bouts of depression. "Dark patches" my mother called them. But he always came out the other side, back to his old self, full of life. Of love. How could he throw it all away and abandon us like that?' She felt the old hurt swelling inside her, pressing against her lungs. 'My mother couldn't handle it. She retreated into herself, barely speaking to me or my brother. She moved away as soon as we were old enough to fend for ourselves.'

Tessa's fingers tightened on hers. 'I am so sorry.' Liquid sheened her eyes, making them gleam in the candlelight. 'That's just . . . utter shit.'

Heather surprised herself by laughing. She felt suddenly lighter, as though gravity's pull had weakened.

'Yes. It is exactly that.' She touched her eyes with a knuckle, dabbing away a tear before it could ruin her make-up. 'I'm guessing Analise was like my dad. On the surface, she seemed bright and bubbly. But that must have just been a front.'

Tessa shook her head, lips pressed together.

'No, it wasn't the same. Obviously she had to have had underlying mental health issues to . . . do what she did. But Analise didn't just *fall* into her darkness. She was pushed. And pushed hard.' She stared into the candle flame and Heather sensed that she was deciding whether or not to tell her something. Heather waited, breath held. Then Tessa nodded, apparently to herself. 'Okay. What I'm about to say can never leave this table.'

'Of course.'

Tessa picked up her champagne, draining it in one gulp. Took a deep breath. 'Analise had a daughter.'

Heather's eyebrows rose. She wasn't sure quite what she'd been expecting, but definitely not this. 'A daughter? Really?'

'Yeah. She was only fourteen when she got pregnant, so she gave the baby up for adoption. But when she became a Winfluencer, she finally had money and tracked the girl down, planning to ask the adoptive parents if it would be okay for the two of them to get to know each other. But something must have gone wrong because she'd ended up in foster care instead, bounced from place to place, with no one properly consistent to love her.'

'Oh, how sad! Couldn't Analise do something?'

'She went to see the girl, offered to look after her, but the kid refused. She's thirteen now, screwed-up. And angry. She's spent her whole life blaming her birth mother for her problems, for abandoning her. Analise didn't give up, though, she kept calling, sending gifts and messages, trying to see her. I'm pretty sure they would have worked things out eventually, except . . .'

'Except the troll found out.'

'Yeah. Comments started appearing on fan sites. Hints really, nothing that would have meant anything to anyone else. But enough for Analise to know her secret wasn't safe.'

Heather rotated the stem of her glass between a thumb and forefinger, thinking.

'Okay, so Analise knew the world might find out she'd given up a baby. That's personal, upsetting, obviously. But for it to trigger a complete mental breakdown?' She shook her head. 'There must be more to it.'

Tessa nodded. 'There is. The troll sent an email to her CelebMail account. She called me up about it, hysterical, the day before the Triple F shipped her off to Sunny Hills. Wouldn't stop crying. She kept repeating "what have I done to her?"' Tessa hunched forward, propping her chin on her palms. 'That's all I know.'

'What did the email say?'

'She wouldn't tell me. She was pretty incoherent at that point.'

'Maybe the Triple F would let us access her account, if we explain why?'

Tessa snorted. 'No chance. They'll just bang on about respecting her privacy. All they really care about is—' Her spine suddenly stiffened, eyes jumping to a spot behind Heather's shoulder. 'Heads up. Photographer moving our way.'

They sprang into action as the lens swung towards them, pushing up smiles and pushing back shoulders, clinking their now empty champagne flutes.

Heather was hoping to continue the conversation about Analise once the photographer had moved on, but then Nima came over to ask Tessa if she was interested in a 'collaboration' involving hair extensions. Amir followed close behind, smiling flirtatiously and carrying a tray of tequila shots. They all knocked one back and the mood of the night changed.

Heather didn't think about Analise again until later the next day.

CHAPTER 18

The water was like satin, flowing across Heather's skin as she swam. There was no pain; her limbs ploughed the pool's turquoise depths in effortless strokes. She rolled onto her back and lay there, suspended between water and sky, gazing at the stars. But when she pulled herself up onto the pool's edge, the London skyline was gone. Instead, the roof terrace was hemmed in by dense, night-black forest. A gust of wind slapped her skin, raising goosebumps. She stared out at the inky spread of trees, trying to work out what to do, how to get through them. Then, from somewhere inside the darkness, came a rustling sound. Heather was suddenly filled with dread.

Something's out there. Something bad.

*

Heather sat up in bed, heart sprinting as she waited for the nightmare to dissolve in the daylight. Then she fell back against her pillow with a sigh. She should never have let Tessa and Amir talk her into that last round of shots; tequila always gave her weird dreams. She groped for the remote control, aiming it at the skylight blind, which rolled back to reveal a thick layer of dark cloud. Heather stared up at it, taking stock of her hangover. A bad one. It felt as though her stomach was on a rollercoaster and her head was in a vice. She threw an arm across her face, wondering whether Tessa's hangover was this bad.

Tessa . . .

Heather probed the tequila fog, slowly reconstructing the night. She had told Tessa the truth about her father's death. She'd done it on impulse, confident that her new friend could be trusted. Now, though, she found herself wondering what exactly that confidence was based on. The two of them had, after all, only known each other for two weeks. And technically, they were competitors, vying for supremacy in the ratings.

Anxiety pressed against her chest as the scale of the risk she'd taken sank in. Heather had handed a rival information she had withheld from the Triple F – knowing it would make the screeners think twice about letting her win. If the truth got out, she could be kicked off of CelebRate. Maybe even charged with fraud.

Heather threw back the duvet and swung her feet onto the floor, the movement sending her intestines on another queasy roll. The F-phone was on the bedside table and she snatched it up, dashing off a DM.

Good morning. Just wanted to say please don't repeat what I said re my Dad. It's v private. You're the only person I've told about his suicide in the 8 years since it happened.

*

Then she sat with her back against the headboard and her fingers around the phone, waiting for a response, anxiety growing as the minutes stacked up. Ten minutes, then twenty. An hour. Heather stared at the silent handset in frustration, wishing she'd thought to ask Tessa for her phone number. But they'd been DMing since they'd met; it simply hadn't occurred to her. An hour and a half. Two.

Then – finally! – came the sound of the message alert and Tessa's name appeared on the screen.

Sorry only just woke up and saw this. Course I won't say anything! Your secret is 100% safe with me. Tx

Heather tossed the phone onto the duvet and closed her eyes, relief coursing through her. She felt guilty now for having doubted Tessa. But it was hard to know who to trust sometimes in this new, unfamiliar world.

The DM alert chimed again. Probably another message from Tessa, wanting to gossip about last night, or perhaps get Heather's opinion on whether to let Nima give her hair extensions.

But the message wasn't from Tessa. It was from Noah, telling her to come to his office straight away. And that it was urgent.

*

Noah leaned forward on the brown leather armchair.

'I'm concerned about you, Heather.'

She straightened against the back of the sofa in alarm, heart surging. Why? What did he mean? Her mind ran through various possibilities before alighting on the issue with her clothes. Duncan had said he didn't give a toss about that, but maybe Noah – and the rest of the Triple F – saw things differently. She had, after all, signed a contract committing to wear whatever the sponsors wanted, no ifs, ands or buts. What if she'd been summoned here because the contest had decided to start enforcing that rule? She drank the coffee Noah had ordered up for her from the lounge – non-fat chai latte, extra cinnamon – eyes avoiding his, drifting instead along the rows of frames above him: Noah on the covers of *Time* and *GQ*, certificates of appreciation from various charities he'd helped, a photo of Noah shaking hands with the prime minister in front of number ten.

'Concerned?' She shook her head. 'What about?'

Noah picked up his juice from the coffee table, leaving a ring of condensation on the smoked glass. 'I've just been informed that you're being offered a new opportunity. And I want to make sure you're ready for it.'

Relief crashed through her. So she wasn't in trouble, after all! Quite the opposite, in fact.

'What kind of opportunity?'

'We've been approached by Casual Elegance, a relatively new label specialising in "modest fashion".'

'Sorry, did you say "modest"?'

'Yes. Long-sleeved tops. Ankle-length skirts. They must have noticed that, unlike most female Winfluencers, you don't wear revealing clothes. So they thought you would make a good brand representative as they look to expand beyond the Muslim market. They want to launch a social media campaign – with you as the main model.'

Heather could feel a smile splitting her face as she absorbed this news. She was going to be a professional model! Who could have seen *that* coming?

I'm concerned about you, Heather.

'But . . . I don't understand. This is good news, right? I've missed having a job. It will be nice to actually *earn* money, instead of living on handouts. Not that I don't appreciate the Triple F payments,' she added hastily.

Noah chuckled. 'Don't worry. I know exactly how you feel about making money. It's part of the reason I took on the consultant role here. My concern is that this will pile added pressure on you. And after what happened with Analise, the Triple F is on high alert where mental health is concerned.'

'You needn't worry about me. I'm fine! And I really want to give this a—'

Noah stopped her with a raised palm. 'Don't worry. I'm not trying to talk you out of this. On the contrary: I think it's a great opportunity. But in light of the added stress it could create, I think you should join the Triple F's support group. As a preventative measure.'

'Sorry, did you say "support group"?'

'Yes. It's called the Winners' Circle. It helps winners adapt to some of the changes in their lives – loss of privacy, disruption of routines, relationship issues. There are also some ex-Winfluencers receiving help to adjust to life after CelebRate. One of our in-house psychologists runs the sessions.'

Heather finished off the latte as she considered how best to respond. This wasn't the first time someone had tried to shepherd her towards therapy – grief therapy, trauma therapy, pain therapy, therapy for people dealing with disfigurement – but she had always resisted, despite having had real horrors to overcome. So why would she relent now, when her alleged problems were wealth and success?

'I'm touched by your concern, Noah. Really. But I'm fine. Better than fine – happy. And I'll be even happier when I start working for . . . the modest company. I'm sure this support group is a great idea for people who are struggling, but I'm not one of them.'

'Then let me ask you this . . .' He leaned forward in his armchair, reducing the distance between them. 'How are you managing the fallout from the incident in the park? Be honest. Duncan told me the police report didn't achieve much. So where does that leave you, emotionally speaking?'

'It's . . .' She was about to repeat the line that she was fine, that she'd moved on and hardly thought about Bill the fan at all any more. But she stopped herself. Because that would have been a lie. Ever since that night, Heather kept finding herself drawn to the front window, heart speeding as she scanned the street. And she'd taken to using the Going Places app for journeys short enough to walk, telling herself she needed to rest her leg. Knowing that wasn't the real reason.

'Okay, I admit that incident has left me feeling . . . unsettled. I even considered moving house, which is obviously an over-reaction.'

Noah nodded. 'An understandable one.' His face wore a look of recognition, as though this were something he'd experienced himself. 'But it wouldn't change anything; ardent fans always manage to work out where you live. So all you can do is learn strategies for managing them . . . and managing the anxiety they create.' He clapped his palms together. 'How about this? Why don't you try one session at the Winners' Circle and see what you think? I sit in on all the sessions myself, so can tell you from experience that they provide an important outlet for stress, as well as a great source of advice. And you don't have to talk if you don't want to. You may find it comforting just listening to other Winfluencers, knowing you're not alone.'

Heather was about to object; he was making her feel pressured. But then she stopped herself. Because Noah knew more about navigating the Triple F landscape than anyone else, so no one's advice on the subject was worth more. And who knew – maybe this group really could help her put that night in the park behind her. Going to the police hadn't resolved anything; there was no CCTV on her street and the camera in the playground had been vandalized. The officer who'd taken her report had said they'd look into it but not to get her hopes up. Heather had left the station feeling more powerless than ever.

And even if this group couldn't help her, it would still be interesting to hear what the other Winfluencers had to say, what problems they were grappling with.

'Maybe . . .' She dragged out the second syllable, still unwilling to commit.

But Noah beamed and said, 'Great! There's a meeting this evening at six. Conference room B on the second floor. I promise you won't regret it.' His expression became earnest. 'But I must first warn you that confidentiality is taken very seriously. Repeating anything said in the sessions – whether through a social media post, tabloid tip, or even just a careless comment to a friend – is punishable by immediate removal from CelebRate and the severing of weekly payments.'

'That's not an issue. I would never share someone else's secrets.'

'Good. In that case, shall I see you there at six?'

'Okay,' she decided aloud. 'Why not?'

CHAPTER 19

Elliot stretched a smile across his face as he nodded along to what Noah was saying. They were standing in the middle of the second-floor conference room, whose sloping window was now covered by blinds to promote a sense of privacy. The conference table had been removed, replaced by a circle of chairs that Elliot had just finished setting up when Noah swanned in with the news that one more chair would be needed.

'… could use your help right away, so I thought it best not to get bogged down in red tape.'

Elliot winched his smile up a couple of notches. 'I appreciate your confidence in the benefits of these sessions, but introducing a new member without telling me first so I can consult her file means I am operating in the dark. I need to understand this woman's background in order to assess her needs and work out the best approach.'

Noah waved a dismissive hand.

'What's to understand? Her name is Heather. She used to be a trainee teacher. She's just been offered a big modelling opportunity that's sure to raise her profile and rating but she's been struggling with the fallout from an unpleasant run-in with a fan, so I'm worried about the added pressure. In short, the usual.'

'There's no "usual". Elliot was usually adept at masking his true feelings, but now he could hear the volume of his voice rising. He counted backwards from five, speaking more quietly when he continued. 'Each client is different. There isn't a one-size-fits-all solution . . .'

But he could see Noah had stopped listening, eyes moving towards the door as the first arrival shuffled through, the ex-roofer whose girlfriend had dumped him when he was photographed snogging a stripper. What was his name again?

'Good evening, Jacob,' Noah said.

Elliot sat on one of the chairs, reining in his anger as he flipped through his notes. Noah stationed himself beside the door, playing the gracious host as group members filed in.

'Hello, Catherine. Good to see you again, Osman. Heidi.'

Heidi, the former Winfluencer who'd developed an eating disorder. Elliot had sent her to see a specialist. He needed to follow up on that, ask how it had gone.

Heidi sat down opposite. If anything, she looked even more skeletal than last time, sunken cheeks rouged, designer clothes hanging from the sharp angles of her body. Not a roaring success, then.

He heard Noah's voice say, 'Heather. Welcome to the Circle.'

Heather, the newbie. Elliot turned to see the profile of a young woman with long hair and a navy jumpsuit, heading towards the chairs. The she sat down and he saw her face.

Elliot's stomach dropped, as if he had just plunged from a high diving board. Or a cliff.

It was her.

She had altered her appearance, grown her hair and stopped dyeing it, allowing the natural chestnut to return. She had lost weight and her normally make-up-free face was layered with liquids and powers. But he still would have known her anywhere.

Rosie.

∗

Elliot!

Shock was scrambling Heather's thoughts, making it impossible to fit words together.

Elliot. Here. Inside the Triple F.

She sat on the chair, frozen. It was as if a hole had been torn between two worlds, a catastrophic breech allowing her past to flood in like black water, filling her lungs, suffocating her.

She was seized by an instinctive desire to run, to distance herself from everything he represented, the terror and the darkness. The lost years. But of course, she couldn't. She would never run again because of *him*. Heather's leg had been quiet since the last pill, but now it began to throb, as though in recognition.

Then the spell that had held her paralyzed broke and she could move again. She might not be able to run . . . but she could still walk. Heather stood up with enough speed and force to send her chair flying over backwards, hitting the ground with a bang that made the woman seated beside her jump.

Then she was heading for the door, limping, shambling, towards escape. His voice was at her back, calling out her name. Her before-name.

'Rosie! Wait!'

She was dimly aware of Noah's baritone superimposed over it, carrying concern and confusion.

'Heather? What's wrong?'

Then she was through the door and away, feet beating an uneven rhythm against the floor as she speed-limped down the corridor. She pushed through a swinging door without thinking and found herself in an empty kitchen with gleaming sinks and ovens along one wall, a metal-drawered counter along the other. Pots dangled from hooks and a giant extractor fan loomed from the ceiling. There were double doors at the far end. They must lead out to the Yellow Lounge. She headed towards them, wanting only to keep moving, to distance herself from Elliot and everything he represented. Then she heard the door behind her open.

'Rosie, please, I just want to make sure you're okay.'

Make sure you're okay.

The words stopped her cold, sending Heather's emotions on a hairpin swerve, from panic to fury. She placed a hand against the steel lip of a sink, her back to Elliot, as rage howled through her in a cleansing blast, whipping away the fear that was hitched to her memories. She spun around, catching him by surprise, making him fall back a step. He stood facing her, wearing a look of confusion, just a few paces away.

'"*Okay*"?' She hissed the word, her rage expanding like a flammable gas. 'Well, allow me to be crystal clear. I am *not* okay. Will never *be* okay. I lost two years of my life and have to deal with near-constant pain. I can't run, can't jump, can't wear shorts or a swimming costume. All because of *you*.'

He was blinking fast. He opened his mouth then closed it again, apparently at a loss for words. For once.

'Rosie . . .'

'My name is Heather.'

'But I thought you hated your first name.'

She began advancing on him, moving slowly through the metal space, spitting out words as she closed the gap between them.

'It gets tedious, trying to tell a constantly changing cast of doctors and nurses to go by your middle name, especially when you're whacked out on pain meds. It didn't seem important, what with the threat of amputation hanging over me.' She saw him flinch and a spark of triumph flared inside her. 'For two *years* I barely left the hospital, having surgery after surgery, not to mention the months of physio. And you know what? After a while I found that the name Heather started to feel right, like it finally suited me. Because heather survives. It clings to rocks, in bitter cold and howling wind. Roses are ornamental. Heather is tough. It doesn't let go.'

He started nodding as she moved nearer, an exaggerated movement, like one of those dashboard dogs.

'That's . . . that's good. It sounds as though you've come through this stronger than before, developed as a person.'

She stopped dead, no more than two steps between them, staring in disbelief. Dear God, was he seriously trying to spin what he'd done into some sort of positive growth experience? No way. No *bloody* way.

'You ruined my body and my life. Do you feel even remotely guilty about that?'

'Of *course* I do, I think about it all the time! About how I lost control . . . I *never* lose control. But I did that day. Control of myself. Of the car. And you paid the price. I wish . . .' His voice faded out. He looked at the floor. 'I am truly sorry. And I just hope that one day, you might find a way to . . .' He looked up, eyes pleading. 'To forgive me.'

'For God's *sake*, Elliot!' Heather threw out her palms. 'You are completely missing the point! This isn't about loss of control. It's about cowardice! You abandoned me to a rising tide. You left me to die.'

'What was I supposed to do? You were trapped, unconscious. Staying with you would have achieved nothing, aside from putting both our lives at risk.' He ran his fingers along the steel counter next to him. 'At least my way, we had a chance.'

'*You* had a chance. You were miles away, still trudging along the road, when the water reached my face. If that fishing boat hadn't spotted the car and called the coastguard . . .'

He raised his arms towards her. 'But it *did*. And we both survived. Surely that's what matters in the end?'

'No. You *abandoned* me. You should have stayed. That's what *I* would have done.'

Elliot shook his head, a series of short, sharp movements.

'You can't know that unless you've actually been in my position. The survival instinct is the most powerful force in nature. Don't underestimate it.'

She took a step forward, intending to square up to him eyeball to eyeball. But he retreated, maintaining the distance between them, one step forward, one step back. As though they were dancing.

'"The survival instinct". So you *admit* you were only thinking of survival, of saving your own neck!'

He opened his mouth but nothing came out. His eyes flicked back and forth, as though searching inside his head for an exit. A feeling of savage triumph flared inside her.

Heather, one, Elliot, nil.

Then he closed his eyes.

'I did what anyone in my position would have done.'

Heather shook her head, a slow, sweeping movement.

'You're wrong about that. I would *never* have done what you did. And I will never forgive you for it.'

Then she pushed past him and went back out through the swinging doors into the corridor, leaving him standing alone in the kitchen.

*

Heather's heart was still racing when she got home. She kicked off her shoes and scooped up her tablet, throwing herself across the red sofa. Then she did something she had expressly avoided for the last two and a half years: she googled Elliot's name. Her failure to keep track of him had been a conscious decision, born of her determination to exile him completely from her life and her thoughts. But now she needed to find out how his career path had veered away from academia and onto a collision course with hers. Was it possible he'd been stalking her – that he'd only joined the Triple F because he'd found out she'd won?

But a quick search showed that not to be true. The top result was a magazine interview, revealing that he'd left his college teaching post to join the contest more than two years ago. The interviewer had gone to Elliot's home and there was a photo of him reading a psychology textbook in 'his penthouse flat in Farringdon's iconic Laynor Building'. Her eyes scanned the photo's background: everything clean, modern, minimalist. He still had an aquarium, she saw. He'd been obsessed with those bloody fish when they were together, always checking the temperature and pH levels. Heather skimmed the quotes from Elliot, talking about the importance of mental health screenings for people taking up high-stress, life-changing roles. There was another photo at the end of the article, Elliot seated behind a desk in his book-lined Triple F office, wearing the forehead crease she'd once affectionately dubbed his thinking-deep-thoughts face. She stared at the image, shaking her head.

What are you doing there, Elliot?

Elliot was an intellectual snob who took enormous pride in his professional reputation. She'd seen him turn down high-paying jobs in favour of less lucrative, more prestigious ones. She propped her shoulders against the arm of the sofa, memory skimming back through the relationship. Now that she thought about it, Elliot had always been fascinated by reality TV and celebrity culture, often joining her as she watched *Love Island*.

'Without talent to support it, this sort of fame is completely at the mercy of public whims and attention spans,' he'd said once, as they'd watched one of the couples being voted off the programme. 'A uniquely stressful situation. No wonder alcoholism and drug abuse are so rampant among former contestants.'

His comments always carried an undercurrent of contempt. But then why—

The tablet's DM alert severed the thought. A chill ran through Heather when she saw the sender's name. *Elliot.* The timing was creepy, as though he could see into her living room, knew she had been looking at his photos.

What could he possibly want to say to her after their showdown in the kitchen? Elliot hated confrontation; it wasn't like him to risk subjecting himself to more of it. Unless . . . what if the message was a confession, an admission that he had knowingly left her to die? Heather's throat felt tight as she clicked open the message.

Dear Rosie, it began, making her lips purse in irritation. She'd

176

told him she didn't use that name any more. God forbid he should respect her wishes. I am truly sorry to have caused you such a shock. Having an element of the past you have so unequivocally broken with invade your present must have triggered some traumatic memories that you have yet to fully confront. And all this while grappling with the enormous challenges that drew you to the Winners' Circle in the first place. Under normal circumstances, I would refer you to another, similar support group. But alas, no such group exists. The Circle is unique because the situation in which you now find yourself is unique. You are being asked to navigate a new social and vocational landscape for which you have no maps. The Circle can help you create those maps, cultivate new skills and, most importantly, express your concerns in a supportive environment, among the only people in the world able to empathize. With this in mind, I would urge you to consider returning, despite my presence there. My role in the sessions is simply to manage the flow of conversation and direct a few exercises. Your focus should be the other members. And perhaps my being in the room could even be beneficial, a form of systematic desensitisation therapy in its own right, affording you the opportunity to confront the traumatic memories you associate with me until my presence ceases to provoke a reaction, thus neutralising them. Obviously, the choice is entirely yours. But I would advise you to weigh the potential benefits of these sessions, the coping tools they could provide at this pivotal point in your life, before casting the opportunity aside. Because whether or not you choose to believe it, I truly care about your well-being and want what is best for you.

*

177

Heather slammed her laptop shut. God, what a bullshit artist – still spewing his psychological jargon all over the shop, flexing his intellect the way other men flexed their muscles at the beach. And was he seriously trying to tell her that just spending time trapped in a room with him would somehow be therapeutic? Please. She remembered his lecture about systematic desensitisation. It was used to treat phobias. The idea was to expose yourself to the thing you feared most – a spider or snake or whatever – keeping it in a box at the opposite end of the room at first, not moving, waiting until the fear reaction it provoked eventually faded with time. Then move the box a bit closer. And closer. Waiting each time for the body's adrenaline alarm to fall silent. Until eventually the spider was crawling on your arm. Was he seriously suggesting that she approach him the same way, as an irrational fear to be overcome? Because as far as she was concerned, there was nothing irrational about it.

Elliot. For two years, she had kept her memories of him weighted down, anchored in the depths. But now she could feel them pulling free, rising towards the surface, carrying her back to the day of the break-up. The day her old life had ended.

*

It was the analysis that finally did it. The relentless analysis. She had enjoyed Elliot's insights at first, felt as though she were being offered a guided tour around the inner workings of the mind. Of *her* mind. But he couldn't switch it off.

'I must have gained half a stone this week,' she'd said on the last day of their holiday, pivoting in front of the hotel mirror, frowning at the muffin top that had appeared over the last few days, protruding over the border of her jeans. 'All these hotel buffets. I can't resist them.'

'Body dysmorphia,' he'd said without looking up from the open suitcase on the bed in front of him, half packed for the journey home.

'Excuse me?'

'A condition characterized by obsession over physical flaws that are in fact imperceptible to others.' He placed a perfectly folded pair of boxer shorts on top of another pair. OCD. You didn't need a psychology PhD to diagnose that one.

Heather gripped the new bulge of flesh between two fingers. 'Are you seriously telling me this is imperceptible?'

He glanced up from the suitcase. 'Ah. Yes, point taken. Well, if it makes you feel any better, I've got one of those myself.' He patted his stomach. 'I like to think of it as a backup energy supply to draw on if I ever get stranded on a desert island.'

Her eyes returned to the mirror. 'Yes, but you're *allowed* to have a gut; you're pushing forty. I've got no excuse.'

She knew the comment was insensitive as soon as it came out; he was self-conscious about their age gap.

He stopped packing and looked down at his stomach. 'It's not that bad, is it?'

'No, it's perfect. Just the right size for my head to rest on. And anyway, we match now.' She patted her belly. 'I lose all self-control in the face of unlimited hash browns.'

He gave her a brief glance then returned to his packing. 'Yes, I've noticed you do occasionally swerve towards B.E.D.'

'Why are you spelling it out?' she'd asked jokingly, lying down sideways on the bed next to the suitcase, striking a mock-seductive pose. 'Is it a naughty word that you're scared to say out loud?'

'It stands for "binge eating disorder". You've shown signs of it over the past week.'

She rolled onto her back, battling a surge of anger. Yes, she had eaten a lot this week. But they were on holiday, for Christ's sake. And who didn't binge eat at hotel buffets? It was practically a rule.

'It would be nice if you could stop being a shrink for two minutes and just be a boyfriend.'

He paused to look at her, a frown creasing his forehead. 'I've noticed you use that word a lot.'

'Boyfriend?'

'Shrink. I can't help but suspect that it's a subconscious way of diminishing me, my professional. To "shrink" me in the literal sense of the word.'

And that was the moment she'd decided the relationship had run its course. That she would wait until they got back to London, then calmly break things off. Maybe try dating blokes her own age. She tossed her suitcase onto the bed, yanking open the zip and throwing in her clothes. She made a point of not folding them and felt a pulse of satisfaction when she saw his jaw tighten as he watched her from the corner of his eye.

'I'm so glad I don't have OCD,' she said. 'Being messy is so freeing. You should try it some time.'

He opened his mouth then gave his head a small shake and closed it again. He zipped his case shut.

'Are you ready to leave?' he asked.

'Yes,' she said quietly. 'I really am.'

*

The downpour had started less than an hour into the journey, drumming against the roof of the Renault, so loud it sounded more like falling gravel than drops of water. They were on a winding road that hugged the Highland coast. She stared out at the dark clouds massed over the sea, dragging nets of rain.

He switched on music, classical, as per usual. She had liked that about him once, back when she'd thought he listened to Vivaldi and Bach because he enjoyed the patterns of sound woven by genius. But she'd later discovered it was because 'studies show it reduces tension and enhances spatial-temporal reasoning'.

Studies show. In the space of their eight-month relationship, those had become the two most irritating words in the English language.

'I've really enjoyed spending time together this week,' he said, putting his free hand on her knee. 'Just the two of us alone, chatting about life, the metaverse and everything. Taking on Scotland's most daunting challenges, vertical cliffs, sideways rain.' He shot her a grin. 'Haggis. It's helped me to crystalize the way I feel about you. The central role you play in my psychological well-being.' His fingers tightened around her knee. 'Which is my admittedly unromantic way of saying that I love you.'

His words sank through her, dragging down her already low mood. Some part of her had hoped that they were both on the same page, that her ebbing affections were being mirrored on the other side of the relationship equation. So that when the time came, they would both nod and smile sadly, as one of them finally said what both had been thinking: 'It was good for a while, but I think we can agree that we've reached the end of the road.'

No such luck.

She stared out of the windscreen. The wipers were fighting

a losing battle against the rain, which had reduced the road to a smear of greys and greens. She couldn't think what to say, so she stayed silent.

'In light of that confession,' he continued. 'I was thinking that maybe it's time we moved in together.'

She turned and stared at him in surprise. 'But . . . we haven't been going out for that long.'

'Eight months is enough time to assess compatibility, don't you think?'

'No.' She shook her head. 'I don't want to move in with you.'

She saw his hands tighten around the steering wheel.

'How about a brief trial period, to see whether we are able to adapt to each other's domestic patterns? Because studies show—'

Perhaps if he hadn't said those last two words, her life would have turned out differently. She would have waited until they were back in London before telling him that she was ending their relationship. In a public place, because she knew how much he hated making a scene. Then they would have gone their separate ways and life would have continued. She would have finished her two years of training and started teaching her own science classes.

But those words ignited something inside her, and suddenly she couldn't wait another day, another hour. Another second.

'I am breaking up with you, Elliot.'

Heather didn't know what she'd expected to happen when she said it, how she would feel, what he would do. But the moment the words left her, she had the sensation of shedding a heavy backpack whose weight she'd grown used to – a sudden lightness, as though she might float. And she knew that this wasn't just an impulse born of annoyance. Her feelings for Elliot were gone. Then she looked at his face. Saw his features twist. She'd never seen that before. Normally he didn't let his emotions gain the upper hand over his 'higher cortical functions'.

'I don't accept that,' he said. 'We can work things out.'

'No, Elliot. It's done.'

'Why don't we discuss this tomorrow?' There was a crack in his voice, letting desperation seep through. 'Sleep on it and then we can talk . . .'

'There's nothing to talk about. I don't want to be with you any more. I – Jesus, Elliot, watch where you're going!' The Renault had swung towards the edge of the road, with its sheer drop to the sea below. She could hear waves slamming themselves against the rocks, like something breaking. Then Elliot gave his head a short shake, as though rousing himself from a light sleep, and the car returned to its lane. She released an unsteady breath. She should have stuck with her original plan and waited until tomorrow. Telling him in the car, when they still had hours left on the road together, had been a big mistake.

'You can drop me off in the next town. I'll get a train back to London.'

She expected him to argue, to tell her that she was being silly or that there wasn't a station in the next town; she'd have to wait. But instead he just stared straight ahead, face blank, as though in a trance.

'Elliot? Did you hear me?' The car swerved again, and for a moment, there was no road beside her, just the thrash of the sea. Fear tore through her. 'Stop the car!' she shouted, not caring about the downpour. 'Let me out!'

'Sorry, what?' His voice sounded blurry and strange, as though coming from far away. The road was heading upwards now, clinging to the cliff edge, North Sea receding below. The Renault slalomed, tracing a giant 'S' across the watery tarmac. Her mouth opened but no sound came out. If someone had been coming the other way, they would have collided head-on. He seemed not to notice. It was as though the break-up had short-circuited something inside his head, disconnecting Elliot from the world around him. She saw a road sign, warped by the raindrops wriggling across the windscreen, a red triangle framing a black arrow bent to the right: sharp curve ahead.

'Slow down!' she screamed, hoping to pierce his daze with sheer volume. 'Please!'

No response.

Her thoughts were a panicky jumble. Should she grab hold of the steering wheel? Pull the handbrake? Throw herself from the car?

But then she saw that it was too late for any of those things, because the Renault was already leaving the tarmac. For a moment it was in the air, held aloft by forward momentum, caught between the sea and the sky. Then gravity reasserted itself and it plunged, nose first, towards the crashing waters below.

CHAPTER 20

Heather was humming to herself as she slid back the door of her walk-in wardrobe and began flipping through the newly arrived dresses and skirts, trying to decide which one to wear. She had hoped to fall in love with Casual Elegance, but if she was being honest, it wasn't really her taste. The colours were too muted and the fit too loose around the middle. Still, nothing a belt and some sparkly jewellery couldn't fix.

She selected a long, greyish-green skirt and matching top with Juliet sleeves, laying them out on her bed. Then she took a pill from the container in her make-up drawer, hesitated, then took one more. She would need the extra help if she was going to be on her feet all night.

There was a chirp from the direction of the bedside table, a DM from Tessa.

Hiya Banner Girl! Throw on those boring clothes and let's hit the town tonight. Txx

Heather laughed and wrote back. **I'll see u there at 8, looking like an extra from Anne of Green Gables**

Banner Girl. When the ratings alert had arrived that morning, Heather could hardly believe her eyes. She had gone to sleep fifth in the ratings. And woken up third, her face featured on the Top

Trio banner that welcomed visitors to the app and website. For as long as she held on-to her place there, Heather would be sponsored by only the most prestigious brands, the ones who could afford to pay the premium rate she now commanded. Interview requests were pouring in; on Friday she would be making her television debut on *The Rule of Three*, *Entertainment Today*'s weekly segment featuring CelebRate's three most popular stars. It was more than she had ever dared imagine. She did a spin around the bedroom in her bra and knickers, socked feet sliding against the oak floor, landing hard on her bad leg and shouting in pain. Damn. She limped back to the bed and pulled on the skirt and top, plucking white hairs from the fabric. How had Mandu managed that? It wasn't as though the Persian ever came near her. The cat had arrived two weeks earlier – along with its pedigree certificate – and had been hiding from Heather ever since, recoiling with a hiss when she reached for him.

She went to the front window and looked out, chest loosening when she saw that the pavement outside was deserted. Her gaze shifted sideways, in the direction of Analise's house. She thought of the friendly, smiling woman she'd met at the New Heights. And the confused, frightened one who'd staggered out of the lilac door. How could one email make someone unravel like that? And what could be the motive for sending it in the first place? The questions that had dogged her since Analise's death kept resurfacing, chasing around her head. There must be a way to find out more. Heather had an hour to kill before it was time to head out and meet Tessa. Might as well use it. She picked up her tablet and sat down on the bed, rereading articles and rewatching TV clips about Analise, her suicide and the events leading up to it, lingering over a quote from Noah in the *Telegram*.

Analise appeared to have been enjoying her role as a Winfluencer, winning over millions of CelebRate fans with her beauty vlogs. Her descent into depression came out of the blue. Nobody could have foreseen it.

*

Heather considered the last line.

Why couldn't they have foreseen it, though? Wasn't that the whole point of having psychological screeners? True, Analise might have withheld information on her background forms – just as Heather had done. But how had she managed to fool all those psychometric tests, when they were specifically designed to pick up on signs of emotional instability?

She skimmed through more articles. Most of them were about Analise's collapse, though one had broken ranks to focus on her successes instead, citing an anonymous Triple F source claiming the contest had been planning to create a new, long-term role for her as a 'brand ambassador' . . . whatever *that* meant. Heather was working her way through YouTube clips when she came across an interview with Analise's mother, Persephone, and sister, Dana: a plainer, less glamorous version of Analise. It had been recorded in their home in Wapping, the pair sitting on a sofa, clutching framed photos of Analise, talking about her in predictably glowing terms: her kindness, talent and beauty. The journalist had concluded the interview by asking Persephone what message she wished she could send to her daughter.

Analise's mother sobbed out the reply. 'I will love you forever, my beautiful, fragile angel.'

Fragile.

Heather's mind snagged on the word. What exactly did she mean by that? Heather rewound the clip, watching the answer again.

Then she googled the Tettersons, finding Dana's TikTok account easily. It was filled with video clips featuring her famous sister dancing, singing, laughing. Heather watched them all, then put the tablet aside and sat for a while, eyes aimed unseeingly at the framed paint splodge hanging above her bedside table – courtesy of a furniture company sponsor branching out into 'designer art'.

Dana and her mother might have the answers she was looking for. But would it be too weird, messaging them out of the blue, inviting herself round? She tapped a freshly manicured thumbnail against her lip, thinking.

Sod it. As Debbie liked to say, 'If you don't ask, you don't get.' The worst they could do was say no. She dashed off a TikTok DM to Dana, offering her condolences, saying she knew Analise from CelebRate. And asking whether she could drop by for a visit.

CHAPTER 21

'Analise was always obsessed with her appearance.' Persephone
Tetterson handed Heather a cup of tea and waved her towards
an armchair before joining Dana on the faded corduroy sofa.
'I sometimes wondered if she was rebelling against me, since
I gave up on that side of things after her dad left. As you can see.'

Heather was about to object out of reflexive politeness, but
then stopped herself. There was no point denying it; Persephone
Tetterson had let herself go. She was overweight, teetering on
the edge of obese, and her hair was dyed a brick-like colour with
a couple of inches of grey at the roots. She wore a denim top
that must have been purchased in thinner times, because the
buttons were straining. Tired tracky bottoms finished the look.
As Heather drank a mouthful of tea, she was wondering why
Analise hadn't thrown some Triple F money her mother's way.
Persephone seemed to read her mind.

'Analise kept bringing me posh clothes and make-up, but I'm
not like her, I'm not a glamour puss. I prefer being comfy.' She
looked around the flat. 'She gave me money – enough to buy a car
and a new telly. She wanted to help us get a proper house too, but
I said no. I don't like change. It makes me feel edgy. And I don't
have the best heart. Moving out of this flat, away from everything

and everyone I know . . .' Persephone glanced around the room with its giant TV and small dining table, the shelves displaying porcelain figures of birds. 'Well, it would be the death of me, I told her that. She was disappointed, though. She wanted to be able to make my life better. That was the sort of person she was.' Tears glimmered in her eyes.

Dana put an arm around her mother's shoulders. Her eyes moved to Heather's.

'So were you and my sister good mates? I've seen a picture on CelebRate of the two of you at a party, with a couple of other girls.'

The question made Heather uncomfortable. Persephone and Dana obviously thought she'd come here because she and Analise had been close. And she had allowed them to believe that. Because the truth was harder to explain. Even she didn't fully understand her own obsession with Analise's death, her compulsion to dig deeper, to get to the bottom of it.

'We were neighbours,' Heather said, side-stepping the question. 'She lived just down the street from me. I liked her.' At least all those things were true.

'It's good she had someone nearby,' Persephone said. 'I didn't like her moving so far away from Dana and me. She wasn't good at being on her own.'

Heather looked down into her mug. It was time, she decided, to get to the point.

'I wanted to talk to you about something. I know that Analise was targeted by a troll. Someone who'd got hold of personal information about her.' She took a deep breath. 'Someone who knew about her daughter.'

Dana's eyes popped wide with surprise. 'She told you about Ellie?'

'It came out one night when she was upset,' Heather hedged. 'She said someone had been hinting about it online. But she didn't know who or why.'

Persephone pressed a knuckle against her lips. Then she nodded.

'Yes, Analise told us about those posts. She was very upset.'

'Did she tell you about the email she received, right before she went to Sunny Hills?'

The two women exchanged a puzzled look.

'No,' Dana said. 'Who from?'

Heather tried to conceal her disappointment. 'That's what I was hoping to find out. I don't suppose you know her CelebMail password?'

They shook their heads in unison, then Persephone's eyes widened in alarm.

'Why are you digging into my daughter's life? Oh God. Please tell me you're not planning to spill her secrets all over the internet! Because Analise would have *hated* that.' Her tear-filled eyes searched Heather's. 'And there's Ellie to think about. You can't tell people about her. That poor girl has been through enough!'

A hot wave of guilt rode through Heather, flushing her cheeks. 'Please don't worry. I'm not going to tell anyone.'

Persephone's hands twisted in her lap. 'Promise?'

'I promise.'

'Good.' Analise's mother sighed. 'Getting pregnant so young, giving up her baby . . . those were things Analise always struggled with, especially on her down days.'

Heather straightened against the chair. 'Down days? Was she . . . did Analise suffer from depression?'

191

The question made Persephone's mouth pull down at the corners.

'I don't want to think of her that way. Most of the time she was happy as a lark. But when the sadness came, she would stay in her room all day. Cry like she was breaking. It didn't happen very often, but when it did she was so . . .' Persephone shook her head, hands cupped around her mug as though drawing warmth from it.

'Fragile?'

'Yes. Exactly that.'

Heather's eyes moved to a framed photo of Analise holding a black cat in her arms, hanging on the wall beside the kitchen door, Persephone's words turning in her mind. *The sadness . . . down days. Fragile.* How had Analise managed to conceal her condition from the screeners? Then her gaze dropped to the dining table beneath. Seeing the three chairs around it made her feel sad.

'Did she have any idea who might have been behind those posts? Or how they could have found out about . . . Ellie?'

Dana shook her head firmly. 'As far as we were aware, no one outside our immediate family knew Ellie existed. Which is why I was surprised she told you.'

Heather drank her tea as fresh guilt seared inside her. She cleared her throat, trying to decide what to ask next.

'Have you spent much time with Analise's . . . with your grand-daughter?'

Persephone shook her head. 'I only met her for the first time after Analise died. I went to tell her what had happened so she wouldn't end up finding out about it on the news. I told her I was her gran . . .' Her voice hitched. She took a mobile phone out of the pocket of her tracky bottoms and tapped the screen. 'Here. Isn't she gorgeous?'

Heather leaned in to look at the photo, which showed a skinny kid in a pink vest and jeans standing in a park, thin arms flung out sideways.

'I took that before I told her about Analise being . . . gone. We'd only just met and I wanted one good moment first.'

Persephone began to cry. Dana took her mother in her arms, stroking her back. The grief in the room seemed to take on weight, thickening the air, making Heather feel suffocated. Then Persephone pulled free of her daughter's arms, dabbing her eyes with a sleeve. 'Anyway. I told Ellie she could come live with us here, since we're her blood, so long as she don't mind sharing a room.'

'So . . . she's moving in?'

Persephone shook her head. 'No. She has friends at her school, and the foster parents she has now are decent folk. So she don't want to move.' A faint smile quivered on her lips. 'She wants to keep seeing me, though. And meet her Auntie Dana. So we're going for a meal this weekend, the three of us.'

'That's good.'

'It is.'

There was a pause. Heather thought about the girl in the photo, remembering Tessa's words.

She's spent her whole life blaming her birth mother for her problems.

Was it possible that Ellie had written those posts herself, to punish Analise for abandoning her? It was difficult to imagine that a thirteen-year-old could be so cold and calculating – but it would explain how the troll knew about Ellie. She rubbed the back of her neck.

'When you told Ellie about Analise, how did she react?'

193

Persephone's whole face seemed to drag downwards, as though it were melting. 'She cried. Floods of tears, like her heart was breaking.' She shook her head. 'Analise was devastated because she believed that girl hated her and would never forgive her. But she was wrong.'

CHAPTER 22

Steve had really let himself go. He needed a shave, his trousers were miles too big and his hair was screaming for a trim.

'You're looking very . . . casual today.' She eyed him above the vase of fresh-cut flowers on their table, noticing the frayed edges of his sleeve, the large moth hole just below the collar. They were in her new favourite restaurant, Lapin, in Westbourne Grove. She was sick of Joe's Café, with its terrible coffee and rubbish menu, so had asked Steve to meet her here instead.

'No more casual than usual,' he said, picking up his coffee in its blue porcelain mug. 'This is how I always look.'

'I'm pretty sure your hair used to be—'

'Nope.'

'Your clothing was definitely more . . .'

'No.' There was an edge of impatience to his voice now. 'It wasn't. I'm scruffy. I've been scruffy for as long as you've known me. You're just noticing my rough edges now because no one else here has any.' Heather glanced around the restaurant, with its big skylights and plush chairs, modernist paintings of rabbits interspersed along pastel walls. Lapin was popular – she'd had to book – and filled almost entirely with women: yummy mummies and ladies-who-lunched. The table next to them broke the trend: a pair of blow-dried, power-suited men sat staring at their laptops.

Steve was right. Everyone here was expensively dressed and perfectly groomed, and she had let it affect the way she viewed him.

'I'm so sorry, that was rude. I don't know what's wrong with me today.' A waitress dropped off a basket of freshly baked rolls ahead of her salad's arrival. Steve had said he only wanted coffee, but leaned over to inspect the bread selection anyway.

'It's okay,' he said. 'You're living in a very non-scruffy world right now, and it's human nature to compare things.' He selected a roll of braided white bread. 'In fact, studies show . . .'

'Don't!' Heather's voice came out louder than she'd intended, making the two men at the next table look up, startled, from their laptops. She squeezed her eyes shut. 'Please can you just . . . stop that sentence right there.' Heather had been making a conscious effort not to think about Elliot, the fact that he was bound up in the contest at the centre of her life, a symbol of her past slithering around in her present. But those two words launched him back to the front of her mind.

Steve's look of wide-eyed surprise compressed into creases of concern. 'Are you okay? You seem . . . stressed.'

'Sorry.' She gave her head a shake. 'That was a complete over-reaction. It's just . . . my ex was a psychologist and he used to say that all the time. "Studies show".'

Steve tore the bread roll in half. 'Good thing he's out of your life. Because studies show that people who keep saying "studies show" make terrible boyfriends.'

Heather laughed. 'Those studies are spot-on. The problem is, he's *not* out of my life. As luck would have it, he now works at the

Triple F.' She skimmed foam from the top of her non-fat chai latte with extra cinnamon, spooning it into her mouth.

Steve grimaced. 'Ouch! Not good. Do you have to deal with him directly?' He took a bite of dry bread, ignoring the porcelain palette in the middle of the table, with its artful display of butter, olive oil and balsamic.

'No. He runs a group I had been thinking of joining, but now that I know he's there, I'll steer well clear.'

'Good. As a wise man once said, don't shit where you eat.'

'A wise man. Your grandfather again?'

'No. Socrates. Or maybe it was Cher.'

Heather laughed and the shadow of Elliot slipped into the background again. She'd missed Steve's sense of humour, their back and forth by the coffee machine.

'But . . . hang on a sec, aren't you yourself flouting the wisdom of Socrates or Cher by going out with my . . . the new trainee?'

He let out a sound that was half sigh, half groan.

'No, that's all done and dusted. Turns out she prefers her relationships open. Wide open. As in, she thinks we should both be able to shag anyone, any time, and when I complained I'd rather it was just the two of us, she called me selfish and controlling.'

'Oh.' Heather pulled a face. 'Sorry to hear that.'

'Yeah, well. I wouldn't have minded so much if she hadn't trolled me. Posted a TikTok video featuring a montage starring yours truly, in which she talked about being "in recovery" from a toxic relationship with a man who tried to put her sexuality in a box. Apparently monogamy comes in boxes now. Anyway, I'm pretty sure the rest of the teachers have seen it because I've noticed a lot of smirking and side-eyes in the staffroom.' He took another bite of bread, washing it down with coffee.

'What a cow! You deserve better.'

'Thanks.' He smiled across the table and she smiled back. There was a pause and for reasons Heather couldn't pinpoint, she began to feel awkward. She ducked her gaze to the flowers on their table, a spray of baby's breath surrounding a trio of white roses. 'Speaking of trolls . . .' She ran a fingertip along a rose stem that had been stripped of its thorns. 'I have a problem with one and could really use your help.'

Steve took another mouthful of bread. 'There's only one way to deal with trolls: ignore, block, move on.'

She shook her head. 'I'm not the victim. A troll got hold of another Winfluencer's secrets and used them to torment her.' The rose had a single leaf and she tore it off without thinking, dropping it onto the table. 'She died.'

'Jesus.' Steve's eyes widened. 'How?'

'Suicide. The final straw seems to have been an email sent to her CelebRate account.' Heather picked up the linen napkin beside her plate, placing it across her lap and smoothing it with her palms, just for something else to do with her hands. 'I was hoping you could use your computer skills to help me access it.'

Steve raised an eyebrow. 'And how, exactly, do you think I would be able to do that without her password?'

'I don't know. Through some sort of . . . back door?'

'I'm flattered by your faith in my computer skills, and if I could, I would jump on this like a ninja . . .'

She rolled her eyes. 'Again with the ninjas.'

'But I'm a trainee computer science teacher, not a hacker.' He selected another bread roll, one with seeds this time. 'Try her pet's name with a number on the end. That's what most girls use for their passwords.'

'That's an outrageous gender stereotype,' Heather said, though to be fair, her CelebMail password was CatMandu3. She'd had to change the number twice because the contest's security system demanded an update every two weeks.

This time, Steve used a knife to divide the bread. 'The thing about gender stereotypes is, they tend to come from somewhere. So . . .'

His voice broke off as his attention shifted to the window beside their table. There was a man standing on the other side of the glass, staring in at them.

Bugger. Heather really didn't feel like dealing with fans right now. Plus she hadn't slept well, so would look washed out in photos. She smoothed her hair, watching the man from the corner of her eye, bracing for the flash of a camera phone. But instead, the stranger vanished from the window, reappearing a moment later just inside the restaurant. Not your typical CelebRate fan: middle-aged with week-old stubble and ginger hair that receded at the front and was too long at the back, hanging past the collar of the jacket he was wearing despite the heat.

Still, a fan was a fan. Heather aimed a polite smile his way. But he wasn't looking at her. He was looking at Steve.

'Jonnie Preston?'

The colour drained from Steve's face. There was a beat of silence. Then he shook his head. 'Sorry, mate, I think you've got me confused with someone else.'

The Lapin hostess came over to greet the new arrival. 'Hello, sir. Do you have a reservation?'

But he waved her away without taking his eyes from Steve.

'I know who you are. I have a gift for recognising faces. It's the eyes. The rest of you looks different, but the eyes are always the same.' He nodded firmly. 'You're Jonnie Preston.'

Heather stared from the man to Steve, trying to work out what was going on.

'Steve? What's he talking about?'

The hostess inserted herself between the intruder and their table. 'Sir, I'm afraid I'm going to have to ask you to leave. You are bothering my customers.'

'It's fine,' Steve said, grabbing his canvas satchel from the floor, standing up quickly. 'I was just leaving anyway.'

'But . . . Steve, wait. Aren't you going to finish your coffee? My salad hasn't even arrived yet and this gentleman is about to leave, now that he knows he's made a mistake—'

'It's no mistake,' the stranger interrupted, head craning around the side of the hostess who was now signalling towards a man with a goatee behind the barista station. He hustled over and stood beside her, frowning at the new arrival.

'Sir,' the barista said. 'I need you to leave right now.'

But the ginger-haired man ignored him too. 'I know who you are, Jonnie. And the things you did.' He grinned craftily.

'Not me, mate.' And before Heather had a chance to react, Steve jumped up, tossed a fiver onto the table and shouldering past the intruder, paused on the threshold to give Heather a brief wave before hurrying out the door.

CHAPTER 23

I should probably go to bed. It's three in the morning and if I go to the office looking exhausted people will wonder why. Rumours might start.

But last month's winner is becoming a problem – a problem that needs to be addressed now, before things develop any further. I read through her DMs then move on to her CelebMail account. Sponsor crap mostly. People fawning, telling her how amazing she is, the usual bullshit.

I pause when I get to an email from Ronan Quentin Davies – a family member, presumably. I open it and discover a long, whiny diatribe, accusing her of 'hoarding fame'.

Interesting.

A line near the bottom catches my eye.

'And what's all this rubbish I'm reading about your refusing to flaunt yourself by wearing short skirts? Haven't you told them the truth? If there's stuff you don't want people to know, maybe you should invite me to one of the Triple F parties so you can brief me on exactly what I can and can't say to the press. Because I wouldn't want to slip up and reveal something you're trying to keep secret.'

That sounds like a thinly veiled threat. Ronan Quentin Davies.

I run the name through a search engine. An actor – or at least, he claims to be an actor on his website. He can't be very successful because there's almost nothing written about him elsewhere online.

I settle back against my desk chair, swivelling from side to side, smiling to myself. A disgruntled, fame-hungry brother with a chip on his shoulder. Perfect.

CHAPTER 24

One more post and she could go to sleep. Heather lay across the Siberian goose-down duvet on her emperor bed, tablet propped against a Cartier cushion. She flicked through the day's images, stopping at a picture of herself and Tessa sharing a piece of cake in the café at Harrods. She considered the photo for a moment, fingers resting on her Bluetooth keyboard. Then she tapped out, *Who needs Breakfast at Tiffany's when you can have lunch at Harrods?*

Mandu slunk into the room and jumped up onto the bed. For a moment, Heather thought the Persian might actually be seeking affection, but instead the cat walked across the keyboard, sending chains of p's and x's across the screen.

Heather held the keyboard in the air, out of reach.

'Nice try, Mandu, but I'm not about to let you start posting on CelebRate. You're only allowed on this keyboard in password form.' She reached out to give her new pet a stroke but he withdrew from her touch, jumping off the bed. Heather sighed and placed the keyboard on her pillow, deleting the surplus letters before submitting the post. A minute or so later there was a soft chime, telling her that the picture had been published.

There. Job done. Time to change into her silk PJs and get to bed. But as she was putting the tablet and keyboard on the bedside table, Steve's words floated through her memory.

Try her pet's name with a number on the end. That's what most girls use for their passwords.

A ridiculous suggestion. Except that she'd done exactly that and she didn't even like her pet all that much. Heather considered the tablet a moment longer, thinking of the photo above Persephone Tetterson's dining table of Analise and the black cat. Maybe . . .

She began scrolling through the 'special collection' of Analise's old posts that CelebRate had put up in her memory. And there it was: a video clip of the black cat batting at a make-up brush in Analise's hand, captioned, 'Midnight is trying to get his paws on my new coral dream blusher!'

Midnight. Heather went onto CelebMail, logged herself out and clicked 'New User'. Then she keyed in username Analise. Tetterson@CelebMail.co.uk

She was greeted by a familiar pop-up box.

'Time to change your password!' Of course. More than two weeks had passed since Analise's death so the security system had kicked in automatically. She looked at the 'Current Password' box underneath. Tapped in 'Midnight 4' into the space, though didn't hold out much hope for that one, since she was pretty sure Analise had been on CelebRate more than a month longer than her. Sure enough, the attempt was met with an 'Incorrect Password' alert. And below that: 'Attempts remaining: 2. After 3 unsuccessful login attempts this account will be locked.'

Damn. Only two chances left. She chewed on a thumbnail, thinking. If Analise had, like Heather, used 1 on her first password and been at Celebrate for eight weeks at the time of her death, that would make 5 the number on her password - assuming she raised it by one each time. She keyed in 'Midnight5.'

Back came the pop-up box. 'Incorrect Password. Attempts remaining: 1.'

So this was it: her final shot. Heather combed her fingers through her hair, thinking. It didn't feel as though Analise had been on CelebRate for more than two months, but if she'd started out low in the ratings, it was possible she'd been there longer, but Heather simply hadn't registered her until she'd risen into the Top Six, joining the Winfluencers whose faces dominated the platform. So maybe she should go with 6 . . . or even jump straight to 7 or 8.

Heather hesitated, fingers frozen above the keyboard. She would just have to guess. It was unlikely to work anyway. She tapped in Midnight7 and waited for the rejecting pop-up box, ready to put down the tablet, put on her pyjamas and crawl into bed, let the custom-moulded memory-foam mattress cradle her to sleep.

There was a pause that felt long, but in reality was probably just a few seconds.

Then a new pop-up box appeared containing two spaces labelled 'New Password' and 'Confirm New Password'.

For a moment, Heather simply stared, taken aback by the unexpectedness of her success as excitement burned away the wisps of sleepiness that had been winding themselves around her. She keyed in a new password and a moment later, the screen filled with rows of names and subjects. Analise's CelebMails. Propping her back against the headboard, she scrolled through the list of senders, heart beating fast. All the most recently arrived emails were unread, mostly from Triple F addresses with names Heather didn't recognize. There was also a flurry of messages marked 'URGENT' from the make-up company sponsoring her. She skipped over the names still in bold – and therefore unread – to the last email Analise had opened before she died. The sender was 'A. Know'. Her heart beat faster. Wasn't 'Know' the surname Tessa had said was on the taunting public posts? The subject beside it said, 'What you did.' There was a file attached.

Heather's heart accelerated. So this was it, the email that had pushed Analise over the edge. She opened it.

You are toxic. You destroyed your child's life by abandoning her. It's too late to try and fix it now. She's broken. Because of you.

She clicked on the attachment, sucking in her breath when she saw the photo. She recognized the girl immediately from the picture on Persephone Tetterson's phone: Ellie, in a sleeveless cotton dress. She was holding a razor blade in her right hand, suspended above her left inner arm. The flesh below it was striped with cuts. Rows of red lines marked the pale skin all the way from her elbow to her shoulder – some fresh, some faded to scars. And mixed in among them, needle marks.

Oh God. How must Analise have felt, scrolling through her CelebMail only to find herself confronted by this image of the daughter she'd abandoned: a wounded child trying desperately to release her buried pain – and obliterate it with chemicals. She imagined Analise's self-loathing and despair as she read the message telling her that irreversible harm had already been done. And that it was all her fault.

Heather dragged a hand across her eyes. How awful. She would have to call Persephone in the morning, warn her that the granddaughter whose photo she had shared with such pride was actually—

A bolt of realisation snapped the thought clean.

The photo.

Heather saw it again in her mind's eye. Ellie in a sleeveless top, pale arms flung wide. The cuts and track marks would have been plain to see.

Except there weren't any. Her skin had been pale and unblemished.

Heather's eyes returned to the image on the computer screen, staring at the marks on the girl's arms. They were flawlessly realistic.

She sat perfectly still for a minute, thoughts galloping, letting the implication sink in. Then she copied the sender's email address and sent it to Steve, with a message asking him to trace the IP address and the sender, telling him to please hurry, that it was urgent.

She had to find out who A. Know was. Because that photo had driven Analise to her death. And it was a lie.

CHAPTER 25

'Modest' Winfluencer Hiding Disfigurement

CelebRate star Heather Davies has been hailed as a new kind of style icon, feted for her refusal to participate in 'the race to the shortest hemline'.

But her own brother has revealed that her choice of clothing has nothing to do with either modesty or feminism.

'She's being portrayed as this beacon of morality,' Ronan Davies, 25, said in an exclusive interview with the London Herald. 'But the truth is very different. Her skirts used to be as short as the next girl's. But then she got in a car accident. The reason she doesn't want people to see her legs is because one of them is hideous. Not to me, obviously, because we're family. To me, she will always be my beautiful sis. But to the rest of the world . . . well, let's just say the surgeons did their best but it was a serious accident so there was only so much they could do. If I could have given her my leg instead I would have.'

Asked whether he thought his sister was a hypocrite for portraying herself as a 'modesty feminist' when in fact she *was simply concealing injuries, he shrugged and said, 'Who are we to judge? In a way, being a Winfluencer is like being an actor. You have an audience and a role to play. And as a seasoned actor myself, following numerous successful theatre productions, I understand how—'*

*

Heather stopped reading and tossed her tablet aside, falling back against the bed and staring up at the ceiling. She had muted her F-phone but could still hear it buzzing against the table. The curtains weren't quite closed, letting in a lance of afternoon sunlight that stabbed her eyes. She pulled the duvet around her, burying herself inside it.

Bloody Ronan. She should have paid him off. Given him more money, a month's worth, on the condition that he keep his trap shut. Although realistically, that might not have worked. Ronan couldn't help himself; when he saw a spotlight, he jumped into it and began to dance. God forbid he should just tell the press that she was his sister and he was proud of her. No, then he wouldn't be giving the audience what it wanted – and getting his face plastered across the *London Herald's* home page. Breakfast shows wouldn't be inviting him onto their sofas to share the inside scoop on his shamed sister; had she always been a liar and a hypocrite?

Heather's followers were abandoning her. Down to 900,000 – ninth in the ratings. It was only a matter of time before she fell into the Drop Zone. Then she would lose everything – her fame, her money. What would happen to her then? She felt as though she was trapped in a nightmare, watching helplessly as everything slipped away. She looked at her F-phone on the bedside table, where it lay like a poisonous snake, ready to strike. She didn't want to see what was on the screen.

From downstairs came the sound of a knock on the front door, hard and insistent. One of the reporters must have worked out that she'd silenced the doorbell. Well, they could knock all day long. She was staying right here.

Then she must have drifted off, because the next time she opened her eyes, the light in the curtain gap had softened to a pearly glow. She could hear the reporters chatting below. Throwing back the duvet, she crossed to the open window at the back of the room, overlooking the park, peeking through the crack in the curtains to see whether any of the reporters had gone behind the house to lurk on the other side of her garden wall, telephoto lenses aimed her way. But there was no one there. Releasing a sigh of relief, she threw open the curtains and stood staring out. Beyond the playground, the falling sun sketched the Shakespeare Estate in watercolour yellows and greys. Debbie was probably making dinner right now, singing to herself as she cooked. She hadn't given up on Heather, messaging a couple of times a week, suggesting a catch-up, saying she wanted to hear all about her posh new life. And Heather kept saying yes, absolutely, let's get a date in the diary. But for some reason it hadn't happened. Maybe she should call a car and head over there now, pour out her troubles while Debbie poured out the wine, just like old times.

Except these weren't old times. Her former neighbour could neither understand nor relate to her current problems. Plus Debbie was sure to ask why, in the ten months they'd been sharing stories and living side by side, Heather had never confided in her about the car accident. And Heather had no answer to give.

Her F-phone buzzed again. She couldn't hide from the truth

forever. Heather crossed the oak floor slowly and stood staring down at the handset, bracing herself. Time to face the music. She snatched it up and looked at the screen. Missed calls. Dozens of them. Mostly unfamiliar numbers and ones labelled 'no caller ID' – journalists. There were also missed calls from Tessa, Debbie, Noah and Lara plus a slew of DMs from other Winfluencers, the 'Are you OK?'s interspersed with the odd sly dig ('I always wondered why anyone would want to wear those skirts!', 'Sorry to hear about your ugly leg 😔 That must suck for you!').

The phone vibrated again in her hand. The latest ratings alert. Her stomach plunged. Twelfth. The bottom. Less than 600,000 followers left. Her fingers tightened around the device. Her dream world was collapsing. Her home, her money and her celebrity status were about to be torn away while millions of fans looked on and said she deserved it.

Heather's jaw clenched. Sod that. She might be losing everything else, but she still had her pride. And she wasn't going to just wait around to be tossed out like so much rubbish. She would become known as the first Winfluencer to quit and walk away with her head held high.

Nausea rolled inside her as she logged on to CelebMail, dashing out an email with trembling fingers, saying she was withdrawing from CelebRate as she no longer felt able to fulfil her duties. The tears in her eyes made the letters shimmy.

Heather was about to send it when she realized she hadn't addressed the email to anyone. Who should her resignation go to? Noah? The legal department? Winfluencer Sales? She could send it to all three. Or she could just go straight to the top. She tapped in Duncan.Caldwell@CelebMail.co.uk

Hit send.

Heather had just stepped out of the shower and was wrapping her hair in a towel when she thought she heard something; a floorboard creaking, somewhere downstairs. Pulling on her robe, she slowly opened the bathroom door and stepped out onto the landing, ears straining. Nothing. Must have been her imagination. She turned and had taken a couple of steps towards her bedroom when she heard, quite clearly, the sound of a muffled cough.

Someone was inside the house.

Heather's heart went into overdrive. Who was it? One of the journalists? It seemed unlikely. Reporters might be pushy sometimes, but she'd never heard of one actually breaking into someone's home. And anyway, she'd peeked out at the pavement before going to have her shower, to see whether any of them were still there. But it was past nine p.m. and they had all given up on her for the day, drifting off to meet their various deadlines.

She had been relieved about that as she'd padded down the hallway to the main bathroom, with its glass-walled monsoon shower – so much more satisfying than the ordinary one in her en suite – to slough this day from her skin. Now, though, she wished they hadn't left, that there was someone nearby she could call out to. She stood statue-still, ears straining, thoughts racing with her pulse. She needed to get to her phone, call 999. She pictured it lying on her duvet, where she'd tossed it after sending the resignation email. Could she make it to her bedroom in time? Or would the intruder hear her footsteps . . . and come upstairs.

Calm down. Focus.

She took a long, steadying breath: in through the nose, out through the mouth. Then she began to move slowly, carefully towards her room. Her ears strained, but whoever was downstairs had gone silent. The hallway had never felt so long. She tried to go faster, but her feet were wet from the shower and she slipped on the floor's polished wood, her left heel coming down hard to keep her from falling, sending out a bolt of pain.

Whoever was down there must have heard it because the silence was replaced by the sound of swift footsteps. The creak of a stair.

The intruder was coming up.

She staggered towards her room, hoping to throw herself across the threshold, lock the door behind her, call for help. But the slip had made her limp worse. She would be overtaken easily. She could scream, but who would hear? She wasn't near a window and the walls were thick, letting no sound through.

'Heather?' a familiar voice said. 'Are you there?'

The build-up of panic and terror left her in a whoosh of air. She placed a palm against the wall to steady herself, closing her eyes in relief. It was okay. She was safe.

Heather hobbled to the head of the staircase, clutching her bathrobe across her throat as she stood looking at the man now halfway up the stairs, his pale face tilted towards her.

'Duncan. How did you get in here?'

He held up a key.

'The Triple F is renting this house to you until the sale goes through. Which means that I am technically your landlord. And it's in your contract that the landlord is permitted to retain a copy of the key and enter the premises in an emergency.'

She closed her eyes for a moment, considering this. Now that her fear had fled, she found she was able to think clearly again, to process what he was saying.

'So your wanting to speak to me counts as an emergency, does it?'

He shrugged, showing no hint of guilt or embarrassment. 'I was worried about you. I called after I got your email but you didn't respond—'

'My phone is muted.'

'—so I came over but you didn't answer your doorbell . . .'

'It's switched off.'

'I tried knocking—'

'I was in the shower.'

'—so I sent a message saying that if you didn't respond within half an hour I was going to use my key to come in and check that you were okay. You didn't. So I did.'

'Well, now you've checked and I am.'

'Yes. And I think we need to have a conversation before you make any rash decisions. Let's go for a drive.'

Heather opened her mouth to object – how dare he think he could barge into her home like this – but nothing came out. Because she could see now that there was a reason she had emailed Duncan, and Duncan alone. She had wanted to reach out to him. He shouldn't have come here like this – was he really her landlord? She should have paid closer attention when the solicitor was talking her through the documents – but the fact that he had rushed over was . . . maybe not exactly romantic, but touching, in a way. It must mean he cared. And she could do with feeling cared for right now.

'Okay,' she said. 'Just give me a few minutes to throw some clothes on.'

'Good. I'll wait in the car.'

*

The last of the daylight had drained from the sky by the time Heather stepped outside. As she approached the limousine, she could see herself reflected in its windows, lit by the streetlights. She looked better than she felt, wearing a navy midi dress and a quick dash of make-up, hair still damp enough to be wavy despite a short blast of the dryer. The driver circled round to open the door for her. She paused, looking up and down the street to make sure all the reporters really were gone. Then she ducked inside.

Duncan was seated beside the far window, watching as she climbed in, holding down her hem. He didn't speak as the car pulled away from the kerb, turned onto Holland Park Avenue and joined the flow of night traffic moving past big houses and small cafés towards the city centre.

'So where exactly are we going?' she asked eventually.

'Does it matter?'

'A man shows up inside my house late at night without warning, bundles me into a car and won't say where he's taking me. That scenario could be described as ominous.'

'Nine-thirty's not that late. And I think "bundle" is a stretch.'

'I may have exaggerated slightly for dramatic effect.'

'Comedic effect.'

'That too.'

'You use humour as a distancing mechanism.'

Heather rolled her eyes. They were passing through the heart of Notting Hill now, its pavements crowded with people hustling between pubs and restaurants.

'You sound like Elliot.'

'Do I?' Duncan appeared thoughtful. 'I have always taken an interest in psychology, the forces that drive people and their varying abilities to withstand pressure. Human nature is a source of endless wonder.'

'This from a man best known for avoiding human contact.'

'I prefer to observe from a safe distance.'

Hyde Park slid past the window. The Saturday picnickers were long gone. The gates were locked and the grass looked grey in the night, pools of deeper darkness filling the spaces beneath the trees.

'You say you prefer to keep your distance, yet here you are, with me, right up close.'

'I had to come, since you didn't answer my calls or email.'

'I told you, I didn't hear your calls or see your email.' She turned away from the window to face him. 'What did it say?'

He gave her a long look. His pale eyes seemed to glow and she thought again of underground creatures, adapted to a world without light.

'Don't go.' He paused. 'That's what it said.'

Heather felt her pulse quicken. 'I'm surprised you'd want me to stay, since I won't be attracting any more sponsors to your company. In case you haven't noticed, I'm nearly in the Drop Zone. My time at the Triple F is up.'

'It doesn't have to be.'

'Did you not see my brother's interview? Everyone says I'm a liar and a hypocrite.'

'They're wrong. I have watched and read everything you've said to the press or posted on CelebRate. And you have never lied. You've said only that you prefer not to reveal your body to the world. That is true. Others labelled your motive as feminism or modesty, but you never did.'

'No, but I went along with it, which is a deception of sorts. And either way, my USP is gone.'

'Then find a new one.'

His gaze was starting to unnerve her, so she looked away, out of the window. They were passing Marble Arch now, heading towards the river. He still hadn't said where they were going. She should probably insist he tell her, but for some reason she didn't want to. She liked being here, with this odd man, moving through London in the night, wondering what would happen next.

'I appreciate that you're trying to help, but no matter what I do, everyone will just see me as the girl with the scars. And that's not what Triple F fans want. They want beauty.'

'I think your scars *are* beautiful, in their own way. Because they tell a story – of adversity and survival.' His eyes moved down her body to her legs, hidden beneath the skirt. He touched the hem. 'May I?'

Heather swallowed, trying to decide how best to answer. But her hormones and her insecurities were sending out clashing messages, making it impossible to think clearly. In the end, she simply nodded, watching as he pulled up the fabric, stopping when it was just below her hips, exposing the gouged and puckered flesh. She shot a self-conscious glance towards the chauffeur.

Duncan must have caught it because he said: 'The driver can't see us. It's one-way glass. Because while I enjoy watching people, I detest being watched.' Long fingers traced their way up her leg, just as they had that day on the roof terrace, his eyes following them. She closed her eyes as Duncan's palm moved across her scars, the sensation coming and going as he passed from nerve-dead patches to sensitive skin.

'Isn't that a hazard, not being able to see through the back?' Her voice sounded breathy.

'There's a camera above the boot that live streams the traffic behind us.' The car stopped at a red light and she became aware of a throng of tourists on the pavement right outside the window, glancing at the limo curiously, perhaps wondering whether there was a celebrity inside. It was exciting being just on the other side of the glass, with half her body exposed, a man's hand moving along her skin. And people just inches away, looking right at them, unable to see. She could be naked and no one would know.

'I find you attractive.' He said it matter-of-factly, as though he were telling her what sort of coffee he liked. 'And if I do, others must too.'

'Not necessarily,' she said. 'You are, after all, very odd.'

He laughed then, his incongruous, deep laugh.

'Yes. Yes, I am.'

Then somehow they were kissing, his weight on top of her. She could feel the seat leather against the backs of her thighs and his hand still on her hip, not wanting to leave that part of her, the wounded part. When she rolled on top of him a few minutes later, pulling the blue dress up over her head and casting it aside, she was dimly aware that they were passing the London Eye, its glass pods now motionless against the night sky. But then she lost track of where they were and what was going on outside.

*

Later, after he'd dropped her back home, she took off her clothes and stood for a while in front of the full-length mirror, considering her body: the curves and plains of her breasts and belly. Then downwards to her legs, pausing on the border where smooth skin gave way to the turbulent reds and purples of the damage zone.

I find you attractive.

The words had been delivered not as a compliment, but a simple statement of fact.

Her phone was still on the bed where she'd abandoned it. She picked it up, ignoring the avalanche of missed calls and DMs, tapping open her CelebMail and skipping straight to the one from him. She opened it and flopped down on top of the bed, still naked, looking at the two words on the screen.

Don't go.

They hadn't discussed meeting up again. Maybe she should send him a reply email, something light and playful? She considered the idea for a moment before discarding it. No. Best leave things for a couple of days and see whether—

There was a firm knock at the front door. She glanced at the time on her phone. Quarter past twelve. Who on earth could it be at this hour? Then her handset buzzed the arrival of a new DM. Tessa. 'You won't answer my calls so you've given me no choice but to come over and hassle you in person. I'm outside and can see your lights are on, so don't bother pretending to be asleep. Let me in.'

Another uninvited guest. This was turning out to be one of life's weirder nights.

*

'I was really worried about you.' Tessa frowned over the crystal wine glass Heather had just handed her. 'I've been calling and messaging.'

'I know. Sorry. I wasn't in a great place today. I sort of . . . hid.' Heather leaned her forearms against the kitchen island's cold granite. They were seated side by side on the stools in front of it, drinking wine and picking at a container of Waitrose olives she'd found in the fridge.

Tessa crossed her legs. 'Well, you're supposed to turn *to* your friends in shitty times. Not *away* from them.'

'I know. I apologize. It's just . . . hard to come to terms with the fact that my life as a Winfluencer is being cut short.'

'Not necessarily.'

'Please. I'm about to breech the 500,000 follower threshold. By Wednesday I'll be begging my old school to let me come back. It's over.'

'No.' Tessa shook her head firmly. 'We can fix this.'

'I'm a liar and a fake feminist.'

'That's not true.'

'True or not, it's the narrative.'

'So change the narrative.'

Heather's laugh was part scoff. 'God, you sound just like Duncan.'

Tessa's frown was puzzled. 'Duncan who?'

'The . . . you know, Triple F CEO?' She felt herself flushing. 'He says I can change my USP.'

An olive stopped halfway to Tessa's mouth. 'You're kidding. You actually *spoke* to Duncan Caldwell? When?'

'Earlier tonight. He . . . dropped by.'

Tessa's eyebrows shot up all the way to her fringe. 'I'm sorry, the famously reclusive Triple F boss just "dropped by"?'

'Mm hmm.' She could feel the warmth in her cheeks, knew she was blushing. 'I met him when I was at HQ one night . . . looking for something. We have a, um, I guess you'd call it a connection.' She hesitated, trying to decide whether to tell Tessa what had just happened between them. But it felt wrong to share the experience so soon, while she was still absorbing it: the intimacy of gliding through the night together in the limo's pocket universe, bodies intertwined, surrounded by the city, yet invisible to it. For now, at least, she wanted to keep their relationship – if that's what it was – to herself. 'I sent him an email, saying I was leaving CelebRate. He came over to try and talk me out of it.'

'Hmm.' Tessa popped the olive in her mouth, frowning as she chewed. 'Okay. So long as that's all it was. You don't want to let a man like that get too close. He's got a reputation.'

Heather took a slug of wine as annoyance rose inside her. 'Yes, he's weird and reclusive. I get it.'

Tessa shook her head. 'That's not what I'm talking about. He's ruthless. The sort of person who'll step on anyone to get what he wants. Even the people closest to him.'

Heather's jaw tightened defensively. What did Tessa know about Duncan? She'd never even met him.

'Well, I have actually spoken with him *and* seen all the articles that have been written about him, but I haven't come across anything backing up that accusation, so maybe you should—'

'You won't find anything online. He's made sure of that.'

Heather rolled her eyes. '*Seriously,* Tessa? I'm aware that Duncan Caldwell has been accused of everything from colluding with the cosmetics industry to causing Covid. But I didn't have *you* down as a conspiracy theorist.'

'I'm not. I just keep my ear to the ground. Word on the street is, he stole the entire Triple F blueprint from his best friend, Brendon Something-or-other. They'd talked about finding a way to commoditize fame, but Brendon was the one who came up with the concept and mapped out a plan for how it would actually work. Duncan had the business contacts so they were originally going

221

to launch it together, as equal partners. But then something went wrong; maybe they fell out or maybe Duncan just got greedy. So he—' Tessa was interrupted by a synthetic trumpet blast: a ratings update. She must have moved up because her features lit as she looked at her F-phone. Then she put it back down and took a mouthful of wine while Heather waited, torn between annoyance and curiosity.

'So? Duncan and his friend?'

'Yeah, so after they went their separate ways, Duncan hacked Brendon's computer, stole all the files and started the whole thing himself, leaving his ex-best friend out in the cold.'

Heather scoffed. 'That's obviously rubbish. Because this Brendon person would have taken him to court or gone to the press. Probably both.'

'That's where things get darker. A couple of weeks before the contest was due to kick off, Brendon told a reporter he was planning to file an injunction to stop the launch. But then his wife received a, shall we say, compromising video of her husband with another woman. So she left him, taking the children. Word on the street is that Duncan was behind it. That he discovered and downloaded the video when he hacked Brendon's computer.'

'Right. So now "the street" is accusing the CEO of the Triple F of sending naughty videos to someone's wife.' She snorted. 'What would that achieve, aside from making his ex-partner even more determined to take Duncan down? It doesn't make sense.'

'Yes, it does. Because Brendon was unstable and a reformed alcoholic. Losing his family pushed him over the edge. He had a breakdown, started drinking again – really heavily. He's a total drunk now, in no condition to launch a legal challenge, let alone convince a reporter to risk publishing such a controversial story about one of Britain's richest men. In other words, threat neutralized.'

Heather put down her wine, the clack of crystal against granite loud enough to make Tessa flinch. 'This is all just Winfluencer gossip. I know Duncan Caldwell and don't believe that he would do something like that.'

There was a pause in which Tessa considered her through narrowed eyes. 'So exactly how well *do* you know him?'

Heather could feel her cheeks warming again. 'Well enough to know that he's a decent human being. Honest to a fault. I was feeling really low when he came over today, but he made me see things differently.'

Tessa tilted her head. 'What things?'

'My disfigurement. I've been hiding it away, feeling ashamed, like I've somehow failed as a woman by not being perfect.'

'Right, so . . . he made you see that your injuries aren't your fault?'

She shook her head. 'No, more than that.' Heather hesitated, remembering Duncan's look of dreamy admiration as his eyes moved along her leg.

I like scars. They show you've been through something.

'What, then?'

Heather took a deep breath. 'I feel like it's time for me to not just accept, but actually embrace my scars, see them as a record of something I've overcome. Personal history, written into my skin. Society shouldn't make people feel less for not offering a perfect picture. Injuries should be a badge of honour, a way of saying "look at me. I went through hell and came out the other side and I'm still here, standing strong. I'm a survivor".' She laughed. Not because it was funny, but because everything was shifting and changing as she said it, weights sliding off, making her feel light, almost giddy. Free.

When she looked at Tessa again, Heather was surprised to find her eyes lit up with excitement, head bobbing in a series of small nods, as though agreeing with her own thoughts.

'That's it!' She grabbed Heather by both arms, giving her a small shake. 'That's *exactly* what you're going to tell them.'

Heather shook her head, baffled. 'Tell who?'

Tessa's smile widened until it took over her whole face. 'Everyone.'

CHAPTER 26

I sit on my sofa, drinking coffee, watching Heather on the wall-mounted TV.

'A car crash,' she's saying. 'It tore my leg apart and left me with agonising pain that comes and goes in waves. For two years I barely left the hospital. My friends got sick of visiting and moved on without me. I fell behind in my career. I was lonely and bitter about the years I'd lost. I felt robbed, cheated. But now . . . I'm starting to see things differently.'

The *UK Morning* host tilts her head, looking at Heather with earnest concentration. 'Different in what way?'

'That accident and its aftermath shaped who I am today. I was trapped, terrified. I came within an inch of drowning.' She laughs humourlessly. 'And I mean that literally. The water was lapping at my face by the time I was rescued. But when something like that happens, life is stripped down to its raw essentials. There's a purity to it. It changes you forever. And having your body breached, torn, that changes you too. But maybe it's something to be celebrated rather than concealed. And make no mistake, I *have* been concealing it, treating it like a dirty secret instead of a symbol of a battle that shaped who I am. So now I am asking myself *why* I felt the need to do that. Are we so shallow as a society that we'd rather see an unblemished surface than evidence of adversity overcome? It's time for me to embrace my scars. Because scars show you've been through something.' Her lips curve into a small smile as she says those last words. Then she lifts the hem of her skirt, revealing uneven, mottled flesh. She stretches out her leg and pushes back her shoulders. 'Scars mark us out as survivors. Not damaged. Strong.'

'Wow,' says the hostess, nodding along as the studio erupts into rapturous applause, the clapping punctuated by whistles and shouts of approval. 'Well said.'

Then the segment ends and a new guest appears, leading in a dog and carrying a 'Best In Show' trophy. I hit rewind and go back to the start, pausing on a close-up of Heather's face. She looks different somehow. It's in the set of her mouth and the lift of her chin. It's a look that says, 'This is me. Take me as I am or sod off.'

I pour myself a whisky and drink it quickly, hoping to still the rustle of disquiet inside me. I've always had a very clear idea of what CelebRate fans want. They are moths, drawn to the glow of beauty, the bright vision of a perfect life. They won't accept ugliness. And rebranding it as courage doesn't change that, whatever an impressionable TV audience might think. This won't work.

It can't.

CHAPTER 27

Heather stared at the rating update in disbelief. 'Wow,' she said. 'Just . . . wow.'

Tessa, who had been doing a victory jig around Heather's living room, came over and snatched away the F-phone, moving it further away, then closer, then further again, like an art collector admiring a small masterpiece. 'Told ya it would work. Though if I'm being totally honest, I didn't think it would work *this* well.'

CelebRate had changed the Top Trio banner so that all three images were now full body shots. Heather had been positioned on the left, using one of the pictures taken by the photographer Tessa had hired, a former warzone photojournalist who'd once had a solo exhibition at the National Portrait Gallery. The lighting made Heather seem to glow as she stared into the camera with a lifted chin and a level gaze, as though challenging it to a duel she already knew she would win, casually holding the hem of her white dress. Her injuries were like a splash of colour on a blank canvas. Modern art. That's how Duncan had described it when he'd called to congratulate her. She had hoped he would suggest going out to celebrate, but he'd told her he was busy 'handling something' and would be in touch after he'd dealt with it. So she would have to wait to see him again. Perhaps it was just as well; her schedule was pretty packed right now anyway, what with all the sponsor meetings and interview requests.

'Number two, baby!' Tessa yelled, picking up her wine glass and spinning across the floor, socked feet slipping against the polished wood. 'You should sack Lara and get me to be your image consultant instead. No one has *ever* rocketed up from the bottom to the banner. And you did it in *three days*! I am clearly a PR master.'

Number two. Three and a half million followers. Heather's phone was ringing incessantly once more, but this time she wasn't under attack. Everyone wanted to talk about her courage, how she had vanquished death, discrimination and her own demons. 'Lady Phoenix' one of the tabloids had dubbed her, risen from the ashes. A charity for people living with disfigurement wanted her to represent it and take a seat on its board.

Last week, the tide of public opinion had swept her onto the rocks. But Tessa had turned that tide, the TV interview propelling her from zero to hero in the space of five minutes – such was the power of breakfast television. A debate over society's unhealthy obsession with perfection had consumed the media, with Heather at its epicentre: proud and unflinching.

'I'm an evil genius,' Tessa declared.

'I think you may be overlooking the complete absence of evil.'

Tessa put on a mock pout. 'Let me have this one, okay? Evil geniuses are sexy, cat-stroking badasses. Run-of-the-mill geniuses are speccy nerds.' She planted her hands on her hips. 'Come on, you owe me this much.'

Heather laughed. She could feel happiness and excitement swirling inside her, making her slightly giddy. Had she ever felt this good?

'Fine.' She rolled her eyes, smiling across the room at Tessa. Her friend. Her saviour. 'You are an evil genius. A total Bond villainess.'

'Thank you,' Tessa said, with a nod of satisfaction. 'That is all I ask.'

CHAPTER 28

'So I tracked down your friend's troll.' Steve pulled back a chair to join Heather at the window table of Joe's Cafe. He'd flat-out refused to return to Lapin ('too poncy, too pricey, too rabbity') and she'd relented; he was doing her a favour, after all.

Heather watched him sit down, heart rushing. She was about to find out who had set out to destroy Analise. She pressed her palms against the table, then thought better of it, retracting them – Joe's wasn't the most hygienic place.

'Go on, then, who is it?'

Steve put on a weird, whispery voice. 'The call is coming from inside the house.'

She stared at him blankly. 'Sorry?'

He rolled his eyes. 'I can't believe you don't get that reference. A horror film classic.'

'It's because you're old; I don't get any of your references.' She waited a moment longer before throwing up her hands in frustration. 'So are you going to tell me or not?'

He tore open a sugar packet to put in the coffee she'd ordered him, accidentally ripping it right down the middle, sending white granules spraying across the table. He swore, swiping spilled sugar into his palm. She watched impatiently. Joe's really should get rid of those stupid packets, replace them with bowls of brown and white sugar cubes served with tongs, like at Lapin.

'The IP address is registered to the Triple F.'

Heather's mouth went dry. '*Who* at the Triple F?'

'That I can't tell you. It's a company-owned computer. There could be hundreds of them.'

'But it's definitely someone who works there? You're sure?'

'Someone who works there or has access to a company computer.'

'But . . . I have one myself. All the Winfluencers are given a laptop, kitted out with the necessary apps, filters and photo-editing equipment.'

Steve opened another sugar packet – more carefully this time – and emptied it into his coffee.

'Do you get to keep it after your six months are up?'

'Yes, I assume so.' Heather considered the information she'd just been given. 'So basically you're saying Analise's tormenter could be someone who works for the Triple F . . . or one of the Winfluencers, past or present?'

'Yeah, that pretty much sums it up.' His spoon chimed against the mug as he stirred. 'Sorry, I know you were hoping for a name. But at least now you know this wasn't just some random.'

'But why? What would motivate someone to do that?'

'Finding out the "who" should lead you to the "why".' He crossed his arms behind his head. 'Any thoughts as to how you're going to do that?'

'Hmm.' She considered the question. 'The obvious next move is to get the Triple F to track down that computer, find out who's been using it.'

'Ye-ess . . . But you might want to bear in mind that it's in the company's best interests to sweep this under the rug. And you'd need help from someone senior there to get the ball rolling. Do you know anyone in a position of power at the Triple F that you're sure you can trust?'

'Yes,' Heather said, feeling a small shiver of excitement pass through her. 'As a matter of fact I do.'

*

If Duncan was surprised that Heather had shown up at reception, demanding to see him right away, he gave no sign. When she stepped out of the private lift, he simply glanced at her from around the open door of the drinks cabinet and said, 'Sauvignon Blanc?'

'Yes please.'

She sat down on the cream sofa and he joined her there a moment later carrying two glasses, handing one across. His eyes fastened onto hers and she felt herself getting flustered, flashes of their encounter in the limo replaying in her head: his fingertips travelling up her leg; her dress, discarded on the floor; the weight of his body against hers as he—

She broke off the thought with a sharp shake of her head.

Heather drank some wine, recalibrating, telling herself this wasn't a social visit; she was here because she needed his help. The trick would be convincing him to provide it without revealing too much. Duncan was the Triple F's founder and CEO, after all; it wouldn't do to start pouring out half-baked theories about suspicious goings-on at his company.

'If I gave you the IP address of a Triple F computer, would you be able to tell me whose it is?'

'Yes. Why?'

'I . . . received an email from someone who works here. But I don't know who. And I need to find out.'

She braced herself for the questions that seemed sure to follow, but he simply cocked his head and said, 'Do you have the IP address with you?'

She blinked, taken aback. Could it really be this easy?

'Yes.' She pulled up the screenshot Steve had sent her. He glanced at it briefly then rose, crossing the thick carpet to his semi-circular desk, sitting down behind the computer.

'Do you need me to read the number out?'

'No. I have a good memory. This should only take a second.' He tapped the keyboard. Then frowned. 'That's odd.'

'What?'

'This address belongs to a laptop that hasn't been allocated yet. So it should still be with the others in Winfluencer Resources, ready to be designated to a new winner.' His long fingers rippled against the keyboard, making her think of pianists. 'I've messaged the team there and told them to locate it.' He rose from the chair. 'We should hear back shortly.'

'So that computer is meant for a Winfluencer, rather than a Triple F employee?'

'Yes. Though employees do sometimes borrow them, since they're not yet in use and have better editing software than standard staff laptops.'

He rejoined her on the sofa. She noticed that he sat slightly closer this time, fixing his pale gaze on hers, making her feel shy. She wondered, had he thought about their night in the limo during the week since? Or was she just one of many women he'd seduced there? If she hadn't shown up at reception, would she ever have seen him again? The truth was, she had no idea. And she couldn't

233

raise the subject now, or it would look as if her laptop-tracking mission was just an excuse to speak with him.

'So . . .' She cleared her throat. 'What have you been up to since we . . . saw each other.'

His phone chimed and she felt a small stab of disappointment when he checked the screen. She had hoped he would stay focused on her for at least a couple of minutes.

'Missing,' he said.

'Missing . . . me, you mean? Because I would have been happy to meet up.'

His lips tugged to the right, a sideways smile. 'The laptop. I've just heard back. It's not with the others. It's missing.'

'Oh.' Embarrassment flamed her cheeks. Of all the idiotic things to say! She tried to move past her mistake, distancing herself from it by pushing ahead with her investigation. 'Right. So you have no idea who's been using it. That's . . . a shame. But maybe you *can* answer my next question: where are the winners' files kept?' It had occurred to her on the way over that the troll's connection to the Triple F could explain how he'd got hold of private information about Analise.

'What files?'

'The finalists' background information and psychometric tests. Our answers to all those probing questions about our biggest secrets and fears.'

'Is this to do with the email you received from a company laptop?'

'In a way. Analise . . .' she began, then stopped herself. She needed to find a way to make her point without breaking her promise to the Tettersons. 'Analise thought someone might have looked at private information in her file.'

Duncan's eyebrows rose. '"Someone"?'

'A troll.' She twirled the glass by its stem, making the wine lap against the sides. 'Could someone have hacked into Analise's file . . . or somehow got hold of a staff password?'

He shook his head firmly. 'There aren't any passwords to use or files to hack. Those documents exist only in their original form, handwritten on paper, locked away in a room to which a very small number of people have access.'

'Where?'

'In this building.'

'No, where *specifically*.'

His eyes narrowed. 'Why?'

'Because all *my* private information is in there too. I'd like to know that it's secure.'

'It is.'

'Then show me.'

A lock of Heather's hair had fallen across her cheek and Duncan leaned closer, hooking it behind her ear with a fingertip. 'Don't you trust me?'

She tilted away from him, determined to stand firm, not get distracted. 'All I'm asking is that you put my mind at rest by letting me see for myself that the secrets I have entrusted to your company are safe. That *I'm* safe. Are you refusing to do that?'

He released a sigh.

'Fine. Come with me.'

*

The file room was unlabelled, behind a blank grey door on the floor below, just off the Orange Lounge.

Duncan was right about security being tight. In addition to the lock, there was a touchpad beside the door. Heather watched from the corner of her eye as his fingers flitted across the grid, tapping in 02-02-22. She wondered whether the numbers were random, or whether the second of February 2022 was a significant date. Then he slotted his key in the lock and turned the handle.

The room was tiny, containing only a small table and chair next to a pair of filing cabinets whose drawers were labelled with letters. She opened one marked 'GA-GR' and saw rows of thick cardboard folders suspended from hanging files, a plastic tab with a hand-lettered name inside it clipped to the top of each one. It was the sort of set-up that belonged to an office in the 1970s, at odds with the high-tech, multimedia world of the Triple F. She flicked through the name tabs, 'Gabel, Mark', 'Ghai, Samesh', 'Gunns, Paulina' . . . then snatched her hand away as the drawer suddenly slammed shut.

'Hey!' She turned to Duncan, who had appeared directly beside her. 'You nearly caught my fingers!'

'Sorry, but those are private. I only brought you here to reassure you that your information is securely stored. The winners' files never leave this room.'

'Surely you must have to take them away sometimes? Aren't screening decisions ever questioned or investigated?'

'Yes, of course. Under those circumstances, an investigator would come here and take handwritten notes, leaving the file behind. It's a no-exceptions rule. And only a dozen people have a key.' He held his up before tucking it inside his cardigan pocket.

'Which dozen?'

'Nice try. But I'm not going to tell you that: you'll only start hassling them. The aim of this visit was to put your mind at rest, and I hope I've succeeded. Now why don't we go find a quiet table in the lounge, get something to eat. He flashed her a grin. 'It's Taco Tuesday.'

She glanced around the small room. There was nothing more to learn here – at least, not with Duncan hovering at her elbow.

'Is it? I must have forgotten to circle it in my calendar.'

*

Heather was halfway through her plate of nachos when Duncan's mobile rang. He frowned at the screen.

'That's reception. Sorry, I better answer it.' He placed the phone to his ear. 'Duncan Caldwell.' There was a pause, then his eyes widened into a look of alarm. 'What? Here, as in this building?' He pulled off his cardigan, as though the room had suddenly become too hot, uncovering the plain black T-shirt beneath. 'What does he . . . Actually, never mind, just tell him I'll be straight down.' He ended the call, slipping the phone into the pocket of his trousers.

'Is everything okay?' Heather asked.

'Yes, fine. Just . . . I need to dash downstairs to deal with something. Are you all right staying here on your own for ten minutes or so?'

'Of course. I'll be right here, mainlining guacamole.'

Heather watched him rush out through the lounge doors, curiosity gnawing at her. Who was at reception? Because whoever it was had clearly thrown Duncan off his stride. She glanced at his cardigan, hanging from one side of the chair, in danger of sliding to the floor. She picked it up and was about to drape it carefully over the seatback when something – part idea, part impulse – hooked itself inside her. She felt inside the cardy's pockets, first one, then the other, until her fingers came up against the hard angles of the file room key. Her hand closed around it. She hesitated . . . but only for a moment. Because if she was going to do this, she couldn't afford to waste any time.

Less than three minutes later, Heather was inside the file room, yanking open the cabinet drawer labelled 'TA-TY.' Her heart beat fast as she flipped through the name tabs. If Analise had written about Ellie in her background report, that would mean her file was almost certainly the troll's information source. And Heather's suspect list would drop from thousands . . . to a dozen.

Tanis, Tesca . . . there! Her fingers touched the name tab: 'Tetterson, Analise'. Excitement was swooping inside her as she reached inside the hanging file for Analise's folder. But there was only an empty V of cardboard. Her eyes returned to Analise's name inside its plastic window. In light of her suicide, the contest must surely be reviewing the screening decision to see whether warning signs had been overlooked. So maybe one of the investigators had broken the rules and taken the file to avoid the bother of handwritten notes.

Or maybe someone was covering their tracks.

Heather slid the drawer shut. How much time had passed since Duncan had left? It felt like less than five minutes, but time could play strange tricks. Her eyes moved to the other cabinet, its middle drawer marked 'DA-GE'. Her own folder would be in there . . . She wondered what the psychologist had said about her. She was aware of time running out; Duncan could be on his way back right now. But this would only take a few seconds. She yanked open the drawer, flicking through the name tabs until she came to her own, groping for her folder. But there was nothing there either. She yanked the front of the hanging file towards her, making the files in front of it crowd together, spreading the cardboard V wide, but the space inside was empty.

The files never leave this room.

She looked down at the drawer filled with thick cardboard folders. What exactly did the Triple F keep inside them? She took one out, being careful to avert her eyes from the name on the front; her goal was to find out what kind of information had been taken from her and Analise's files, not snoop into someone else's secrets. She flicked past the familiar pages of tests, self-evaluations and background reports until she arrived at a document she hadn't seen before, on the very last page, entitled 'Assessment Result'. Her eyes dashed along the lines of handwritten notes.

'Strong family unit and peer group'. 'High scores on adaptability matrices borne out by successful move to Hong Kong for two years in early twenties'. 'Career-focused mindset but should be able to transfer ambition to Winfluencer role'.

At the bottom of the page were three boxes labelled 'Red', 'Amber' and 'Green'. The green box had been ticked. Beneath was a signature: 'SJ Hudson.' One of the psychological screeners, presumably. She returned the file to the drawer, thinking. She could understand why someone might want to remove Analise's records. But why take hers? Unless she and Analise had something in common that—

'What are you doing?' Duncan's voice was like an electric shock, jolting right through her. Heather's head turned slowly towards the door. He was standing just inside it, arms crossed, watching her. How did he get in without his key? 'The handle doesn't lock automatically,' he said, as though reading her thoughts. 'You have to turn the switch underneath it.' Heather looked at him with her mouth ajar, fingertips still resting on the lip of the open drawer. Caught with her hand in the proverbial cookie jar. Duncan's eyes were flat and cold. 'Well? Are you going to tell me what you're doing?'

Her mind raced through various excuses, none of which seemed particularly plausible.

'I . . . I wanted to find out what the psychological screener wrote about me,' she said in the end – which was at least true, if not her motive for coming here. 'To see whether any concerns were raised.'

'And were they?'

'I don't know. My file is missing.' She watched him blinking rapidly in the silence that followed. Was that surprise? Guilt? Or fury that she'd used his key and gone behind his back? She had no idea. Heather pushed ahead, thinking, *attack is the best form of defence*. 'I know I shouldn't have taken your key, and I am sorry for that. But you told me my information was here, safe. And it's not.'

He looked at the two cabinets. 'I'm sure it's here somewhere. It must have been misfiled.'

She crossed her arms. 'In that you have failed to reassure me that my information is secure, perhaps you could instead tell me yourself whether my assessor raised any concerns?'

'I can't, I'm afraid. I haven't read your file. That side of the business is dealt with by my assessment team.'.

'But don't you need to know about any risks associated with the people being chosen to represent your company?' *The best form of defence . . .* 'I'll be honest; I'm really surprised you're not more across this.' She threw her palms to the ceiling. 'Do you even know *who* assessed me?'

'As a matter of fact, I do.' He moved away from the door to

stand in front of her next to the open filing cabinet. 'There was an issue with the assessments from your Final Fifteen group; one of the screening psychologists got sick, so her files had to be reassigned last minute. We were in danger of missing the scheduled Winner announcement, so I dealt with it personally. Yours was among the five reassigned files.'

Heather's heart beat faster. 'So who assessed me?'

'I'm not going to tell you that.'

She crossed her arms. 'Fine. Then you give me no choice but to track down all three screeners, ambush them one by one and demand answers.'

He smiled then, a weak smile, but a smile nonetheless. 'You're a very stubborn person, aren't you, Heather?'

'I've been told I make mules seem chilled out.'

Duncan's eyes flicked sideways to the open drawer with its missing folder, staying there through the long silence that followed. His voice, when he spoke, was so quiet she had to lean forward to catch the words.

'Dr Leyton did your assessment. Dr Elliot Leyton.'

*

When she got home, Heather poured herself a glass of Sauvignon Blanc. She swirled her wine around the curved crystal, thoughts circling with the liquid. Was there a connection between Elliot doing her assessment and her documents going missing? Even before one of the other psychologists got ill, there had always been a one-in-three chance he would screen her, so obviously it could just be a coincidence. But if he'd assessed Analise too . . . Well. That would be a bigger coincidence.

Her tablet was on the coffee table and she picked it up and went to the CelebRate home page almost without thinking – she checked it at least a dozen times a day – lingering over her banner image and latest follower numbers. She scanned the ratings to see if anyone had moved up or down since her last check, before turning her attention to the main photo collage, eyes pausing on a group shot, half a dozen Winfluencers raising their champagne glasses towards the camera, all laughing or smiling, looking happy. Like Analise had, that night at the mixer. She stared at the faces in the photo, wondering why the troll had chosen Analise, out of all the CelebRaters. She had been flying high right before the troll struck, so the motive could have been simple jealousy – some overlooked worker, slaving away in a forgotten corner of the Triple F empire, seething with resentment over Analise's shiny new life. But in that case, why wait until two and a half years into the contest? There would have been plenty of other successful Winfluencers to envy before her. Heather sipped her wine, mind working at the puzzle, picking up and discarding various theories. Maybe the troll was new to the company. Or maybe the resentment had built up slowly over the years, until it reached boiling point.

Or maybe Analise wasn't the first.

The idea sank through her, gathering weight. Bubbles of memory rose to the surface, snippets of conversations she'd dismissed as Winfluencer gossip.

'Mei Lin swears that the photo must have been a deepfake . . . but then her family's Nazi past was outed on social media . . . she couldn't handle the backlash . . .'

'Omar totally denied he actually got with that prostitute, said he never even met the woman with him in that picture . . .'

'. . . turned from a Top Trio babe into a train wreck drunk after *that video of her slagging off working mothers went viral. She tried denying saying it . . .'*

What if those denials weren't just the desperate protests of Winfluencers caught in a downward spiral? What if someone really had created AI fakes to bring them down – someone with access to their private information and all the latest image-editing technology?

Heather took a swig of wine, staring at the smiling faces in the collage, hoping she was wrong, that she was putting two and two together and making five.

Because if Analise really wasn't the first, then chances were, she wouldn't be the last.

CHAPTER 29

How has this happened?

I stare at the CelebRate home page, glowing on my computer screen. The brother's revelations should have blown up her USP, sending her plummeting into the Drop Zone. But instead, Heather stares out at me from her place on the banner. When she first shot up the ratings, I assumed it was just a knee-jerk reaction, a woke reflex, and that in a few days she would fade away with the sympathy that had propelled her there. But I was wrong.

She's turned everything around. *They've* turned it around. Because I happen to know that this was all that bitch Tessa's idea. She sabotaged my plan. And for now, at least, there's not a lot I can do about it. The occasional deepfake photo or troll attack is random, an accepted fact of life online. But if it starts to appear targeted or systematic . . . Well, let's just say I could do without the attention.

My gaze drops to the photo collage under the banner. There's a picture of Heather and Tessa, at a club somewhere, grinning like Cheshire cats. The seed of an idea takes root and begins to grow. I close my eyes and work through angles, as it blossoms into a full-grown plan. Then I look at the picture again: the two bitches with their smirking faces, celebrating their victory over me, no doubt, the power of their alliance.

But the thing about alliances is, they can be broken.

CHAPTER 30

Heather was sitting on her sofa watching *Disfigured Figures* – a sponsor's documentary series about people living with deformities – trying to think of a 'powerful personal quote' to promote it when her phone rang.

She looked at the screen and was surprised to see an incoming videocall from Candi Cane, a Winfluencer whose trademark move was tossing her head to one side so that her blonde mane (mostly hair extensions) fell across one shoulder while kicking the opposite leg backwards so that her heel hit her bum. What on earth could she want?

Heather answered and was greeted by a view of Candi in what must have been her bedroom: a red and white space centred around a bed covered in heart-shaped cushions, a large teddy bear in pride of place.

'Hey there, Heather,' Candi said, as though they chatted all the time.

'Hello, Candi, how are you?'

'Oh, you know. A little bruised since you knocked me down.'

Heather stared at the face on the screen, confused. The last time the two of them had crossed paths was at the beach party. Was it possible that she'd collided with Candi, hard enough to knock her off her feet, yet somehow failed to notice?

'I'm really sorry, Candi. I had no idea I did that. The New Heights gets pretty crowded. I must have pushed past you without realising.'

Candi rolled her eyes. 'No, silly, not like *physically*. I mean in the ratings. Because I was, like, number three. And then you steamrollered past with your hurt leg thing and now I'm down to four and you've got my spot on the banner.'

'Ah. I see. Well, it wasn't my plan to displace you. I just wanted to be honest about my disfigurement.'

'Oh well.' She gave Heather a smile that looked more like a grimace. 'No biggie. I heard your podcast – what was it called again? "Look at my Scars"?'

'"Facing my Flaws",' Heather said, already regretting having taken the call.

'Oh yeah. It was super cute.' There was a pause, then she said slyly, 'Maybe you should make one about your dad.'

Heather felt her insides turn cold. 'My dad? What do you mean?'

'About, you know, what it's like when your parents commit suicide? Something like that must cause *so* much damage, except like, on the *inside*. I'm sure you can use it to make yourself sound brave and strong.'

Heather struggled to keep her features from betraying her shock and horror. The worst thing she could do right now was let on that her father's suicide was supposed to be a secret. That would only set Candi off on a mission to spread it.

Heather forced a cheery tone. 'That's a great suggestion. I'll take it on board. Do you mind if I ask where you heard about my dad, since I . . . I don't remember posting about it.'

Candi turned her head from side to side, pushing her lips into a pout, clearly checking out her own image on the call screen.

'Tessa DMed me about it. I think she was worried that Analise doing the same thing might trigger like, flashbacks or whatever.'

The words were like hot coals, burning all the way to her core. *Tessa*. Her new best friend and Triple F saviour. Why would she betray Heather like this – and to Candi of all people? It was incomprehensible.

'Annnnywaaaay,' Candi continued, 'I was calling because I see you're also invited to the Bond premiere tonight, and I wanted to let you know that I'm planning to wear a red dress, so it would be super helpful if you could like . . . *not* wear red too? We don't want to look all matchy-matchy.'

Heather was trying to follow what Candi was saying, but shock was whiting out her thoughts, making it impossible to focus. She needed to end the conversation now, before her facade of indifference crumbled.

'Sorry, Candi, I'm afraid I have to go. I have a Zoom meeting with a new sponsor.' She had just enough time to see Candi's lips inflate into a pout before severing the call.

Heather sat staring at the silent phone, heart beating fast. What had happened? Had Tessa somehow forgotten that Heather's family history was supposed to be kept private and let it slip without thinking? She tapped open her DMs, scrolling back through the conversation, pausing when she came to Tessa's final message on the subject.

Of course I won't say anything! Your secret is 100% safe with me. Tx

*

How could she say that then turn around and tell Candi? It didn't make sense. There had to be an explanation. Heather's fingers were trembling as she tapped out a DM to Tessa.

Hi – just spoke to Candi, who says you told her about my dad?! WTF? Did you forget that was supposed to be just between us two? Please tell me what happened. I don't understand.

Then she lay back on the sofa, waiting for Tessa's reply, staring blankly at the TV screen where a girl with a badly burned face was playing the piano. Heather didn't have long to wait. A minute later, the F-phone's two-tone alert sounded. *Tessa.*

Heather jumped on the message, reading it with growing disbelief.

Yeah, may have mentioned it to Candi. Didn't think it was a big deal. Frankly, I don't appreciate the tone of your message. It's pretty toxic, TBH. Makes me think our friendship has run its course. We can be civil at mixers but it would be best if you didn't speak to me or try to contact me again.

*

'What the hell?' Shock made her say the words out loud, drawing a glare of annoyance from Mandu who'd been dozing on the rug, having abandoned the sofa as soon as Heather arrived. She read and reread the DM, trying to make sense of it. What part of her message had been 'toxic'? Maybe 'WTF' with its implied swearing? But surely that was just something people wrote all the time? No. This had to be a joke. That was the problem with messages; you could misinterpret the tone. Best call and speak to her in person.

But Tessa's phone rang once then went to voicemail. Weird. She fired off a fresh DM: **Please call me ASAP. We need to talk.**

*

She could feel nausea churning inside her as she tapped 'Send'. Heather watched the screen, waiting for the 'Delivered' status to appear, hoping that 'Read' and 'Typing' would be close behind. But nothing happened. She frowned. Maybe there was a problem with the messaging system? She went onto Tessa's CelebRate page to try and send a message from there instead, expecting to see Tessa's latest profile photo featuring one of the leather jackets she was sponsoring. But the space where the image should have been was blank. And her follower count had disappeared. CelebRate must be having major technical problems. She went to Candi's page to see whether the same thing happened there. But no, there she was, sucking coyly on a candy cane. An uncomfortable suspicion began to take root. Heather put down the phone and picked up her tablet, logging herself off CelebRate, re-entering as an anonymous visitor. And there was Tessa, side-smiling over a leather-clad shoulder, her follower numbers below. Just to be absolutely sure, she logged back on as herself and tried again – to find the image gone. This was no technical problem. Tessa had blocked her.

She put the tablet down beside her on the sofa, thoughts tumbling, trying to work out how things between them had gone so wrong so quickly. Was Tessa really so defensive and weak that she would rather end a relationship than admit a mistake? It didn't seem like her. But then – as she kept having to remind herself – they had only known each other a short time. Heather must have completely misread her. She stared unseeingly at the TV screen, where the pianist was bowing towards a cheering audience. Fine, if that was how Tessa wanted it. Tonight it was definitely her loss, because Heather had been planning to invite her to the premiere as her plus-one. She would bring Debbie along instead, make up for having cancelled their plans again last week. But just as she was about to call, Heather hesitated, trying to picture Debbie strolling along the red carpet in one of her wigs. Did she even own a formal dress? What if she showed up wearing something cheap and inappropriate, stained by the painted fingers of toddlers? The night would end up embarrassing them both.

But if not Debbie, then who? It went without saying that Steve would be a nightmare at any event involving the rich and famous, heaping scorn on everyone and everything around them. Best stick with someone from CelebRate who knew what to say and how to look good for the cameras. But as she scanned the list of names, Heather realized the extent to which she had placed all her eggs in Tessa's basket where Triple F friendships were concerned. There were plenty of people she got on with at mixers, people she chatted and drank with. But no one close enough that she could call up and suggest a night out together without it seeming odd and out of the blue. Her already low mood sank deeper. Maybe she should pull out, say she wasn't feeling well. She'd been looking forward to getting glammed up and swanning around with film stars. But that was when she'd thought her best friend would be by her side.

Her phone rang, setting off a spark of hope that Tessa had seen sense and wanted to talk. But it was snuffed out as soon as she saw the screen.

'Hi, Noah.'

'Hello, Heather. I just checked Friend Finder and see you're still at home. Aren't you supposed to be livestreaming at the Bond premiere tonight?'

'Yes, I was. Am.'

'You don't sound very enthusiastic. Everything okay?'

'It's fine. Just . . . my plus-one has let me down. And it feels awkward going on my own.'

'Ah. Yes, I know how that can be.' A brief pause. 'Tell you what, why don't I swing by your place and the two of us can go together? It will give us a chance to catch up.' She heard the smile in his voice as he added, 'Call it a Bonding experience.'

Heather laughed, louder than the joke deserved, her mood lifting. Imagine: her arriving at a film premiere on Noah Fauster's arm! That was sure to get tongues wagging and followers flocking. Take that, Tessa.

'Thanks, Noah. You're a star.'

*

'Look, it's Heather! Heather Davies!'

Arriving at the premiere with Noah was like stepping into an alternate universe where the line between fantasy and reality had disappeared. Crowds had gathered in front of the Leicester Square cinema, security holding them back as the parade of celebrities moved past. Tom Hardy and Ana de Armas were right in front of her, mere steps away, pausing to greet the dense throng of photographers. Kylie Minogue was there too, and gave Noah and Heather a cheery wave as she went by.

Then it was her turn – *her*, walking down an honest-to-God red carpet! She could feel excitement surging through her veins as she strode along it on Noah's arm, chin lifted, shoulders back, not limping at all, thanks to a strategically timed pill. Cameras flashed, CelebRate fans held their phones in the air and voices called out their names. She had expected Noah to attract that sort of attention – he was properly famous, after all – but hearing her own name shouted too came as a complete surprise. She felt dazzled, transported.

Heather's emotions must have shown on her face because as they reached the doors of the cinema, Noah murmured in her ear, 'You never forget your first walk down the red carpet.'

She beamed up at him. 'I just can't believe this is my life. What have I done to deserve it?'

'You've been yourself,' he said firmly, leading her through the doors. 'That's more than enough. I'll have the Triple F cameraman send you the red carpet footage so you can post it tonight.' He glanced at his watch. 'Doesn't your livestream start soon?'

She checked the time on her phone. 'In four minutes. I hope people here don't mind being in it.'

'They won't. These are film folk; if they're not comfortable around cameras, they're in the wrong job.'

He was right. No one paid the slightest attention as she swept the F-phone's lens across the glittering crowd, describing the scene for her followers. Noah seemed to know everyone, introducing Heather – and her watching fans – to directors and actors, sound technicians and make-up artists. She had just wrapped up the stream and was tucking away her phone when a videographer came by to 'collect their thoughts' on the enduring popularity of Bond films. Noah spoke about their energy and beauty, about escapism and the human yearning to believe that one man could change the world. Then the videographer turned and pointed his camera at Heather.

'How about you? What do you think makes this franchise so special?'

She smoothed her hair as she gathered her thoughts, flattered that he wanted her opinion too. 'It transports you to a dazzling world where everything is exciting and beautiful,' she said, remembering the media trainer's advice to look at the camera as if it were a friend. 'Reality seems a bit flat and banal by comparison. It's an experience no one should miss out on.'

'Good answer,' Noah whispered, giving her a nod of approval as the camera moved away. Then someone rang a bell and they were all herded up the crowded staircase to the screening room, with its rows of reclining armchairs, each with a built-in table for snacks and drinks, a swag bag of 007 merch lying on the seat. Noah peeked inside his, taking out a Martini glass and raising it towards her in a mock toast, one eyebrow arched in a convincing James Bond impression.

'You'd make a great 007.' She smiled, moving her bag onto the floor and sitting down. 'You have that Bond vibe.'

Noah settled into the seat beside her. 'I'd rather play the baddie than Bond. Baddies are more interesting and seem to have more fun.'

Her smile faded as Noah's words set off a flash of memory: Tessa, spinning around the living room, high on triumph at having beaten Heather's troll.

Evil geniuses are sexy, cat-stroking badasses.

Fine. You are an evil genius. A total Bond villainess.

Thank you. That is all I ask.

She felt a throb of loss.

The director appeared at the front of the room and gave a speech heaping praise on the film's stars, who responded by standing up in their VIP seats to wave at the audience. Then the director moved aside, the curtains swept back and the screen lit up.

'Here we go,' Noah whispered. 'Prepare to be shaken but not stirred.'

And she laughed, even though it wasn't a great joke, because Noah was so kind and she was so grateful to him for bringing her here. And for those two hours, her fight with Tessa was forgotten.

*

'Heather Davies! Is that you?'

Heather gritted her teeth before turning to face the speaker. Ruth was squeezed into a strapless satin dress that was at least a size too small. Pale cleavage bulged over the top. Heather had seen her arriving at the premiere, pivoting in front of the throng of photographers as if she were one of the celebrities, but then she'd lost sight of her in the lobby crowd and thankfully they hadn't been seated near each other.

Now, though, cornered beside the bar at the New Heights after-party, there was no escape.

'Hello,' she said as Ruth air-kissed her cheeks. 'Nice dress.'

'Can you believe I'm a size twelve now?' Ruth twirled around. 'I've jumped on the intermittent-fasting bandwagon. It's not easy, but it works!'

'Mm. Yes. I can . . . see that.' She scanned the crowd around her, trying to locate Noah; he'd been pulled aside by a man in a business suit who'd said there was 'an urgent matter' they needed to discuss. That was nearly an hour ago and Heather hadn't seen him since. Her eyes returned to Ruth. 'So what's new on your side of the business? How's Dunc . . . Mr Caldwell getting on?'

Ruth eyed her shrewdly over her cocktail glass. 'Getting on with what exactly?'

Heather flushed. 'The American version of the Triple F? I've seen some articles about it in the press.'

'Oh God.' She rolled her eyes. 'Don't even *ask*. The poor man had to fly off to New York last night, where he's trapped in endless meetings that seem to go nowhere. It's taking *forever*. Between you and me, the Americans are being *such* a pain in the arse, trying to change everything. Which is fine for them, but they want *us* to change *our* model to bring it in line with theirs! Can you believe the cheek?' She hiccupped and covered her mouth, putting on a look of little-girl embarrassment. 'Oops. I may have had one drink too many. I can never resist Franco's margaritas.' She turned towards the bar, eyeing a handsome bartender pouring cocktails in front of the throng of non-champagne drinkers. 'They're to die for.'

Heather drank some champagne, trying not to let Ruth see that she was thrown by the news that Duncan had left the country without telling her. But then, it wasn't as if she was his girlfriend.

She cleared her throat. 'What do the Americans want to change? I thought they were just copying our format?'

'They were,' Ruth sighed. 'Until the investors saw how much legacy winners cost.'

'Sorry, legacy winners?'

'Past winners, no longer on CelebRate, ergo no longer promoting products and bringing in money – but still getting their five grand a week. Obviously that adds up. So the Americans want to cap it at five years. Which makes financial sense, but doesn't sound anywhere near as exciting as "wealth for life", so fewer people would enter the contest. But they want *us* to do the same so they don't look like a budget version of the Triple F.'

Heather's eyes widened in alarm as the implication sank in.

'So . . . winners could be cut off after five years? Can the contest really do that?' Her mind raced through the calculations. Five years at a quarter of a million or so a year. Not enough to pay off her mortgage and cover her living costs – not even close. And when the money stopped, how would she earn more? She hadn't finished her teacher training and she wasn't qualified to do anything else.

Ruth gave Heather's arm a squeeze, crimson fingernails biting. 'Don't worry. If the execs *do* decide to go along with it – and I'm not saying they will – it would only apply to new winners. We'd still have to honour our commitments to people like you.'

'Ah. That's . . . good to know.' Heather affected a casual tone, as though the money wasn't really that important. But Ruth's words were an uncomfortable reminder that she was no longer capable of supporting herself, that she was dependent on a lifetime of handouts. The pain in her leg had been slumbering all evening, but now it suddenly woke up and began shouting for attention. Time for a pill. 'If you'll excuse me, I need to dash to the loo, so . . .'

But Ruth's eyes had already moved past her, scanning the crowd, alighting on the next target. 'Sunita! How fabulous to see you! I have some exciting news about an Asian make-up promotion that I just can't wait to share with you!'

*

The powder room of the New Heights looked like a film star's dressing room, with its velvet stools in front of a giant mirror framed by globe-shaped lights, the counter beneath lined with marble trays of brushes and sprays.

A woman was seated on the middle stool when Heather arrived, her familiar face reflected in the mirror as she leaned towards it.

'Mrs Shul— Veronica. Hello.'

Eric's mother turned towards her while continuing to apply burgundy lipstick.

'Ah, Heather.' She patted the stool beside her. 'Join me. I needed a break from all the highbrow debate raging out there.'

Heather sat down and pulled the stool closer to the mirror, placing her bag on her lap so that it was concealed by the counter.

'Which debate is that? Actually wait, let me guess: which James Bond is the hottest?'

'No, that would have been vaguely interesting, though obviously the answer is Sean Connery. This was about Bond girl bodies and how to buy one.'

'Ah. To boob job or not to boob job.'

'That *is* the question.' She put the lipstick away then rummaged inside her alligator clutch, clearly looking for something. Heather used the opportunity to reach inside her own handbag, twisting off the lid of her pill container, fishing out a tablet and popping it in her mouth, swallowing it dry. But when she looked up again, Veronica was staring straight at her.

'Oh.' Heather could feel her cheeks flushing. 'I was just . . . My medication . . .'

'I don't suppose you have any coke on you?' the older woman interrupted. 'I've run out.'

Heather paused, analysing this unexpected response. She concluded that it was Veronica's way of being kind. She clearly assumed that whatever Heather was sneaking into her mouth was on a par with coke, so was letting her off the hook with a show of solidarity. Of course it wasn't the same thing, though; Heather's pills were legal. She had a prescription.

'Sorry, I'm afraid I don't have any.'

'Hardly anyone does since they started the random bag searches.' She turned back to her reflection, smoothing her hair. 'I've heard the club's back office has a safe packed with confiscated powders and pills.' She met Heather's eyes in the mirror. 'I don't know whether anyone told you. About the searches.'

Heather flushed, torn between annoyance and embarrassment; Veronica clearly thought Heather was doing something wrong and was trying to help her avoid getting caught.

'That doesn't really concern me. What you just saw . . . that was oxycodone.'

Veronica's manicured brows dipped. 'You're on Oxy? You should be careful. It's very addictive. I've never tried it myself, but I doubt it's worth the high.'

'I don't take it to get high. It's for pain.'

A light dawned in her features. 'Ah. Your leg. I saw your interview. That was a smart move. You didn't mention needing pain medication, though.'

'No, I didn't. It's private. You're the first person I've told. Ever.'

Veronica smiled. 'I'm honoured. Thank you for sharing that with me.'

'Well, you did kind of catch me in the act.' She shrugged. 'Plus I didn't have any coke, so thought I should share something.'

Veronica laughed her throaty laugh before walking out of the powder room, heels clicking against the marble floor, leaving behind a faint smell of perfume. Something with lilies.

Heather sat staring at herself in the mirror, replaying their conversation.

You should be careful. It's very addictive.

And suddenly she needed to get out of the club. She wanted quiet and space to breathe. To think. She checked her watch, with its weirdly plaited gold frame – not her taste but she was sponsored to wear it for another two weeks – and saw that it was ten past twelve. Early, by Winfluencer standards. She had already uploaded her red carpet footage and a picture from inside the cinema, so just needed one more post to meet her daily quota. Might as well get that out of the way now. She headed out onto the terrace, grabbed a glass of champagne from a passing waiter and positioned herself beside a circle of actors she recognized from the film: small roles, but still. She waited, F-phone camera at the ready, until one of them told a joke. Then she leaned into the circle, taking a group selfie as she threw back her head and laughed along with them. There. She would wait and post it later, so that it looked like she was still out. She pocketed the phone. Job done. She was free to go.

*

A light breeze played with the hem of Heather's dress as she strolled along the path beside the pond, inhaling the smell of fresh-cut grass. Hard to believe she was just a few minutes' walk from the New Heights. The Chiswick Business Park pond was flanked by landscaped gardens and inhabited by ducks, coots and geese, a pocket of wildlife hemmed in by high-rises, roads and railway lines. She was halfway round the water, wondering how many hours it took the business park's gardeners to keep all the bushes so trim and tidy, when she saw that she wasn't alone.

There was a man standing under a tree near the water's

edge, smoking a cigarette. He was facing the waterfall linking the pond's upper and lower halves, his back to her. Then he must have heard her footsteps because he turned and looked straight at her.

'Heather? Is that you?'

'Hello, Noah.' She crossed the grass to join him. 'I didn't know you smoked.'

'I don't.' He dragged on his cigarette, making the ash wink orange. 'At least, not officially. I have maybe one fag a week. I find it . . . meditative. But I'd appreciate it if you didn't tell anyone that. Smoking doesn't really fit with my brand.'

'Your brand?'

'You know.' He waved his hand around, dropping ash. 'Clean-living, vice-free . . .'

'Vice-free? Is such a state even possible?'

'Only if you're exceptionally boring.' Noah reached inside his jacket and produced a cigarette packet, flicking open the lid before holding it out to her.

'Fancy one?'

'No thanks, I—' Then she stopped herself. She used to smoke the occasional cigarette at parties before the accident. The nicotine itself didn't really do anything for her, but she'd enjoyed the ritual of it all: the click of the lighter, cupped hands sheltering a flame, that first drag, making the ash glow. 'Actually, sod it. I will.'

She took one and he lit it using a silver lighter with an enamel pattern that gave it an art deco feel. Noah must have noticed her looking because he said, 'It's Rathbone. They're a sponsor.'

She drew in a deep, dizzying breath, releasing it in a plume of smoke. Her first drag in years. She felt light-headed as she watched Noah tuck the lighter back in his pocket.

'Do you ever get tired of having everything chosen for you, not being able to pick your own clothes?'

'God yes.' He blew smoke at the sky. 'Last year a company that makes Hawaiian shirts in a particularly lurid selection of colours paid the Triple F a small fortune to have me wear their entire summer selection: twenty of them, hanging in a row. I swear I had to put on sunglasses every time I opened my wardrobe.'

She laughed. It was good, standing with him in the quiet dark. She'd enjoyed their time together at the premiere, but they hadn't had much chance to talk, surrounded as they had been by celebrities, journalists and filmmakers. This was different. Intimate, but not in a sexual way. It made him feel less like a mentor and more like a friend, someone she could confide in. She hesitated, then took the plunge.

'Do you ever think there might be something about the contest that's . . . not quite right?'

He chuckled. 'I'd say "not quite right" is a major understatement. There are plenty of things about it that are positively bonkers. But it's still one hell of a ride.'

'No, what I mean is . . . have you ever noticed how many people end up . . .' She paused, hunting for the right word. 'Self-destructing?'

He inspected the tip of his cigarette. 'You're talking about Analise.'

'Yes, but not *just* her. There was that girl, Mitzu, last year, who was about to start her own fashion label, until she got stoned on a boat, fell off and drowned. That made headlines because it happened while she was still on CelebRate. But the ones that happen afterwards barely make the news. Like Blake Drayford, who got drunk and crashed his sports car a year after winning.

261

And Ellie Palek, who passed out on a snow bank and died of hypothermia.' She took a short drag. It was less dizzying this time. 'Those are the worst ones, the deaths. But there are quite a few others who suddenly went off the rails for no apparent reason. Like Ozzie and Jim, for example. And Omar. And you know what I find interesting?'

Noah blew smoke out of the side of his mouth to keep it from going in her face. 'Go on.'

'They were all successful. I mean *really* successful. Every single one of them made it into the Top Trio. And not just that: Analise was being offered a 'female brand ambassador' job. And Sara Kalin was up for a similar role until that crying toddler video came out. Mitzu broke CelebRate's record for follower numbers. And Jim was meant to star in the next Triple F advertising campaign. They were the contest's biggest success stories. But then something went wrong and they just . . . fell. Down the ratings and off the radar.'

He was silent for a moment, drawing on his cigarette. 'Life on CelebRate isn't easy – as you well know. The loss of privacy, falling out with friends over money, the stress of competing in the ratings. And all the while knowing that it won't last, that the celebrity status you are working for and obsessing over will be snatched away after six months, casting you out into obscurity. It obviously strikes the most successful Winfluencers the hardest, because they have the most to lose.'

Heather crossed her arms as she considered this. Noah's logic made sense. Should she tell him her theory: that the most successful winners were being trolled by someone inside the contest – someone who was weaponizing their secrets against them? She knew how it would sound: outlandish, even paranoid. And she couldn't share the only piece of evidence she had without breaking her promise to the Tettersons. Heather stared out across the pond. It was a clear night and a fat slice of moon lay on the water. Then a Canada goose swooped down from the sky, feet trailing across the surface as it came in to land, breaking the image apart. She decided to try a different tack.

'Having to deal with trolls all the time doesn't help. And top Winfluencers do seem to be the main targets, brought down by damaging photos and videos spread across social media. A lot of them claim to be victims of AI-generated deepfakes. Do you think that's true?'

Even in the darkness, she could see his frown.

'It's difficult to say. Because the reality is, some of the winners don't like the way they come across when they're caught on camera drunk or high or angry, and the easiest solution is to cry fake. Deepfakes are obviously a hot topic at the contest, what with all the rumours about the Triple F having started with one, but if you want my personal opinion, the numbers have been hugely exaggerated.'

Heather blinked, puzzled. 'Sorry, I don't know what you mean. I haven't heard those rumours.' Her throat was starting to hurt from the cigarette so she stamped it out, putting the butt in her bag to dispose of later. 'What's this about a deepfake starting the contest?'

'Nothing really, just some unproven claims that the Triple F's founder used doctored video footage to stop a court case that could have derailed the contest's launch.'

She thought of Tessa's warning, the rumours about Duncan. 'You mean the sex tape sent to his former partner's wife?'

'Ah, so you *have* heard about it.'

'Sort of. In the version I heard, the video was hacked rather than faked.'

He waved a hand in the air. 'Hacked, faked, either way it's all just gossip, unworthy of close consideration. There are plenty of unsavoury stories about Duncan Caldwell, not helped by the fact that he refuses to address them. He's not the most communicative person.' He took another drag, exhaling smoke through his nose, dragon-style. 'Or perhaps you disagree, since I understand the two of you have spent time together? I'd be interested to hear your impressions of him.'

Heather was glad of the darkness; it meant he couldn't see her blush. 'Well, he's clearly highly intelligent. Dry sense of humour. Honest.'

'I agree about the intelligence and humour. I do like Duncan. Though there are times . . .'

She braced herself for his next words, not sure she wanted to hear them. But Noah fell silent.

'Yes?' she prompted. 'Times when . . . what?'

His sigh was a stream of smoke. 'I don't know. There's this other side to him . . .' He shook his head. 'Never mind. He's clearly under a lot of pressure, especially now, with the Americans. And Analise's death was obviously a PR disaster as well as a human tragedy.'

'Yes, about Analise . . . there's something I wanted to ask.'

Noah tilted his head. 'Go on.'

'Why didn't the screeners weed her out? Because if she was capable of suicide . . . surely there must have been *some* signs of instability? And not just her. The others I just mentioned. Didn't their psychometric tests raise any red flags? Because I thought the whole point of the assessment process was to stop vulnerable candidates from winning.'

Noah was silent for a moment, forehead creased in thought. Then he nodded.

'You're right, of course. I have already requested a thorough review of Analise's assessment to see whether signs were missed. But in light of our conversation . . .' His eyes met hers and there was a look of determination there. 'I'm going to ask that the investigation be broadened out to include the other cases you've highlighted. Thank you, Heather, for bringing your concerns to my attention. We need to make sure there are no more sad outcomes like these.'

She smiled out at the night, warmed by his praise and the knowledge that he was taking her seriously – and taking action.

'Thanks for listening to me, Noah.' Heather was surprised to feel a prickle at the back of her throat, threatening tears. The fight with Tessa must be catching up with her, making her emotional. 'Your support means a lot.'

He patted her shoulder. 'It's what I'm here for.'

CHAPTER 31

Heather looked down at the rows of faces spread across her coffee table. She'd printed up images of past winners who'd gone off the rails. Some of them were still out there, grappling with drug addiction, alcoholism or mental breakdowns. Others were gone . . . killed in car crashes, boat accidents, overdoses . . . Her eyes paused on the picture of Analise . . . And suicides.

What if whoever had targeted Analise was tormenting a new victim at this very moment, driving one of her fellow winners down a path to self-destruction? She lay back on the velvet sofa with an arm across her forehead, gazing up at the white plaster petals of the ceiling rose, thinking. There was only one way to find out whether the troll was still active: by questioning the other CelebRaters. They would all be at this weekend's mixer, so she could speak to them there. Except that would probably violate the ban on negative conversations at the New Heights. And even without that rule, she couldn't really imagine the other winners opening up to her in that setting. They arrived at those parties with their guards up, focused on raising their profiles and boosting their ratings, competitive instincts sharpened like claws, hair tossing and teeth flashing as they put on a display of easy-going confidence for the photographers. So they were hardly going to share their fears and secrets with a rival.

She could DM each of the CelebRaters individually, invite them round for one-on-one drinks at her place, then try to draw them out. But even if they came – and she suspected most wouldn't – they were bound to wonder what she was up to, contacting them out of the blue then pumping them for information about their problems. No, if she wanted to find out what was really going on, she needed to speak to the Winfluencers when their guards were down – in a place where there was no risk of being ambushed by photographers or fans.

Heather could see where this train of thought was carrying her and struggled to divert it; there had to be another way.

Maybe she could pretend to be doing a research project about online abuse and send everyone a questionnaire.

But even as she ran through options, she knew she was just putting off the inevitable. The solution was simply too obvious to ignore.

Heather rubbed the back of her neck, releasing a sigh. There was no way around it. She knew what she had to do.

CHAPTER 32

If Elliot was surprised to see Heather walking through the door of the second-floor conference room, he didn't show it, greeting her with a neutral expression and a small nod. She ran an internal assessment of her reaction to seeing him again as she crossed the room. She felt . . . nothing. As though he were a complete stranger she was meeting for the first time. She wondered what had happened to deactivate the screaming alarm bells that had gone off the last time they'd met. Obviously she had known he would be here tonight, which had removed the element of surprise. And their confrontation in the kitchen had released some of her pent-up anger. Plus she had come here tonight on a mission – one that had nothing to do with him. She didn't forgive him – she never would – but his emotional power over her was gone.

Heather looked around at the Winfluencers seated in the circle, pausing to make eye contact with each one. Sandra, a plus-sized model – now fifth in the ratings – was seated directly opposite. There was an empty chair on Heather's left and Nima – now seventh – was seated on the other side of it, toying with her hair, which was today worn in tight twists, frosted pale blue at the tips. A guy the tabloids had dubbed 'Bob the Builder' was sitting just beyond, hands fidgeting in his lap. Next to him was Vlad, a former personal trainer who posted workout videos and was tenth in the ratings. The rest were ex-CelebRaters, winners whose six months had passed.

'Let's begin,' Elliot said. 'Does anyone have something they wish to share with the group?'

Heather listened closely, fingers locked around her knees, as one by one, the winners began pouring out their problems. Nima was here because she needed a 'safe space' to vent about her followers and how rubbish they were at replicating her elaborate hair styles. 'Why do I even *bother*?' she asked, voice quavering. Bob the Builder – formerly a construction worker named Robert – was missing his ex-girlfriend now that the novelty of 'hot birds on tap' was finally wearing off. Vlad was worried about not being able to find a good platform for his workout videos after his time on CelebRate ended. And Sandra had developed an eating disorder after being fat-shamed online.

'You wouldn't believe the names they called me,' she told the group. She bit her lip. 'I mean, I knew there would be haters . . . but I didn't think they would be *this* bad.'

Heather saw her opening. 'Was there one troll in particular who stood out, maybe knew things about you he or she shouldn't have?' She watched the model's face closely. 'Because I've heard there's a particularly nasty one who only targets Winfluencers.'

Nima waved a dismissive hand. 'There are lots of those.'

'Yeah,' Bob said. 'I have one bloke who keeps posting on fan forums saying my ears are too big and I don't deserve the money. Like the two things are somehow related.' His hands drifted to his ears, touching the lobes self-consciously.

Heather ignored them, her words aimed at Sandra. 'So there's no one whose name has come up more than once? Maybe going by "A. Know"?'

'No.' She shook her head, looking puzzled. 'I don't think so.'

So not Sandra then. Heather turned her attention to the others, scanning the circle of faces. 'How about the rest of you? Have any of you come across a troll who somehow got hold of private information? Maybe knew something from your past that—'

'Where exactly is this coming from, Heather?' Elliot interjected, frowning. 'If you'd like to talk about your own experience of trolling, please feel free to do so. This is a place for sharing and support. But not—' the frown deepened, '… for interrogation.'

'It's not interrogation,' Heather snapped. 'I was just trying to see if we all have a . . . a common problem that we could discuss. Because trolling is probably the most corrosive part of life as a Winfluencer. So I wanted to know whether anyone here has been trolled by someone who . . . stood out in some way.'

Nima snorted. 'You sound like Analise.'

Heather's spine straightened. 'Sorry? What do you mean?'

The hair artist shrugged. 'Just that she asked similar questions the last time she came to a session.'

'Yeah,' Bob nodded. 'That's right. It was weird, because she never seemed bothered by trolls before that. She was always telling us not to let them get in our heads. But one of them definitely got into hers.'

'Did she have any idea who this troll was?'

'No, she just—'

'I feel we are once again drifting off topic,' Elliot interrupted. 'We are here to share our own experiences, not speculate about the struggles of others who, sadly, are no longer with us.'

'I happen to think we are very much *on* topic,' Heather shot back, making no effort to hide her irritation. 'What happened to Analise could also be happening to others in this room. So I think it's important that we find out whether there's a link—'

She was interrupted by the sound of the door opening. Heather turned to see a pair of late arrivals enter the room. The first was Noah, wearing a navy suit and an apologetic smile.

The second was Tessa.

She was dressed in designer-torn jeans, her favourite DMs and a top layered with silver loops of metal. When she spotted Heather, she stopped suddenly, eyes springing open in surprise. Heather looked back at her, unsure how to feel. Because although she was still hurt and angry at Tessa for sharing her secret and turning her back, there was no denying that she'd missed their friendship. Triple F life just wasn't the same without her.

Ignoring the empty chair next to Heather, Tessa chose the only other free one, between Noah, who'd just sat down, and Elliot.

'Sorry I'm late,' she said breezily into the silence that followed. 'What did I miss?'

'We were discussing trolling and the pain it can inflict,' Elliot said. 'Have you had any experiences with trolls that you'd like to share with the group?'

Tessa's eyes narrowed as she appeared to consider the question.

'Do friends count?'

Elliot tilted his head. 'Are you saying that a friend of yours has had an issue with a troll?'

'No.' She crossed her arms tightly across her chest. 'I'm talking about friends who suddenly start *acting* like trolls.'

'So you've had a friend – or a former friend, presumably – post negative comments about you online?'

'Not exactly. The comments weren't posted publicly. More like abusive DMs.'

'Ah, I see. That's a different issue: abuse inflicted privately, by a friend or family member, after the relationship turns toxic.' He tented his fingers in front of his chest, looking at Tessa. 'Would you like to share your experience?'

'Actually, no, I don't think I would.' She shook her head firmly. 'That is all I have to say on the subject.'

There was a brief silence during which Tessa's eyes slid towards Heather before retreating again. Heather stared at her former friend's averted face in disbelief. Was she seriously implying that *Heather* was behaving like a troll – after Tessa had betrayed her trust?

'I think this would be a good point at which to move on,' Elliot was saying. 'Why don't we go to the Secret Space? Today's exercise is to describe a self-destructive pattern you would like to rid yourself of.'

Around the circle, people began nodding, taking out their F-phones. Most were tapping words onto what looked like a notes app, though Nima was using handwriting mode, scrawling on the screen with a finger. Bob and Vlad had both brought Bluetooth keyboards.

Heather took her mobile from her pocket and looked around, baffled, her anger at Tessa momentarily forgotten. 'I'm sorry, what's going on?'

Elliot gestured towards the handset. 'You'll find there's an app pre-installed on your F-phone with a large blue "S".' She looked down at the screen, flicking through the rows of apps. There it was, right at the end. 'Open it,' Elliot continued, 'then write about a self-destructive pattern, along with any fears or insecurities associated with it, that you wish to banish. Once you've done that, you can tap one of the three icons in the top right corner to purge the negative thoughts you've just captured . . . Do you see the icons?'

'I see a flame, a wave and . . .' She squinted at the screen. 'Is that a pineapple?'

'A grenade. It lets you watch whatever you've written being blasted apart. The flame burns your words to ash and the wave dissolves them and washes them away.'

'Right. So it's basically a fancy delete button.'

'Externalising and then destroying negative thoughts and emotions in this way can be very cathartic.'

Heather frowned at the screen. 'So just to be crystal clear: no one else will see what's written here? Once we've blown it up or whatever, it's gone?'

'Yes. It's the equivalent of writing your darkest thoughts and fears on a piece of paper and then setting it on fire . . . minus the health and safety issues.'

Heather considered the blank note page on her screen, with its three symbols of destruction tucked in the corner. She'd only come here to dig for information, so hadn't really thought about participating in the exercises. She looked around at the others, seeing the play of emotions on their faces as they wrote, brows dipping, lips twitching, eyes blinking back tears. Then she heard the sound effect of a bomb going off and saw Sandra flop back against her chair with a sigh of relief. Then there was the whoosh of a wave and Bob's face took on a look of sour triumph, as though he'd just won an important argument with a hated enemy.

Well, she was here anyway. Might as well give it a go. She

thought for a moment about what to say. A self-destructive pattern . . .

She crossed her legs without thinking and was hit by a bolt of mind-blanking pain. Stifling a gasp, she uncrossed them quickly and waited for it to fade. She needed another pill. But that would make four today. Again. She used to be fine with one or two. She could feel unease gnawing at her as she returned her attention to the blank page waiting to be filled with her insecurities and fears.

She began to write. '*My oxycodone's not working like it used to, so I keep taking more. I think I've been on it too long, but I can't imagine life without it. I don't tell people I use it because they'll think I'm an addict. I don't know what to do.*'

There. She'd done it, pushed out her 'negative thoughts'. Now to wipe them from the face of the earth. She looked at the three icons. No destruction by water, thank you very much. She tapped the grenade, watching with satisfaction as it blew her words apart, leaving only an image of a mushroom cloud. She grinned. Elliot was right. It *was* cathartic.

*

There was coffee after the hour was up, so Heather stayed for a while, hoping to find out more about what Analise had said at her last meeting. But the moment the session ended, everyone seemed to suddenly forget about their problems, milling around Noah instead, vying for face time.

After a couple of failed attempts to direct conversations towards Analise and trolling, Heather gave up. There was nothing more to learn here. Picking up her bag, she slipped out into the yellow-striped corridor. Tessa must have left right before her because she was just ahead, moving in the direction of the lifts, a battered rucksack pulled up over her arm. *Strategically* battered, Heather thought sourly, in keeping with her grungy brand. But Tessa must have grabbed it by the wrong strap because the bag tipped sideways, spilling its contents through the draw-stringed top. A hairbrush, make-up bag, wallet and silver hip flask hit the floor, along with a scatter of change. Heather bent down reflexively to help, gathering up the coins and picking up the flask, handing them across. Tessa's lips were pressed tight as she accepted them silently, stuffing everything back in the bag.

Unbelievable.

'I think you'll find "thanks" is the traditional response,' Heather snapped.

Tessa was yanking at the strings of her bag, pulling the top shut. 'Well, seeing as you've made it clear that you never want to hear my voice again, I assumed I was doing you a favour by keeping quiet.'

'Oh, give me a break. How does asking why you told Candi about my dad translate into "I never want to hear your voice again"? And anyway, *you're* the one who ended our friendship and blocked me.'

Tessa's fingers froze on the strings. She lifted her head and stared at Heather, brows drawing together.

'No, I didn't.'

'Didn't what? Didn't gossip to Candi about my dad's suicide? Or DM me, saying our friendship had run its course? Or block me right afterwards? Because I think you'll find you did all three.'

And Heather turned on her heel and began walking away in the direction of the loos, old hurt and fresh anger churning inside her, knee shrieking in protest.

She was already halfway there when Tessa's next words hit her back. 'I didn't tell Candi about your dad. And I didn't say that about our friendship or block you. *You* did that to *me*.'

Heather stopped short. Turned around. Stared at Tessa along the length of corridor.

'What are you *talking* about?'

'Are you seriously trying to play innocent? Because you may have deleted the original, but I have a screenshot of your last message right here . . .' Tessa waved her mobile in the air, 'stating quite clearly that you were calling time on our friendship.'

'But . . . that's impossible.'

Then her voice faded out and they stood looking at each other, faces mirroring the shift from brow-creased confusion, to blinking analysis, to the widened eyes of dawning realisation.

'We need to talk,' Tessa said.

*

'I can't believe it.' Heather shook her head slowly as she reread the message on Tessa's screenshot. 'How did this happen?'

The Yellow Lounge was closed for the night but she'd remembered the unlocked kitchen leading onto it from her confrontation with Elliot so they'd gone through there. The sofas were pushed against the walls with the chairs lined up beside them, the dim lighting turning their yellows grey. They had dragged two of the chairs over to a table, then Tessa had shown Heather what was on her phone.

There was no sign of the message Heather had sent asking about the revelations to Candi. Instead, there was a DM under her own name, rebuking Tessa for showing up late to the last mixer and 'leaving me hanging', accusing her of 'selfish behaviour'. This was closely followed by a message similar to the one Heather had received.

I've given it a lot of thought and decided that we really don't have much in common and our friendship has run its course. We can be civil at mixers but I'd rather you didn't contact me or speak to me again outside of group settings

'Wow,' Heather said after reading it. 'What a bitch!'

Tessa laughed, the sound amplified by the empty lounge. 'Megabitch! I tried to call you right after this came, but I was already blocked. Ditto on CelebMail. Then the original messages were deleted, which I assumed was you concealing the evidence of your bitchery.'

'I hadn't even noticed that the ones on my phone were deleted too; they made me feel sad so I never looked at them again. How creepy!' She glanced around the closed lounge. The floor gleamed with fresh polish in the night-glow passing through the glass wall. She lowered her voice. 'We need to get straight onto the IT department. I can't believe someone can just crawl around inside our phones like this, sending and deleting and blocking. There is clearly a serious security loophole somewhere.'

'Actually . . .' Tessa put a knuckle against her lip. 'I'm not sure we should. Get onto IT, I mean.'

Heather stared, baffled. 'Why not?'

'Think about it. Whoever did this was able to access our F-phones. It had to be someone hijacking the AI software that's supposed to scan our messages for, you know, nasty shit—'

'Abusive content?'

'Yeah. And besides scanning, you know what else that program does?'

Heather nodded grimly. 'Deletes the messages and blocks the sender.'

'Exactly.'

'But surely the IT department is best placed to track down whoever has been misusing the system? Plus we really should tell Noah. He'll want to help.'

Tessa drummed her fingers against the table, eyes narrowed in thought.

'I don't think we should tell *anyone*. At least, not yet. The way I see it, whoever did this either works in IT or is senior enough to have access to all the contest's programs. Either way, do we really want to tip off the saboteur to the fact that we're on to them, giving them a chance to cover their tracks? Wouldn't it be better to hold on to that knowledge, let them think they got away with it, while we come up with a plan to draw them out?'

'Okay, now you really *do* sound like a Bond villainess.'

'Hashtag goals.' And she made a gun out of her thumb and index finger, blowing imaginary smoke from the tip.

Heather laughed. 'I've missed you.'

'Yeah, well. Kinda missed you too.' They smiled shyly at each other and Heather felt a warm glow of happiness. Then she folded her arms behind her head and gazed towards the floor-to-ceiling window, thinking. It began to rain, striping the darkened view of warehouses and low-rise office buildings.

'The email that pushed Analise over the edge was sent from a Triple F computer,' she said eventually.

Tessa's brows shot up. 'You're kidding! How do you know that?'

'It doesn't matter. What matters is that it's true. And surely that can't be a coincidence? Whoever sent it must be the same person who messed with our phones.'

Tessa picked up her mobile and held down the button on top.

'What are you doing?'

'Switching off my phone so no one can look at Friend Finder and see that we're together.'

'Shit. I didn't even think of that.'

Tessa tapped her temple. 'Which is why I'm the brains of this operation.' She turned and gazed across the shadowy lounge. The other tables looked strange without chairs, a pool of shadow beneath each one. 'Hard to believe that someone inside the contest would do these things.'

'I know. Why, do you think? What's the motive?'

Tess shrugged. 'Causing trouble for the sheer sport of it. Or jealousy because we're hot and have money and whoever's doing this isn't and doesn't. In other words, the usual shite.'

Heather's eyes returned to the window, now blurry with rain. Was it really that simple? Because she had a strange sense that there was a purpose behind those DMs, a goal. But the feeling was like a shapeless cloud that broke apart as she poked at it. She gave her head a shake. 'Yeah,' she said. 'The usual shite.'

CHAPTER 33

Heather needs to be stopped. Not just slowed down. Stopped dead. Which means harsher measures are needed. I swivel back and forth in my chair, eyes moving across the faces pinned to the wall beside my computer. My Icarus gang. They flew too close to the sun and came crashing down. It's amazing the way human weaknesses can be harnessed, made to take over. Like a self-destruct button that just needs a gentle tap. It's been surprisingly easy. Until now.

Heather's been tricky, countering my moves, throwing me off my game. But now that I've got her away from that bitch Tessa, she won't have anyone to scheme with, so things should get easier. And Heather will be feeling low, abandoned. So this is the time to strike.

I enter a chatroom I've been keeping tabs on and join the conversation using one of my online identities, sharing my made-up backstory. Express sympathy. Stoke rage. I wait until the conversation takes the right turn, so that it feels natural when I spill Heather's secret. I post the video clip. That gets them fired up. But then, 'fired up' is their default setting. They have lost loved ones, after all. By the time I'm done, they feel like it's all her fault.

I pour myself a whisky. It's amazing, what you can do with just a few key strokes. You can unleash a whole army.

CHAPTER 34

Heather threw out her arms and spun in a circle, sending Regent's Park wheeling around her, filled with a soaring sense of wonder. She was a model – an *actual* model! Talek, the photographer, dashed back and forth shouting instructions and encouragement.

'Give us a spin . . . lovely, lovely . . . now look at me over your shoulder . . . perfect, perfect . . . now throw out your arms and look at the sky . . . beautiful, beautiful.'

She'd taken an extra pill today, knowing the Casual Elegance shoot would be too hard on her leg otherwise. Which wasn't good, but it was the only way she could be here now, striking various poses among various roses while Talek looked at her as though she were a piece of art and marvelled at her every move. She giggled and flicked her long skirt from one side to the other, waiting for the photographer to pour out more praise, since he seemed to have a lavish supply. But this time he didn't react. Instead, he slowly lowered his camera, wearing a puzzled frown, staring at a point behind her shoulder. Heather turned to follow his gaze. A crowd armed with placards was moving through the park. Must be a protest of some kind. Animal rights activists maybe, heading to the zoo?

Then she read the signs and her confusion deepened. 'Down with Drugs'. 'High's not Mighty!' Weird. Why come here? Had drug dealers been taking over Regent's Park? But then she saw a woman marching straight towards them, features etched with rage. Her sign said 'Oxy Moron'.

A chill swept through Heather. The crowd was moving nearer, all of them wearing white T-shirts with photos across the front. *It's just a coincidence*, she told herself firmly. *In a minute they'll walk past and we'll continue the photo shoot.*

Except they didn't walk past. The crowd – easily forty of them – surrounded her like an angry swarm.

'You're supposed to be setting an example, you junkie bitch!'

'I heard what you said on your video! You should be put in jail!'

'Pill-pushing cow!' That last one shouted by a short, middle-aged woman whose T-shirt showed a photo of a teenage girl above the words, 'My Lucia. Took drugs, then taken by them'. She grabbed Heather by the arms and shook her with surprising strength. 'Stop it, stop it, stop it!' Her voice was a hybrid of anguish and fury. She turned to the people around her. 'We can't let her keep saying those things! More people will die, more families like ours will be destroyed! We need to make her stop!'

The crowd picked up the words, began to chant. 'Make her *stop*! Make her *stop*!'

Heather turned in a helpless circle looking for a gap, a way past the wall of rage-twisted faces, the signs brandished like weapons. But there was none; she was trapped.

'Let me go!' she shouted, eyes moving from one person to the next, searching for some sign of sympathy. The circle was getting tighter, pressing in. A couple of people were holding up their phones, filming her struggle to escape. 'Please! I haven't done anything!'

Then a hand appeared through a gap in the bodies and grabbed her wrist. Terror snatched Heather's breath away as she was dragged forward. But then she saw Talek's shocked face, his wiry body angled sideways, wedged between an elderly man and an overweight woman with a photo of an acne-spotted youth stretched across her stomach ('My Jake. Took drugs, then taken by them').

Heather clung to Talek's hand like a tow-rope as he pulled her out through the tight maze of bodies, the crowd jostling against her. She smelled BO, sun cream and a whiff of beer.

Then they were gone, replaced by empty grass and the rose bushes beyond. She had broken through.

There was a brief moment of relief, of open space and fresh air on her skin before Heather's attackers registered that she had been pulled from their midst.

'Hey! Come back here!'

Talek shot a frightened look behind them. 'Can you move faster?'

She laughed then, a harsh sound that was half sob. 'No. I can't.' He tried to hurry her along, but she was staggering and their pursuers could run. They would be caught in a matter of seconds. Engulfed. Probably beaten – or worse. All because of her lame, useless leg. Hopelessness overwhelmed her. She looked at the photographer, clearly terrified but still doing his best. 'I'm so sorry,' she said.

'Make her admit what she's done wrong!' someone shouted.

Heather stumbled and fell, landing hard on the grass. She covered the back of her head with her hands, bracing for the blows that she felt sure were about to rain down.

But then there were other voices, different voices, shouting from somewhere to her right.

'Leave them alone!'

'What the hell is wrong with you people?'

'I've called the police! They'll be here any second!'

She lifted her head, expecting to see the mob encircling her. But there was only Talek, bending down, offering her his hand. She took hold of it and he pulled her to her feet. Heather turned to see a line of people standing with their backs to her, shoulder to shoulder: good Samaritans, creating a human barrier between her and the angry crowd, keeping them at bay.

'Don't protect her!' shouted a woman on the other side. 'She's a junkie, popping pills and telling her followers they should do the same, making addiction sound glamorous. More vulnerable people will die if she's not stopped!'

Then a man's voice, calm, reasonable. 'You need to leave now, before the police arrive.'

As if to underline the point, a siren began to warble in the distance. Faint at first, but growing louder.

'We don't give a toss about the police!' a man with a neck tattoo shouted back. But Heather could see the mob was losing cohesion, gaps forming as they drifted outward, glancing in different directions. A woman at the back turned and walked swiftly away, onto the path that bisected Regent's Park, her 'Drugs = Death' sign resting against her shoulder. Another followed. Then another, moving faster as the sirens grew louder and then stopped, replaced by the sound of car doors slamming.

Neck Tattoo was the last to leave, retreating slowly backwards. The picture on his T-shirt looked like a younger version of him. 'My brother started taking the same pills as you after his surgery, until he took too many and ended up dead.' His voice shook. 'Your followers will do what you tell them and follow you into their graves.'

CHAPTER 35

Heather lay on the sofa with the curtains drawn against the reporters. She could hear them on the street outside, chatting amongst themselves.

The only other sound was the buzz of her handset, muted but vibrating against the coffee table. She should probably check it. No doubt Tessa would be trying to reach her, using someone else's phone – they'd agreed to avoid all contact on their F-phones – offering sympathy and support. But Heather didn't feel like talking to anyone right now. She couldn't face seeing the latest ratings update, telling her that her beautiful new life was coming to an end. She looked around at the marble fireplace and the sweep of French silk curtains, the Georgian chaise longue with its arched mahogany back. And the chandelier, like a cloud of diamonds floating above the room. When the payments stopped, she would have to leave this place. Then where would she go? Someone else was living in her old flat. And someone else was doing her old job. So she would be left with nothing when she breeched the 500,000 threshold. Which was sure to happen soon.

The oxy junkie. That's what they were all calling her. It didn't seem to matter that the drugs were prescribed, that she used them to tame her near-constant pain. All anyone saw was a woman swilling champagne and popping the same pills addicts used to get high. One of the papers had interviewed a medical expert who'd said that no responsible doctor would have kept prescribing such an addictive drug for such an extended period of time, that he should be investigated, perhaps have his licence revoked. So now there was a real risk that her supply would be cut off and she would be exiled to a world of endless torture. But she couldn't think about that right now. She needed to focus on finding out how this had happened – and who had set the wheels in motion.

The reporters had done much of the legwork for her, tracing the attack to a post on the message board of 'Families Fighting Drugs', or FFD, a militant group made up of people who had lost loved ones to narcotics. Her heart had lurched when she'd seen the name behind the post. 'A. Know'. There it was, proof that she had been brought down by the same troll who had driven Analise to suicide.

'Influencers do just that,' A. Know's post had said. 'They influence. And right now one of the most influential of them all is gobbling oxy and urging her followers to do the same – all while passing herself off as a role model. She will lead vulnerable young people down a dark path of destruction . . . unless we stop her. On June 13 at 2 p.m. Heather Davies will be near the Regent's Park rose garden, posing for a photo shoot that glorifies her druggie lifestyle. We must meet her there. Drown out her dark message with our own. Tell her how we feel and what we have lost, because of people like her.' There was a video attached labelled 'Heather tells fans why they should try oxy.' She'd clicked on it, expecting to see an AI-generated fake, but had instead found herself looking at a familiar clip: her own face lit with excitement, wearing the satin dress she'd bought for the Bond premiere.

'It transports you to a dazzling world where everything is exciting and beautiful,' she told the camera. 'Reality seems a bit flat and banal by comparison. It's an experience no one should miss out on.'

The interview from the cinema lobby. The videographer had DMed Heather the next day, thanking her for her contribution and sending a link to his YouTube page where all the clips from the premiere were posted. At least the press had figured that part out. The video had been debunked but her junkie status had not. Heather's 'Secret Oxy Shame' was all over the headlines.

She put one of the sofa cushions under her head as she lay looking up at the chandelier, mind working through the three questions the FFD post had raised.

Question one: how had the troll known where she would be? She'd told her followers about the shoot in a CelebRate post, but said only that it would happen 'in a park' – not which park or at what time. Maybe her sponsorship schedule was stored somewhere accessible to Triple F staff? It made sense. Winfluencer Sales would need to know her availability before booking club and restaurant appearances.

Second question: who had notified the press? They had arrived at the same time as the police, half a dozen of them, armed with cameras. Had Families Fighting Drugs summoned them? Or had the tip-off come from the troll, to ensure that news of her oxy use was spread across the nation's screens?

Then came the third and most important question of all: how had the troll known she took oxycodone in the first place? Because while she sometimes admitted to taking pain medication, she never revealed what type it was – or how regularly she took it. She wasn't quite sure why she'd kept it secret. Maybe because she knew the drug had a reputation, and didn't want people to get the wrong idea. Or because the pills were a constant reminder that the crash was still controlling her life. Or maybe she was simply afraid to think about her oxy use too closely. But whatever the reason, Heather hadn't told a single soul.

Until the night of the premiere.

She smelled again the scent of lilies. Heard the click of heels against marble. And a husky voice speaking.

I doubt it's worth the high.

Veronica Shulman.

*

Heather walked along the outside of the iron railings separating the pavement from the school's 'recreation zone', keeping an eye out for teachers. Eric always hung out alone in the corner furthest from the school building. Or at least, that's what he'd done when she was working here.

She wanted to speak to him before confronting his mother, to try and get a sense of what she was dealing with. Because she could think of only one reason for Veronica Shulman to use Heather's secret against her: maternal revenge. She had claimed not to blame Heather for getting her son suspended, that it was for the best. But that must have been an act designed to lower Heather's guard. Then she'd outed Heather as a drug user – just as Heather had outed her son. The Shulmans had strong ties to the Triple F, so it may have been possible for her to get hold of an unused company laptop. But there was one piece of the puzzle still missing; if Veronica really was A. Know, that meant she'd targeted Analise as well. And Heather was at a loss to come up with a motive for that.

Watch yourself, bitch. Or I'll make you sorry.

If Heather was right, that email hadn't come from Eric after all. His mother had sent it, using her son's computer. But she needed Eric to help confirm that theory. Her eyes darted among the teenagers playing table tennis, hanging out on the arched bridge in the 'Japanese garden', ducking behind the bushes at the far end of the 'zone' to furtively look at their phones. Eric had to be around here somewhere. Unless he was sick or bunking off school. What if—

Wait. *There.*

He was walking along the outer edge of the grounds, fingertips trailing along the bars of the railings. It struck her for the first time how lonely he looked, how isolated. He'd had a gang of boys backing him in class, jeering along with his antics. But at lunchtime, the others played football. Eric never joined them.

She stood waiting until he came within earshot. 'Hello, Eric.' She kept her tone light and friendly. He stopped and looked at her through the fence, wearing an expression of extreme wariness.

'What are you doing here, Miss? I thought you quit.'

'Just passing by.'

His fingers fidgeted along one of the bars. 'So you . . . what, saw me, your favourite student, and thought you'd come say hello?'

'Something like that. I did want to tell you that reporting you for bringing drugs to school – that wasn't personal. I would have done the same no matter which student it was.'

The familiar sly smirk. 'Except it turns out I wasn't the only one bringing drugs to the school. I used to get my weed from a dealer on your estate. Did you get your drugs from him too? His flat was well scruffy. I saw you coming home once, through his window. Bet you're glad not to be living in that shithole any more. Now you can afford dealers who deliver pills to your door on a silver tray.'

She'd forgotten how quick he was, how cutting. Heather looked down at the ground for a moment, centring herself.

'My pills are medicine, prescribed by a doctor.'

'Yeah. Just like Heath Ledger and Prince.' He shoved hands in his trouser pockets. She gritted her teeth, determined to stay cool, not let him get to her.

'What I'm trying to say, Eric, is that I was just doing my job and didn't wish you any harm. I genuinely want you to do well.' She took a breath, watching his expression closely as she said the next words. 'So I think your email was out of order.'

His face was blank. 'What email?'

'The one you sent me after you were suspended.'

One eyebrow rose, making his forehead crease: that look she remembered from her teaching groups when she was explaining a complicated idea. It was the look of someone who had absolutely no idea what she was talking about.

'How could I send you an email? I don't have your email address. And even if I did, I wouldn't bother. There was nothing to say.'

She stared at his face, looking for an evasive eye-flick, the twitch of a lip. But there was nothing. Unless he was an outstanding actor, Eric was telling the truth. Which meant her theory was correct: Veronica Shulman had played her, pretending not to care about her son's suspension – and the family shame that must have accompanied it – while sending threatening emails and plotting her revenge.

'That's odd, because I received a message from your computer. Maybe one of your parents borrowed it? Do either of them know your password?'

Eric looked at her as if she was completely mad. 'Course not! No one knows my password.' The sly smirk again. 'Wouldn't want anyone checking out my porn collection, would I, Miss?'

Typical Eric, trying to shock and embarrass her.

'Fair point,' she said breezily. 'I keep my password secret for that exact reason.' She had the satisfaction of seeing his eyes spring open in surprise.

Then, behind Eric's shoulder, she saw Steve emerging through the back door of the school. He stationed himself beside it, hands on hips, scanning the recreation zone. Damn. He was bound to come over if he saw her talking through the railings to her least favourite student. She needed more time so she could build a fuller picture of the woman she was dealing with.

'I met your mother,' Heather said. 'At a party.'

She watched Eric's reaction closely. Saw a small flinch.

'Oh. She likes going to parties. She likes going out generally.'

'She cares about you.' In the corner of her eye she could see Steve's head turning her way. 'She's protective. Mothers will do anything to defend their children, attack anyone who threatens them. It's instinctive.'

Eric's laugh had a bitter edge. 'I think that's just bears. The only thing my mother attacks is a G&T.'

Now Steve was shading his eyes with a hand, looking straight at them. Damn. She returned her attention to Eric, speaking quickly.

'Was she very upset about your suspension?'

He frowned. 'Why do you care? That was ages ago and you don't even work here any more.'

'It's just . . . I like your mother and was thinking of suggesting we meet up for a chat, but wasn't sure she'd be open to it, given the trouble I caused you. But I was hoping she might because the two of us recently lost a mutual friend. Analise Tetterson. Has your Mum ever mentioned her?'

Eric gave her a suspicious frown. He opened his mouth, but before any words came out, Steve appeared.

'Everything okay?' he asked, looking through the bars with a quizzical expression. 'What are you doing here, Heather? Shouldn't you—'

The school bell sliced the sentence. She'd forgotten how harsh that sound was.

'Hi, Steve. Actually, I wanted to speak to you.'

'So you decided to lurk around the playground instead of just sending a text?'

She pushed past the question. 'Do you have time for a coffee after work?'

He shrugged. 'Sure, if you can lower yourself to Joe's. Four-thirty?'

'Perfect.'

*

'He's lying,' Steve said, biting into his cheese toastie, talking as he chewed. 'He must have sent that email. Eric is in my computer class and I can tell you he is obsessed with security. We're talking multiple passwords that change all the time. It verges on paranoia. So unless his mother has a secret identity as an MI5 hacker, I don't see her getting into his computer.'

Heather shook her head. 'I saw the look on his face when I accused him. He had no idea what I was talking about. You're *sure* you got the right IP address?'

'Yes. That was the easy part. Getting the name was the

challenge, and I may have entered a bit of a grey area, legally speaking, so best not go into detail. The point is, I got it.'

He took his phone from his pocket, tapped and swiped at the screen, then slid the device across the table towards her.

'See for yourself if you don't believe me. I took a screenshot.'

'It's not that I don't believe you . . .' She picked it up. 'It's just . . . there has to be another explanation.'

The waiter, a ginger-haired man with an Irish accent, appeared beside them. 'Are you ready to order?'

Heather put down the phone and picked up the laminated menu, already knowing there was nothing on it she fancied. But she felt guilty taking up a seat and not ordering anything. Maybe a drink.

'Can I have a non-fat chai latte with extra cinnamon?'

Steve let out a snort of laughter and the waiter stared at her as if trying to work out whether or not this was a wind-up.

'We have coffee and tea,' he said.

She flushed. 'Sorry, force of habit. Just a coffee, please.' The waiter walked away and she scowled at Steve, who was still chortling. 'I forgot how basic this place is.'

'It never bothered you before.'

'I'd never tasted a chai latte before.' She picked up his phone, glanced at the screen, then held it out towards him. 'It's auto locked.'

Steve squeezed ketchup onto the side of his plate from a plastic bottle, ignoring the phone. 'Satan squared.'

'Excuse me?'

'My password. 666-666.'

'Ah. Very amusing.' She tapped it in and was rewarded with a screenshot showing a string of numbers and dots with a name and address below. Heather frowned. 'It says "Shulman E". Just "E". Not "Eric".'

Steve shrugged. 'So? What else would it stand for?'

'Edmond. Eric's father.' And suddenly, it all made sense. 'Edmond Shulman sent me that email.'

Steve put down the ketchup bottle and parked his forearms on the table.

'Just so we're clear – you're now saying that the head of the Shulman media empire decided to take a night off from pulling the levers of British economic power to threaten his son's teacher?'

She thought of Eric's father standing outside the head's office, dark eyes drilling into hers.

'Yes, that's exactly what I'm saying. Think of all the money he poured into the school just to make everyone think twice about clamping down on Eric's behaviour. I was the first person who refused to toe the line. The other students must have told their parents about his suspension: rich, important people gossiping about how the Shulman heir is a druggie, how his father failed as a parent. He would have felt angry, humiliated. Vengeful.' Her mind was working fast now, moving along a chain of possibility.

I'll make you sorry.

What if Veronica Shulman had gone home drunk after the party and spilled Heather's oxy secret to her husband, unaware of the strength of his animosity towards her . . . then Edmond Shulman had utilized that information to mobilize a mob against her? He could have exploited his position as a major shareholder to demand access to Triple F computer programs – and then used it to manipulate her DMs and settings. Was everything that had happened nothing more than a bully's revenge on the woman who'd dared defy his wishes?

But her theory came up against the same wall it had run into with Veronica: the fact that 'A. Know' had targeted not just Heather, but Analise as well. Why would a man like Edmond Shulman want to destroy the life of a beauty vlogger? It didn't make sense.

The waiter dropped off her coffee and Heather poured in sugar, drinking absently, barely noticing the burnt taste.

Steve sawed off a piece of toastie. 'Okay, let's say for now that Shulman really is out to destroy you. Does that mean he's responsible for the video on the anti-drugs site too?'

Heather's mouth pulled to one side. 'I don't know. He's the best suspect I have right now. But there are things that don't fit.'

'What do the police say? When will they know who's behind that post?'

'Never.' Heather grimaced at the memory of her last conversation with the officer in charge of her case. His polite sympathy. Her helpless frustration. 'The post stopped short of inciting violence, so technically it didn't break any laws. They've already tracked down and cautioned the people who physically came at me, so as far as the police are concerned, it's case closed.'

'Oh.' Steve put down his knife and fork. 'I'm really sorry. That sucks.'

'Thanks.' She dropped her eyes to the table, feeling defeated. Every time it seemed like she was getting somewhere, her search for answers hit a wall. And that search was the only thing keeping her mind off her problems – and the fact that #Heatheroxyaddict was trending on social media.

'Sod the police,' Steve said. 'We can solve this mystery ourselves, Scooby Doo style. Or maybe Sherlock Holmes style, since the Scooby gang only really deals with unscrupulous property developers.' He leaned down to rummage inside the canvas satchel at his feet, digging out a pen and plucking a paper napkin from the metal dispenser on their table. 'Let's start by narrowing down the suspect list. How many people have you told about your oxy use?'

'That's easy. One. Veronica Shulman.'

He nodded, jotting her name on the napkin with 'Friend? Family?' beside it. 'So if we rule out Eric, that leaves Veronica, her husband and any close friends she could have passed that information along to.' His thumb clicked the button on top of his pen, sending the tip in and out of its sheath. 'But I think the more likely suspect is your phone hacker. Have you ever mentioned taking oxy in a DM?'

'Definitely not.'

'What about emails?'

'No, never.'

'Triple F documents? Didn't you have to fill in a health declaration form of some sort when you joined the contest?'

'Yes, but I . . . left out the part about my medication, since I didn't see how it was relevant.' She drank her coffee in the pause that followed, avoiding his eye. 'I'm telling you, I have not written down a single word about my oxycodone use anywhere . . .'

Then her voice faded out as it dawned on Heather that this wasn't strictly true.

She stared out the window at the traffic creeping past, building towards rush hour, thoughts spinning.

No . . . It couldn't be . . . Could it?

'Even so,' Steve said, drawing her attention back to the table, 'I'm adding the hacker to the suspect list.' He jotted 'Phone hacker' on the napkin under 'Veronica Shulman/hubby/friends'. 'Because I find it hard to believe—'

Then the words stopped and his pen froze above the napkin. Steve's eyes were aimed at something behind Heather's shoulder. She turned round to see a man walking straight towards them, carrying his jacket at a strange angle. He was about Steve's age, overweight and unshaven, wearing jeans and a shirt in need of an iron. She had just enough time to wonder why he was carrying such a long jacket on a warm day before he whipped it aside like a magician, revealing the professional camera beneath.

Heather's stomach plunged. A paparazzi ambush. And she knew exactly how this scene would look: the fallen Triple F idol in a cheap café with an unknown, unkempt man, possibly her drug dealer. She should never have agreed to meet at Joe's, with its shabby tables and unflattering light. The photographer was probably from one of those terrible magazines specialising in photos of celebrities popping to the shops in the morning before they'd put on their make-up or with their skirts blowing up to reveal a patch of cellulite, helpfully circled in red, just in case the reader had missed it.

She combed fingers through her hair. Was her lipstick still on, or had it been washed away by the coffee? Too late to do anything about it now. She remembered Noah's advice for dealing with these situations; the trick was not to react, to maintain a serene facade no matter what. The last thing she needed was a viral photo showing her face twisted with shame and fury. The photographer raised his camera.

But he didn't aim it at Heather. He aimed it at Steve.

She stared in baffled disbelief as Steve's features performed a series of rapid shifts in the volley of clicks and flashes that followed, from shock to fear to anger, concluding with a look of grim determination. Then he lunged.

'Hey!' the photographer shouted, as Steve grabbed hold of the camera, wrestling him for control. 'Let go! That's my property!'

'Yeah, well, this is my face.' His voice was a snarl. 'And I do *not* give you permission to photograph it, so you can tell that to the lawyers at whatever shitty rag you work for.'

The ginger-haired waiter dashed out from behind the counter, then drew to a halt, clearly unsure what to do next. 'Stop this right now!' His eyes darted back and forth between the grappling men. 'Or . . . or I'll call the police!'

The photographer yanked his camera free and sprinted to the door, pausing on the threshold to give the waiter a nicotine-stained grin. 'No worries, mate. I was just leaving anyway.' Then he ran off down the pavement with the camera in his hand. Steve returned to his chair and sat down heavily, burying his fingers in his hair.

Heather stared at him, thoughts tumbling, trying to make sense of what had just happened. Why would a tabloid photographer target Steve?

I know who you are. And the things you did.

She'd done an image search after that strange encounter, curious to see who Jonnie Preston was – she'd assumed a criminal of some sort – and whether he and Steve really did have the same eyes. She'd found a decent-sized crop of John and Jonnie Prestons, most notably a world-class flautist, a child actor and the head of a defence company. But no one who resembled Steve. So she'd dismissed the incident as mistaken identity.

Now, though, it appeared she may have been wrong.

She toyed with a sugar packet, tipping the grains from side to side. 'You okay?'

'Yeah.' A weak chuckle. 'Sorry I lost my rag there. You know how I hate having my picture taken.' He picked up the remains of his toastie with his hands, biting into it and chewing slowly, taking his time. 'Now, where were we?' He looked down at the napkin, with its two lines of notes. 'Okay, so either a Shulman or a hacker.'

'Steve—'

'Or one of the Shulmans could have been in league with the hacker. Remember that big hacking scandal at Shulman Media? Actually, you probably don't, since you would have been a mere sprog. Shulman Media reporters broke into the phones of bereaved relatives and listened to their phone messages. It was a whole big thing.'

'Steve—'

He slumped back against the chair. 'Okay, fine. I'll tell you. The thing is . . .' He folded up the napkin, with its short suspect list. 'Have you heard of a TV programme called *Five's a Crowd*?'

'Of course. Who hasn't? It came out before my time but I remember bingeing on the box set when I was a kid. I had a crush on the oldest boy, what was his name?'

'Mackie. Yeah, everyone fancied him.' His face curdled. 'A total dick in real life.'

'How . . .' Then she stopped. Because pieces of the Steve puzzle were flying together. The contempt for celebrities. The resentment towards his mother. The sour certainty in his voice when he talked about life in the spotlight.

You might not be so desperate for fame if you actually knew what it was like.

'You were a child actor.' She stared hard at his face. 'Which . . . Were you . . . You're not . . . George?'

His lips pulled down at the corners as though the name itself tasted bitter. 'Yeah.'

She gestured towards the window. 'So that photographer . . .'

'I changed my name, but he's tracked me down somehow. They must be doing a "Where are they now?" piece. Either that or it's one of those clickbait things where they say "Remember that loveable lad from the telly? You won't believe what a fat bastard he's turned into".'

'You're not fat.'

'I used to be, a few years back. Why do you think all my trousers need belts?'

'Just FYI, I've heard there are these magical people who can make clothes fit better with a wave of their enchanted needles. They're called tailors.'

'I don't go in for such witchcraft. And anyway, I've already trademarked the too-big-and-belted thing.'

'Well, far be it from me to interfere with a man's trademark.'

That seemed to lighten the mood a bit. He managed a smile.

'Look, I know you felt like I was trying to burst your Triple F bubble, and maybe fame is a good thing for you, but for me it was destructive. It ripped my childhood apart. All I wanted was to be normal and go to a regular school, instead of being tutored on the edge of a set.'

Heather drank the rest of her coffee, watching Steve slumped against his seat, seeing him through the prism of fresh understanding. 'Is that why you decided to become a teacher – to experience the school life you'd missed out on as a child?'

He rolled his eyes. 'Thank you for your analysis, Dr Davies.' Then he laughed, a soft, bitter sound. 'But you know what? You may be right about that.' The waiter walked past and Heather asked for an orange juice; she'd hit her caffeine limit. Steve waited until they were alone again before continuing. 'Safe to say that my life was pretty dysfunctional back then. I changed my name at fifteen, after the glamour model I was dumb enough to think was my girlfriend gave a tell-all interview about taking my virginity. But there is one advantage to being a child star: you eventually grow into someone people don't recognize.'

'Until a tabloid runs a photo of you as an adult.'

He rubbed his forehead with his fingertips. 'Yeah. Hence my overreaction. Actually, sod that, my reaction, since I actually think it was fair enough.' He was quiet for a moment. 'But on the plus side, my miserable past does make me better equipped to offer advice on your current bad-press situation, since I'm a world-class expert on what *not* to do.'

'Thanks, but there's no fixing my situation.' Heather plucked a napkin from the dispenser, dabbing at a drop of spilled coffee and avoiding Steve's gaze. 'I've been written off as a druggie and a fraud. I'm nearly in the Drop Zone.'

'You've turned things around before. I do follow your progress, you know. You took a huge hit when your brother gave that interview. But then you bounced back stronger than ever.'

'I can't bounce back from this.' The weight of shame and sadness pressed down on her. The waiter arrived with her orange juice and she lowered her eyes to hide the liquid sheen there.

'Yes, you can,' Steve said firmly. 'You can and you will.' He stared out of the window again, but this time he looked thoughtful rather than morose. On the other side of the glass, freshly released office workers were moving along the pavement, overtaking cars now caught in rush hour's grip. The pollution level must have been bad because the sky had a sickly, yellowish tinge. When he looked at her again, the spark in his eyes told her that he'd thought of something. 'Okay, here's what you need to understand. Britain's celebrity culture is weird. The only thing people love more than tearing someone down is a redemption story, ideally with some serious hardship and soul-searching along the way. So you've been taking dodgy pills. Fine. Admit to that and say you didn't think of it as addiction, but now that you've learned the error of your ways—'

'What error? A doctor prescribed—'

He wagged a finger back and forth in front of her face. '*Now that you've learned the error of your ways* . . . you want to free yourself from them. But it's going to be a long, hard journey and you need support if you're going to make it. Which is why you're asking everyone to share it with you. Drag your followers along for the ride as you kick the habit.' He clapped his hands together, clearly pleased with himself. 'Easy-peasy.'

She took a small mouthful of her juice before putting it aside. Now that she'd grown used to freshly squeezed, anything else tasted stale.

'Giving up pain medication when you actually suffer from permanent, near-constant pain is *not* easy. Peasy or otherwise.'

Steve sat back in his chair and folded his arms across his chest. 'Then let me ask you this: if the pain is indeed permanent, do you plan to keep taking this hardcore and highly addictive opioid for the rest of your life?'

Heather opened her mouth to snap back a retort. Then closed it again as his words sank in. *Could* she imagine life without those pills? The thought filled her with horror. The pain always drew her to them. And if she was being completely honest with herself, there was something else there too, something separate from the pain: a pull, as if her blood was calling out for those chemicals.

A *need*.

'I'm an addict.' She said the words out loud. The rest of the country had been saying it, writing it, chanting it. But she hadn't believed it herself.

Until now.

'That could be the name of your blog,' Steve said. He was watching her closely from across the table. She blinked, her mind still grappling with the enormity of her realisation.

'Sorry, the name of my what?'

'Your blog. Or vlog, or whatever you decide to do. You could call it "I'm an Addict". Take people through your journey to get clean.' He polished off the last bite of toastie, washing it down with coffee. 'I'm telling you, this is the solution to your problem.'

Heather propped her chin on a palm as her mind circled this idea. Could there really be a way out of the corner she'd been forced into? She retrieved the orange juice and took a mouthful, noticing that her hand was trembling slightly. It had been doing that more and more often lately. Was it because of the pills? Was she developing a tremor that was only going to get worse as the months on oxy stretched into years . . . into decades? She put the glass on the table and held on to it with both hands, grip tightening as she reached a decision. Heather could feel adrenaline building in her blood: the fight-or-flight response. Well, she was done with flight. She raised her chin.

'I'm going to do it.'

'Do what? Give up oxycodone? Or start a vlog?'

'Both.'

CHAPTER 36

Who does the little bitch think she's fooling? I watch the post again, from the beginning. A ridiculous piece of theatre.

Heather, standing in her bathroom, opening the mirrored cabinet above the sink and taking out a vial of pills.

'So this is oxycodone,' she tells the camera, holding up the container. 'An opiate-based painkiller. I had multiple surgeries after my car accident. Skin grafts. Without these, I would have been in constant agony.' She takes a deep breath, as though steeling herself for what comes next. 'But I've been out of hospital for eleven months now. I still have pain . . . but my leg is as healed as it's ever going to be, so things won't get much better than they are now. Which means I have a choice. Either I keep taking these . . .' She shakes the container, making the pills rattle. 'Or I learn to manage without them. Accept the fact that having pain doesn't make me any less of an addict.' There is a pause as she stares intently at the container, her expression a mix of fear and yearning. Then it's back to the camera. 'My doctor suggested slowly scaling back, but I don't want to drag this out. I'm ready to start a fresh chapter. A clean one. So I've decided to go cold turkey. I'm scared. But also determined. It's going to be tough. I just hope I'm strong enough.' Heather pours the pills into the toilet and flushes, aiming the camera phone at the cistern as they swirl around the bowl a few times before disappearing. Then her face fills the shot again, nervous and exhilarated. 'Wish me luck.'

The vlog is posted on her CelebRate page under the heading 'Getting Clean: Day One'. Nearly a million views already, but that's probably just morbid curiosity, because her rating hasn't bounced back like last time. She has moved up – from twelfth to tenth – but she's still languishing near the bottom. Hardly surprising, given that this is her second attempt to recover from scandal and deception. People are more sceptical now. I read through the comments. There are some positive ones, but most are denouncing the video as a PR stunt.

'I felt bad for her when she went on TV and admitted her modest image was a lie and showed her gammy leg,' one said. 'But I'm not biting this time. #Foolmetwiceshameonme.'

I smirk. Fine, let her have her little vlogs. Everyone can see them for what they are. The desperate flailings of a woman caught in a downward spiral.

She can't save herself this time.

CHAPTER 37

Heather was trying not to snap at Tessa, aware that pain was putting her on edge, making her unreasonable.

'But this is an amazing opportunity,' she argued, resting her leg across the sofa seat. 'The only reason Sky is even offering me a slot is because they're doing a special on opioid addiction. I may not get another chance like this. You're seriously saying I shouldn't do it?'

Tessa's headshake was firm. Before winning the Triple F, she'd worked at a digital marketing agency, the head of a team responsible for getting new brands noticed. Now she was channelling that experience into 'Operation Redemption' – making feedback notes, working through options, planning their next move. 'It may seem counter-intuitive, but you need to trust me on this. You can't afford to look as though you've only been doing this to raise your profile and get on TV.'

Heather scowled, disappointed. It was day five of the video diary. Her viewers – one and a half million of them now – had watched Heather emerge from the hospital's outpatient clinic after she'd gone there seeking alternatives to pain medication. They had listened to her talk about her first Narcotics Anonymous meeting. And yesterday she had edited together a short video of her pain management session. She had followed Tessa's advice about not wearing make-up. 'This isn't about glamour,' she had told Heather earnestly, jotting down notes on the comments under the latest vlog. 'This needs to be real and raw.'

And the approach was starting to work. The negative comments were melting away as viewer numbers rose. But Heather's rating was slower to respond. Ninth. So people were listening, but still unsure – not yet willing to give her the vote of support that a follow represented.

'Okay, if not a TV interview, what *should* I do next?' Heather reached for the wine bottle on the coffee table, only to find it empty. She got up to get another one, sucking air through gritted teeth as her leg took the weight.

Tessa looked up from scribbling notes in the armchair opposite. 'You okay?'

'I'm fine. It's just . . . the pain is hard.' Heather dragged the side of a hand across her forehead. She'd been sweating a lot lately.

Tessa was watching her more closely now. 'It's not just the pain, though, is it? You're going through withdrawal.' Said in a different tone, the words might have thrown Heather on the defensive. But there was no sting of judgement there – only concern.

'Yes,' Heather said. 'I am.'

Tessa picked up her F-phone from the coffee table, aiming the lens at Heather, centring the shot.

'Talk to me about that. Be honest, no brave fronts. And don't hold anything back.'

'Are you seriously filming me right now? I look terrible; I'm sweating like a pig and I haven't even washed my hair.'

'I know. Trust me.'

She looked at Tessa, the firm set of her mouth as she channelled all her energy into trying to save Heather. The troll's plan to tear them apart had failed; they were closer than ever. She ignored the camera, seeing only the pale oval of her friend's face. Felt something open inside her.

Heather spoke without thinking, letting the words rush out, completely unfiltered.

'Everything hurts. It's like my bones are grinding against each other. And my leg feels . . . less like it's on fire this time, more as though there's a knife buried inside it, sawing into my muscles. I'm scared. Scared it's going to get worse. Scared that I won't be strong enough or brave enough to handle it. Scared that without those pills, I'll be trapped in a life of constant agony, barely able to walk. But also scared of the way that drug calls to me. Like my blood is screaming for it. I'm scared of the future, because it sometimes feels like there's no good way out of this.' She took a deep breath. 'But there's something else. Something equally strong, maybe stronger. Hope. Because I have to believe that this can end, that I *can* win somehow. And I know I'm not alone. I have a weapon in this battle.' She felt herself tear up, heard her voice catch as she looked Tessa in the eye. 'I have friendship.'

CHAPTER 38

'I know we're here to talk about our own problems,' Josie said, 'but can I just say that I think Heather is so brave.' There were nods from around the circle. Heather smiled at Josie, a new Winfluencer who'd been complaining about 'mean comments' targeting her nose, which was, unfortunately, rather on the large side. 'I actually cried watching your last vlog. Like, *actual* tears.'

'Thanks, Josie,' Heather said. 'This last week has been really hard, but I feel stronger for having gone through withdrawal and come out the other side. And I'm glad my story has encouraged other people to talk more openly about their struggles with prescription drugs.'

She glanced over at Elliot, who was watching this exchange with a look of extreme focus, as though it were a puzzle he was trying to solve.

'Yes, I think we can agree that Heather is a source of inspiration,' Noah said from his seat next to Elliot. 'Critics of the Triple F say that being a Winfluencer is all about displaying a perfect mask. But Heather has proved them wrong. She has taken off her mask and shown that vulnerability can be a form of strength. And although I know it's not the way things are usually done at these sessions . . .' he shot a sideways glance at Elliot, whose features remained still, betraying nothing, 'I think Heather deserves a big hand.'

Noah and Josie began applauding enthusiastically and the others quickly joined in. Heather looked around the circle at the beaming faces and clapping hands of everyone except Elliot, whose fingers remained tightly folded in his lap.

What are you up to, Elliot? she thought. *Are you using these sessions to steal people's secrets? Is it all part of some psychological experiment?*

When the applause had died down Elliot rolled his shoulders as if releasing trapped tension.

'What Heather has done in her videos can be very cathartic,' he said. 'By opening up about the things that scare us, we external-ize them, preventing them from growing and festering within. With that in mind, does anyone have something they'd like to share with the group? Perhaps a fear that's preventing you from achieving your goals, or anger that's—'

'Why don't we write it down?' Heather interrupted. 'In the Secret Space? That way we can think about what we want to say more carefully before deciding whether or not we're ready to take the next step by reading it aloud.'

'That wasn't really what I—' Elliot began.

'That's a good idea,' Josie said. 'I'm not great at words. Writing them down first would help me to get things right in my head.'

And now everyone was nodding and Noah was saying, 'Yes, an excellent suggestion,' so the decision was being taken out of Elliot's hands. Heather suppressed a grin of triumph. He must be hating this, control freak that he was. But his features remained perfectly composed as he said, 'Very well then, if you believe it would be helpful.'

'I do,' Heather said. 'I really do.'

*

Steve answered her call without bothering to say hello.

'So? Did it work?'

'Yes.'

She heard breath leave his lungs. 'Good. The trap has been baited. Now we just have to wait and see if anyone bites.' A pause. 'Three hours. Then we'll know.'

CHAPTER 39

I stare at the computer screen. I can't believe it. She's number one. Number one! A lying junkie with the whole country eating out of her hand. I stare at her face on the screen: hair greasy, gleaming with sweat, not a scrap of make-up. The Triple F is supposed to be about glamour and aspiration – not flaws and personal struggle. How has she changed the rules? My fingers shake as I pick up my glass and down a shot of whisky. If I don't stop this now, she could ruin everything.

I wipe my lips, take a deep breath, count backwards from five. True, things with Heather haven't gone to plan. But whatever brave front she's putting on now, I know the truth: that she's weak underneath, damaged. So eventually she'll crack, like the others. I close the page and open the special folder. Today's crop of confessions should have downloaded by now. Maybe there's something there I can use. I skip past the other files to the one with her name on it. Begin to read.

CHAPTER 40

Heather tapped nervous fingers against the dashboard as she gazed through the windscreen of Steve's Mini. They were in Harlesden, on a stretch of road untouched by gentrification: fast food, pound shops and a bookie advertising 'best odds guaranteed on UK & Irish racing'. The car was parked in a space meant for clients of a dental surgery, now closed for the night. Across the street, a group of teenagers in hoodies jostled each other in a good-natured argument outside a chicken shop.

Steve watched them through the windscreen. 'So who are you expecting to show up tonight?'

'The press. Maybe the police too.' Heather's palms were sweaty and she rubbed them against her jeans. 'If we're *really* lucky, we might even see the troll himself, watching the drama play out.'

Steve drummed his hands against the steering wheel. 'Mm, not sure about that last one. I think of him as more of a shadowy, puppet-master type, sitting in a windowless basement, pulling strings.'

'Even shadowy puppet masters have to get out of the house once in a while. Go for a lurk. And where better to lurk than on the fringes of some mayhem you've created?'

'Well, we'll know soon enough.'

Heather's new mobile made a beeping sound in her pocket. She and Tessa had bought pay-as-you-go handsets so they could contact each other without their Triple F mobiles. 'Burner phones', Tessa had dubbed them. 'Like criminals and spies.' There were just two numbers programmed into Heather's, each with its own shortcut button: press one for Tessa, two for Steve.

She read the text message in the window above the keypad.

What's happening?

Heather tapped out, **Nothing yet. Will keep you posted** before slipping the device back into her pocket.

Steve glanced at his watch. 'T minus four minutes. And no sign of anyone so far.'

'If no one shows up, at least we'll have learned something: that the troll isn't using the Secret Space after all.'

She took out her F-phone to keep an eye on the time, then couldn't resist rereading her email from Duncan – not that there was much to read. It had arrived in the morning, subject-headed 'Number One'. The message said, 'Congratulations. Well played. I will be back in London shortly. We must celebrate. D.'

Well played. What did he mean by that? Did he think her vlogs were a game, that her journey to get clean was nothing more than a cynical PR stunt? She'd thought about replying, asking for an explanation. Then decided against it. They could speak in person when he got back. Hopefully by then, she would finally be able to tell him about the traitor inside his company – with proof to back it up. Then they could decide together what to do next.

Across the street, the teenagers had moved on. A lone man stood in front of the chicken shop, wearing a bucket hat and eating a kebab.

'Nine fifty-eight,' Steve said. 'Show time.'

Heather pulled her bag over her shoulder and opened the door. 'Wish me luck.'

'Good luck. I'll be watching. Ready to jump in at the first sign of trouble.'

'Like a ninja.'

'*Exactly* like a ninja.'

Heather stepped out onto the road, wincing as she put pressure on her leg. In the car, the pain had been a scratch, easily pushed aside. But now it was sharpening its claws. She limped across the road and made her way past the chicken shop and a boarded-up pub, focusing her attention on the street corner up ahead, heart accelerating as her destination drew near. Soon she would know.

She reached the corner and stopped. This was a quieter stretch of road: no late-night fast-food shops with their spill of light and noise. The only businesses were a darkened hairdresser's and a job centre. Beyond lay a graffitied bridge over the railway. Heather checked the time on her F-phone – ten p.m. exactly – before returning it to her bag. She stood with her hands in her pockets, nerves stretched tight. Then came movement from the other side of the bridge. A figure appeared and began walking towards her across it. She sucked in a deep breath, thinking, *Here we go*.

The figure moved closer, a slight frame dressed in jeans and a raised hoodie, face draped in shadow. Heather waited. They were perhaps twenty steps apart now. She looked around to see if anyone else emerged. A dozen steps apart. Half a dozen. Still nothing. Maybe she was wrong. Maybe no one else was coming because no one had read what she'd written.

Two steps.

The figure in the hoodie stood facing her.

Contact.

'Hello,' Heather said. 'I believe you have something for me?'

She was answered with a nod, then a hand groping in a pocket, taking out a vial. She could see the outlines of pills pressed against its clear walls. Heather reached for the container. Her fingers touched the plastic.

And that's when it happened. She was hit by a volley of flashes as a photographer burst through the back door of a parked van. There was a TV cameraman too, moving in for the money shot of Heather, the reformed addict, caught with her hand in the oxy jar.

Triumph rose inside her. She had been proved right – because there was only one way the press could have known she would be here. She turned in a circle, scanned the small crowd that had suddenly appeared out of nowhere, then looked behind it to the street beyond. Until she found the person she'd been hunting.

He was standing in the doorway of a closed pawn shop, watching the scene unfold. At first she wasn't sure it was him. But then the TV reporter swung a light into position, briefly catching his face in the glare. Their eyes met and time seemed to stop as she stood, absorbing the fact of his presence. What it meant.

She mouthed his name.

Elliot.

CHAPTER 41

Elliot sat in his living room, mind replaying the scene on Station Road again and again. Heather's eyes meeting his. The look that had passed between them before she'd turned towards the cameras and turned on her smile. The person with her – a woman, as it turned out – had pulled down her hood and introduced herself as the head of 'SAD' – Students Against Drugs. Heather had opened the vial she'd been handed and pulled out the folded and tightly coiled banner crammed inside it, whose background photo of pills had been pressed against the vial's transparent walls, making it look as if the container was filled with oxycodone. The two of them had unfurled the banner, which said, 'Silence Kills: Let's Talk About Pills'. The student had told the journalists a very moving story about the day she'd come home from primary school to find her mother lying on the floor after taking too much Valium. Then she and Heather had shared a tearful hug while the photographers went into a feeding frenzy before a final statement from both of them about how pleased they were to be joining forces in this uphill battle.

Elliot didn't understand it. Heather was supposed to be meeting a drug dealer. Was it possible he had somehow misinterpreted her Secret Space entry?

He reread it, seeing the words through fresh eyes.

I can't handle the pain any more. It's too much, more than one human being should have to carry alone. I've tried managing without help, but it's too hard. So I've made a call, arranged a meeting in Harlesden. I'm at a crossroads, so it seems fitting that we're meeting where the road crosses the railway. Now I just have to get through today, keep smiling, try not to scream. At ten o'clock tonight, I'll get the help I need.

*

The intercom buzzed, the sound jolting him like an electric shock. Was that a delivery of some kind? He didn't remember ordering anything.

He went to the door, pressing the button mounted beside it. A voice entered the room, made tinny by the speaker.

'It's me. Open the door.'

Heather! What was she doing here? How did she even know where he lived? He heard her speaking to someone in the background, then a muffled male voice. Elliot caught the words 'wait in the car' before her voice became clear again. 'Let me in right now.'

He gritted his teeth, feeling trapped. She had obviously come here to demand an explanation for his appearance in Harlesden. What was he going to say?

'Just so we're clear, Elliot, I'm not leaving. I'll press all these buttons and hassle all your neighbours if I have to.'

He closed his eyes and counted backwards from five, releasing a deep breath as he buzzed her in. Then he opened the door to his flat and stood waiting on the threshold, pulse surging unpleasantly.

A moment later the lift pinged and Heather was marching towards him down the short stretch of corridor, moving with an uneven gait, chestnut hair unkempt, as if she'd been caught in a high wind, though the air outside was hot and still.

She hobbled past him into the flat, stopping in the middle of the living room, between the fish tank and the black leather sofa. She planted her hands on her hips.

'I know what you're up to, Elliot.'

His heart didn't so much sink as go into free fall, thumping into the pit of his stomach, where it lay like a stone. *She knew.* Somehow, she had worked it out. Heather's tone was acid. 'You read what I wrote in the Secret Space. And you called the press to shame me, thinking I'd be caught on camera in the middle of a drug deal.'

'What? No!' He moved to stand directly in front of her, straightening his spine and raising his chin, hoping to reverse the power dynamic. 'I went because I thought you were in trouble and I wanted to help.'

Her lips pulled sideways into a sneer. 'Well, there's only one way you could have found out I would be there and "in trouble". By reading my Secret Space entry.'

Elliot flinched. His worst fears were coming true. He tried to deflect the conversation, to buy himself time to come up with an explanation.

'As long as we're explaining our movements, care to tell me how you know where I live?'

'From a magazine interview. It mentioned your 'iconic' building. And your name is beside the bell. Now quit stalling and answer me.'

So much for throwing her onto the back foot. He scratched his jaw, trying to think what to do next. She was going to ruin everything, unless he found a way to manage the situation. To manage *her*.

'Okay, yes, I admit that I . . . glanced at what you wrote. To see how you were coping. I misinterpreted your entry and thought you were about to relapse. So I went to Harlesden to talk you out of it and offer my help – my *professional* help. But as for the press . . . that had nothing to do with me. I thought you'd contacted them yourself to record your PR stunt.'

Heather's laugh was scornful. 'You're unbelievable. Are you seriously trying to portray yourself as some sort of . . . good Samaritan?' She spat her next words. 'How *dare* you, Elliot! You pretended the Winners' Circle was a safe space where we could let go of our secrets, when in reality you were harvesting them to use against us.'

'Really, Heather. I think "against us" is a bit strong.'

'Are you bloody joking? You guilt-tripped Analise into a mental breakdown and made a violent mob attack me!'

'What? No! Okay, I admit that the Secret Space entries are downloaded into a file. But that wasn't even my idea. The app was set up that way so the Triple F could anticipate and manage PR risks; there are more than a dozen of us with access. I know it's a bit of a grey area ethically . . .' this was met with a high-pitched laugh that made him wince, 'but it does allow me to better understand and help people.'

Heather fixed him with a cold, unwavering stare. 'Help people,' she echoed.

She limped towards the large dining table near the back of the flat, a slab of black wood supported by two stainless steel

X's. Heather took a sheath of papers out of her bag and began spreading them across the table's dark surface like a dealer with a deck of cards.

'So are these the people you've helped?'

He went to stand beside her, eyes moving across the news clippings, jumping from one headline to the next.

Drink-Driving Blamed for Triple F Horror Crash

Tragic Teddy: Former Social Media Star Dies of Heroin Overdose

'The Pressure is Killing Me': TF's Tiffany Withdraws From CelebRate

He was, of course, well acquainted with all of these cases; they were part of his project, after all. But seeing them laid out together like this, while Heather glared accusingly, made Elliot's stomach squirm.

'Care to explain how, exactly, these people were helped?' She folded her arms over her chest, wearing a 'case closed' expression.

He cleared his throat, waving a hand towards the cuttings. 'Well, as you know, sudden fame creates a huge amount of upheaval in a person's life. It's hardly surprising that some winners buckle under the pressure.'

'All of them were in the Winners' Circle. Quite a coincidence, don't you think?'

'Not really. They would have been drawn to it precisely because they were struggling.'

She banged a fist against the table, making his pulse jump.

'Oh come *on*, Elliot! Give up! I've figured it out. You used a support group to steal people's secrets and then terrorize them until they broke. I'm guessing it's some sort of sick psychological experiment you've devised to see how much pressure a person can withstand. I used to think you were just a selfish coward. But now I see that you're something far worse. You're a monster.'

Elliot's mouth fell open. 'Jesus, Heather, how can you possibly . . .' He stopped. Took a breath, gathering himself. 'Okay, I'll tell you the truth.' Another breath, deeper this time. 'I'm writing a book. A psychological study of sorts, but in a form accessible to the layperson. About the damaging impact of sudden, unearned fame.'

There was a pause. She looked as if he'd thrown a bucket of ice over her, leaving her blinking and disoriented.

'A book,' she repeated. 'Really?'

'Yes, really. I have a three-year NDA . . .' Seeing her blank expression he added, 'Non-disclosure agreement. All Triple F staff sign one. But once I've gathered all the case studies and information I require, I'm going to resign and spend three years working on it. I believe my book will have mass appeal. Because this type of celebrity is a relatively new phenomenon, one that hasn't been written about with any depth or expertise. My working title is "Toxic Fame".' He saw disbelief scrawled across her features. 'Here, I'll show you.' He strode across the living room to his study on the other side of the fish tank, opening the door that led into the small, windowless space. Heather appeared on the threshold a moment later, eyes moving along the row of photos pinned to the wall. Just as well he'd decided not to put hers there.

'These people are my central focus, the most compelling cases.'

He waved his hand towards them, hoping to draw her attention away from the stack of folders beside his computer. No such luck. She picked up the top folder, flipping it open.

'Don't touch that,' he snapped. 'It's private client information.'

Too late. She was already scanning the pages inside, eyes widening. 'These are Triple F finalists' files – the psychometric tests and background reports! This stuff is never supposed to leave the file room in HQ . . . and you're telling me you're putting it in a *book*?'

Elliot cleared his throat. 'I understand why you might disapprove of my decision to draw on private material. But I don't plan to use it in a way that would identify the person it's linked to. Unless I get permission, of course, but there's no point thinking about that until further down the road.'

'So these stolen files—'

'Not stolen. Copied.'

'Where are the originals?'

'I returned them to the file room.'

Heather made a scoffing noise. 'Yeah, right.' She walked her fingers down the neatly stacked cardboard spines. 'You're seriously hoping to convince me that this is all just research material for a book?' Scepticism steeped the words.

'Take a look at my introductory chapter if you don't believe me. It's still very rough, but you get the idea.' Elliot bent over his keyboard, logging in and clicking on the file labelled 'Toxic Fame'. Then he watched Heather's face as she leaned towards the screen, eyes moving along the lines of text.

Fame is as old as humanity. For as long as there has been exceptional talent – whether as a caveman hunter or virtuoso pianist – there have always been those who were elevated above their peers, admired and envied. But only recently has this status become uncoupled from flair or expertise, creating a new breed of celebrity: those described as 'famous for being famous'. But without the underpinning of talent, this fame is wholly dependent on the whims of a fickle public

Elliot was hoping she'd say something about the content or writing style, but instead she returned to the folders, picking them up one by one, reading the names on the covers before placing them aside to form an untidy pile, corners sticking out at random angles. Elliot fought off an impulse to line them up, knowing it would only inflame her.

She had almost reached the bottom of the stack when she froze, staring at the cover of the folder in her hand. He could see the name: Analise Tetterson. Heather opened it and began flipping through, pausing when she reached the background file.

'Anorexia as a teenager.' Her eyes moved across the page. 'No mention of a child, but I'm assuming you know all about that from the Secret Space.' Elliot stayed silent, not wanting to add fuel to the fire. Of course he knew about the girl. Analise had written about her incessantly. Another page flip. 'And look, it's right here in black and white, "periods of depression"!'

He cleared his throat. 'Yes. Although she did say none of the episodes were recent.'

Heather flipped to the end. 'Where's the screener's assessment?'

She held up the sheath of documents, shaking the pages in front of him. 'It's not here. Where did you put it?'

Elliot lifted his shoulders. 'None of the files I copied contained assessments. Management must store them separately.'

'No, they're supposed to be at the back of the folder.' Her tone was inexplicably certain.

'Well, they weren't at the back of these ones.'

She returned Analise's documents to the folder and then tucked it inside her handbag, giving him a look that dared him to tell her to give it back. Then he watched her flip through the last few folders in the stack, frowning when she reached the end.

'Mine's not here.'

'No. I had thought about including you, given the challenges you've faced. But in light of our past relationship, I decided against it. Objectivity is crucial.'

She perched on the edge of his desk, folding her arms. He had knocked her off her stride by telling her about the book, bought himself some breathing space. But he could see she was regaining her mental footing.

'Really?' She leaned on the first syllable. 'Then why is my file missing from the—' She stopped, appearing to reconsider her words, started again . . . 'How can I believe anything you say after you lied about the Secret Space entries being deleted, then violated my privacy by reading what I wrote there? Tonight is proof that you've been snooping around on me, including me in your sick experiment.'

'I told you, it's not an experiment. It's a research project. And as for reading your entries, I admit to having used them as a therapeutic resource. Access to concealed information enables me to help patients more effectively, offering targeted treatment that wouldn't be possible otherwise.'

'*Treatment?* Please. You use people's secrets to troll them until they break. Is that to make your book more exciting? It's not much of a story if everyone goes off and lives a quiet life after their six months are up. Far more interesting if they fall apart or get attacked by a mob. A mob incited by *you*.'

'How many times do I have to say it? I had nothing to do with any of that. This information is for research. Nothing more.'

She moved to stand right in front of him. So close he could smell her breath. Minty. Her eyes narrowed.

'Okay, let's just pretend for a moment that I believe you. It still doesn't explain the assessments.' Heather yanked a photo from his wall, tearing it between the pin and the edge of the page, making him wince. She held it under his nose: inflated lips and artfully applied make-up. Analise before her breakdown.

'She was let through. Despite obvious red flags in her background report. Flags *you* chose to ignore. Because you've been manipulating this entire process, letting vulnerable people through, knowing they would fall apart. Instead of doing what you're supposed to do, which is protect them by keeping them out.'

And suddenly, Elliot had had enough. He was a trained psychologist, a respected professional. What did she know about the work he did? He snatched the photo of Analise from Heather's outstretched hand and laid it on the keyboard, smoothing the edges where the pin had ripped it.

'That is outrageous, insulting and completely untrue. I didn't assess Analise. There are only two files here that I recognized as mine, both of which I rated amber. But having read Analise's file, I agree with you that she should have been red-lighted. One of the other screeners must have made a mistake. A serious mistake. But it wasn't me who made it.'

Heather's voice was quiet. 'She might have lived a long, happy life if she hadn't won the Triple F.'

Elliot leaned against the wall beside the desk, suddenly tired. 'I'm just one of three screeners, so you can't blame me for every vulnerable candidate that makes it through. And the psychologists don't even have the final say. We just rate the finalists as green, amber or red and then send the files up the executive chain. We don't even receive the names or photos of the candidates we're assessing. So aside from the two whose background information I recognized among these,' he waved towards the stack of files, 'I couldn't tell you which Winfluencers I've assessed.'

Heather was quiet for a moment as she appeared to consider this.

'What about the taglines? Do you see those?'

Elliot pursed his lips. 'Yes. The theory is that the candidate might unconsciously reveal something through the slogan. But in reality they are banal and meaningless.'

'What did you think of mine?'

'I didn't do your assessment. I would have recognized your history from the background report.'

'You're lying. I know for a fact that you screened me. And you're wrong about the taglines. I chose "Class Act" because my teaching career was part of my identity. It meant something.'

Elliot blinked. '"Class Act"? That . . . that was *you*?'

She scoffed. 'You're seriously trying to pretend you didn't know?'

'I didn't.' His forehead creased. 'But I do remember the tagline. "Class Act", the trainee teacher. It couldn't have been you, though; there was no mention of a parent committing suicide, nothing about a car accident or years in hospital.'

And for the first time since she'd come through his door, Heather looked flustered. Her face reddened and her gaze dropped. 'Yes, I . . . decided those parts of my life weren't the Triple F's business.'

He gave her a level stare. 'In other words, you lied to improve your chances of winning.' He was starting to feel better now, back in control. 'That's fraud, Heather. Let's hope no one at the contest finds out or I shudder to think of the consequences.' He let the implied threat hang in the small space, knowing she was smart enough to read his message: *If you tell on me, I'll tell on you.*

It worked. She fell back a step, settling on the edge of his desk again, stretching out her leg. When she next spoke, her voice had lost some of its heat.

'So tell me, Elliot, what did you think when you read my file?'

He squinted, casting his mind back. *Class Act.* They stuck in your head, those bloody catchphrases.

'I thought, this is a young woman without a strong support system. Father, deceased. Mother living somewhere remote. The Orkney Islands?'

'Yes.'

'I thought she lived in Wales?'

'She moved last year.'

Elliot sucked in his lips as he probed his memory. 'I thought, she has a sibling, but they're clearly not close. No real social media experience. A recent move and a new job, so disrupted peer groups. And an unexplained gap in the timeline.'

'That sounds like a lot of red flags,' she said softly. 'And yet you green-lighted me.'

'No,' Elliot shook his head firmly as his memory fleshed out the final details, adding in the moment of judgement. 'I didn't.'

'Ah. So you rated me amber and the Triple F decided to take a chance anyway. Why? What was it about me that they liked so much?'

'That's not right either.' He squeezed the back of his neck, seeing himself on the sofa holding a pen above those three boxes. Green. Amber. Red. Thinking about the power he'd held in that moment: a young woman's future in his hands. 'I had no idea it was you at the time, but I do recall your assessment, and I know I didn't give you amber either. I couldn't risk it with so little support and signs of deception. So I red-lighted you.' He watched her face as the implication of his words sank in, saw the look of confused disbelief. 'That's an automatic ban – no ifs, ands or buts. But you won anyway.'

CHAPTER 42

'That's mental.' Steve said, after Heather had filled him in on Elliot's revelations. He took a swig from the bottle she'd handed him then pursed his lips in disgust, looking at the label. 'What the hell have you given me?'

'I don't know. Something experimental from a Welsh micro-brewery.' Heather collapsed onto the sofa with a yawn. It was late and she was exhausted. But she'd invited Steve in anyway so the two of them could talk through the night's events while the memories were still fresh. 'They're sponsoring me in the hope of attracting more women.'

Steve had driven her to Elliot's flat straight after the impromptu press conference in order to catch him off guard, not give him time to think up an explanation for his appearance in Harlesden. He had wanted to come with her to the penthouse 'just in case', but Heather had insisted that he wait in the car and let her confront Elliot alone.

Now, two hours later, Steve was seated on a box labelled with the name of an interior designer she'd never heard of, drinking beer as they tried to make sense of everything that had happened.

'Why don't you come join me here on an actual piece of furni-ture?' Heather said, patting the sofa beside her before returning her attention to the press cuttings she'd shown Elliot, now spread across her coffee table, alongside the copy of Analise's file.

'I'm good here. I like thinking outside the box.' She groaned and he smiled around the neck of the bottle, shuddering a moment later as the beer entered his mouth. 'God, that's rank.' He put the bottle down on the box. 'Okay. Let's review your theory.'

'My *facts*, you mean.'

'Facts you are using to construct a theory. Fact number one . . .' he held up a finger, 'you were allowed to win despite having been deemed an unacceptable risk.'

'Not just me,' Heather said. She waved a hand above the news cuttings. 'I'll bet most of these people were red-lighted too. Which explains why their assessments were removed. Someone let them through, knowing they would eventually buckle under the strain.'

'Okay, let's move on to fact number two.' He held up another finger. 'Your ex has been sneaking a peek at the Winfluencers' secrets. And he showed up, along with the press, when he thought you were meeting a dealer.'

'He claims he went there to talk me out of it. And swears he wasn't the one who contacted the press.'

Steve snorted. 'Well, he would say that, wouldn't he? Are you sure you're not giving him the benefit of the doubt because you still fancy him?'

'God, no.' She grimaced. 'He says he's been using the Secret Space information for a . . . separate project. It *could* still be him, but . . .' She shook her head. 'I really don't think so. Which means someone else at the Triple F has been letting vulnerable candidates win and then pushing their buttons. The same person who hacked mine and Tessa's DMs to engineer our fight. Presumably because once I'm isolated, I'm easier prey.'

Steve rubbed his eyelids. '*Why,* though? What would motivate someone at the Triple F to sabotage their own contest? Unless . . .' His forehead contracted in thought.

'Unless what?'

'Well . . . executives and shareholders must save a bundle every time a contestant dies. No more lifetime payouts.'

Heather took a first sip from her own beer bottle before quickly setting it aside. Steve was right; it tasted disgusting. 'So you're saying the Triple F promises winners money for life, then tries to drive them into an early grave . . . as a *cost-cutting measure*?'

'Well, yeah, pretty much. It's been all over the news that the Triple F is trying to turn itself into a global franchise. Getting some of those lifetime payouts off the books would make the company look more profitable, and therefore more attractive, business model-wise. Plus TV detectives always say you should follow the money.' Heather could feel herself resisting Steve's theory, blocking it with walls of scorn. But was that because she truly didn't believe it was possible – or because she didn't like the direction it was taking her? Noah's voice echoed in her memory.

There's this other side to Duncan . . .

She gave her head a sharp shake. 'No,' she said firmly. 'This isn't about money.'

'Okay. What *is* it about, then?'

'Psychological manipulation for the sheer sport of it? A mega-lomaniac's power trip?'

'Riiiiight. So you're going with cold-blooded psychopath – a *Silence of the Lambs* type thing?'

'A toned-down version. Less eating people.'

'I'm not convinced those game-playing psychopaths actually exist outside of Netflix. In the real world, there's usually a boring,

332

sensible motive. But let's assume for now that it's not your shrinky ex and head straight to fact number three . . .' Steve picked up his bottle, then thought better of it, putting it back down. 'We are going to catch the bastard.'

Heather lifted an eyebrow. 'That's a fact now, is it?'

'Yes. If this really is the same person who messed around with your DMs, then chances are all your messages are being read, as well as your secret sesh stuff. So we can use that to lure this toerag out of hiding.'

'Lure . . . how exactly?'

He held up a finger. 'Shh. Genius at work.'

Heather rolled her eyes, suppressing a giggle. Honestly. But a look of intense focus had taken hold of his features so she stayed quiet, watching Steve's eyes flicker back and forth as if seeing a scene play out in front of him. He cracked his knuckles – God, she hated that sound – and nodded a few times, as though agreeing with his own thoughts. Then he turned to her wearing a wide grin of pure triumph.

'We are going to draw this troll-person to an isolated location, where you will dupe them into confessing while I film the whole thing from a secret hiding spot.'

'Right, because London is so well known for its isolated locations and secret hiding spots.'

'I see your cynically raised eyebrow. But I happen to know the perfect place.'

CHAPTER 43

'I used to love being by the river,' Heather said, watching the Thames flow past. She turned towards Steve, who was crouched on the other side of the floating dock, fiddling with the cover of the speedboat moored to it. 'When I was little my family would go for lunch on the bank in Putney and I always brought my swimming costume, hoping my parents would let me swim across. But they never did.'

Steve yanked at one of the cover's zips, frowning as it remained stuck. 'Just as well. You wouldn't have made it.' He wiped his sweat-glazed forehead. The sun was dropping towards the horizon but the built-up heat still hung in the air, refusing to budge.

'Yes, I would have,' Heather said. 'I was a very strong swimmer. I even won medals.' *Before I learned to hate the water*, she thought but didn't say. She turned her gaze to the riverbank, with its messy piles of building materials and tarpaulin-covered machines. An old furniture depot was being redeveloped into waterfront flats, diverting pedestrians away from the river to a road behind the construction site. Heather and Steve had ignored the 'Men Working' sign blocking the path, picking their way over stacks of bricks and around a small cement mixer, a major undertaking now that she wasn't using oxy. Steve gestured towards the water without rising from his crouch beside the boat. 'Don't let the innocent surface fool you. It's okay further inland, but this part of the Thames is dangerous: the tides are really strong, and the uneven bottom makes for nasty currents and undertows. An entire graduation class was swept away around here in the Eighties, when their party float sank. They weren't far from shore, but even so, only a few survived. The rest were dragged under.'

'Jesus.' Heather's gaze returned to the river's gently rippling surface, thinking of those long-ago graduates flailing in dark currents, fighting for air as the water closed over them. And just for a moment, she was back in the car, in those last few seconds before the coastguard arrived. The water was right below her face by then, so she'd had to hold her breath with every wave, gasping for air in between, wondering each time the water smothered her whether this would be the wave that didn't recede, whether she had just drawn her last breath.

She gave her head a shake, pulling herself back into the present, taking comfort in the solidity of the boards beneath her feet. The dock they were standing on had been built as a mooring point for a floating seafood restaurant – gone now, brought down by a high-profile bout of food poisoning. Steve had chosen this location because of something a woman from his pub quiz team had said to him, that getting to her speedboat was a nuisance now that the towpath was closed off. And that she found walking home afterwards unnerving, because there was never anyone else around. She let Steve borrow the keys to the dock gate after he'd told her he loved fishing and it sounded like a perfect spot to angle for carp.

Steve gave a shout of victory as the zip finally came unstuck. He opened the side of the cover nearest the dock, throwing it back to reveal a steering wheel with two seats behind it. 'I'll film from here.' He indicated a space behind the seat nearest the dock. 'The range on the microphone is good, so sound shouldn't be a problem. Try and position yourself so that he turns towards the boat. We want to be able to see his face.'

See his face.

She shivered in spite of the heat. Was she really going to stand on this very spot, staring into the eyes of the person who had destroyed so many lives . . . and who had tried to destroy hers? The thought set off an electrical storm in the pit of her stomach. A wave of unease suddenly swept over her, a powerful sense of having overlooked something. Something important.

We need to get out of here now, before it's too late.

She gave her head a sharp shake, trying to toss the thought away. She was being paranoid, letting fear hijack her imagination.

'He might not even show up,' she said, more to calm herself than anything else.

'He will if you're right about him reading your DMs.'

Heather took out her F-phone, reading back through the carefully worded messages she and Steve had exchanged.

Steve: Wish you'd share the deets about the 'undeniable proof' you're giving this hotshot hack.

Heather: You'll find out soon enough. Everyone is going to learn the truth about the contest being rigged. Plus he can use my evidence to track/ID the troll.

Steve: 100% sure you don't want me to come with?

Heather: Thx but no. I need to do this alone. Will get there at 8

to do a recce, double-check there are no CCTV cameras or people etc before he comes at 9. I need to show my face at tonight's mixer afterwards but will swing by yours when done for full debrief.
Steve: OK. Promise you'll be careful?
Heather: Promise

*

She slipped the phone back into her skirt pocket. 'He could send someone else to do his dirty work, like he did with the anti-drug group.'

'He won't.' Steve reached inside the pocket of his thin water-proof jacket, taking out a tiny, clip-on microphone. 'That was different. He was just using those people as a weapon to attack you. This time he thinks you've got something that could incriminate him. He won't want anyone else getting hold of it.'

Her bag strap slipped down her shoulder and she moved it over her head so that it was slung diagonally across her chest. 'Of course, you're right. I'm just nervous.' Heather tried not to think about the pain screaming inside her leg. At least it had eased since the morning. She had woken up feeling as though her nerves might actually be tearing, that they'd been pulled so tight they were starting to fray, like strands of rope.

Steve handed her the microphone and she attached it to the vest top she was wearing under her blouse, so that the tip jutted through the buttonhole. The vest and the blouse were both black, as per Steve's instructions, to camouflage the mic.

Then he stepped from the dock onto the speedboat, making it sway in the water as he crouched down to take his position behind the seat. She helped him close the boat cover back up, leaving only a tiny gap between the two zips for the phone's camera lens. Heather checked her watch. Seven-fifty. The troll would be expecting her to arrive in about ten minutes . . . and he would want to get to her before the journalist did.

Heather's pay-as-you-go phone rang in the pocket of her skirt, making her jump.

Steve's name appeared on the screen. She looked at the boat as she answered, but couldn't see him under the cover.

'Hello,' his voice said. 'I'm going to stay here now, just in case he shows up early. Let's test the range. Can you walk to the far corner of the dock and say something?'

She went to the edge of the wooden platform, trying not to think about the tide pulling at the water just below her feet. This was the only dock in sight, but Heather knew there were others further along, linking multimillion-pound riverfront homes to their owners' private boats. There had been a time, not so long ago, when the thought of people enjoying that sort of wealth and luxury would have brought an acid twist of envy.

She turned, eyes pausing on the river wall, with its green stain marking the tideline, now perhaps half a metre above the water's surface.

'Testing, testing . . . come in, Steve. Do you think the tide's going in or out?'

She looked towards the boat. There was a pause. He didn't answer her question, but made a hand signal through the gap in the zip to let her know the sound had worked.

She put the pay-as-you-go on mute – she didn't want to risk having it ring when the troll was here – and tucked it back in the pocket of her skirt with her F-phone. Then she stood facing the riverbank. She had the sense of standing on the border between 'before' and 'after'. Because in a moment, someone would appear on the shore. Perhaps they would be familiar – another Winfluencer whose smile she knew from posts and parties. Or a stranger who, for reasons she couldn't comprehend, had set out to destroy her. Or – and she felt something turn in the pit of her stomach as she allowed the thought in – someone who knew her intimately.

Her eyes searched the blocked-off towpath, the throb in her leg keeping time with the beat of her heart.

CHAPTER 44

There she is, standing on the raft, wearing one of her long skirts. Amazing how she managed to turn that disgusting leg into a selling point. There's a bag slung across her chest. Whatever evidence she has must be in there. I'm going to have to tread carefully. She's tricky, Heather. Unpredictable.

She's not looking in my direction, focusing instead on the blocked towpath. I'm approaching round the side of the old furniture depot, skirting along the wall. There's no one else around. She chose her location well.

Then her head finally turns and her eyes find me. I'm close enough now to see the surprise on her face. I push through a gap in the orange plastic barriers separating the site from the path, being careful not to spill anything from the coffee cup I'm carrying. Then it's just a few more steps until I'm through the gate and walking down to the dock.

She cocks her head, a puzzled frown creasing her forehead.

'Noah,' she says. 'What are you doing here?'

CHAPTER 45

Damn, Heather thought. Noah was going to ruin everything.

He was smiling at her as he walked down the ramp, carrying a takeaway cup. A sense of unreality washed over her. What on earth was he doing, strolling up to her with a drink as though they were meeting for a chat in the Blue Lounge?

A breeze stirred the heat-baked air, ruffling his hair as he stepped down onto the dock.

'Hello, Heather.' He handed the cup across. 'I brought you a drink: non-fat chai latte, extra cinnamon. Just the way you like it.'

'Oh. Thanks.' She looked down at the cup as she tried to regain her mental footing. She had been completely focused on seeing the troll, senses on heightened alert, leaning towards the moment of revelation. Noah showing up out of the blue had crashed into all that, knocking her off course. She drank some of the latte, which was sweet and warm.

Just the way you like it.

He had obviously seen her location on Friend Finder and come looking for her. Why? Had he found out about her plan and come to offer help? Or the opposite – to talk her out of it, warn her not to put herself at risk? But no, that couldn't be right.

Aside from Steve, the only person who knew what she was really up to tonight was Tessa, who was providing her cover story at tonight's mixer – the other Winfluencers were bound to notice her location – saying Heather had gone to check out a boat she was thinking of buying.

'What's going on, Noah?'

He stared at her intently, as though searching for something behind her eyes. Then he put his hands in his pockets and sighed.

'Look . . . Dr Leyton called me. He's concerned about you.'

'I'm sorry, he *what*?'

'He says your behaviour has become erratic and he's afraid you might fall off the wagon. So when I checked to see if you were on your way to the mixer and instead saw you miles away in a remote location . . . well.' He shook his head. 'Let's just say I was worried. I came to make sure you're not about to do anything . . . self-destructive.'

'Why would . . . I can't believe . . .' Fury and frustration tore through her. What the hell was Elliot playing at? Was this his way of undermining her credibility, so that he could claim she was unstable if she grassed him up to the Triple F? Bastard! He already had her background report, with its glaring omissions. Wasn't that enough? She breathed in through her nose, exhaling through her mouth, trying not to let her anger show. It would only feed into Elliot's narrative. 'Look, Noah, I'm touched by your concern. But Dr Leyton is wrong. I'm fine. Truly! I'm just meeting someone here. *Not* a drug dealer. And if you don't mind, it's . . . kind of private. So I'd really appreciate it if you could just trust that I am 100 per cent okay and leave me to it.'

She stole a glance up at the riverbank to see whether anyone was arriving. But it was deserted. A fresh breeze rode in off the water, pushing a lock of hair across her eyes. She raised a hand to push it back and found that her fingers were shaking.

Noah frowned. 'You're trembling. Your blood sugar's probably low. Finish your latte. I bought it for you specially.'

'Fine.' She chugged the drink, more to speed things along than anything else, then looked at the time on her F-phone. Twenty-one minutes past eight.

'Thanks for coming all this way to check on me, Noah. It's kind. But I do really need you to go now. I promise I'm not doing anything stupid and I'll see you at the mixer later. Okay?'

Noah scratched the back of his shoulder. Glanced towards the towpath.

'Look, I'll level with you. I've been briefed about your meeting with the reporter. And I have to ask: have you considered the repercussions?'

Heather's mouth went dry. 'But you just told me you were here because Elliot said . . . Wait, is Dr Leyton the one who briefed you? Has he been reading my DMs? Or . . .' She swallowed. 'Was it Duncan? Did he send you here?'

He dismissed the questions with a wave of his hand. 'It doesn't matter who told me. The important thing is that I know. And I've come here to help you make the right choice, to really think things through. Because slagging off the contest in the press . . . It won't just end *your* career at the Triple F. It will put every Winfluencer's future at risk. And what do you actually *know*? What proof do you have?'

His blue-green eyes fixed on hers.

'I know that someone at the Triple F is helping fragile people win and then trolling them until they break.'

His eyes moved along the river bank. 'As I've said before: the

343

screening process isn't perfect. We already knew that. And as for trolls . . . well. They're an unavoidable part of life online. Chances are you were trolled or threatened at some point before you even became a Winfluencer.'

'Only once,' Heather began, 'but that turned out to be . . .' And then she stopped, as an image popped to the surface of her memory. The screenshot on Steve's phone: 'Shulman E.'

And picturing the name laid out like that triggered something, made her mind flip the troll's name the same way round.

From A. Know.

To Know A.

'Know-a. *No . . . ah.*' She said it out loud, voicing the realisation as it dawned. 'You . . .' But the next words broke apart, dissolved into an exhalation.

No.

Her fingers tightened around the takeaway cup. It wasn't conceivable. Noah was the heart and backbone of the contest. Always there to offer a helping hand, talking to the Winfluencers about their problems, sitting in on all the Winners' Circle sessions. But it suddenly occurred to her how little she actually knew about him. She'd read somewhere that he used to be a carpenter, but found that hard to picture. It felt as though his life began the day the Triple F launched.

'Noah,' she said, when she finally trusted her voice again. 'Are you . . . are you the troll?

Nothing. Silence. Some small part of her had clung to the hope that she was wrong, that she would look into his eyes and see shocked disbelief there, telling her that she had made a terrible mistake.

But Noah didn't look shocked. He didn't even look surprised. His expression was flat, unruffled. Then he smiled.

344

That's when the last spark of hope flickered and died. And Heather knew that no one else would be coming tonight because the person she'd been waiting for was already here.

She was dimly aware of cardboard crumpling beneath her fingers as they clenched around the cup.

'Why?' Her words came out as a whisper.

He tipped back his head, sighing up at the darkening sky. 'Your problem, Heather, is that you aren't able to see the big picture. People used to say "knowledge is power" but that's no longer the case. These days, *popularity* is power. I have seven million followers. That's more than the prime minister has on X. Think of that! Millions of people watching my every move, quoting my every word. The Triple F made me the man I am today. And that man is too important to be pulled down by you or anyone else.'

Heather felt as though she'd been rocked by an explosion, shattering everything she thought she knew about the person standing in front of her. She needed time to sift through the rubble, stare down at the truth hidden beneath. And come to terms with it. But time was a luxury she didn't have. She was going to have to absorb this shock – right here, right now.

Noah was the troll.

No one would believe her – not without rock-solid proof. She fought off an impulse to glance towards the boat.

Stay calm. Focus

Okay. Tonight's plan was to catch the troll on camera. The fact that it had turned out to be Noah – someone she'd trusted and admired – didn't change that.

'Yes, you're worshipped and adored right now,' she said. 'But not for long. This sort of fame never lasts.'

'Mine does,' he snapped, and she saw a flash of anger in his eyes. 'Other Winfluencers disappear from the radar when their time runs out. But not me. I am unique. And I intend to keep it that way.'

And that was when she finally understood what this had all been about – that it was never anything to do with money or jealousy or psychological games. All of it – rigging the results, stealing winners' secrets, mobilising the press – had been about one thing and one thing only: Noah, protecting his own celebrity status.

'You backed vulnerable candidates, knowing they'd be easier to get rid of if they ever threatened your position as top dog at the contest.' Her theory was solidifying as she voiced it, puzzle pieces slotting together. Noah stared silently out at the river. She needed to get him talking, make him confess. 'But how were you able to get red-lighted finalists through? Was one of the screeners working with you?'

Noah inspected his manicured nails. 'Heather, Heather, what you fail to grasp is just how important I am to the Triple F, how central. As executive consultant, I go through the finalists' files and make recommendations, tell the selection panel who I believe will attract the most followers and sponsors. I'm good at it; my opinion is highly valued.'

And there was her answer. Noah hadn't needed any help from the screeners. Because the Triple F had already handed him all the power he needed. 'I'm not just a pretty face.' He flashed a smile as though to underline the point. But for the first time, Heather didn't find him handsome. It was as though she could see something else now, something warped and knotted, straining beneath the surface of his skin, trying to break through.

She repositioned herself so that her back was towards the

speedboat; she wanted Noah to be facing her – and facing Steve's phone camera – when he answered her next question.

'Just so I'm clear . . . you've been pushing through red-lighted finalists – concealing their screening status from the selection department – knowing they'd be popular . . . but also that they'd be easy prey should they ever become *so* popular that they threaten your position as the most famous name at the Triple F?' Now that Heather's shock had faded, anger was moving in to take its place. She'd come here expecting to meet someone driven by the usual dark forces: greed, bitterness, jealousy. But this . . . The scale of the betrayal was breath-taking. She unzipped her bag, which contained the press cuttings and the copy of Analise's file she'd taken from Elliot's flat. Not the damning evidence she'd pretended to have, but something to bluff with at least. She took out Analise's background report, shaking it in front of him. 'She admitted to having had an eating disorder and episodes of depression. But you made sure she won anyway. Then, as soon as your bosses started talking about making her the contest's female face, you decided to get rid of her, stealing her private thoughts and fears from the Secret Space, tricking her into believing she'd destroyed her child's life.' Anger had completely taken over now and she fired the words like bullets. 'Did you tell the press she was at Sunny Hills as a final humiliation? Well, congratulations, it worked. You killed her.' She shoved the file back inside her bag.

Heather wasn't sure exactly what she'd been expecting from Noah in response to this barrage. Guilt perhaps. Annoyance, that she'd had the audacity to call him out. Perhaps sneering indifference.

What she hadn't expected was for him to jump at her.

The move was swift and silent, like a cat pouncing. He snatched the bag's strap, pulling it over her head, the sudden invasion of her personal space sending her heart into a wild dash. Then, with the bag in his hands, he stepped back and began rifling through the pages inside. His look of pursed concentration gave way to relief as he reached the end. He held up a handful of papers.

'Is this all you've got? One contestant file and some press cuttings about forgotten Winfluencers?' He chuckled. 'This isn't evidence of anything. I feel sorry for whichever reporter you're dragging down here. Because you are wasting their time.' That must have reminded him that he was up against the clock, that a journalist was supposed to be on the way. He looked at his watch, a large, illuminated circle. She could see the digital numbers across the middle. Eight thirty-two. Heather could feel the sore imprint of her bag strap between her shoulder and neck where he had yanked it against her skin. She felt as though she'd been mugged, adrenaline chasing through her veins. At least he hadn't dislodged the mic.

'I disagree.' She pushed back her shoulders, determined not to let him see how his sudden show of force had rattled her. 'A decent journalist won't have trouble proving you've been helping redlighted finalists win, knowing they'd be easier to take down.'

He shrugged. 'That's one interpretation. The other is that I decided Triple F policies were discriminatory, unfairly depriving finalists from troubled backgrounds of the opportunity to transform their lives. So I decided to take a chance on them, while making sure that, as their mentor, I was on hand to help if they started to struggle. I even set up the Winners' Circle as another means of support.'

'Please! You set it up so you could mine the Secret Space for information to use against them.'

'That group helped a lot of people cope. *I* helped a lot of people cope.'

'Yes. The ones who didn't threaten your lone star status.'

Another shrug. 'I can't be held responsible for the frailties of others.' Noah held up Heather's bag by the strap, letting it dangle in front of her for a moment before flinging it over the side of the dock without breaking eye contact. It landed in the water, riding the surface for a moment before disappearing beneath it.

'For the record,' he said, 'I was genuinely upset when Blake – he was one of the first winners whose success I had to rein in – lost the plot and crashed his car. I genuinely didn't mean for that to happen. But the head of marketing had suggested I let him take over some of my PR gigs and press conferences, and I couldn't let that happen, so I invited him to the Winners' Circle, and found out that . . .' Noah frowned. 'The point is, I just wanted Blake to fade away, like the two before him. But later, after Mitzu drowned, I began to see things differently. It was better, in a way. More humane. Because it's not as though their lives were worth anything any more. Once you have known true fame and adoration, your every word repeated and reposted a thousand times . . . to then be thrown on the scrapheap, forgotten, knowing you will never shine again. Well. You really are better off dead.'

The last words made Heather's stomach drop. She and Steve had based their plan on the assumption that the troll didn't pose a physical threat, the keyboard his only weapon. But what if they were wrong?

Better off dead.

Heather glanced around, suddenly conscious of how vulnerable she was. They had the evidence they needed. It was time to get away from here. She took a step towards the angled walkway, intending to leave as swiftly as her leg would allow.

But Noah, it seemed, had other ideas. He moved with her, stepping back every time she stepped forward, like a dancer mirroring his partner until he'd reached the base of the walkway. He stood facing her, holding the wooden handrails, blocking her exit.

'I must say, Heather, you've been quite a spirited competitor. Each time I think you're down for the count, up you jump. Like a boxer who doesn't know when to quit. You could have gone quietly, like the others. But instead,' he lifted a palm from the railing, waving it in a small circle before dropping it back down, 'here we are.'

She met his gaze, determined not to let him see that he'd rattled her. She pictured Steve, crouching under the boat cover just a few metres away, watching her through the camera. Knowing he was there made her feel calmer. Stronger. She lifted her chin.

'Sorry I wouldn't lie down and play dead for you.'

Noah shrugged. 'Well, we got there in the end. That's the main thing.' And something about his tone – the casual certainty of it – sent a chill right through her.

'What do you mean by that?'

'Heather,' he sighed, shaking his head in mock sadness. 'There are only so many lies the public will tolerate, only so many redemptions they're willing to stomach. How disappointing, after all those vlogs, that you've relapsed. It's not really your fault; oxy is a powerful opiate and you're an addict. But it's sad that the drug has made you delusional, reduced to badgering reporters with wild conspiracy theories.'

Relief washed through her. So *this* was his play? Noah must be more desperate than he was letting on. Because he should know that a lie like that could be easily disproven. She folded her arms across her chest.

'You can make whatever baseless claims you like. A blood test will prove I'm clean.'

His smile was a slow crawl of triumph. 'Will it?'

'Of course it—' Then the words froze in her throat as she suddenly became aware of something. Her leg had stopped hurting. For the first time since she'd stop taking oxy, there was no pain at all.

She looked down at the scrunched takeaway cup on the dock. *No.*

'This isn't just a job, Heather. I matter. People need me in their lives.'

Perhaps it was the outrageousness of that last statement, given the catastrophic damage he'd caused. Or the fact that it was just now sinking in that she'd been drugged. Or maybe, after all the shock and disappointment, it was simply the final straw. But whatever the reason, hearing those words – *People need me in their lives* – flipped a switch inside her. And Heather found she couldn't put up with another second of Noah's shameless, self-serving lies.

'You couldn't be more wrong!' She leaned towards him, reaching for the words she knew would strike hardest, loading them with contempt. '*Nobody* needs you. You're just a sad, shallow sociopath whose fame will fade with his looks. It's only a matter of time before you're yesterday's news. And no one will even remember your name.'

That's when the thing beneath the surface broke through. Noah's features twisted and his mouth pulled downward, half snarl, half grimace. He lunged at Heather, grabbing her by the shoulders, fingers digging in. Then he began shaking her, hard enough to make her head rock back and forth.

'You shut your mouth! You don't understand a thing about what I represent. How could you? You're nothing but a junkie from the reject pile.'

Heather had just enough time to register the thought that goading him had been a terrible mistake, that she had put herself in real danger, when she saw a blur of movement in the corner of her eye. Heard the thump of feet landing on wood. Then Steve's voice, shouting.

'Get your hands off her, you psycho!'

Noah's face changed all at once, the gritted teeth parting, knotted eyebrows rising as surprise shunted aside rage.

The grip on her arms was knocked away as Steve flung himself at Noah, a sideways tackle that brought both of them down. There was a hollow thud as they hit the dock together.

Then they were wrestling, rolling across the boards with Heather standing over them, trying to work out how to intervene. She managed to land a kick on Noah's shoulder but he barely reacted, his attention riveted to Steve – skinny, out-of-shape Steve. What chance did he have against Noah's gym muscles? She needed to jump in, wrap her arms around Noah's neck and pull. But the two men kept rolling back and forth, Noah's back alternating with Steve's, making it impossible to time her move.

Something fell from Steve's trouser pocket, skidding across the wooden planks. A metallic rectangle.

The phone, Heather thought. *The footage.*

For a moment, she feared it would slide right off the edge and into the water, but it came to rest near the edge of the dock.

She had just enough time to make up her mind to dive for it

when the flurry of movement stopped abruptly. She froze, paralysed by the tableau in front of her: Steve, face down on the dock, his cheek pressed against the boards, one arm twisted behind him at an unnatural angle; Noah, holding her friend's wrist up between his shoulder blades, one knee planted on the base of his spine.

Then Noah spoke to Steve. His tone was conversational, as if the two men were having a casual chat.

'So I'm guessing you're Steve? Care to tell me what you're doing here? Because I thought she told you not to come.' Silence. Noah yanked Steve's wrist higher, eliciting a gasp of pain.

'Let go of him!' Heather shouted, moving forward ready to throw herself at Noah, kick and bite until he released his grip.

He glanced over at her. 'I'd stay there if I were you. Otherwise I might end up twisting this arm right out of its socket.' That stopped her. She stood on the dock feeling completely helpless. Noah gave her a bright smile. And somehow it was more sinister than the most vicious sneer. 'So, who's going to tell me what game the two of you are playing? Was this whole hiding-in-a-boat pantomime for the journalist ... or ...?' He shot a glance towards the shore, frowning. 'You know, I'm starting to wonder whether there's a reporter coming at all. A bag with no real evidence. A man hiding in a boat. Was all this for my benefit? He stared at the back of Steve's head. 'Were you *spying* on me?' He used his free hand to grope inside Steve's trouser pockets, but came away with nothing other than a set of keys and a couple of coins. Heather's eyes darted to the edge of the dock. The falling sun threw stripes of shadow across the wood, draping Steve's device in grey. Maybe Noah wouldn't notice it. And anyway, the main thing now was to defuse the situation, convince him to let Steve go. To let *both* of them go.

'Of course we're not spying. I just . . . decided I didn't want to come here alone after all. So I brought Steve to keep watch. Just in case.' A flimsy lie. In case *what?* She was supposed to have chosen the spot herself and was theoretically meeting a trusted journalist. But Steve's gasps of pain were short-circuiting her thoughts and it was the best she could come up with.

Her gaze jumped to the unguarded walkway. She could try to escape on her own, head for the road beyond the construction site as fast as she was able, call 999, flag down passing cars and come back with help. Except she couldn't run. Noah would catch her easily.

But in order to catch her, he'd first have to let go of Steve.

She moved towards the walkway. Put a foot on the bottom of the ramp.

'Bad move,' Noah said from behind her. She turned around just in time to see him release Steve's wrist and grab hold of his hair with both hands, using it to haul Steve's head up with enough force to raise his shoulders right off the dock, neck stretching at an unnatural angle.

Then he brought Steve's head down again in one swift, terrible movement, slamming it against the dock: once, twice, three times.

Heather felt as though a sinkhole had opened up in the pit of her stomach, pulling everything inside. She had come here expecting to meet a sly coward who hid in the back alleys of cyberspace, relying on trickery and deceit, avoiding face-to-face confrontation. She had made a terrible miscalculation – one that Steve could be paying for with his life.

The world seemed to shrink until it felt as if there was nothing in it but this tiny wooden island. And the three of them: Steve, one bloodied cheek against the boards, eyes closed; Noah, calm, kneeling over him, fingers still buried in his hair. And Heather, paralysed by her own guilt and horror. With absolutely no idea what to do next.

Noah moved first, standing up and stretching his arms out sideways, giving them a shake.

'That was your fault, Heather,' he said conversationally. 'You put your friend in danger by dragging him into . . .' he glanced around, taking in the boat, the river, the towpath, 'whatever *this* is.'

She tried to move past the gridlock in her mind, to think of something, anything, that could reverse this, turn him back into the Noah of before.

'You didn't have to do that. He's just here to keep an eye on me.'

'An eye on *me*, you mean. I'm assuming at least one of you has been recording this little chat.' He held out his hand. 'Give me your phone. And don't even think about running off or your friend goes straight in the river.'

She took out her F-phone, easing it past the pay-as-you-go. 'I wasn't recording you.' Heather said, holding out the device. 'Check for yourself if you like. My passcode is—'

But he must have known what it was, because he was already tapping at the screen, swiping through images and videos before slipping it inside his pocket.

'Okay, if *you* weren't recording our conversation, that must mean your friend was. So where's his phone? On the boat?'

The movement was involuntary. At the mention of the word 'phone', Heather's eyes flicked to the corner of the dock. She caught herself immediately, looking in the direction of the boat instead, hoping Noah hadn't noticed. No such luck.

'Aha.' His voice was triumphant. 'So *that's* where it went.'

He stood up, stepping over Steve's unconscious form and turning his back on Heather. She might not get another chance. She pulled out the pay-as-you-go phone, unlocked the screen and pressed down hard on the number one, praying Tessa was keeping an ear out for it, that she answered right away.

Noah stepped slowly, casually, towards the far corner of the dock.

'Yo,' Tessa's voice said. 'What's happen—'

'Get help!' she shouted, then shoved the phone back in her skirt pocket as Noah wheeled around to face her.

'What did you say?'

She could feel the muted handset vibrating in her pocket: Tessa calling back.

'You heard me. I told you to get help. Because there's something wrong with you, hurting people who haven't done anything . . . You're not right in the head.'

Noah's eyes were flat and cold. 'I knew you wouldn't be able to understand.'

'Look, it's not too late to fix this. I promise I won't say anything about what happened here tonight.'

'You can say whatever you like. The fact of the matter is, no one will believe you without this.' And with one swift kick, he sent Steve's device flying into the water. There was a tiny splash as the river swallowed it.

All our evidence . . . gone.

Her eyes returned to Steve, motionless on the dock. The recording didn't matter. The only thing that mattered was convincing Noah to let her take Steve to a hospital. And to do that, she needed to make him believe that the two of them no longer posed a threat. She took a deep breath – in through the nose, out through the mouth. Chose her next words carefully.

'You're right,' she said. 'Without that phone, no one will believe a word I say. You've won. I admit I got Steve to film this meeting. I never dreamed it would be you who showed up, I just wanted to catch whoever had been reading my DMs. But your secret is safe. Because I know how it will look if I say anything – a junkie with blood full of oxy and a head full of conspiracy theories, trying to distract the public's attention from her own addiction. So tomorrow I'm going to step down from CelebRate, leave with my tail between my legs. You've won, Noah. So please, just let me take Steve to the hospital. I'll say it was an accident, that he fell down some stairs.'

She had hoped this would appeal to his ego, make him feel more in charge, and therefore calmer. But when his eyes met hers, there was nothing in them but cold calculation.

'I'm afraid that's not going to work for me.'

She felt her breath catch. 'Why not?'

He looked down at Steve, slumped on the wooden boards. Was he even breathing? She thought she'd seen his chest rise and fall. Or was that just wishful thinking?

'Yes, it's safe to say that *your* account of tonight's events would be discredited and dismissed. But not his.' He prodded Steve in the side with the toe of his shoe. 'He's a witness. He'll go to the police.'

Heather shook her head emphatically, frightened by the direction this was heading.

'No, he won't! I'll tell him I won't be able to back up his version of events, because of the oxy. So it'll be his word against yours, and you're the one the whole country trusts and adores. He's just a nobody.'

Noah crouched down next to Steve and took hold of his arm, pulling it across his shoulders before straightening up with Steve beside him, head lolling. Relief crashed through Heather. Her strategy had worked. Noah was helping her get Steve off the dock to safety. She smiled at Noah, grateful. But Noah didn't smile back. Instead, he fished her F-phone from his pocket and wiped it with the tail of his shirt before dropping it onto the dock. She waited for him to kick it into the water, as he had Steve's. But he just left it lying on the boards.

'You have a big PR challenge on your hands, Heather.'

She looked from Steve's blood-streaked face to Noah's, trying to work out what he meant, where this was going.

'Yes, I probably do. But everyone will forget about me once I leave CelebRate. Right now, though, I just want to take my friend to hospital.'

But he ploughed on, ignoring her. 'A big PR challenge. What will people think when they hear that you fell back into drugs on the same night you were linked to a suspicious death?'

There was a gap of time during which she was unable to process his words – as though her mind had thrown up a barrier, refusing to let the implication pass through.

She stared from Noah to Steve, now hanging beside him like a puppet with cut strings.

'What do you mean?'

But instead of replying, Noah turned and strode to the far side of the dock, Steve's trainers scuffing against wood as he was dragged along. For a moment Noah stood with his back to Heather, looking out at the sunset with Steve sagging against him. Glowing pink wisps rode the horizon.

'Noah,' she said. 'Don't—'

But it was too late. With one swift movement, he heaved Steve over the edge of the dock and into the river. There was a splash as the water took him.

'Look what you made me do,' Noah said. 'You should have—'

But Heather never found out what she should have done. Because before he had the chance to tell her, she had dived off the dock.

CHAPTER 46

The first thing to hit her was the cold. She kicked her legs as she floundered beneath the water's surface, trying to stay calm and get her bearings as her body adjusted to the temperature. She tipped back her head and saw the pink smudge of sunset, rippling through the water. Moving further away. She was sinking. Heather was suddenly conscious of the weight of her sodden clothes dragging her down. Her shoes were slip-ons – *thank God, thank God* – so she pushed them off with a toe to the heel and fought to reach the surface. Her love of swimming had ended with the accident, but the muscle memory was still there, the strong efficient strokes, lung capacity stretched by underwater laps.

She reached the surface, gulping for air.

Steve. She looked around desperately but there was no sign of him.

Oh-God-oh-God-oh-God.

Grabbing a deep breath, she dropped under the water again and turned in a circle, eyes straining to pierce the murk. At first she saw nothing, just silt-clouded layers of water and the vague shapes of rocks below. A school of fish flickering past. Then she turned around and suddenly, there he was: a human shape floating near the bottom.

Trails of bubbles were leaking from Steve's mouth as she

reached his side: not a good sign. Grabbing him under the arms, she towed him towards the surface, his weight pulling at her, slowing their progress. Heather's lungs were starting to burn. Don't panic, she told herself. Panic burns oxygen. She kept her eyes fixed on the wavering pink sky, arms wrapped around him from behind. Just a few more kicks . . .

They broke surface and she gasped for air, legs working hard to keep them both afloat.

'Steve?' Her voice was a gasp. He was still and silent in her arms. *Oh God.*

Helplessness overwhelmed her. If she could make it to shore, perform CPR, she might be able to revive him. But here, fighting just to stay afloat, there was nothing she could do.

Unless . . . Her hands were clasped across his ribcage. Now she shifted her grip downward, to just below it, pulled her joined hands in and up with all her strength, forcing them under the ledge of bone, shoving them against his lungs: a floating Heimlich manoeuvre. Nothing happened. Maybe she hadn't used enough force? She tried again. And again.

Suddenly, water jetted from Steve's mouth and then he was gasping for air, eyelids flickering.

Relief swept through her. He was alive. Thank God.

'Steve? Can you hear me?' But there was no reply other than the rasp of his breathing. They were being carried along by the current, drifting past waterfront houses, the riverbank tantalisingly near. She could see people wandering along the towpath, enjoying a sunset stroll. Lights in the windows of homes. And stone steps against the river wall just ahead, leading up to the path. Hope soared through her. Just a few more moments and they would be safe.

Then a powerful undertow grabbed them and she was clinging

to Steve as they were pulled and rolled, ducked below the surface and then flipped back up above it again, the water hissing in her ears now, dragging them along as—

A violent, jarring blow knocked the air from her, as though she'd been slammed into a wall. Steve was jolted from her grasp but she managed to grab hold of his arm. For a moment the world seemed to swoop away, careening around her in dizzying circles as she gasped for air. Then everything settled back down and she was able to look around, to try and work out what had happened. The water was pushing her up against some sort of barrier. She looked up and saw the underside of a pier; they had been swept into a metal strut connecting two of the pier's iron legs. The river was trying to carry them onwards, but she grabbed hold with one hand, ignoring the scrape of barnacles against her palm, clamping her other arm around Steve's bicep in a tight V, bracing for a fresh game of tug of war with the current. But Steve didn't move. It was as though his back was stuck fast to the pier leg itself. How was that possible?

'Steve?' She clung to the strut beside him, water racing around her middle, watching his face and hoping his eyes would open. They didn't. She surveyed his body, trying to work out what was going on. Why she was fighting against the current while he remained motionless, as though locked in place. Then she saw the blood staining his shirt just below his shoulder. As she watched, the stain grew bigger, spreading outward. And in the centre, a piece of metal, protruding from beneath his collar bone. A long bolt or nail must have been sticking out of the pier leg and Steve had been swept into it with such force that it had cut right through him, impaling him there.

'Steve,' she croaked, knowing he couldn't hear her, that he was far away, drifting somewhere in the depths of his unconscious. Just as well, in a way. This wasn't a reality anyone would want to wake up to.

Slowly, tentatively, Heather let go of him, ready to lunge if he somehow pulled free. But he was stuck tight, head lolling on his bloodstained shoulder, water surging around his chest.

She hung from the metal strut, catching her breath, gathering her thoughts. Looked around. They were in a wider part of the river now; the pier jutting perhaps fifteen metres out from the shore. This stretch of the riverbank must be private property, because there was no towpath here, no couples and dogwalkers strolling. So no good Samaritans running to wrap her in a coat or blanket as she staggered ashore, no saviours hurrying along the pier with ropes and ladders to rescue Steve. If only the struts ran the whole length of the pier, instead of just the final section, she could have used them to pull herself towards the shore. She stared at the short stretch of water separating her from solid ground. About fifteen metres. But this wasn't like doing laps in a pool. Swimming against the tide and the currents would require every ounce of her remaining strength. She could do it alone. But with a full-grown man in tow . . .

From out of the dark came the hum of a boat engine. Hope swooped through her. She leaned away from the pier, waving her free arm over her head as the engine grew louder. A white cruiser moved into view, light pouring from its windows. She could see a passenger leaning against the side railings, staring towards the shore. Heather's arm movement became more frantic.

'Help!' she shouted, though she knew her voice would be buried under the noise of the engine.

The boat swept past, pushing out a frothy swell that lifted her for a moment. She tried again when a small ferry went by a few minutes later, with the same result. She was on her own.

She returned her attention to Steve, pinned to the metal leg like a butterfly in a collector's box. Pulling him off the spike would be dangerous; he might bleed out. But she couldn't just stay here with him, clinging to the pier as the darkness deepened and her grip began to fail. The only logical solution was to leave him and go for help.

Like Elliot had.

The thought sent a wave of nausea rolling through her. And following in its wake, a realisation.

The tide.

She looked at Steve, suddenly noticing the barnacles pocking the metal pillar behind him, studding the weed that rose to the tideline just above his head.

Above his head.

She looked around desperately, trying to get her bearings. She had thought the tide was rising when they'd arrived at the dock, but that was probably just her own fear, tainting her perception. What if she'd been right, though? How long would it be before Steve woke to find himself alone, impaled in the darkness with water rising around his neck, his chin. His mouth.

Heather's memory catapulted her back to the car, trapped, racked with unimaginable pain but unable to scream because the water had reached her face . . .

She threw back her head and screamed now, up at the night sky, a long wailing note of horror and helplessness, the sound snatched up and carried away by the breeze riding the river.

CHAPTER 47

I'm making sure my presence is registered at the New Heights. Mingling with the Winfluencers. Smiling for the cameras. I came here earlier too, before the river, chatting with the staff while they were setting up, telling them I had some business to attend to in the back office. Hunting through the confiscated drugs in the safe until I found what I needed. No one saw me slip out. I'm sure about that.

I head out to the roof garden, dispensing smiles as I go. Tessa is on her phone, looking stressed.

I could swear I hear her say 'Heather Davies'. Probably just my imagination, fired up by nerves. I count backwards from five, one of Dr Leyton's stress-fighting tips from the Winners' Circle. I find it helpful.

I approach Tessa wearing a look of friendly concern. 'Everything okay? You seem worried.'

'It's . . .' She hesitates. Shakes her head. 'Forget it. I'm just having a weird night.'

I chuckle. 'You and me both.' I pat her shoulder and move on through the crowd.

No, there's nothing to worry about. I've covered my tracks. I took black cabs to the river and back, wearing sunglasses and a baseball cap, pulled low. Paying in cash. Just in case there's an investigation.

Not that I'm expecting one. A known addict with drugs in her system is fished out of the river with her friend. Perhaps they'll decide he was a hero who jumped in to try and save her, but ended up smashing his skull on a dock or the underside of a boat. Such a tragedy. I'll be quoted and photographed, sombre and sorrowful about the promising life cut short by opioid abuse.

Case closed.

'Noah, did you hear the news? I'm going to be on telly! A Channel 4 miniseries!' The new bloke, a wannabe actor, appears in front of me. Been in a couple of plays. Not terrible, apparently. His face glows with excitement. 'Think of the posting possibilities: a behind-the-scenes look at the life of a TV actor. I'm thinking video diaries, live streams . . . the lot! Let the followers feel like they're part of it all, sharing in my success!'

I clap him on the back. Kyle Waters. Handsome, with bags of charismatic charm. I didn't want to let him through, but he was such an obvious choice, it would have looked strange not to.

'That's fantastic news, Kyle. Congratulations! Why don't we set up a meeting with your image consultant tomorrow, do some brainstorming about ways to spin this to your best advantage?'

'Thanks, Noah!' His eyes brim with gratitude. 'You're the best! I don't know how any of us would manage without you.'

'Just doing my job.'

Then someone draws him away towards the bar. I watch Kyle go, moving through the crowd. Women touch his shoulder and smile, tossing their hair. Men laugh and shake his hand.

Tomorrow I'll suggest he join the Winners' Circle, just as a precaution, an outlet for the stress of his new role.

I'm going to have to keep a close eye on that one. A very close eye.

CHAPTER 48

The cold had seeped through to Heather's core, making her shake, teeth clacking. How long had she been here, clinging to a piece of metal in the dark, paralysed by indecision?

She couldn't afford to wait any longer. The logical move was to swim to shore alone and get help. There was bound to be a road somewhere nearby. This was the outer edge of London, for Christ's sake, not the Scottish coast.

She turned to Steve, hoping against hope that he would wake up so she could tell him her plan. That he would nod and tell her to leave, saying it was for the best.

'I'm going to swim for it,' she said, despite knowing he couldn't hear. 'Then I'll come right back with help and we'll both—'

Then the words stopped as she noticed something. The top button of his shirt was no longer visible. She'd been looking at it earlier, wondering whether she should undo it, whether his wet clothes were making him warmer or colder. Now it was hidden beneath the water's surface.

Because the tide was rising.

A high moan escaped her throat, like the sound of an animal in pain. Because she knew what this meant: she couldn't leave him behind. No matter how great the risk, she had to bring him with her. The question was, how? She would need both arms to swim if they were going to have any chance of making it to shore. And the front crawl was by far her strongest stroke. So how was she going to carry him? If only she had a rope, she could tie him face up on her back. Maybe she could take off her blouse and twist it up tightly? But that wouldn't be long enough. Maybe Steve's trousers would do the trick. They were loose, so should come off easily once the belt . . .

The belt.

Of course. What an idiot she was. Heather groped around Steve's waist for the buckle, which had slipped to one side. The waterlogged leather was reluctant to pull free but she worked at it with her fingers until finally it came out and she was able to open the belt and take it off. Then she reached behind him and worked the length through the two back loops of his trousers, leaving it there unbuckled. Once she had prized his shoulder free of the pier leg, she would tie the belt around her own waist, so that they were joined, back-to-back, Steve facing the sky as she swam. Hopefully he wouldn't slip sideways and become submerged. Hopefully the water would help carry his weight, keeping him from pushing her under. *Hopefully, hopefully.*

Wrapping one arm around the pier leg, she used the other to grab hold of his pinned shoulder, grimacing at the sight of the metal jutting through it. Heather drew in a deep breath, filling her lungs. Then she pulled with all her strength.

It was easier than she'd anticipated; the metal must not have been wedged too tightly between his bones because he fell forward, briefly pushing Heather under. She grabbed on to him and realized, with a stab of dismay, that they were moving away from the shore, being carried back towards the middle of the river. She held his head above the surface with one arm, legs kicking, while her free hand groped for the belt behind him. Panic and doubt were teaming up, attacking her as she fought to stay afloat. How had she thought this was possible, fastening an injured man to her back while being swept along a river? Ridiculous. Impossible. But she hoisted him up onto her back, his weight pushing her down beneath the surface as she pulled the two ends of the belt in front of her waist. Her cold fingers stumbled against the buckle, but somehow she managed to thread the leather through. One pull would lock it in place – and lock their fates together.

Don't do it. Once you're attached, he'll drag you down to the riverbed.

She hesitated, hand frozen on the belt, lungs screaming. But then her memory fired off one last salvo: the moment of awakening. There had been a brief window of time, perhaps only a minute or two, when the pain had hidden itself behind a veil of shock, giving her time to absorb what was happening: that the car was full of water, that she couldn't move. She felt once again the creak of vertebrae as her head turned slowly towards the driver's seat. The gut-punch of horror when she saw that it was empty.

Heather pulled at the belt.

The metal prong slid into one of the holes. The belt was loose around her waist, but it would do. They were bound together. A surge of energy rode through her, propelling her upwards through the water, sending the two of them popping to the surface like a cork. She gasped in the night air, filling her lungs. Blinked her eyes clear of water. Then she surveyed her surroundings. They were closer to the bank now, no more than ten metres from a stretch of riverfront lined with houses. She saw lights in windows. Heard a snatch of music. Relief filled her. She struck out towards the shore. Her legs were tired; they'd been working too long. But her bad leg still didn't hurt. Noah had unwittingly done her a favour by slipping her a hefty dose of oxy. Heather doubted she could have done all this while wrestling with her own agony. She smiled at the lit windows, thinking, *It's almost over.*

Then her smile fell away. The current was just a few metres from shore, a wall of turbulence that pushed them backwards then – suddenly, horrifyingly – downwards. She tried to fight her way back up, but she didn't have enough air or energy to do it with Steve anchoring her down.

I'm going to die.

She flailed helplessly, lungs burning, shrieking at her to open her mouth. To let the river in.

Something brushed against her hand and she grabbed it instinctively, fingers tightening in a death grip. A rope. The river tried to carry her away from it but she clung on, discovering reserves of strength she hadn't known existed. The belt linking her to Steve dug into the bottom of her ribcage as she began pulling herself along the line, hand over hand, praying it would take her to the surface. If it was attached to something under the water, her last hope of survival would hit a dead end. The scream of her lungs was overpowering now. She would drown in a matter of seconds. One last hand over hand, one last pull . . . Heather's face lifted out of the water. She sucked in air, filling her searing lungs with oxygen in hoarse, tearing gasps, fingers frozen around the rope, which was secured to a ladder – a ladder! – attached to a private pier. She grabbed on to the bottom rung, holding tight. Now all she had to do was climb up four rungs and they would be saved.

But even as the thought entered her mind, Heather knew she couldn't do it. Not with Steve attached to her. Dragging him through water had been hard enough. Outside of it, she would be carrying his full weight. It was taking every last ounce of her remaining energy just to keep holding on to the bottom rung. Soon, in less than a minute probably, she would lose her grip and they would both slip beneath the surface. And all her struggles would have done nothing but prolong her terror. Maybe Steve was gone anyway, maybe he had drowned or bled out, just so much dead weight. She looked towards the bank. The lit houses, filled with people who could help. She thought she smelled barbecue smoke. Friends and families, enjoying the sultry night, perhaps gazing out over the river. One of them might have spotted her, if night hadn't fallen. But the last shred of daylight had gone, shrouding her in darkness. She tried to call out, but her voice came out as a rasp.

She looked up the ladder. Just four rungs. But with Steve on her back, it might as well be Mount Everest.

Which left her with only one option: she had to undo the belt and let him go. There was no other way. Tears made her vision waver, an overflow of horror and frustration. To have made it so far, only to fail now. It wasn't fair.

Her right hand went to the belt buckle, yanking at the leather, pulling. She was so weak. So cold. But yes, she'd managed it, the leather was out of the top half of the buckle. Now all that remained was for her to pull it back, free the prong from the hole, let the belt fall open. Then he would be gone.

Her body was shaking now and she was starting to see things, flickering lights on the edge of her vision. Except . . . *was* it a hallucination?

'Help.' Her voice was a whisper. She closed her eyes, reaching inside herself, gathering up her last meagre scraps of strength.

Like a gambler scrabbling for the last bits of change, throwing it all down on one last desperate roll of the dice.

Heather ploughed everything she had left into her voice, into one word, tilting back her head as it rose from her throat and out into the night.

'*Help!*'

And that was it. The tank was empty. White spots danced in front of her eyes. Then they cleared for a moment and she saw the night sky. Stars looking down.

Her last glimpse of the world.

Her fingers finally gave out and she splashed back into the river.

Goodbye, she thought, closing her eyes as the water rose above them. She had fought the tide, but in the end the tide had won.

She felt the pull of the current and, simultaneously, a scorching pain across the top of her scalp. Then something inexplicable happened. Her clothes began pulling against her, blouse rucking up under her arms, digging into the soft flesh there as she was borne miraculously upwards. She was rising out of the water, the belt pulling against her, night air slapping her skin.

Then everything went black.

CHAPTER 49

Just before Heather opened her eyes, she had the strange sensation of having travelled back in time. She was in the hospital again, after yet another surgery, another attempt to fit a missing piece into the jagged puzzle of her leg.

It was because of the sounds: the too-loud tick of the clock. The click and whir of an IV bag dispensing its load. The warning beep of a machine as someone rolled over in bed, disrupting the flow. And from right nearby, the unmistakable sound of a cubical curtain being pulled around a suspended rail.

A dream. It had to be.

Then she opened her eyes and saw, with an unpleasant jolt of surprise, that it wasn't a dream after all. She was lying in a hospital bed, the familiar too-stiff sheets pulled up to her chest, an IV line attached to her arm. A nurse was standing beside her, one hand still holding the edge of the curtain she had just dragged back.

'Ah, you're awake.' She picked up a jug of water from the wheeled table at the end of Heather's bed, filling a plastic cup and passing it across. 'Drink this.' The nurse pressed the control button attached to the bed and the top half rose, lifting Heather into a sitting position.

'I'm not thirsty.'

'Drink it anyway. You were dehydrated when they brought you in. You've been given intravenous fluids, but there's no substitute for a good old-fashioned glass of water.'

Heather took a couple of gulps, mainly because she didn't have the energy to argue. Snatches of memory were coming at her, not in order, but all at once. Noah holding out a coffee cup; lights sweeping the shore; Steve's face pressed against the dock, smeared with blood.

Steve.

'My friend, the man I was with. Where is he?' Dread filled Heather's chest as she braced for the answer.

But the nurse smiled. 'He's out of surgery, resting comfortably.'

'Surgery? For his shoulder?'

'Yes. But also for a head injury. There was some swelling on his brain that needed to be relieved immediately. But he's in recovery now.'

Heather fell back against the pillows, closing her eyes as relief flowed through her. Steve was here, safe. They had made it.

As her fear faded into the background, she became aware of aches and pains throughout her body. Her leg was complaining the loudest, as usual, striking up its chorus of razor-sharp notes. But now all her other muscles were throbbing along to the beat. And something else too, a burning sensation on the top of her head. She touched her scalp and came up against a gauze bandage.

'What's this? Do I have a head injury as well?'

'No.' The nurse chuckled. 'More of a hair injury. The police officer who rescued you grabbed you by it. Took out a fair-sized chunk.'

'The police,' she echoed. Heather looked at the closed door to the room, wondering whether officers were loitering on the other side. 'Are they still here?'

'No, they left. They said they'll send someone to take a statement whenever you're ready.'

'Oh. All right. I thought they'd want to speak to me as soon as I woke up. But maybe that's just on TV.'

She had to tell the police about Noah. She saw his face in her memory, the way it had changed and twisted. Saw him heaving Steve into the river.

Look what you made me do.

A wave of dizziness rolled through her. Maybe it was just as well the officers had left. She could report what Noah had done later, when her head felt less jumbled. Make a statement laying out the facts clearly and calmly. Then, once Steve was out of recovery, he could do the same.

She took another sip of water as she looked around, taking stock of her surroundings. She was in a semi-private room, but the bed next to hers was stripped, with nothing on it but a mauve overnight bag. The window just beyond showed a daytime view of a car park, a row of houses on the other side.

What time was it? She instinctively scanned the room for her phone, before remembering that Noah had taken it and dropped it on the dock. Even her pay-as-you-go was gone, in the river somewhere.

Her eyes alighted on a folded slip of paper on the bedside table.

'That's from a friend of yours.' The nurse unhooked Heather's chart from the end of her bed. 'She was here for hours yesterday afternoon and again this morning.'

Heather put down her water and picked up the note.

Are you okay? WTF happened?! Call me as soon as you wake up and I'll come straight over. At Mum's (it's her birthday) but can be there in 20 minutes. Tessa xx

Heather put the note back, warmed by the thought of her friend keeping watch over her. She'd have to borrow a phone to tell Tessa she was okay and not to ruin her mother's birthday; they could speak properly tomorrow, when Heather was feeling more alert. Her eyes returned to the travel bag on the next bed. It looked familiar.

The nurse followed Heather's gaze.

'Someone from the Triple F dropped that off,' she said. 'They thought you might want some fresh clothes and toiletries.'

The penny dropped. The bag was part of a luggage set that had arrived last week, from a Spanish designer known for his love of purple. Whoever had brought it must have gone into her house using the 'landlord' key – presumably on Duncan's orders. Or maybe he had packed it himself. Heather felt a warm glow as she pictured him carefully selecting shampoo bottles and face creams.

'The man who brought it. Was he—' Then she stopped. Rephrased the question. 'Did anyone from the Triple F visit while I was unconscious?'

The nurse jotted something on Heather's chart, lips curved in a small smile. 'As a matter of fact, yes. Mr Triple F himself. He arrived about an hour after you were brought in and hasn't left the hospital since.' Heather felt a grin spreading across her face as she pictured Duncan pacing back and forth in the waiting area, consumed with worry. 'If you're feeling up to it, I can let him in.' The nurse flushed pink. Odd. 'But of course, it's your decision.'

Heather ran fingers along the side of her hair that wasn't bandaged. It felt greasy; she needed a shower and some make-up.

'I'd rather not let him see me like this. I look terrible.'

But the door was already opening. 'Nonsense,' said a familiar voice. 'You look absolutely fine.'

Noah stepped inside the room.

CHAPTER 50

Adrenaline crashed through Heather's veins as Noah moved closer. She opened her mouth to speak, but no sound came. The smiling nurse withdrew, eyes glued to Noah, leaving her trapped, weak as a kitten, tethered to an IV stand and pinned to the mattress by tightly pulled sheets.

Noah gave Heather the easy smile she knew so well as he settled into the armchair beside her bed. She groped for the call button to bring back the nurse, but he gently removed it from her hand, placing it aside.

'There's really no need for that. I'm just here to check that you're comfortable. You'd been put on a ward with three other people, but I saw to it that you were moved.'

He gestured towards the unused bed.

'All the private rooms were taken, unfortunately, there was nothing I could do about that. But I got you an empty semi-private one, which is better, in a way, because you have more space.'

She looked around the room, bewildered. Had she somehow imagined the scene on the dock? Because this was the Noah of *before*. The caring mentor who would do anything to help. Heather closed her eyes, trying to herd her thoughts together, to separate memory from imagination. She replayed the scene on the dock . . . saw Noah slamming Steve's head against the boards. Heard the terrible sound it made. She couldn't have imagined that. She opened her eyes. It was all true; Noah had admitted to being the troll and pushed Steve into the river.

So why was he here now, acting as though none of it had happened?

She lay against the raised back of the bed, inspecting his face. The shock of seeing him step through the door was starting to fade, taking much of her fear with it. Noah wouldn't risk attacking her here, with doctors and nurses popping in without warning. So he must have something else up his sleeve. Heather watched him cover a yawn as he leaned back in the blue armchair, crossing his legs at the ankles. What Noah had done to Steve was attempted murder, plain and simple. And nothing he said now was going to prevent her – or, more importantly, Steve – from reporting it. Noah's life was about to implode. Yet there he sat, looking as if he didn't have a care in the world.

'You had a lucky escape,' he said. 'Very lucky. I'm told Tessa called 999 and the police used Friend Finder to trace your phone.' He took something out of his pocket, placed it on the side table: her F-phone. 'They found it on the dock. So the police feared the worst and did a sweep of the river's edge, allowing for the current. Sounds like they showed up just in time.'

'My phone.' She stared at the device in confusion. White flares blotted out her vision for a moment and she blinked them away. 'It shouldn't be here. It's evidence.'

He gave her a look she couldn't read. 'Evidence of what, exactly? The police will, of course, want to take a statement, get your version of events. But I've already explained the situation.'

She raised an eyebrow. 'I see. And what did you explain, exactly?'

He looked her in the eye then, and she felt something cold sink down through her chest, all the way to the pit of her stomach. It was the face of a poker player about to reveal an unbeatable hand.

'I told them how worried I'd been, suspecting you might be headed for a relapse. Which is why I came looking for you. And as feared, I discovered you incoherent, hallucinating, spouting crazy conspiracy theories. That's how I knew you were using again. That you'd taken too much this time. But then your friend arrived, so I made my exit, thinking he could probably handle your mental state better than I could, since he wasn't making you hysterical the way I was. Unfortunately it appears you must have lost control after I left. I'm sure you didn't *mean* to knock him into the water – and you clearly regretted it immediately, since you called a friend for help and dived in after him.'

Heather surprised herself by laughing. It was just so ridiculous. Was this really the best he could come up with? Surely he must know how easily his lies could be disproved? Steve was in recovery. She had a witness.

But if Noah was concerned about that, he gave no sign. He got up to pour himself a glass of water from the plastic jug before settling back into the chair.

'They've seen the results of your blood tests, so they know I'm telling the truth.' He shook his head, as though in disappointment. 'That was a lot of oxycodone, Heather, a risky amount. But don't worry. I'll do my best to keep that part of the story out of the press.' He drank some water. 'That's the thing about friends. They keep each other's secrets.'

She raised her chin, determined not to let her disquiet show through.

'I think my having been tricked into ingesting painkillers isn't going to get much press. Not when it's competing for clicks with the news that the Triple F's most famous name tried to kill a man. Oh yes, and that he's been rigging the contest, pushing damaged people towards an early grave, just so he can cling to his place in the spotlight.'

Noah propped an ankle on his knee. 'My goodness, what an imagination you have! But amusing though it is, you can't go around saying stuff like that. I know you've been on a drug trip and may have suffered some hallucinations, but throwing wild accusations around in public is . . . well, slander. Which is a crime.'

'It's not just me, though. Steve will tell everyone what you did. What you *are*.'

'Ah yes, Steve. He's doing very well, all things considered. It was touch and go for a while there: pressure on the brain, loss of blood. But he's okay now. Aside from his memory.'

The air in the room seemed to turn to ice, stealing her breath and tightening her chest.

'His memory?'

'Oh, don't worry. He knows his name and what year it is. It's just short-term stuff. He remembers arranging to meet you, but nothing after that. It's very common apparently, with head injuries, for the hours leading up to them to be erased.'

Heather slumped back against the pillow. So this was why Noah had sauntered in looking so relaxed and smug. Steve couldn't back her up. Their footage was somewhere on the bottom of the Thames, inside a ruined phone. And hospital blood tests proved that she had ingested a drug that, when taken in large enough doses, could cause hallucinations. Without that video, anything she said would come across as the ravings of an addict, attacking the man who had tried to help her get clean: a celebrity and pillar of the Triple F community. No one would believe a word she said.

It was over. Noah had won.

*

'I'm sorry I can't remember,' Steve said. 'It's weird, having blank spots in my head. The last time that happened I stopped drinking for a month.' He broke off a piece of the KitKat she'd brought him from the hospital shop. 'Or maybe it was a week. But the point is, it scared me then and it's scaring me now.' He was out of recovery, installed in a semi-private room identical to hers. His roommate was off having an X-ray, leaving them alone together.

Steve reached for the coffee cup she'd placed on his bedside table before falling back against the pillow, wincing and swearing.

She got up from the chair – the same wooden arms and fake blue leather as the one in her room – and handed him the cup.

'How many times do I have to say it? Use your right arm! Pretend your left arm's not even there.'

'I can't. I'm a lefty. Using my right arm is like . . . giving in to the machine.'

'You think a machine makes people right-handed? Just as well you don't teach biology.' She picked up the KitKat from the blanket beside him, ignoring his 'hey!' of protest as she broke off a finger before returning it. 'You lost a lot of blood.'

'Yes, but what I lacked in blood, I more than made up for in surplus brain fluid.'

She bit into the chocolate, watching him as she chewed. He looked pale. Ghostly.

'That's not funny, Steve. You nearly died.'

'But I didn't. Thanks to you. That was some serious bravery, Davies. Jumping in after me. Belting me to your back . . . bloody hell! You could have drowned trying to save me.' He rolled onto his right side and, his face taut with pain and determination, moved his left hand onto hers, giving it a squeeze. 'Thank you. I wish there was a bigger word than that, but it's all I've got. I owe you my life. You're a hero.'

She shook her head, shame flooding her, filling her up. 'Don't call me that, it's not true. I'm . . . I . . .' She tried to fight the tears, but there were too many of them. They overflowed, escaping down her cheeks.

'Sorry.' He sounded bewildered. 'The last thing I wanted was to upset you.' Then, when she began to quake with sobs, 'Jesus, Davies, what is it? What's wrong?'

She wiped her eyes with the sleeve of her hospital gown.

'When you were pinned to the pier, I thought about leaving you behind, going for help alone.' Her gaze dropped to the floor; she couldn't look him in the eye.

'Well, yeah, that makes sense. And hey, you would have made it back in time. Probably. But that's not what you did. I don't know how you got me off there and strapped to your back but . . . it took some serious balls. Wait, that's sexist. Ova.' His eyes were filled with admiration. 'You're pretty amazing, you know that?'

'No.' She shook her head. There was a deep ache in her chest that had nothing to do with her injuries and she sensed it was where the tears were coming from, that many more were about to follow and she would be powerless to stop them. Because her past, the car accident, was part of it, mixed in with what had happened in the river. And then the next wave of tears did come, not a trickle but a downpour, landing on Steve's blanket. He passed her a box of tissues and it was clear from his face that she was scaring him.

'Are you in pain? Should I call a nurse?'

She shook her head. 'No. I'm sorry, I just need to . . . let this out.' The words came in short gasps. She stood up, swaying on her feet. 'Sorry, I'll go to the bathroom.'

But he caught her hand. 'You don't have to hide away. I'm not scared of emotions. Well, maybe a bit. But that's my problem. You can stay if you want.'

So she sat back down at his bedside and cried, not holding back, mopping her eyes and nose with tissues, neither of them speaking. She waited until the tears had emptied themselves out and she could trust her voice again.

It was time for the truth.

'You don't know the whole story. Right at the end, before we were rescued. I couldn't get up the ladder. In the river the water took most of your weight, but climbing out with you on my back . . . I knew I wouldn't be able to do it.' She sucked in a deep breath before plunging ahead. 'So I was going to let you go. My hand was already on the belt buckle, about to release it, when the police arrived. If they hadn't come right when they did, I would have let you drown to save myself.' Shame and self-loathing were churning inside her, but saying the words out loud had released some of the emotional pressure, making it more manageable. Her head drooped forward.

Steve's hand was still on hers. Why hadn't he snatched it away, she wondered, now that he knew the truth?

'Why didn't you just buckle me to the ladder instead?'

She wasn't quite sure what she'd been expecting: a sombre pronouncement of disappointment or shocked intake of breath. But his question – delivered in the same tone he used to use in the staffroom to ask why she hadn't used a scanning app instead

384

of faffing around with the photocopier – took her completely by surprise.

She raised her head to stare at him. 'What?'

'Why didn't you just unbuckle me from your waist and attach me to the ladder, then go for help. Simple. I may not be a science teacher like you . . .'

'Not teacher. Trainee. Not even that.'

'But, you know . . . *logic*.' He clicked his tongue and rolled his eyes in that exasperating way that always used to irritate her.

She surprised herself by laughing. 'Well, thank you, Captain Hindsight. If only you'd been this helpful and communicative at the time.'

Heather tugged another tissue from the box and blew her nose. She drew in a long pull of air, filling her lungs. There seemed to be more space inside her now, more room to breathe.

'Look,' Steve said, 'you were superhuman. And then you were human. When faced with the choice of staying alive or dying pointlessly anchored to some biscuit dunker from work, you made an entirely sensible decision. A decision anyone would have made.'

'Anyone too dim to think of the belt–ladder thing you mean.'

'Well, yes. But logic and life-and-death situations don't always go together.' He squeezed her hand. 'I am now going to do something out of character by being very serious for a moment. So you need to listen carefully because this may never happen again.' He looked her straight in the eye, holding her gaze as he said the next words. 'You did everything in your power to save me and didn't give up until it really did look like the only option. I am incredibly grateful and you have nothing to be ashamed of.'

She gave him a wobbly smile. 'Thank you. But I still feel . . . like I need you to forgive me.'

'No. You really don't.'

'I do, though. It's important. *Please.*'

He shrugged, then swore at the resulting pain in his left shoulder. 'Fine. If you're going to be stubborn about it . . . I forgive you.'

She felt a weight lift. 'Thank you.'

There was an awkward silence.

'For God's sake, can we please talk about something else now? I'm a shallow bloke and all this big emotion stuff is way outside my comfort zone. At this point, I just want someone to catch me up on the footy.'

Heather laughed softly, dropping the damp wad of tissue into an empty water cup.

'I'm afraid I don't follow football. So why don't *you* catch *me* up on the latest goings-on at the school?'

He relaxed visibly as he shuffled down in the bed, tucking his right arm behind his head.

'Well, the end-of-year science fair and bake sale is on Friday, so I need to get out of here before then since people will be counting on me; my Smarties fudge is legend.'

'The science fair.' She smiled nostalgically. 'Remember the Year 7 one before Christmas? Ali's bloody ant farm.'

'God, of all the places for it to break.' His face pursed in disgust. 'I found an ant in my coffee weeks later.'

'That's because they got into the biscuit tin. And you will insist on dunking them.'

'Well, as a wise man once said—'

'"Tea's too wet without biscuits",' she finished, thinking back to their coffee breaks in the staffroom. It seemed like a lifetime ago.

'Oh!' Steve snapped his fingers, grinning. 'Speaking of science fair disasters, I haven't told you about the blood drama.'

'Sorry, blood drama?'

'Eric's science fair project. There was, shall we say, an incident involving Susan Moyles, which culminated in her flat-out refusing to have Eric in her class next year. She even spoke to the head. It's a whole thing.'

'Oh God, what's he done now? But . . . hang on, isn't Susan Moyles on maternity leave?'

'Yes, but she dropped by the school to show off her baby while everyone was in the middle of setting up their projects.'

'And?'

'Well, there she was, carrying the baby and pretending to admire Eric's frankly sub-par drawings of blood cells when he asked her if she and her husband knew their blood types. So she says yes, she's A negative and hubby's B negative. To which our little Prince Charming says . . .' Steve drum-rolled his right hand against the metal bedframe. 'If the baby turns out to be Rh positive, you better hide it from your husband, or he'll know you've been playing away.'

'*No!* He *did*n't?' She burst out laughing.

'He did. And when the head called him in about it, he said he was just making use of knowledge he had acquired during the course of his education, and that we should be glad he was able to put theory into practice in real-life situations.'

'Cheeky sod!' She laughed. 'He is right, though. Two parents with negative blood types can't have a baby with a positive one. I taught him that.' The realisation that Eric had listened, had carried that knowledge out of the classroom and into the world made her feel oddly proud.

Steve must have picked up on it because he said, 'Get you, teacher of the year!'

'Not a teacher. Just a trainee. Not even that.'

'You would have been a great one, though, this proves it. And shows that you don't need CelebRate to be an influencer.'

She pressed both palms against her cheeks in mock horror.

'Oh. My. God. Did you *actually* just say that? That is the soppiest thing you have ever said. Possibly the soppiest thing *anyone* has ever said.'

'I blame the head injury.'

She eyed his bandage for a moment. 'You jumped out of hiding and attacked Noah.'

'Did I? Why? Sounds like a bonkers thing to do.'

'He was shaking me and you came to my rescue.'

'God, I'm heroic.'

'Yes, you were. Though in hindsight, it would have turned out better if you'd been armed in some way.'

'I suppose I could have clubbed him with my battery pack. Or with an actual club, ideally.'

'Yes, a cricket bat . . .' Then she stopped, forehead creasing. 'Wait . . . battery pack? I didn't know you'd brought one.'

'Yeah, my phone battery's on its last legs. Dies at 5 per cent and filming drains it at warp speed. I didn't want to risk blowing our Watergate-style exposé.'

Heather could feel her heart accelerating as she asked, 'What does this battery pack look like?'

Steve had the presence of mind to do a half-shrug this time, leaving his left shoulder in peace.

'Like a rectangle.'

'Yes, but . . . is it around the same size and shape as your phone?'

'Well, yeah. Why?'

Her heart was in overdrive now. She tried to pull up the

memory of the fight on the dock, the object lying on the ground wrapped in shadow. Then skidding into the river. Had she actually *seen* a phone? Or just assumed that's what it was?

'You're looking very excited, Davies. If I'd known describing phone battery shapes had this effect on women, I would have worked it into my chat-up lines years ago.'

She laughed, jumping up from the chair and kissing him on the forehead, just below the edge of his bandage. He gave her a smile that looked oddly shy.

'See you later, Steve. I've got to run off.'

'Run off? Don't you mean "lie down"? Aren't you supposed to stay in hospital for at least one more night?' His eyes narrowed suspiciously. 'What's going on?'

'I'm not sure. It's just . . . there's something I need to check. It might be nothing.' But she could feel hope and excitement churning inside her as she limped back down the hall to her room. She opened the mauve bag, pulling out a designer T-shirt, baggy black trousers, matching flats and a Lagerfeld canvas tote, changing into the clothes and tossing her hospital gown onto the bed. There was a short mac in the bag too and she pulled it on over top. It was probably hot outside, but after her night in the river, she was determined to avoid being cold at all costs. Then she picked up her F-phone, lying on the bedside table, the battery at 12 per cent. She'd burned through 6 per cent right after Noah had left, checking her latest follower numbers, heart pounding, fearful that news of her blood test results had been leaked. Instead, Heather had been amazed to find that, not only was she still in pride of place on the banner, but she had somehow gained another 300,000 followers! A quick Google search revealed why. Heather was all over the headlines:

Winfluencer Risks Life in River Rescue.

**CelebRate Star in Hospital After
Saving Friend.**

Hero Heather's Near-Death Horror.

So everyone knew about her ordeal in the river – but not about the drugs in her system. Noah was clearly holding on to that card for now, using it to keep her quiet.

Heather did another quick follower check (up another 20,000 since bedtime yesterday) grimacing as the battery dropped to 10 per cent. Her eyes returned to the purple bag. What if . . . She unzipped the side compartment, grinning when she discovered her charger inside. Heather dropped it into the tote bag. Ready.

She opened her door a crack. She wanted to sneak out while the nurses weren't looking, to avoid an argument about leaving against medical advice. She waited until the nurse at ward reception had turned her back before making her escape, limping towards the side exit. Then she took a lift to the ground floor, following the signs towards the main entrance, moving as fast as her leg would allow.

And walked straight into Elliot.

CHAPTER 51

Elliot had been nervous approaching the hospital, carrying a box of Heather's favourite salted caramel truffles. Or at least, they *used* to be her favourite. So much about her had changed. He could feel his stress levels rising as he walked through the main doors. It hadn't gone well the last time he'd visited her in a hospital, shortly after the accident. He remembered how her features had twisted as she'd grabbed the nearest object – a plastic jug – and hurled it across the room, narrowly missing his head, bringing nurses running.

Get away from me, you fucking coward! You saved yourself and left me to die alone!

He hadn't gone back after that.

Maybe coming here was a mistake. Perhaps he should just leave the chocolates with the nurses. Being in hospital must be triggering old memories for her, tapping into unresolved issues surrounding the accident. And the last thing he needed was—

Someone walked right into him, making him drop the box. Why couldn't people look where they were going? Then he saw who it was and his stomach lurched.

'Ros . . . Heather.' The crown of her head was bandaged, her skin deathly pale below it.

'Elliot. What are you . . .?' She looked down at the truffles on the floor. 'Are those for me?'

'Yes.' He picked up the box, holding it towards her awkwardly. 'I heard about your accident. Just wanted to drop by . . . make sure . . .' He was babbling, incoherent. Damn it, she had caught him completely off guard. What was she even doing down here? 'Have you been released already?'

'Not exactly.' She took the chocolates from his outstretched hand – which was something, at least.

He expected her to rush off then, brush past and leave without a backward glance. But instead she remained statue-still in front of him, her eyes searching his.

Something was happening. He could see it in the dip of her eyebrows, the lips tightening then loosening again, the short volley of blinks. As if she were trying to work through a long and complicated puzzle.

Everyone else seemed to fade into the background, leaving only the two of them, standing just inches apart, halfway between the main doors and the information desk. Then her features relaxed and something extraordinary happened. She placed a hand on his arm.

'I understand it now, what you did that day. You were scared, and felt like you didn't have a choice.' She spoke as though thinking aloud, realising the words as she voiced them. 'You were human. And we're both still here. So,' she lifted her chin and said her next three words carefully, enunciating each syllable, giving each the same weight, 'I forgive you.' Then she withdrew her hand, put the chocolates inside her bag and walked past him with her uneven gait, the hospital doors parting to release her.

Elliot didn't move. He stood where she'd left him, trying to absorb what had just happened, the strange wonder of it. He could feel powerful emotional currents churning inside him, tearing through the knotted webs of guilt and self-loathing.

'Sir? Are you all right?'

Elliot became aware of his surroundings again, of the woman at the reception desk, now wearing a look of polite concern. How long had he been standing here, thunderstruck, staring at nothing?

'Yes, I'm fine, thank you.' He dabbed at a tear that had appeared on his cheek. How had that got there?

'Was there something you needed?'

'No.' Elliot shook his head. 'No, I'm fine now.'

CHAPTER 52

Nausea was swirling in the pit of Heather's stomach as she slowly worked her way along the riverbank, past slabs of concrete and construction equipment, towards the dock. Competing emotional forces were clashing inside her, as an echo of the terror she had felt the last time she was here jousted with the wild hope that had brought her back.

The lock on the dock gate was broken, presumably by the police who'd come searching for her. Heather could feel her heart banging as she walked through it and down the ramp, stepping carefully along the wooden struts to the bottom. Steve's pub quiz friend clearly hadn't been here in the last couple of days, because the speedboat's cover was still partially open.

She took a deep breath before bending down to unzip it all the way, tossing back the cover, exposing the interior. The boat was a simple model, two seats, a curved windscreen and a white fibreglass floor. Orange lifejackets along the sides and an engine at the back.

She scanned the floor quickly, then more slowly, eyes searching with growing desperation.

Please be here, please be here.

Nothing. She stepped carefully onto the boat, which rocked

as it took her weight. She moved around the small space in a crouch, peering around the seats, covering every inch of floor before finally giving up.

Steve's phone wasn't here. She felt the downward suck of despair. There went her last hope of catching Noah. She stared desolately around the empty boat for one more moment before climbing back onto the dock. She should probably call the hospital, apologize for leaving without saying anything, promise to return and stay in until they discharged her. She was zipping the cover back around the side when she saw something: a flash of red paper jammed between one of the life jackets and the boat's inner wall. She pulled it out. A KitKat wrapper. Trust Steve to be eating chocolate in the middle of a covert mission. She shoved it in her pocket to throw away later and was about to finish closing the zip when she saw something else wedged behind the life jacket – a metallic line of black.

Heather's mouth went dry. Volts of excitement charged through her as she reached for it, fingers stumbling, accidentally pushing it lower before shoving her hand all the way behind the life jacket, grabbing the object trapped there, pulling it free.

Then she sat down heavily on the dock, staring in wonder. Steve's phone. The screen was blank, of course, the battery flat. But it was dry and appeared undamaged. So in theory, all she had to do was charge it and she would have the evidence she needed to unmask Noah. She heard a mobile phone ringing. For a confused moment she thought it was Steve's, somehow returning to life.

Then she realized the sound was coming from her pocket. She took out her F-phone and saw Duncan's name on the screen.

His tone was abrupt, urgent. 'It's me. Are you still in hospital?

I was held up in New York so only got back last night. I want to see you.' His voice softened. 'I've been really worried.'

She closed her eyes, suffused with a feeling of well-being. Only yesterday, it had felt as if her world was shattered beyond repair. But now all the pieces were flying back together.

'I'm fine. I've just left hospital.'

'That's great news! Can we meet? Or are you still too weak?'

'Where are you?'

'In my office.'

Heather slipped Steve's phone into the front pocket of her trousers, thinking. The storm of controversy she was about to unleash was going to have a direct impact on Duncan, as CEO of the company Noah represented. So the least she could do was warn him. Perhaps they could file the police report together, to show that the Triple F was taking full responsibility for what had gone wrong – and allow Duncan to take a stand against the man who had corrupted his life's work.

'Actually, why don't I meet you there? I need to show you something.'

*

The first thing Heather did when she arrived in Duncan's office was put Steve's phone on charge, plugged into the socket beside the bookcase. She propped the handset on the shelf against some book spines and stood next to it, so she could keep an eye on the screen. In just a few minutes, she would be able to see the footage. Assuming it wasn't damaged. Assuming the microphone had worked. *Assuming, assuming.* It seemed to be the dominant word in her life these days.

Duncan took Heather gently by the shoulders and inspected her from top to bottom, as though checking for damage. The skin under his eyes was bruised with fatigue. Was that just jetlag . . . or had he lost sleep worrying about her?

'Are you sure you're okay?'

'I'm fine. Honestly.' She took a deep breath. 'But there are some things you need to know.'

His hands dropped from her shoulders to the pockets of his cardigan: navy this time.

'What kind of things?'

She glanced sideways at the phone screen. Still black. Damn. What if it wasn't just a flat battery? What if the handset was broken?

Please-work-please-work.

As if in answer to her plea, the logo glowed on the screen. Thank God. She could show the video to Duncan – right here, right now – while it was plugged in. But the thought of doing that without checking the footage first made Heather uneasy. What if there was no sound, or something had gone wrong and the recording didn't exist at all? She would look like a fool. Or worse, a lunatic. No, best nip to the loo once it was charged enough and make sure it was there and working before boldly proclaiming she had evidence to back the declarations she was about to make. But whether the video was there or not, she had to tell Duncan the truth.

'Look, there's no easy way to say this . . .' Heather saw his shoulders tense and was suddenly struck by the enormity of what she was about to reveal, the fact that it would shake his empire to its foundations. 'I wasn't in an accident. My friend and I were attacked.'

'What? Oh my God!' His head rocked back in surprise. 'Was it a mugger or . . .' his eyes widened, 'not . . . your stalker?'

'No. It was someone from the Triple F.'

'Someone . . .' He squinted, as though trying to bring something into focus. 'You mean another Winfluencer?'

She glanced at the phone: 3 per cent. 'I'll get to the "who" part in a minute. Let's start with the "why".' She touched the surface of her bandage. Her scalp felt tender, but the burning sensation was gone. 'I recently discovered that the contest has been rigged to let red-lighted contestants win.'

Duncan frowned, looking irritated. 'I accept that our screening process needs to be tightened up, but—'

'No, you misunderstand. These finalists weren't let through *in spite* of the risk. They were put forward *because* of it.'

Duncan shook his head. 'You're mistaken. Most of our ex-winners thrive. Of course there will always be a small minority who struggle—'

'Oh, come *on*. You must have noticed how many have gone off the rails? The nervous breakdowns, drug overdoses, alcohol abuse and . . .' she swallowed before saying the word, 'suicides.'

Duncan tilted his head, blinking rapidly as he appeared to consider this. Then he gestured towards the cream sofa. 'Why don't we sit down?'

Her eyes dashed to Steve's phone: 6 per cent. 'No thanks, I'm good here.'

'But what would motivate someone to let vulnerable candidates win? Unless . . .' He appeared to consider his own question. 'I suppose someone on the screening panel could have taken the view that it's unfair to exclude them.'

Heather's jaw tightened. That was exactly the excuse Noah had come up with. But it wasn't going to fly.

'I'm afraid it's nothing so altruistic. Because the person who pushes them through also goes on to troll them, using private information extracted from their DMs, Triple F files and Winners' Circle sessions.'

Duncan began pushing his fingertips slowly up and down his forehead, clearly struggling to process it all.

'That's . . . well, shocking, obviously. If true.'

'It *is* true.'

'You keep saying "someone". Does this someone have a name?'

'Yes.' Another eye flick: 8 per cent. It would have to do. She disconnected the phone and put it in her pocket.

Duncan was watching her quizzically. 'Well?'

'I'll tell you everything, but first . . . do you mind if I use your loo?'

'It's broken, I'm afraid. The flush. Maintenance is sorting it out tomorrow. You'll have to use the public one downstairs.'

'It's just to splash cold water on my face.'

'You're not feverish, are you?' He moved closer, placing a hand on her forehead. She could smell his soap and the faint tang of alcohol. He must have had a drink before she'd arrived. 'Your temperature feels okay.'

'I'm fine. I just need a couple of minutes to . . . refresh myself.'

'In that case, be my guest.'

*

A wave of dizziness broke over Heather as she entered the bathroom. She closed the door and sat down on the lid of the toilet – there was a ribbon of paper across it saying: 'Out of Order: Do Not Use' – waiting for it to pass. Steve was right; she should really be in her hospital bed right now. She would go back as soon as she was done here; have a doctor check her over. She took out Steve's mobile. Tapped in 666-666, hearing his voice in her head saying 'Satan squared.' Then she took a deep breath and opened the photo app, pulse spiking as her eyes skipped to the last thumbnail image.

The video was there. The thumbnail showed the first frame: Noah standing on the dock, coffee cup in hand. The duration said thirty-two minutes and forty-seven seconds, so the camera must have been left to film the back of the lifejacket until the battery died. Her heart was surging as she tapped the thumbnail.

'Noah, what are you doing here?' Heather's words were crystal clear. But what about Noah's? The footage would be worthless if the mic hadn't picked up his voice. There was an achingly long pause. Then, quieter but distinct, 'Hello, Heather… I brought you a drink: non-fat chai latte, extra cinnamon. Just the way you like it.' She continued watching the video until she saw her own face change, marking the dawn of realisation. She slumped forward in relief. She had the evidence she needed.

Duncan was on the sofa when she returned from the bathroom, so she hobbled over to join him. Just as well she could sit now. Her muscles felt watery and there was a tremor running through her.

'So?' He turned his palms to the ceiling. 'Are you going tell me who's behind this . . . scheme?'

She could hear the doubt in his voice. Noah must have told him about her blood test. He probably thought that the combination of opiates, oxygen deprivation and terror had left her confused, delusional.

But that was about to change.

She held Steve's phone between them on the sofa, angling the screen his way.

'Why don't I *show* you.'

She put the volume on full, watching Duncan's face as the video began to play. Saw his puzzled frown as Noah offered her the latte. The flinch of shock when he revealed his true colours. He began shaking his head slowly as the man whose name was synonymous with his company admitted to having sabotaged it. At the point where Noah yanked the bag from her shoulder, Duncan took the phone from her hand and stopped the video.

'That's enough,' he said quietly, slipping the mobile into his cardigan pocket.

'I'm sorry.' Heather placed a hand on his knee. Poor Duncan. It must be such a shock. 'I know it's a lot to take in. But I think it would be best if the two of us went to the police together.'

She watched his face, saw his eyes flicker back and forth, as though watching something play out inside his head. Then he sighed.

'Of course, on the face of it, that seems the right and obvious thing to do. But this is a serious situation so we need to give it serious thought. Consider the consequences.'

'Consequences,' Heather repeated, frowning. 'For who?'

'For the contest and by extension, you, me and everyone else whose livelihoods depend on it. Thousands of Triple F staffers, not to mention all the winners, past and present. Because make no mistake. That video is a bomb that will blow up the Triple F. Bankrupt it. The company could be criminally liable. I could even be personally liable. Everything that both of us have built our lives on will be ripped away. So we need to decide: is this really what we want?'

Heather blinked rapidly. This wasn't the response she had been expecting, and she found herself struggling to process it. A fresh wave of dizziness broke over her, sending a swarm of white dots swimming across her vision, like a school of burning fish.

'But . . . people are dead because of this. Noah deliberately pushed them over the edge. Not to mention the small matter of him attacking a man and throwing him into the river unconscious.'

'Yes, and now that I know what's been going on, I will personally make sure nothing like this ever happens again, that red-lighted candidates stay red. That private information remains private. And Noah is quietly sidelined.'

'"Quietly sidelined?" *That's* his punishment?!'

'Believe me, I am as horrified as you are. Probably more so, since I've known Noah for years. Well, I *thought* I knew him.' He turned to face her on the sofa, taking her hand between both of his. 'But destroying the contest won't fix anything. Quite the opposite: it's only going to make things harder for the vulnerable winners who are still here.'

She stared at him, thunderstruck. Where was the man who'd insisted she report her stalker? Who had told her that the truth mattered more than the contest's image? That *she* mattered more? It was as if he'd disappeared. Disappeared . . . or never existed in the first place.

'Can I have the phone back, please?'

'I'd like to hold on to it for now, if you don't mind. I'll need it to confront Noah, show him that the game is up, that all of this stops right now. Trust me, this is the right approach.' He reached out to gently tuck a lock of hair behind her ear. 'You *do* trust me, don't you?'

His eyes moved over her face, one of his analysing sweeps.

Heather struggled to formulate a response. But it was as though a fog had wrapped itself around the inside of her skull, muffling her thoughts. It occurred to her that what she said and did in the next few minutes would decide the shape of her entire future.

The thought brought back a line from a GCSE poem, sending it skittering across her memory like a leaf in the wind.

Two roads diverged in a yellow wood.

The Robert Frost poem had resonated with her – the idea that once you started heading down one path, it became impossible to go back. And you could spend the rest of your life wondering how things might have been different if you'd chosen the other one.

She closed her eyes, shutting out the room, trying to focus. She could hear the rustle of Duncan's clothes as he shifted beside her. When she opened her eyes again, the fog had cleared. She knew what she was going to do.

Duncan's features were tense, his grey eyes locked on hers.

She put a hand on his arm. 'Of course I trust you. And of course I don't want to destroy the Triple F. Especially now that I fully appreciate how much it means to you, what you're willing to sacrifice to defend it. I know how hard you've had to fight already, what with so-called friends trying to steal it from you.'

'Ah. You've heard about Brendon.' He looked down at his hands, the fingers tightly interlocked against his lap. 'What exactly were you told?'

'That he created the blueprint for the contest.'

Annoyance flickered across his features. 'Only after *I* suggested we find a way to commoditize fame. The lottery idea would never have occurred to him otherwise. And anyway, thinking up a plan is one thing. Having the tools to actually implement it is quite another. Without me, the Triple F would never have been more than words in a computer file. Worthless. But he failed to see that. His behaviour left me with no choice but to take matters into my own hands.'

'By hacking his computer and stealing his work?'

Duncan's lips tightened. 'By doing what was necessary to create all this.' He waved a hand to indicate the room, with its art deco furniture and sloping glass walls, the fountain below, with its spray-pummelled Fs. 'He could have been a part of it, running the company by my side.'

'But instead he turned into a drunk after losing his wife and kids.'

Duncan's mouth twitched to one side. 'You seem to have been well briefed by the water-cooler brigade. What else did they tell you?'

'That you sent her the video that ended their marriage.' She propped a shoulder against the sofa's cream upholstery, facing him. 'Did you?'

'Yes.' He swirled wine around his glass. 'And I make no apologies for it. I liked Laura. She had a right to know the truth.'

'If it actually *was* the truth.'

Duncan appeared genuinely puzzled. 'Of course it was. Why would you suggest otherwise? Brendon was stupid enough to make sex tapes of himself with a nineteen-year-old cocktail waitress. I merely . . . passed them along.'

'I heard—' Then she stopped as realisation sank in. That Noah had been planting seeds of doubt, deflecting suspicion from himself. She shook her head. 'Nothing. Just . . . rumours.'

Duncan's lips tightened. 'I'm sure this story has been framed in a way that puts me in a bad light, but the way I see it, Brendon betrayed both me and Laura and got what he deserved. The fact that his alcoholism prevented him from disrupting the launch of my company was simply an added bonus.'

Heather laughed softly, leaning closer, tracing his jawline with a fingertip. 'You have a ruthless streak, don't you, Duncan?'

He tilted his head, watching her intently. 'I prefer to think of it as "pragmatic".'

'Let's stick with "ruthless",' she said, slipping her arms around his waist. 'Ruthless is a lot sexier than "pragmatic".' She put her lips to his, the kisses building and deepening as she swung round to straddle his lap, burying her fingers in his hair. His hands slipped under her T-shirt, palms skating up the sides of her rib cage. She could hear his breath coming faster. Heather rested her forehead against his.

'At the risk of spoiling the mood, I need the loo.' She disentangled herself from him and headed for the bathroom, drawing up short as she reached the threshold and confronted the taped-up cistern. 'Damn. I forgot it was broken.'

When she turned back around, he was standing directly behind her, making her breath catch in surprise. Duncan's arms encircled her, pulling her close, breathing words into her ear.

'Are you sure it can't wait?'

She detached herself gently. 'It really can't, I'm afraid.' Heather crossed the room to press the lift button. 'But don't worry, I won't be long.' She struck a playful pose as she waited for the lift to arrive, back pressed against the wall, arms stretched above her head. 'And the next time you see me, I may not be wearing quite so many clothes.'

The door slid open and she stepped inside. Duncan moved in with her, and for a moment, she thought he was going to come along, escort her to the ladies' and wait for her outside. But instead he touched his card to the sensor, pressed the button for the fifth floor and retreated with a small wave. Then the door closed and she was alone.

Heather released a shaky breath. There was a discreet camera in the lift, so she waited until she had stepped out into the fifth-floor lobby before taking Steve's handset from the pocket of her trousers. She wondered how long it would be before Duncan noticed it was missing. She needed ten minutes. Maybe fifteen. And the strength to make it down to the third floor. She switched off her F-phone to remove herself from Friend Finder, then pushed through the door to the stairs. With everything that had been going on, she'd managed to divert her attention away from her leg. Now, though, the pain was moving into the spotlight, making the staircase look like a treacherous cliff. She hesitated. But only for a moment. Because she couldn't afford to waste a second. Gripping the handrail, she began working her way down the two flights of stairs. Every step set off a starburst of pain, like terrible fireworks. She gritted her teeth, focusing on the task ahead, telling herself that the neural messages from her leg didn't matter. The only message that mattered was the one she was about to send.

Nearly there. Three steps, two steps. One. Made it. She shouldered through the door to the third-floor lift lobby, pausing on the other side to get her bearings. By now, Duncan would probably be starting to wonder what was taking so long. And once he discovered that Steve's phone was gone and she wasn't in the ladies', he would come looking for her. She hobbled along the corridor, praying that she didn't run into anyone. But it was late and the third-floor hallway was deserted.

Her destination was just around the corner. She reached it and stopped, breath coming fast, all her attention now focused on the keypad beside the door. It seemed like a year had passed since she'd last stood here, watching Duncan tap in the code. 10-09-08. Like a rocket countdown. She copied it, then waited, tension humming through her. What if the combination had changed? It must be switched regularly, for security's sake. There was an agonising pause. Then the light turned green. She rolled her shoulders to release the tension. Shot a look down the corridor, half-expecting to see Duncan running towards her, telling her to stop. But no one was there and a moment later she was through the door, pulling it shut and leaning back against it, heart hammering.

The room was just as she remembered, the glowing collage casting shifting patterns of light across the walls and along the conference table's white surface, making her think of churches: sun falling through stained glass. She looked at the wall screen and felt a sour jolt as she saw a picture of herself getting into a Triple F car outside the hospital, face white, hair limp beneath the cap of gauze bandages, features twisted into a grimace from stepping too heavily on her leg. Whoever had taken it must have been hiding because she'd scanned the street and hadn't noticed any phones aimed her way. Not that an image like that would have made it beyond this room.

She took out Steve's phone: 7 per cent. Would it be enough to send the video? She thought of her charger, still plugged uselessly into the wall of Duncan's office. If the file was too big and the phone died before it sent . . . She pushed the thought aside. There was nothing she could do about that. And anyway, she had other things to worry about. Because by now, Duncan must be looking for her, checking that she hadn't collapsed in the loos.

Focus-focus-focus.

She opened the CelebRate app on Steve's phone then clicked 'Submissions', eyes dashing to the top of the screen and the battery image with its thin red bar. She selected the video icon and a note popped up, warning her that submissions could not exceed four minutes. Damn. She'd forgotten that rule. She did a quick edit, starting where Noah had told her she was failing to see 'the big picture', ending where he'd grabbed her arms and shaken her. Three minutes and fifty-two seconds. Had it really only been that long? She selected the cut-down video – damn, 6 per cent! – and tapped 'Submit'. Then she held her breath.

Nothing happened. The phone's screen appeared to have frozen. The battery dropped from 6 to 5 per cent.

No, no, no, don't fail me now!

She gritted her teeth in frustration and, just for a moment, her eyes squeezed shut. When she opened them again, the screen was dark. Had the video gone through before the battery died? Her eyes flew up to the wall collage. It occurred to her that she had no idea how long it took for public submissions to appear in the filter. It could be seconds, minutes . . . or hours. All she could do now was hope it had sent . . . and that it arrived before Duncan did.

She limped to the computer at the end of the table and tapped the spacebar, making the welcome screen glow. Then she moved the cursor to 'Username'. For a moment, she had no idea what to put there. Nerves were scrambling her memory, so she had to force herself to calm down, breathing in through her nose, out through her mouth, sending her thoughts travelling back to that night, standing beside Duncan in the room's kaleidoscopic glow, watching his slim fingers move across the keys. Relief washed through her as the memory returned.

She tapped 'FFFCeX'. The password came more easily, since she'd typed it herself. Heather remembered her confusion when he'd said the words.

What's it for?

Now the question seemed to take on new layers of meaning. She tapped 'Whatsit4?'

And experienced a sick jolt of dismay as the words 'Invalid

Password' appeared. *Damn.* He must have changed it. She slammed her palm against the table in helpless frustration. To come this far, only to fall at the last hurdle.

Unless . . . Was the 'I' supposed to be capitalized? Her fingers trembled as she carefully tapped out 'WhatsIt4?' Clicked 'Access Filter'. Waited.

There was a pause, followed by a three-note chime as the wall collage was briefly mirrored on the computer screen. Then the montage faded away, replaced by rows of thumbnail images, framed in red: unfiltered and unpublished. And there it was, at the top, Noah standing on the dock, a 'Play' button superimposed over his image. The video had gone through. Her hand shook as she clicked on it. A pop-up box appeared. 'Select this video?'

'Yes,' she said aloud, clicking through to the next box: 'Publish to CelebRate?' Below were the two options, 'Confirm' and 'Cancel'.

She moved the arrow to 'Confirm'.

'Stop.'

Everything inside her seemed to plunge, as though she had fallen from a great height.

Duncan was standing in the doorway at the other end of the room, his fingers still on the handle. Light from the hallway spilled across the threshold. Then he stepped inside and closed the door, cutting it off. He took a careful step towards her, palms raised in front of him – like a hostage negotiator approaching someone armed and dangerous.

'I know what you're about to do. And I urge you to reconsider. Because if you publish that video, your life as you know it will be over. No more parties. No more fans. No power to influence people. And no more money. You'll lose your house.' Another slow-motion step. His voice softened. 'Work with me, Heather.

You can take over Noah's position, become the new face of the contest. A mentor to the winners. You'll be everything that he was supposed to be. An example, a leader. Someone for the whole country to look up to.' He was close enough now for her to see his eyes. The fear there. 'The Triple F needs you. The fans need you.' A pause. '*I* need you.'

His words froze her hand. She had come here riding a wave of righteous fury, determined to show the world what the Triple F's poster boy had done. But now she found herself weighing up Duncan's offer. Tempted by it. Imagine . . . *her*, the face of the Triple F! Its one forever star, her fame stretching across years instead of months, a living example of adversity overcome, admired and adored. She would have everything she'd ever wanted and more. And what would exposing Noah actually achieve? She couldn't undo the damage he'd caused. But by taking his place, acting as a true mentor to the winners, she could make a real difference in people's lives, use the role to help rather than hurt.

And maybe, just maybe, that was more important than the truth.

Popularity is power.

She looked at the cursor, now floating in the no-man's land between 'Confirm' and 'Cancel'. Then up at the video wall at the red-rimmed image of Noah, frozen in the moment before he'd revealed himself, after handing her a drink laced with drugs. She would never be like him because she would never allow herself to become addicted to fame, corrupted by it.

Duncan had drifted closer; only two steps away now. A sense of unreality took hold of her, as though all this might be a dream.

Her eyes returned to the computer screen. Amazing to think

that her entire future now hung on a single click. Left or right. Publish or cancel.

Two roads diverged in a yellow wood.

Duncan stopped. Gave her one of his abbreviated smiles.

'I can tell that you're starting to see sense, to understand how amazing your life could be if the two of us joined forces.' His voice softened. 'And not just professionally. I think what we have is special and will only get better with time. But this contest . . . It's part of who I am now, and I could never love someone who took it away from me. So I am asking you – *begging* you – not to do this.' He held a hand out towards her. 'Together, we can make the Triple F bigger and better: a global brand that will spread social media lotteries all around the world. You won't just *have* fame. You'll also *control* it, a precious resource for you to dispense as you see fit. I am offering you a life of power, adulation and luxury. And, let's be honest, what other choice do you have? Without the contest, you'd have to go back to teaching, condemned to spend your life in a low-paying, thankless job. No more parties or photographers. No more fans following your every move. So you need to ask yourself, after everything you've seen and experienced here, could you really turn your back on this life . . . and live *that* one instead?'

Heather stared at Duncan's face, seeing the tension in it, the muscles taut beneath the skin's surface, grey eyes glowing in the room's strange light.

She nodded. 'Thank you. That helped. I wasn't sure. But now I am.'

She saw the stress flee his features. 'It's because I care about you. I want you to make the right decision.'

'I have.'

The arrow swerved out of no-man's land. She clicked.

Two roads diverged in a wood and I—

Duncan was looking more like his usual self. Calm. Back in control.

'Shall we return to my office? Pick up where we left off? We can discuss your new role a little later. After we—'

Then he broke off, apparently registering that Heather wasn't looking at him, that her attention was now focused on the other end of the room.

I took the one less travelled by.

He turned around just in time to see Noah's image fill the screen. The words 'Video Published' blossomed over it for a second before the picture shrank back down to join the others, now framed in black. Heather watched the views tick up, passing a thousand in a matter of seconds.

Duncan stood frozen, like a pale waxwork, staring at the screen, face slack with disbelief. He stayed like that even when Heather brushed past him on her way out, the poem finishing itself in her head as the door closed behind her.

And that has made all the difference.

CHAPTER 53

'So do you ever miss it?' Steve asked. The coffee hadn't finished brewing, but he yanked out the pot. There was an angry hiss as drops fell from the filter onto the hotplate.

'Parts of it,' Heather admitted as he filled her mug. 'It was a bit of a shock how quickly Winfluencers were forgotten, once the app and site shut down.'

'Well, there is an important new season of *Love Island* underway.' Steve opened the biscuit tin, easily locating a Hobnob; it was the first day of the new school year, so a fresh selection had been provided. 'People can only obsess over so many strangers at a time.'

'I knew I could count on you for empathy.'

He dunked the biscuit in his coffee. 'All part of the service.' Heather's eyes drifted to the jagged line on his forehead. It looked better, the skin pink where it had healed. But he would always have it. Battle-scarred, like her.

He must have noticed because he said, 'Looks pretty cool, I reckon.' He pulled back his hair to expose the scar's full length. 'Gives me a gangster vibe. Plus it gives me an excuse to keep telling people how I got it fighting Britain's most hated man, skipping the part where a girl had to rescue me.'

'I'm—'

'*Woman*. Not girl.'

'Good catch.'

'I'm learning.'

He took a bite of Hobnob. 'Can you believe it? Two teachers, not even that at the time, single-handedly . . . double-handedly bringing down the Triple F.'

'Yes, well. The novelty of talking about it has definitely worn off. I spent four hours at the police station yesterday, going over the same questions again and again until I started fantasising about throwing my glass of water in the DCI's face.'

'Yeah, I've been lucky on that score. My interview was a lot less time-consuming. Mostly I just said "I don't remember a thing about that" while the policeman looked irritated and scribbled down notes that I can only assume said "useless twat".' Another dunk-bite. 'The bottom line is, he underestimated you. A fatal mistake.'

Heather frowned, puzzled. 'The policeman?'

Steve rolled his eyes. 'No. Noah. He thought your past, the stuff you've been through, made you weak. Easy prey. But he was wrong. It made you tougher, more resourceful.'

She flushed, stirring sugar into her coffee. Compliments had never been a part of their staffroom banter, so she found herself unsure how to react.

'Thanks.' She glanced around the room, suddenly conscious of the fact that the two of them were alone; the other teachers were busy with last-minute preparations, getting their classrooms ready for the first day. Heather seemed to be the only one who'd come in a week early to set up.

Steve drank some more coffee, watching her over the cup's rim. 'So are you ready for today?'

She fiddled with the top button of her navy blouse, part of the new work wardrobe she'd bought in the H&M sale.

'I've done all my lesson planning and prep work so . . . as ready as I'll ever be, I guess.' Nervous excitement was making her stomach flip. Which was ridiculous really. She'd just spent more than two months living the life of a celebrity, had a near-death experience in the river and would next year be taking the stand in the trial of the decade. So why was the thought of teaching science to teenagers sending volts of nervous energy charging through her veins?

Maybe it was because Heather felt she had something to prove. Veronica Shulman had really gone to bat for her, wielding her family's financial clout, putting pressure on the school board not just to take their former trainee back, but also to use their prerogative, as an independent school, to let her skip the rest of her training and start teaching classes immediately. Heather didn't want to let her down.

'So are you still in touch with any of the CelebRaters? Or have they all lost interest, now that you're no longer providing each other with human photo props?'

'God, you're such a cynic. I'll have you know that Tessa and I are still very close.'

He ate the last bite of Hobnob. 'So just the one, then?'

'Yes,' she conceded, sighing, 'just the one.'

'Well, if you ever get desperate for someone to go drinking with, there's always me.' He ducked his head, appearing to consider the contents of his mug. 'In fact, I was thinking we could maybe go for a pint after work, if you fancy it. Celebrate our first day as real teachers by moaning about how underpaid and thankless the profession is.' He cleared his throat. 'Or we could go to that rabbit place you like. Maybe have dinner.'

Heather felt a smile growing across her face as a new kind of nervousness joined the first-day jitters already firing inside her.

'I would love to, but I have plans after work that I absolutely cannot cancel.'

His eyes were still aimed downwards, as though something interesting was happening inside the cup. 'Of course, no problem, it was just a thought . . .'

'How about tomorrow? We could have dinner at the pub?'

He looked up quickly. 'Sure.' He lifted his left shoulder in a half-shrug; he could do that now without flinching. 'Tomorrow works.'

'Great. It's a da— um, a plan.' Her face felt warm. There was an awkward silence that ended when her mobile chirped: a text from Debbie.

'Good luck today. You'll be awesome! Looking forward to full debrief over wine tonight.'

She sent a quick reply – 'Can't wait!' – before tucking the phone back into her pocket. Her nice, normal phone, its contents and location nobody's business but her own. The time on the screen said 08:11.

'The students will be arriving soon.' Heather poured out the dregs of her coffee. 'Shall we go out front and greet them?'

Steve shook his head in mock dismay. 'You missed them, didn't you? God help you, you actually *missed* the little monsters.'

She washed her cup, placing it upside down on the tea towel beside the sink. 'I wouldn't call them little. Most of them are taller than me.'

'Still monsters, though.'

'Oh, most definitely.' But she could hear the affection in her own voice.

Steve drained his coffee and put the dirty cup in the sink, then seemed to think better of it, washing it out and placing it beside hers. 'All right, then, let's go confiscate some phones and feign some outrage over swearing.'

*

Heather and Steve stationed themselves beside the school's main door. The head was at the other end of the courtyard, just inside the school gates, welcoming nervous Year 7s and their parents. A group of Year 9 girls – no, Heather corrected herself, Year 10s now – strode past her, uniforms freshly pressed for the first day of school. Marianne Coleman had clearly raised the hem on hers to display a non-regulation amount of thigh. They were moving across the courtyard, gossiping with noisy bravado when one of them, Alesia Baig, caught sight of Heather.

'Look, it's Miss Davies!'

'Miss Davies! You're back!' And then they were running towards her and Heather had to struggle to keep her features arranged in a professional smile as she was ambushed by the gang of girls, all loud voices, shrill laughter and restless energy, breath minty with illicit chewing gum.

'Are you very sad about CelebRate? I can't believe Noah Fauster turned out to be such a dickhead. He looks so hot!'

'What's it like being back, are you very disappointed? You must miss all the parties and people taking your picture and that.'

'Can I be in your class, Miss? You're the only teacher who makes physics sound like it actually *means* something.'

'Welcome home,' Steve whispered in her ear – he was pushing her buttons, the bastard, he could see she was already emotional

417

– before turning to address the teenagers in a tone of mock outrage. 'What about me? Isn't anyone excited about sharing tech adventures with a brand-new, fresh-off-the-presses computer science teacher?'

He received a blank stare. Then Sarah – the softie of the group – said, 'Well, I like the way you make learning Python funny.'

'Funny!' Steve put on a stern tone. 'I will have you know I am a serious educator. Now stop badgering Miss Davies, lose the gum and get to class. Go on.' He waved them towards the doors. 'Scat!'

The girls scowled, moving away reluctantly.

'Bye, Miss!'

'See you later, Miss!'

Then they were gone. Steve sighed dramatically. 'Computer science teachers are so unsung. Everyone loves the Coding Corner equipment but not the person who brings it all to . . . Oh. Damn.' He glanced at his watch. 'The Coding Corner. I forgot to pick up the key. Can you hold the fort while I dash to the office?'

'Consider it held.'

A bus must have arrived right after he left because a wave of students suddenly poured through the gates, their overlapping shouts and laughter echoing around the courtyard, the sound reminding Heather of seabirds. Within minutes, her nerves were gone and it was as though she'd never left. There was a fight to be broken up, a thrown hat retrieved and returned to its owner. Kevin Pritchard from Year 8 tried to smuggle in his pet ferret, claiming it 'got too lonely' when he wasn't there.

She waved them inside one by one, until she was alone on the school steps, listening to the cloud of chatter drifting out through the open door behind her. Then the first bell rang and the sound was replaced by hurrying feet, the bang of lockers and the geography teacher's voice shouting 'No running!'

Heather was about to turn and head inside herself when she saw a lone figure slouching past the head and through the gates, clearly unconcerned about being late for the first day of school.

Eric.

His dark eyes watched her as he approached. She was expecting him to breeze past without breaking his stride, perhaps casting a sly remark her way as he did so. But instead, he stopped beside her on the step, turning his head towards her.

'My mother said you were back.'

'She's right.'

'Because you're not rich any more.'

She flirted briefly with the idea of telling him that her weekly payments were still coming in, as the liquidators attempted to continue honouring the company's commitments. But she'd been warned that it wouldn't last much longer. The Triple F's money was almost gone.

'No,' she conceded. 'I'm not rich any more.'

'You must hate being stuck back here, after all those months of doing whatever you want.'

'Maybe being back here *is* what I want.'

His mouth twitched sideways. 'Well, that can't be true, can it? Or you wouldn't have left in the first place.' His tone was accusing.

'Sometimes you have to leave a place to find out that it's actually where you're supposed to be.'

He snorted. 'Yeah, right. Next you'll be saying you missed me.' He poured sarcasm over the words. But she thought she sensed something else, hidden underneath.

He talks about your lessons. You inspire him to think.

Eric Shulman. She'd discarded him, written him off as a soulless monster. When really he was just a lonely child with a bullying

419

father and an unhappy mother, filling his lunch hours with solitary walks around the school grounds. A boy who liked science but struggled with exams, reshaping his sadness into anger.

'You know what, Eric? I *am* going to tell you that. Because it's true. I did miss you and I'm really pleased you're in my class this year.'

And she caught the briefest flash of a surprised smile before he pulled up a scowl to cover it.

ACKNOWLEDGEMENTS

I must start with Cat Camacho at HQ, my wonderful editor. Thanks for all the insightful feedback, invaluable guidance and intelligent editing. Her talent made this book so much stronger. And thank you to my agent, Teresa Chris, for her support and advice, and for always fighting my corner.

A special shout out to Eddie Batha, provider of feedback, contributor of ideas, creator of my writer website. I can't think what I've done to deserve such a generous donation of time and energy, but I am incredibly grateful for it. Also to Lotte Pang, who helped hammer out the kinks in my plot during brainstorming sessions over wine and feedback sessions over Zoom.

Thank you to author and playwright Ness Lyons, who made writing a less lonely business, working alongside me in London cafés and Brighton hotel lobbies.

And, most of all, to my mother Jean and sister Claire, whose love and pride mean more than I can say.

ONE PLACE. MANY STORIES

Bold, innovative and
empowering publishing.

FOLLOW US ON:

@HQStories